Wealth, po...
and ...

CONNELLYS: DANIEL, BRETT & CATHERINE

Three award-winning and bestselling authors deliver three delicious, sensual romances.

We're proud to present

MILS & BOON®

SPOTLIGHT

a chance to buy bestselling novels
by favourite authors every month
– they're back by popular demand!

THE CONNELLYS: DANIEL, BRETT & CATHERINE

Tall, Dark & Royal
LEANNE BANKS

Maternally Yours
KATHIE DeNOSKY

The Sheikh Takes a Bride
CAROLINE CROSS

MILLS & BOON®

*MILLS & BOON and MILLS & BOON with the Rose Device
are registered trademarks of the publisher.*

*This collection is first published in Great Britain 2007
Harlequin Mills & Boon Limited,
Eton House, 18-24 Paradise Road, Richmond, Surrey TW9 1SR*

THE CONNELLYS: DANIEL, BRETT & CATHERINE
© Harlequin Books S.A. 2007

The publisher acknowledges the copyright holders of the
individual works, which have already been published in the UK
in single, separate volumes, as follows:

Tall, Dark & Royal © Harlequin Books S.A. 2002
Maternally Yours © Harlequin Books S.A. 2002
The Sheikh Takes a Bride © Harlequin Books S.A. 2002

*Special thanks and acknowledgement are given to Leanne Banks,
Kathie DeNosky and Caroline Cross for their contribution
to the Connellys series.*

ISBN: 978 0 263 85673 6

064-0407

*Printed and bound in Spain
by Litografía Rosés S.A., Barcelona*

Tall, Dark & Royal

LEANNE BANKS

LEANNE BANKS

is a bestselling author of romance. She lives in her native Virginia with her husband, son and daughter. Recognised for both her sensual and humorous writing with two Career Achievement Awards from *Romantic Times Magazine*, Leanne likes creating a story with a few grins, a generous kick of sensuality and characters that hang around after the book is finished. Leanne believes romance readers are the best readers in the world because they understand that love is the greatest miracle of all. You can contact Leanne online at leannebbb@aol.com or write to her at PO Box 1442, Midlothian, VA 23113, USA. An SAE with return postage for a reply would be greatly appreciated.

Prologue

Merry Christmas. You're the new ruler of Altaria, his mother might as well have said.

The snow fell outside the window of Daniel Connelly's Chicago high-rise condominium as he tried to make sense of his mother's announcement. Not every man in America had a mother who was a former princess. Although she'd always been Mom to Daniel, and she'd given up her title thirty-five years ago when she'd married his father, Emma Rosemere Connelly had never lost the regal poise drilled into her by years spent as Princess of Altaria. Even now, faced with the news that her father and brother had been killed in a boating accident, she held herself together as she sat beside her husband on the brown leather couch.

"You're going to have to repeat that, Mom," Daniel said, sinking into his favorite chair.

His mother took his hands in hers and leaned toward him intently. Her cold fingers and the glint of pain in her blue eyes betrayed her emotions. She gave a sad smile. "I've told you many stories about Altaria. You've even visited a couple of times."

Daniel nodded, his mind filling with vague childhood memories. "I remember Altaria as a beautiful island off the coast of Italy with a great beach," he said. "But how in the world can I be its new ruler?"

"Altarian law stipulates that only male descendants can assume the throne. My father and brother are dead," she said, and squeezed his hands in a moment of telltale grief. Out of the corner of his eye, Daniel saw his father squeeze his mother's shoulders in a gesture of support. Grant Connelly had made his fortune in textiles, but his backbone was made of steel. His mother took a quick breath. "My brother had only one daughter, Catherine. He had no male children."

Daniel thought about some of the gossip he'd heard about his uncle, Prince Marc, over the years. "I don't want to speak ill of the dead, but are you sure Uncle Marc didn't have any other children? He really seemed to take that playboy-prince role to heart."

His father made a sound between a cough and chuckle.

His mother frowned. "Daniel," she said, her tone just a shade sharper. "Marc may have had his flaws, but he would never turn his back on his own child. You are the heir to the throne of Altaria."

Daniel's head reeled. In all his thirty-four years, he'd never imagined being a ruler of a small kingdom. Chicago-born and -bred, he'd always assumed he would spend his life in America. He glanced at his father, a man who had taken the family textile company and turned it into a Fortune 500 corporation. His father had always possessed a passion for the family business, an unrelenting zeal to make it grow.

Daniel had not.

He had succeeded in competitive sports in college, and he had succeeded as Vice President of Marketing at Connelly Corporation, but he'd always had the sense that something was missing, that he wanted something deeper, more. Could this possibly be it?

King? Lord help him.

He looked at his parents and shook his head. *"King?"*

His father nodded and leaned forward. "You've got what it takes to lead a country if that's what you think you should do. It's your choice."

His mother squeezed his hand again. She looked at him with a mixture of pride and concern in her eyes. "Consider it carefully. My father had such dreams for Altaria. When he founded the Rosemere Institute to research cancer treatment, he not only provided a beautiful memorial to my mother, he also brought Altaria into the scientific age. Ruling will be a heavy responsibility, and once you start down this road, your life will be changed forever."

One

She was late, but anxious to meet her assignment. Erin Lawrence bit her lip at her slip. *Begin* her assignment, she mentally corrected. His Majesty might not appreciate being regarded as an assignment. Even if that were true.

She adjusted her hat, then showed her identification to the security guard on the bottom floor of Daniel Connelly's high-rise condominium. Despite the jet lag from her delayed flight, she felt a rush of anticipation as she entered the steel elevator. Even though she'd arrived at night, she couldn't help noticing how different Chicago's architecture was from the Mediterranean-style houses and buildings in her homeland, Altaria.

The elevator doors whisked open, and she walked down the hallway to Daniel Connelly's condo. She lifted her hand to ring the buzzer, and her heart hammered in her chest. Taking a deep breath, she couldn't escape the sense of history surrounding this moment. She was about to meet the royal heir to the throne of Altaria.

Squaring her shoulders, she pressed her index finger into the buzzer and waited.

And waited. A dog barked in the background.

She counted to twenty, then pushed the buzzer again and waited. The dog continued to bark.

The door opened and a tall man with tousled hair and jade-green eyes met her gaze. His chest was bare and muscular, and the only item of clothing he wore was a pair of lounging slacks slung low on his narrow hips. "You rang?"

"Perhaps I'm at the wrong—" She broke off, totally fixated on his wide shoulders and all that naked skin. A dusting of chest hair arrowed down to the top of his slacks. Leaning against the doorjamb with indolent ease, he gave the impression that he was comfortable with his half-naked body. Something told Erin he knew his way around a woman's naked body. This was the kind of man all her headmistresses had warned her against. This was the kind of man who inspired all the bad girls to sneak out of their windows at night.

Tearing her gaze from his impressive body, Erin rechecked the number on his door. The address was correct. She swallowed over a knot of apprehension. "Your Majesty?" she said weakly.

His gaze cleared, and he lifted his head in realization. "You must be Erin Lawrence, the royal etiquette rep."

"Royal etiquette and palace liaison," she said, fighting a twinge of irritation at his casual description of her position. She gave a slight dip. "At your service, sir."

His gaze swept over her in brief masculine assessment that hinted at banked, yet powerful sensuality. She held her breath, until he looked into her eyes again with a glint of amusement. "For some reason I thought you were supposed to arrive earlier today."

"Yes, of course, sir. I apologize. My flights were delayed."

"Happens to everyone," he said generously and held the door for her to enter. "Come on in. Sorry I'm not dressed for the occasion. I had nine meetings today, so I decided to hit the sack early. Don't worry about the dog. I put Jordan in his kennel when I answered the door," he said, referring to the barking dog.

"Jordan, sir?"

"In honor of Michael Jordan, the best basketball player the Chicago Bulls were sorry to lose."

Erin made a mental note to bone up on American basketball. She knew nothing about it. She stopped midway through the doorway and gazed expectantly at him. "The rule of protocol is the king should precede, sir. One should never turn one's back to the king."

"Oh." He gave her another once-over. "Well, that could be a damn shame."

Erin felt a rush of heat to her cheeks and prayed he didn't notice. "Please do proceed, sir. I will follow."

He gave a slow nod, then led the way through a luxurious living room furnished with contemporary brown leather furniture and oak end tables. She followed him into a clean, well-equipped kitchen. He opened the refrigerator door and pulled out a carton of milk. "You want something to drink? Or a sandwich?"

The man was almost completely unaware of his position, she thought, and wondered how he would change once he began to exercise his power as king. *If* he exercised his power as king. Daniel Connolly struck her as a man who didn't need a title or decree. Staring at his wide shoulders, she caught her mind wandering and gave herself a mental shake. The king was offering to fix her a drink or a sandwich. That would never do. "No, thank you, sir."

He grimaced slightly. "Do you mind me asking how old you are?"

She stiffened her spine. "Twenty-two, sir."

"You're young, but we're both adults. Do you have to call me sir?"

"It's proper, sir," she said.

He sighed. "Okay," he said and took a swig directly from the milk carton.

Erin's eyes widened in horror.

He must have caught her expression because he gave her a grin. "Don't worry. Last sip," he told her and tossed the empty carton into the trash container.

Erin practiced what had been drilled into her from years at the finest Swiss boarding schools: she kept her mouth shut. This was the new king of Altaria— a good-looking American who had a body that would make any woman's temperature shoot up ten degrees and who clearly had zero knowledge about royal protocol. She wondered how many of his Altarian ancestors would be spinning in their graves.

Heaven help Altaria.

Heaven help her.

"I'm not exactly sure what your role is," he said.

"I'm to fill you in on royal protocol and also to learn as much about your preferences as possible so that the palace is well prepared for your arrival, sir."

He raked his hand through his hair. "Translate *royal protocol*."

"Traditional royal etiquette, sir. It's my job to inform you about how the people of Altaria will greet you and how you will be expected to respond."

He sighed again and rubbed his hand over his face. "Etiquette lessons. I'll have to fit them in sometime after an airport expansion plan and a budget review. How about if you take a couple of days to take care of your jet lag and we can get together then?''

''I'm quite able to perform my duties immediately, sir.''

''Tell you what, get settled and we'll talk tomorrow or the next day.''

Erin felt as if she was getting the brush-off. That wouldn't do. Her father, the foreign minister of Altaria, had assigned her this job—in spite of her unfortunate nervous response that had been the bane of her existence as long as she could remember. She couldn't fail her father. This was her opportunity to forge a closer relationship with him. ''I can be useful to you, sir. My father is Altaria's foreign minister, so I'm quite familiar with the political climate.''

Daniel Connelly gave her a considering glance. ''Okay. I'll call you after I get through the most critical matters. Welcome to the Windy City.'' At her puzzled look, he clarified, ''Welcome to Chicago.''

''Thank you, sir.''

''Are you sure you don't want something to drink?''

His insistent hospitality disconcerted her. ''Quite sure, sir. Thank you.''

He nodded and picked up a phone. ''Then I'll tell security to get you a cab.''

''Oh, that's not necessary, sir. I can do that.''

"I'm sure you can, but *my* protocol won't allow me to send a young lady visitor out into the streets of Chicago without transportation to her destination."

A gentleman? A secret warmth slid through her. She'd been surrounded by so many men more concerned with their own self-importance that she almost didn't know how to respond. "Thank you, sir," she murmured as he gave instructions to the security attendant.

Daniel led her to the door and opened it for her. "Why does your accent sound British?" he asked.

"Although I attended Swiss boarding schools, the headmistresses were British."

"Your bearing is similar to my mother's," he said.

"I take that as high praise, sir," she said. "I attended the same boarding school she did years earlier. Princess Emma has always been much beloved and admired by the people of Altaria."

"Even though she gave up her title to marry a rough American upstart?" he asked with a sly, yet appealing grin.

"She may have officially given up her title as princess, sir, but she is always a princess in the hearts of Altarians."

He chuckled. "You're very good. Are you sure you're not a public relations specialist?"

"Knowledge of public relations is required for my position, sir. As I told you, however, part of my job is to learn what pleases you so you will feel at home in Altaria.''

"I'm not hard to please. A Bulls game and a Chicago hot dog, and I'm happy."

Erin blinked, trying to imagine the palace chef preparing a Chicago hot dog. Whatever it was. "I'll make note of it, sir."

"I'm sure you will. Good night."

Daniel winced as he listened to his voice mail messages two days later. Three of them were from Erin Lawrence. He remembered what a prim but curvy little package she'd been. She was so proper, his contrary mind couldn't resist visualizing her stripped of her perfect manners and clothes. Daniel had also noticed, however, that while Miss Lawrence was a babe, she also gave the impression of innocence, forbidden fruit.

He hadn't deliberately pushed her aside, but his transition from Vice President of Marketing at Connelly Corporation to King of Altaria had him swamped. To ensure continuity of succession, the successor to a monarch was normally required to be present immediately, so it seemed odd that the foreign minister had told Daniel they weren't quite ready for him yet. Daniel decided to bide his time with his questions. He had plenty to do with the loose ends he had to tie up in Chicago and the preparations he needed to make for Altaria.

Glancing at his packed-to-the-brim schedule on

his electronic organizer, he saw that dinner was clear and punched out the telephone number for Erin's hotel. "Daniel Connelly here," he said when she answered the phone.

"Thank you for calling, Your Majesty," she said in a proper, but well-modulated tone. Daniel wondered what it would take to ruffle her perfect poise. He wondered what kind of underwear she wore, but pushed the thought aside.

"Sorry it took so long. I've been swamped, and today's not much better. Can you join me for dinner? I'll order pizza and we can meet at my place."

A long paused followed.

"Problem?"

"No, sir," she said, her voice clearly reluctant.

"I hear 'problem' in your voice, Miss Lawrence," he said, feeling a twitch of impatience. "What is it?"

"I'm just trying to determine the propriety of my giving you a protocol lesson in your private quarters, sir," she replied.

"Didn't you tell me earlier that you wanted privacy?" he asked.

"Yes, sir, but—"

"Do you need a chaperone or something?"

"Absolutely not, sir," she said with a trace of defiance in her voice. "I'll meet you for dinner. What time?"

"Make it late," he said. "Seven-thirty."

"Very good sir. I'll see you at seven-thirty."

Daniel hung up the phone and groaned aloud just as the door to his office pushed open to reveal his brother, Brett.

"How's it going, YM?" Brett asked and cracked a half-grin. "The king stuff getting to you already?"

Daniel threw his brother a dark look. "YM?"

"Short for Your Majesty," Brett said. "The press is sniffing around big-time. They all want an interview, but I should be able to hold them off a little longer."

Born with a silver tongue, Brett had been the perfect choice for Vice President of Public Relations for Connelly Corporation. He not only reveled in the ability to work the press to the advantage of Connelly Corporation, he also enjoyed his single playboy status to the max—something Daniel had grown weary of during the past couple of years.

"You think Justin is ready for the world of marketing?" Brett asked.

Their straitlaced brother Justin was steady and responsible and more than willing to climb the Connelly Corporation corporate ladder. "Justin will do a great job replacing me or he'll die trying," he said.

"All of us will miss you, but—"

"—but don't let the door hit me on my way out," Daniel said with a wry chuckle. Whether the game was sports or business, there'd always been a friendly combination of camaraderie and competition among the Connelly males.

"You've done a terrific job," Brett said. "Don't

get me wrong. But I always got the impression you wanted something different. You think this is it?''

Surprised at his brother's insight, Daniel nodded. ''It's got to be. I have to believe fate is at work here. I always wanted to make a difference, not necessarily in the textile world.''

''Those Altarians are damn lucky to get you,'' Brett said.

''I don't know about that. I get the feeling the foreign minister isn't dying for me to move in. He's been slow to send information I've requested, but he did send his daughter,'' Daniel said, unable to mask a slight grimace.

''Daughter? What for?''

''Royal protocol.''

Brett blinked, then barked with laughter. ''She's going to try to teach you everything you tried not to learn from Mom.''

''And more, I'm sure,'' Daniel said, and waved his hand. ''I really don't have time for this right now, but I don't want to be rude.''

''What's she like?''

''Prim and proper,'' Daniel said, then added, ''with killer curves.''

Brett's mouth lifted in a wolfish grin. ''Then maybe there will be some fringe benefits with the lessons, after all.''

Although the prospect of intimately exploring Erin's curves tempted the hell out of him, Daniel shook his head. "I don't think so. I've never seen a woman so determined to make me perfect."

Erin juggled a large pizza box with two volumes on royal etiquette along with a photo book on royal uniforms as she twisted around to push His Majesty's buzzer with her elbow. Since the pizza had arrived at the same time she had, she'd suggested delivering it herself.

Daniel opened the door, and she was struck again by his height. His eyes widened.

"Let me help you—"

Just as he reached for the heavy books, a blur of something large and brown raced across the room and careened into her. Erin toppled toward the floor.

"Jordan, heel!" Daniel yelled, and the dog abruptly backed off.

Her knees hit the hard stone floor, and pain shot through her, but she automatically squeezed her fingers around the pizza box. Her face was going to hit the floor or the pizza box, she thought in despair, just as strong hands caught her shoulders.

Daniel swore under his breath. "I'm sorry," he said. "He smelled the pizza and went nuts. He's spooked by all the visitors that have been in and out of here over the last week."

She felt him lift her as if she were a flower. He carried her to the couch and she was acutely aware of his muscular chest pressed against her. She couldn't recall the last time she'd been carried, not even by her father. She felt an odd, but gentle stroke at a hidden tender spot inside her. It mystified her. She felt Daniel try to pry the box from her fingers.

"You can let go of the pizza now," he said, furrowing his eyebrows.

Still distracted, she felt heat rise to her cheeks. "Oh, I'm sorry, Your Majesty."

He looked at her quizzically. "I'm surprised you didn't drop it when Jordan crashed into you."

She blinked. "Training, I guess, sir. Don't lose your dignity, but if you do, don't spill your tray."

His lips twitched. "Your teacher should be proud." He set the pizza box on top of an entertainment center and turned to the dog. "No pizza for you tonight. That's no way to treat a lady," he muttered.

Erin took a long look at the contrite dog. The animal was huge, with dark soulful eyes and large paws. "I'm not sure I've ever seen that particular breed, sir," she said, unable to mask her curiosity. The beast looked like a combination of a brown bear and a bulldog.

Daniel ruffled the dog's ears. "He's a mixed breed," he said, then shot Erin a look that mixed humor and undiluted masculine sex appeal. "Mixed breed. Kinda like me. Half Altarian royalty and half American rebel," he said and led the whining dog to another room.

So true, she thought, except Daniel was much better-looking than his dog. Erin tried to collect her wits. Taking a deep breath, she wasn't sure which had rattled her more, the dog rushing her or Daniel carrying her to the couch. Her books, she suddenly remembered, reining in her strange feelings. Focus on the job, she told herself, not His Majesty's distracting body. Glancing toward the doorway, she saw the books on the floor. Daniel must have dropped them to catch her.

She moved her legs to rise from the sofa and felt a twinge. She looked down at her stockings. They were shredded and one of her legs was scratched and slightly bleeding.

Daniel returned to the room at that very moment. He swore again and rushed toward her, then bent down and gingerly touched her leg. "Damn. I'll get some antiseptic and a bandage."

Flustered, Erin shook her head. "That's not necessary," she said to his back as he strode from the room. She jumped to her feet to follow him. "Sir, this is not at all proper protocol," she protested, but might as well have been talking to the dog for all the attention Daniel was paying her. As he entered the bathroom, she paused outside the door, uncertain what to do next.

She watched him collect some items from the medicine cabinet and run some water over a washcloth. He turned to face her. "Go back to the sofa," he said, meeting her with a gaze that said he meant business.

"But, sir—"

"But nothing," he returned, striding past her. "My dog did this to you. I'm responsible."

Distressed, she followed him into the living room again and resumed her seat on the sofa. "Sir, this truly is not appropriate."

"What would be appropriate? For me to order a servant to take care of your scratch?"

"Yes, sir, or I could do it myself."

He shook his head and knelt in front of her. "Neither of those choices work for me. I'm king, I'm pulling rank." He glanced at her leg, then met her gaze. "You need to ditch your stockings."

Erin's heart climbed into her throat. Seeing the unswerving determination in his eyes, she held her breath for a full moment. She opened her mouth and closed it, then cleared her throat. "Could you please turn around, sir?" she asked in a voice that sounded high-pitched to her own ears.

Realization crossed his face. He shrugged. "Sure. Let me know when you're ready."

Try never, sir, she thought, as she pushed her stockings down her legs with unsteady hands. The horrified face of her finishing-school teacher flashed before her eyes. Erin had known this assignment would be challenging, but she'd never imagined finding herself in such an awkward position. Stepping out of her pumps, she pulled the shredded hose off her feet and tried again to collect herself.

"Ready?" he asked as if he had eyes in the back of his head.

"Yes, sir," she said reluctantly.

He turned around and lifted his hands just above her knee to the scraped place on her leg. Her leg automatically stiffened. His gaze shot up to meet hers. "Sore?"

"A little, I suppose, sir," she managed, too aware of the fact that His Majesty was kneeling before her. She felt the threat of her dreaded secret nervous response and closed her eyes. She took slow, soothing breaths and pictured a peaceful Swiss snowfall.

An odd intimacy seemed to swim between them when he touched her thigh. His hands were gentle as he cleaned the scrape and applied antibiotic ointment. He put on the bandage and Erin opened her eyes. She caught him looking at her painted toenails.

She couldn't resist the urge to curl her toes into the carpet.

He skimmed his hand down her leg to her feet, sending an odd ripple through her. "These are going to get cold. I can give you some socks," he offered, rising to his feet.

He looked down at her and held her gaze for a long moment in which the world seemed to turn on its axis. Erin held her breath. She watched his gaze dip to her lips for several heart-stopping seconds before he glanced away. Briefly, he shook his head, almost as if he'd considered kissing her, then come to his senses.

Erin wondered when she would come to *her* senses.

"Socks," he muttered. "They may not make the kind of fashion statement you usually make, but you'll be more comfortable." He narrowed his eyes. "Come to think of it, you're not going to want to go back to your hotel with bare legs. I'll get you a pair of sweatpants and a sweatshirt."

Erin felt a rush of panic. Wearing His Majesty's clothes? How had this situation gotten so totally beyond her control? "Thank you very much, sir, but it's truly not necessary."

"Of course it is," he said. "It's January in Chicago. No one in their right mind faces the elements with bare skin," he said, then his eyes glinted with masculine intensity. "Although it's a damn shame to cover legs as nice as yours with sweatpants."

Erin's heart skipped over itself, and a rush of emotions swam through her. How was she supposed to accomplish her job, maintain appropriate distance and, as her father had requested, subtly discourage Daniel from accepting the throne, when Daniel was clearly determined to treat her as a human being more than as a protocol instructor? How, in heaven's name, was she supposed to maintain her equilibrium when this man emanated enough electrical energy to burn her to a crisp?

Two

As Erin sat on Daniel's couch, it occurred to her that it was tough to remain proper and starchy when she was wearing a sweat suit that swallowed her. She stiffened her back. "I brought several books for your reference, sir," she said. "This one is the most complete. I have another on royal etiquette, and I brought a book with pictures of the military uniforms you'll wear for a variety of occasions. Some people absorb information more easily if it's introduced in a visual manner."

Daniel thumbed through one of the books and gave her a considering glance. "You thought I might need a picture book?"

Oops. She hoped she hadn't insulted his intelligence. "With all the information you're being given, sir, I thought it might be easier if some of it weren't delivered to you in such a dry manner."

One side of his lips lifted in a half grin. "I'm curious what you've been told about me."

Erin sifted through half a dozen things her father had told her that couldn't be repeated. "I know you're thirty-four years old and you are Vice President of Marketing for the Connelly Corporation, sir. I've been told you attended college with a football scholarship and you're as American as—" She searched her brain for the correct term. "As popcorn," she said. "Or is it pie?"

He flashed his teeth in a grin. "Both will do."

"The most important thing, sir, is that you are the eldest son of Princess Emma, which makes you the natural heir to the Altarian throne. And you are consenting to relinquish your life as an American to serve as King of Altaria."

He nodded. "Just to fill in a couple of blanks, I graduated from Northwestern with degrees in Business Administration and Philosophy. Do you have a laptop at your hotel?"

She nodded, wondering where this was leading.

He gave a careless shrug. "If you're interested, Northwestern has an informative Web site."

Erin had the uncomfortable feeling that there were quite a few gaps in the profile of Daniel she'd received. "I'll do that, sir."

Daniel glanced back at the book. "Let me get this

straight. Part of my job is to appear at various events in these military uniforms.''

''Yes, sir,'' she said. ''Traditional decorum provides a certain security for the people.''

''Okay. Will there be someone at the palace who will be knowledgeable about what uniform I wear when?''

''Of course, sir. You will have at least two royal dressers at your service.''

''In that case, I could safely delegate the task of whether I wear red or blue to one of the royal dressers, right?''

''I suppose, sir. I thought that since there will be a significant difference in your attire, you would prefer to be informed.''

Daniel shut the book with a smile. ''As long as nobody puts me in a pink tutu, I really don't give a damn.'' He laced his fingers together and leaned toward her. ''I'd really rather know more about the people of Altaria.''

Erin blinked. This definitely wasn't going as planned. Her father had instructed her that if she couldn't discourage Daniel from accepting the throne, then she needed to convince him that the position of king was more decoration than substance. ''The people of Altaria, sir?''

''Yes. You're Altarian. How would you describe your people?''

''Warm and caring, sir,'' she said, thinking of the island people who provided services to tourists and fresh fruit and vegetables. "They're very family-oriented. Because of the isolation of the island, they're not especially sophisticated in terms of higher education."

"Why not?" he prompted.

"We have no schools of higher learning on the island, sir."

"Why not?"

"There never have been. Anyone who wants to send their children to school sends them to the continent."

Daniel frowned. "So if someone was motivated and intelligent, but their family didn't have the means to send them to a university in Europe, then they wouldn't get to go at all?"

She nodded. "Correct, sir. Such a person would likely continue to do whatever his or her father or mother did."

"And what is the parliament's stand on this?"

"The parliament is slow to change without considerable provocation."

He frowned again as if he didn't like her answer. "What do you think the people of Altaria want in a king?"

She felt a distressing tug in opposite directions. Part of her was drawn to Daniel's sincere interest in her people, while at the same time she couldn't forget her father's wishes. Erin found she could only answer him honestly. "Sir, I believe the citizens of Altaria want a king who will provide a bridge from the past to the future. Even Americans understand that tradition can be a source of comfort in times of grief. Altaria takes great pride in the unbroken line of succession the Rosemeres have provided. Altarians want a ruler who appreciates where they have been and where they need to go.''

Daniel nodded slowly. ''I guess that means I need to bone up on Altarian history. You said you were familiar with the political climate. How does the parliament feel about an American taking the throne?''

Her stomach tightened, and she glanced away. ''The official stance is that the parliament is pleased there is a healthy heir ready and willing to take the throne, sir. Many were surprised that you would agree to give up your privacy and freedom to accept the job.''

Daniel sighed and stood. He moved toward the huge picture window and glanced out. ''I don't believe in shirking family duty. My parents drilled into all of us that we have responsibilities to fulfill. I wouldn't be able to look myself in the mirror if I didn't fulfill mine, but—'' He broke off and glanced at her. ''But I've always felt I was biding my time at Connelly Corporation. God knows, I wouldn't have chosen to be king, but it appears the job has chosen me.'' He turned to meet her eyes, and she felt the intensity in his gaze clear down to her toes. ''I'm a Connelly. I can't do less than my best.''

His words vibrated between them, and Erin began

to sense that there was far more to Daniel Connelly than she or her father could have imagined.

His green gaze shifted like the Chicago wind as he moved toward her. "You've told me the official position of the parliament. What's the unofficial stance?"

Erin's mind locked in panic. She needed to obey her father and follow his wishes, but... She tried to find a way to protect her father without undermining her own sense of integrity. "Unofficially and officially, the parliament embraces tradition and is very slow to change, sir."

"A nice way of saying I probably make them nervous," he said.

"I didn't say that, sir," she protested.

"You didn't have to." He cocked his head to one side. "I make you nervous, too."

Confounded was a more accurate description, she thought. "No, sir. Of course not," she said, but felt she wasn't exactly telling the truth.

"Not at all?" he asked, sitting down on the couch next to her.

Her stomach fluttered nervously at his closeness. "Well, perhaps a little, sir. You're not exactly what I expected."

"How am I different?" he asked, his gaze so intense she wondered if he could see straight through her.

Erin barely resisted the urge to squirm. "It's truly not my place to say, sir," she said.

Irritation crossed his face. "Well, I'm king, so what happens if I'd like to know?"

She bit her lip as her stomach churned. "Is that an order, sir?"

"Is that what it takes?"

"Yes, sir," she said reluctantly.

He nodded decisively. "Done. How am I different from what you expected?"

Erin took a deep breath and wished she could fly away through that huge plate-glass window. She looked away from him. "You're more intelligent than I expected, sir," she admitted in a low voice, then added an explanation. "Football scholarship."

"Northwestern is a highly competitive university. The academic requirements are high for everyone, including the football team."

"Oh," she said.

"What else?"

"You have a sense of honor that surprises me, sir. Your interest in the Altarian people is... unexpected. You are kinder and less self-absorbed than I would have imagined," she continued and took a shallow breath. Her chest felt tight with anxiety. "You look at me when I talk to you. You pay attention to what I say."

"That surprises you?" he asked.

She met his gaze and nodded silently.

"Why would I not pay attention to what you say?" he asked.

She shrugged and thought of how many times

she'd felt that her father looked past her instead of at her. "I don't know sir. I guess I'm just not accustomed to it."

He frowned thoughtfully for a moment, then met her eyes again. "What else?"

Erin had the frightful urge yet again to fidget. She clenched her hands together in her lap. "You are taller, sir," she said. And better looking, she thought, but she refused to utter those words.

"What's the height of the average Altarian man?" he asked.

"I don't know, sir. Shorter than you."

He chuckled. "How have I not surprised you?"

Erin's stomach tightened with dread. "Is that an order, sir?"

He nodded and cracked a grin. "Yeah."

"You are very American, very casual, and you couldn't be less interested in learning royal protocol. Sir," she added, and relaxed. She was finished. No more honest and potentially embarrassing disclosures.

"You're right about that," he said. "To keep it fair, I'll tell you how you're different from what I expected."

Erin's stomach immediately twisted into a square knot.

"Even though I knew you were the foreign minister's daughter, I imagined you would be a lot older."

"Older, sir?" she managed.

"Around fifty with orthopedic shoes, and annoyingly prissy and proper."

His words stung. Annoyingly prissy and proper hit a bit close to home.

"Instead, you're this blue-eyed blonde with killer legs who is annoyingly prissy and proper," he said, softening his assessment with a sexy grin. "But maybe it's your job to be prissy and proper. I can't help imagining what you're like when you're not on the clock or on guard," he said, putting his hand over hers and gently prying her fingers from their locked position. "In time, maybe I'll find out."

Erin's heart stuttered. Not if she could help it.

An hour and a half later, after Erin had returned to her hotel room and scoured the Northwestern University Web site, she paced the floor of her small suite. Her phone rang and she knew immediately who it was. Her father.

"Have you met with the American?" he asked without preamble.

"Yes, I met with His Majesty tonight."

"Are you making progress with him?"

Not much, she thought, pushing her hair from her face. "I find I wasn't given adequate information about our new king," she said, unable to keep her irritation from her voice.

"What information?" her father asked.

"I was led to believe he wasn't particularly bright."

"He isn't," her father insisted. "He's a football player."

"Father, this man graduated with honors from a prestigious university." She still felt like a fool because of her wrong assumptions about Daniel.

"That doesn't qualify him to rule Altaria," her father said.

"No. The only thing that qualifies him to be King of Altaria is the fact that he is the eldest male Rosemere. He could easily be an eighteen-year-old inheriting the throne. Instead he's an intelligent, experienced thirty-four-year-old man."

"An eighteen-year-old would likely be easier to manage," her father grumbled. "Do you think you'll be able to discourage him from taking the throne?"

Erin's chest tightened with conflicting feelings. She understood some of her father's reservations about Daniel. He was an American, after all, with very little knowledge or appreciation of Altaria's history. Her father feared Daniel would move in like a bull in a china shop, disrupting the peace and tranquillity of the kingdom. Erin remembered the determined expression on Daniel's face when he talked about taking the throne. "I don't know, Father. I sense His Majesty views his role as king as an act of duty and honor."

Her father's disapproving silence stretched on, and Erin closed her eyes.

"You're not switching loyalties, are you?" he asked quietly.

"No," she said, but she wondered how she would settle the conflict tugging at her. Her father wasn't here, dealing with Daniel Connelly in the flesh. "You are my father and Altaria is my country."

"Remember, Erin, just because he is a good man doesn't mean he would be good for Altaria. Get some sleep, child. I will call again," he said and hung up.

Erin returned the phone to the cradle and stared out the window at the lights of the Chicago skyline. She hugged her arms around herself. Her father had called her child. She hadn't felt like a child for years. Her mother had died when Erin was so young that she only had vague memories of softness, gentle laughter, sweet touches and perfume.

Spending her childhood in boarding school had made her grow up quickly, forced to depend only on herself. She'd spent a lot of years hiding her loneliness. Now she finally had a chance to forge a bond with her father, and she wasn't at all sure she would be able to accomplish it.

She absently rubbed the soft fleece sweatshirt and glanced down at the too-large sweatpants she still wore. It was odd, but wearing Daniel's sweat suit made her feel as if she were wrapped in a big, warm hug. She wondered what it would be like to be wrapped in Daniel's arms. She wondered how his lips would feel on her mouth, on her skin. The thought nearly gave her hiccups.

Ridiculous, she thought, rolling her eyes at herself. She went to the bathroom to brush her teeth and tried to dismiss her unsettling thoughts about His Majesty. She chanted the title to drill it into her mind. "His Majesty, His Majesty, His Majesty," she murmured as she pulled out a nightgown and changed her clothes.

Erin immediately noticed that the big, warm hug was gone. She dashed under the covers and pulled them up over her head just as she'd done a thousand times as a child. She tried not to think about Daniel, but she couldn't forget how gently he'd touched her thigh and how he'd insisted she wear his clothes. She couldn't forget that when she talked to him, he looked at her, not past her. She couldn't forget *him*.

"I know it's short notice," Daniel said the following morning. "But if you're not doing anything tonight, would you attend the Big Brothers' charity ball tonight with me?"

Since Erin had arrived in Chicago, she hadn't been less busy in her life. She struggled to mesh her job description with Daniel's last-minute invitation. "A Big Brothers' charity ball, sir?" she echoed.

"It's one of my family's pet charities and I promised I would attend before I got the king assignment. I told my mother I would still attend as long as I can keep it low profile. In other words, we'll arrive late and leave early. Are you game?''

Her mind still reeling, Erin twisted the phone cord around her finger. ''But why me, sir?''

''There are other women I could take, but I'd spend the evening dodging any discussion of my future plans. I'm leaving this world and going into another. You're the one who understands that best.''

Flattered despite herself, Erin felt her heart swell in her chest.

''So, yes or no?''

She fought a thread of panic. ''I didn't bring anything appropriate to wear to a ball.''

''This is Chicago, a shopping Mecca,'' he said, countering her concern. ''Put what you need on my tab and make sure you get a wrap too. The ball begins at eight. I'll pick you up at eight-thirty.''

''Yes, sir,'' she said, wondering which turn this roller-coaster assignment was going to take next.

Ten hours later, a knock sounded at Erin's door and her heart rate sprinted. She opened the door and her breath caught at the sight of Daniel in a black tux with a black overcoat and a white cashmere scarf. The image of the American upstart was immediately replaced with that of a sophisticated, dangerously handsome man.

His gaze trailed over her. ''You clean up very nicely, Miss Lawrence,'' he said with a sensual edge to his voice.

''Thank you, Your Majesty. So do—'' Appalled,

she bit her tongue at the inappropriately personal remark.

His lips curved in a hint of a smile. "Damn. Don't tell me it's improper to compliment the king?"

Erin wondered if her entire body was blushing. His expression made her feel as if he were hungry and she was the first course. "Of course not, sir, but I am in your service."

He nodded. "So what's the proper way to compliment a king?"

Erin took a careful breath and tried to unscramble her brain. "If I may say so, Your Majesty looks quite dashing this evening."

"Dashing," he said. "Sounds like something out of an old English novel. I guess that means it wouldn't be proper to say you look hot enough to start another three-alarm fire in downtown Chicago?"

The same was true of him, she thought. "That's correct, sir," she said.

"But you won't mind if I give the fire department a call to warn them about you," he said, his mouth unsmiling, but his eyes full of masculine humor.

"Me?"

His gaze fell over her with dangerous awareness. "Yes, you."

Three

Daniel led Erin through the grand lobby of the hotel where the ball was being held. Sweeping her into a brass-lined elevator, he tugged at his collar as soon as the doors closed. "We won't stay long. I've grown impatient with these affairs during the last couple of years. I'd rather do almost anything than just make an appearance."

"Pardon me, sir, but you know that your appearance at state and social functions will be quite important to the people of Altaria," Erin pointed out.

He nodded. "I know. I can dress to suit the occasion. But I also know that the personality and vision of the man wearing the crown determines his role. I plan to spend as much time doing things as I will spend making appearances."

Erin felt a ripple of uneasiness as she thought of her father's diametrically opposed view of Daniel's role as king. She looked at the strong, dynamic man in front of her and wondered how she would be able to convince him that he would be more of a figure-head. Not bloody likely. Especially when her own opinion was beginning to waver. She felt a light-ning-fast jab of pain and slammed the door on her thoughts. She had a job to do for her country, for her father.

Daniel led her away from the main entrance to the ballroom down the hall and to another door. "We decided it would call less attention to me if I weren't announced," he said. "The press will have to search for me."

Erin glanced at him and couldn't help shaking her head at his comment.

He stopped. "What?"

"Nothing, sir," she said.

Daniel sighed. "I really don't want to have to do this, but—"

Erin cringed. She suspected she knew what was coming.

"I order you to tell me what you're thinking," he said. "For the rest of the evening."

Erin gaped at him in shock. "The entire evening, sir?" she echoed, aghast.

He nodded. "So cough it up. Why did you shake your head when I said the press would have to search for me?"

Erin closed her eyes in embarrassment. "Must I, sir?"

"Yes."

She swallowed a howl of frustration. "If you want to avoid attention, sir, you need to shrink your height and intelligence. And you would have to do something to make yourself look more plain. You draw attention just by entering the room."

He dipped his head close to hers. "You're a lot more fun when you're honest," he murmured and took her hand. "Let's go."

He pulled her into a huge room filled with beautifully dressed party-goers. Music emanated from an orchestra playing on the far end. The marble-floored ballroom was decorated with mirrors and crystal chandeliers. Tables of appetizers and pastries lined one corner of the room while waiters carried trays of champagne throughout the crowd.

Erin remembered when she had accompanied her father to other parties. Her job had been essentially to disappear once the announcements had been made. "I can excuse myself while you make your necessary rounds, sir," she offered, disengaging her hand from his.

He frowned at her. "Why?"

"Because I'm certain there are people with whom you must speak, sir."

"Is there a reason you can't speak to them too?"

Confused, she slowly shook her head. "No, sir. I thought my purpose for the evening was to provide the appearance of an escort and stay in the background as much as possible.''

"No," he said. "Your job for the evening is to make this bearable, and you can start by ditching the 'sir.' If anyone overhears you, it will make them curious. You probably need to pretend to like me.''

Her stomach twisted, and, at a loss, she nervously twined her fingers together. "If I may ask, si—'' She broke off. "How am I to make this bearable? And how should I pretend to like you?'' she asked, determined to keep the panic from her voice.

He shrugged. "Damned if I know. Here comes my brother Brett. You can practice with him.''

Brett patted his shoulder. "Good of you to show up, YM,'' Brett said, abbreviating the royal address.

"How are you keeping the press at bay?'' Daniel asked, surveying the room.

"There are a few here, but they're wearing special name tags and red roses. Who can resist a rose?''

"Clever,'' Daniel said, admiring his brother's savvy. "I'd like you to meet Erin Lawrence. Erin, this is my brother Brett. He's the master of public relations for Connelly Corporation and the reason I'm here tonight.''

Daniel watched his lady-killer brother give Erin a glance of approval and felt a swift jab of protectiveness toward her.

Brett took Erin's hand and lifted it to his lips. *"Enchanté mademoiselle.''*

"Merci beaucoup, Your Hi—'' Her eyes widened

in alarm as she looked at Daniel. "I'm sorry, si—" She shook her head. "I'm sorry. It slipped."

"Years of breeding," Daniel said dryly.

"I don't mind being called Your Highness," Brett said smoothly. "Particularly by such a lovely young woman."

Daniel fought a ripple of irritation. "Excuse us just a moment," he said to Erin, then moved a few steps away with his brother. "Stop hitting on her. She's young."

"Not that young," Brett said. "Her accent is sexy and that body—"

"She's only twenty-two, and she's spent her life in boarding schools. She might as well have been raised in a convent."

Brett lifted a dark brow. "Who are you trying to convince? Me or you?"

Me, Daniel thought. The last thing in the world he needed right now was to be sexually distracted by his prim and proper protocol instructor, but damned if he wasn't. "How's Mom?" he asked, knowing his mother was still struggling with the double loss of her father and brother.

Brett's face grew serious. "Perfectly composed. Just don't look at her eyes very long or your gut will start to ache for her."

Daniel quickly glanced around the room and spotted his parents. "Dad's sticking by her side."

"Like glue," Brett said.

"That will help," Daniel said.

"Knowing that you're accepting the title and the job that goes with it helps too," Brett added quietly.

Daniel felt a gnawing impatience to get on with his transition, but he knew change took time. "Go make your rounds," he said.

"Thanks for coming. I know it's a strange time for you. If you're smart, though, you could take a little solace from Erin Lawrence."

"There'll be a heat wave in Chicago in January before I take romantic advice from you."

"She looks pretty hot to me," Brett shot back, then scooted through the crowd to avoid Daniel's wrath.

Sighing, Daniel returned to Erin. "I see my parents. Let's go say hello."

Erin lifted her hand to her throat. "Your mother? The princess?"

"My mother, Emma Rosemere Connelly," he said, although he was accustomed to the star-struck response. Emma inspired admiration of mythic proportions. "Remember to ditch the titles," he said, guiding her through the crowd.

His mother was dressed in a black gown. Most would admire her sophisticated beauty and miss the grief, but Daniel immediately caught the sadness in his mother's gaze and felt a twist inside him. He kissed her cheek. "You look beautiful."

Emma smiled. "I'm going to miss you," she said, and turned her gaze on Erin. "Ah, you must be the woman with the formidable job of teaching my son royal protocol. Erin Lawrence. A pleasure to meet you.''

Daniel felt Erin start to dip into a curtsey and slipped his arm around her waist to prevent it. She shot him a look of dark chagrin.

''It's my honor to meet you, Your Hi—'' She broke off and smiled. ''Mrs. Connelly. At the boarding school I attended, you're greatly revered.''

''Not always,'' Emma said with a smile of reminiscence. ''Years ago, the teachers despaired over my lack of interest in those tiresome etiquette classes. It's amazing what time and distance can do. Please meet my husband, Grant.''

Daniel's father greeted Erin and shook his head. ''You're so young for such a challenging job,'' he said, glancing pointedly at Daniel.

''I was just thinking the same thing,'' Emma said. ''It can be lonely in a different country. You must join us for dinner. I'll call Daniel soon to arrange a time.''

''Thank you,'' Erin said, appearing stunned as Daniel led her away.

He snagged two glasses of champagne and lifted one glass to Erin's lips. ''Drink up. Having a father as foreign minister, you must have met plenty of renowned people before.''

She took a quick sip, then another. ''I have,'' she admitted. ''But your family is so kind. Your mother, your father, your brother, they obviously care for you so much and it's clearly reciprocal. How can you bear to leave them for Altaria?''

Daniel glanced away. She'd unknowingly touched a tender spot he kept concealed. So far, the most difficult part of accepting the throne would be moving far from the people he trusted most to a place where he wasn't sure there would be anyone he could trust. He met her gaze. ''I guess a big part of the reason I choose to leave is to honor my family's bond. Nothing will change it, titles, oceans, nothing.''

Erin's eyes grew shiny, and she glanced at the floor. He wondered what was racing through her mind.

''Say it aloud,'' he said.

She looked up at him in surprise. ''Pardon?''

''Say what you're thinking.''

''I'm trying to imagine what it would be like to have a family like yours, to share that kind of love.''

''Don't you have that with your father?''

He looked into her eyes and in one swift moment, he saw a mile-wide streak of loneliness that shook him. As if she were afraid he'd seen too much, she looked away. ''Of course,'' she murmured, but the words were spoken too late with too little conviction.

Daniel would have to think about that later, he decided. When he wasn't thinking about the three hundred other items on his to-do list. He downed the rest of his champagne and glanced at her averted head. "You're falling down on your job," he said.

Her head immediately shot up. "Pardon?"

"You're supposed to make this ball bearable."

"I hadn't quite figured out how to do that," she said and took another sip of her champagne. "What do you usually enjoy doing at these affairs?"

"Figuring out how to leave early," he said. "What do you usually enjoy doing at these affairs?"

Her lips twitched. "I make a game of guessing what's in the appetizers, and sometimes I waltz."

"Let's head for the food," he said, guiding her toward the tables laden with food. "I'm not big on waltzing."

"You must waltz," she said firmly. "You will be expected to lead the first dance for many occasions."

"I'll appoint an official waltzing representative," he joked, and chuckled at the look of disapproval she shot him.

They drew near the tables, and Daniel chose an appetizer. He lifted the small bite to his mouth, but Erin stopped him halfway.

"The game is to guess the appetizer *before* you eat it," she said.

"I thought I was supposed to guess after I ate it."

"That wouldn't present as much of a challenge," she said. "Unless the food is very bad." She eyed the small morsel of food. "I guess that's crab and mushroom."

"I agree," he said.

She looked at him and groaned. "You are supposed to guess something different."

"You stole the best guess," he said with a shrug.

"I didn't steal anything," she protested.

"Let's see if you're right." Daniel lifted the appetizer to her mouth.

Her eyes widened in surprise, but she opened her mouth. Daniel watched her tongue curl around the bite of food and felt an unsettling twist of arousal. Her attempted perfection goaded the hell out of him. She made him want to tease her. He wanted to pull down her hair, make her laugh and mess up her lipstick by kissing the breath and starch out of her.

He had to keep telling himself she was only twenty-two, twelve years younger than he.

She swallowed and licked her lips, and Daniel felt another twist of arousal. The sight of her pink tongue generated a dozen forbidden images in his mind.

"Definitely crab and mushroom," she said. "I choose the next one." She glanced over the table and pointed to a dessert tray. "Your turn to guess."

"That's easy. It's a puff pastry," Daniel said.

"But anything could be inside," she said. "What's inside?"

Daniel lifted one of the pastries and scrutinized it. "These remind me of you. Easy to see what you are on the outside, but I can't help wondering what's inside," he said, searching her eyes. At times, she reminded him of a lost little girl. Other times, he wanted to strip off her clothes and know her every way a man could know a woman.

She looked away as if she didn't want him to see too much. "I'm not that complicated," she murmured, then glanced back up at him. "Are you stalling with your guess?"

"Butterscotch swirl," he said and lifted the pastry to her lips. He didn't have time to be curious about this woman, but he was.

She opened her mouth and accepted the small bite of dessert. "How did you know it was butterscotch?"

"Insider information. Butterscotch is my father's favorite. The menu planners try to please him when they know he'll be attending."

"What is your favorite?"

"Variety," Daniel said as he caught sight of a press representative. "I see someone with a rose. Let's head for that alcove."

Daniel led her into a small, dim room and closed the doors behind them. The outer wall was lined with windows that allowed the city lights to shine into the room, and the orchestral music was piped in from a speaker in the ceiling.

Aside from the music, the only sound Erin could hear was her pounding heart. She was alone with Daniel Connelly. She'd been alone with him before, but the thick veil of formality had always provided her with protection and comfort. Tonight Daniel had insisted on dropping the formality, and he had treated her more like a date than an employee. More like a woman than a protocol teacher.

She'd watched the tenderness he'd extended to his mother and couldn't help but feel moved. She'd seen the combination of camaraderie and mutual respect he shared with his brother and felt acutely the lack of the family she'd always wanted, but never had.

She was supposed to discourage Daniel from taking the throne because he was wrong for Altaria, but the more she learned about Daniel, the more confused she became. Heaven help her, she felt his eyes on her and could hardly breathe.

She heard the first strains of a familiar waltz and an idea hit her. Desperate for a diversion from her thoughts, she grasped at it. ''This is a waltz,'' she said. ''I can teach you how. You'll need to know how once you move into the palace.'' Biting her lip, she lifted her arms into dance position.

''You're going to teach me?'' he echoed, taking her hand and curling his other hand around her waist.

His closeness halted her breath all over again and second thoughts slammed through her. She cleared her throat and trained her eyes on his left shoulder. ''Yes, the waltz is done in steps of three. One-two-three, one-two-three.'' After years of training, her feet moved automatically. Thank goodness. She continued counting and he slowly followed. Before she knew it, however, he was leading her.

Erin looked at him suspiciously. "I thought you said you didn't waltz."

"I said I'm not big on waltzing," he said. "Do you really think Emma Rosemere Connelly would allow her firstborn son to take a pass on social dance lessons even if he'd rather be playing football?"

An image played across her mind of Daniel at a younger age futilely protesting dance lessons. She smiled. "I suppose not. But you actually waltz quite well for someone who dislikes it."

The music slowed, and so did Daniel. The blatant male sexuality in his expression made her heart race. He lowered his forehead to hers and whispered, "Maybe I needed a different dance partner."

Four

"**I** know there's more work to be done during this transition, and I'm ready to get on with it," Daniel told his brother Brett three days later as he made another note on a new marketing proposal for Connelly Corporation.

"What do you mean?" Brett asked.

Unable to sit, Daniel stood as he struggled with a nagging impatience that was becoming all too familiar. He was tired of feeling split between two worlds. "I mean the facade is wearing thin. If I were doing this my way, then I would be in Altaria now. I'm still not getting the information I want from Erin's father, the foreign minister, as fast as I want it. It's almost as if everyone's throwing logs on the road in front of me to slow me down."

Brett threw him a cautious glance. "You know you're not going to be able to change everything in a day."

"I know," Daniel said. "But until I get all the information I want, I can't do anything. I'm letting you know because I'm cutting back on Connelly time. I'll tell my assistant sometime during the next week."

Brett nodded his head slowly. "You know your succession to the throne will hit the news right away."

Daniel took a deep breath. He knew his life would be turned upside down once the media found out he was accepting the throne. "It's going to be part of the job. Just like all this royal protocol Miss Perfect Erin is trying to teach me."

Daniel glanced up at that moment to catch Miss Perfect right behind his brother. He saw the look of hurt on her face and swallowed an oath. He shouldn't take his frustration out on her, but damn if the woman hadn't said Your Majesty and sir to him so many times since the ball he thought he could break a window.

"Let's finish this later," Daniel said to Brett.

Confusion crossed Brett's face. "But—"

"Hello, Erin," Daniel said meaningfully and watched realization cross his brother's face.

"Oh." Brett nodded. "Later. Keep me posted. Hi, Erin," he said as he strode out the door.

"Your Highness," she murmured to his back.

"Your Majesty," she then said to Daniel in a voice that dripped ice. "Begging your pardon. Perhaps you forgot that we were to meet for an hour just before lunch."

"I did forget," he admitted and closed the door behind her. "And I offended you. I'm sorry."

She waved her hand. "Oh, no, sir. It's my job to present the best possible example to you, and you are certainly more than entitled to your opinion. It's unfortunate that I've been unsuccessful in conveying to you the importance of tradition and royal protocol in your new role as King of Altaria."

Erin's clipped voice cut his conscience like knives. Why did he feel as if he'd just kicked a puppy? He rubbed his face. "You're right. I don't put the same priority on tradition as you do. But just because I don't buy everything you tell me doesn't give me the right to hurt your feelings."

Her eyes widened. "No, sir. You didn't hurt my feel—"

"I damn well did," he said, cutting her off. "And I don't like that I did it. We need a truce."

"A truce, sir?" she echoed doubtfully.

"We're not going to get anywhere if you stick to your guns and I stick to mine. I'll work on understanding why this royal protocol is so important if you'll work on figuring out how to bring part of my world to Altaria."

Her eyebrows furrowed in confusion. "I'm not certain what you mean, sir."

Daniel tossed his pen on his desk in frustration. "I mean we're going to take turns. I'm going to try to look at things from your point of view and you're going to look at things from my point of view."

Erin frowned. "But how can we accomplish that, sir? I know very little of your life."

Daniel wondered if part of the reason it drove him nuts for Erin to call him sir was because it reminded him of their twelve-year age difference. "You're going to have to spend some extra time with me, and the first new rule is no more 'Your Majesty' or 'sir' unless we're specifically discussing royal protocol."

She lifted her chin. "Begging your pardon, sir, it is entirely correct for me to address you as Your Majesty."

"It may be correct, but it bugs the hell out of me."

"Begging your pardon again, sir, but you must know that everyone in Altaria will address you in this manner."

"Unless I request them to address me differently. Correct?"

Reluctance shimmered in her eyes. "Yes, sir."

"Drop the sir," he told her. "If you need to fill in the gap, say my name. Daniel."

"Yes-s-s—" She drew out the word as if adding sir was compulsory. She glared at him. "Yes, Daniel."

"Thank you, Erin. Tomorrow's Saturday. I'll pick you up around 11:00 a.m. Wear jeans."

Erin blinked. "I don't have any jeans. The schools I attended didn't allow them and my father doesn't approve of them."

"Well, you've graduated from boarding school and Daddy's not here," Daniel said, struggling to keep the edge from his voice. He had more than one reason to be irritated with Erin's father. "You need casual clothes to blend in where we're going, and the closest to casual I've seen you wear was my sweat pants. Buy a couple of pairs of jeans and whatever else you need and put them on the Connelly account."

She gave a slow, reluctant nod of agreement. "When will we have our next royal protocol consultation?" she asked, determination in her voice.

"After our outing tomorrow," he said and figured they were even. Erin would probably dislike their field trip as much as he detested the protocol lessons.

The following morning Daniel pulled his sport utility vehicle up in front of Erin's hotel and opened his car door only to spot her striding through the revolving door to meet him. She wore jeans, a cuddly sweater and a casual overcoat, and her hair hung in a shiny curtain to her shoulders.

"Good morning, Daniel," she said, meeting his gaze so directly he felt as if he'd been broadsided.

"Good morning, Erin." His attention caught by her hair, he helped her into the car and got in. "You look good,'' he said as he pulled the car out into traffic.

She lifted an eyebrow in disbelief. "My father would probably disown me."

"Is your dad that uptight, or is he afraid he's going to have to beat the men off you?"

Erin did a double take. "Beat the men off me?" she said in disbelief.

"Yeah. If you wear your hair down like that all the time and bag the perfection syndrome, you'll have to fight them off."

Erin turned silent. "That problem hasn't presented itself so far. Besides, my father is well aware of the fact that I'm not perfect. You've said your family is competitive. You should understand the drive for perfection."

"My father always taught us there's a difference between striving for perfection and doing your best. Doing your best means you recognize you can make a contribution by pushing yourself to be the best you can be. Striving for perfection just makes you cranky."

Erin looked at Daniel and swallowed a sigh. She so wanted not to like him. Disliking Daniel would make her job so much easier. When he spouted something about perfection that went against everything her father had taught her, yet somehow resonated in her heart, she was at a loss to maintain her disapproval of him. "You're very fortunate to have grown up with such supportive parents."

"You've said that more than once. What's your mother like?"

Erin laced her fingers together. "She died when I was very young. My father's professional position was demanding, so I've spent most of my life in boarding schools."

Daniel was silent for a long moment. "That must have been tough."

Erin felt her heart tighten. She didn't want him to feel sorry for her. "I was actually quite fortunate. I've been given the best possible education."

Daniel nodded, but he didn't look convinced. He pulled into an alley behind an older building and stopped the car.

"Where are—"

He took her hands and looked into her eyes, causing her words to stall. "Just because you didn't get the same kind of support I got growing up doesn't mean you didn't deserve it."

Her heart squeezed tight again at his combination of strength and gentleness. It was almost as if he'd known the words she'd longed to hear. But he couldn't possibly, she told herself. He couldn't possibly.

"Yo! Daniel!" a man called outside the car, interrupting the moment that seemed to move her ever closer to Daniel. "Open the trunk."

Erin looked at Daniel in confusion. "The trunk. What are we doing?"

"We're at a soup kitchen that operates out of the

basement of a church. I get donations from some of the local restaurants, pick up sandwiches on Saturday morning, and we feed some people who need a meal.''

Astonished, Erin stared at the men unloading the back of Daniel's vehicle. ''You do this every Saturday?''

''For the past four years,'' he said, exiting his side of the car and coming around to open her door. He offered his hand to assist her. ''You look surprised.''

Erin accepted his hand to make the big step to the ground. ''I don't know what I expected, but I didn't expect this,'' she said, as their eyes met.

He skimmed his fingers down a strand of her hair. ''I'm a hands-on kind of man.''

Erin felt a dip in her stomach. Her father would be less than thrilled with that information. She pulled her hand from his. ''How can I help?''

''You can watch. You don't have to do anything,'' he told her, striding past her to pick up a huge tray of sandwiches.

Erin hurried after him. ''But I'd like to help,'' she said.

He met her gaze and assessed her. ''Okay, but you need to understand you'll see all kinds of people in there today. College graduates, homeless families and a few alcoholics, but no royal titles.''

Slightly affronted by his tone, she frowned. ''I'm not a snob.''

He lifted a dark eyebrow. ''Could've fooled me.''

"I may be a bit strict about the rules of protocol, but I'm not a snob," she insisted.

He nodded, although he didn't appear entirely convinced. "Okay. If you want to help, I'll introduce you to the soup kitchen leader. Joe!" he called as he walked through the open entrance into a large room filled with tables covered with white paper.

Erin followed Daniel and couldn't help noticing the way his jeans molded to his long legs and muscular backside. She blinked at her observation. Heaven help her. She was ogling His Majesty. Again. Her cheeks burned with a mixture of consternation and self-consciousness.

A tall man with a scrubby beard and friendly eyes approached them. He thumped Daniel on the back. "Good to see you."

"Same," Daniel said and cocked his head toward Erin as he set the huge sandwich tray down on a long serving table. "I brought a visitor with me this time. Joe Graham, meet Erin Lawrence. She wants you to put her to work."

"It's a pleasure to meet you, Mr. Graham," Erin said.

Joe beamed. "My pleasure. Call me Joe. Love the accent and so will the masses. You don't have to serve. I just want you to talk for the next two hours."

Daniel groaned.

"Pardon?" Erin said, confused.

Daniel returned to her side. "Joe likes your accent. American men in general like your accent. It's sexy."

Astonished, Erin gasped and shook her head. She swallowed her amazement. "There is nothing sexy about my accent," she said, and lowered her voice. "There's nothing sexy about me,"she said more to herself than to him. She should never forget that Daniel was light-years ahead of her in sexual experience.

Daniel's gaze was so intense he could have leveled a forest with it. "Who told you that?"

Erin got an odd jumpy feeling in her stomach. "Well, no one. But no one has told me differently either."

"Hm," he said, and the sound was short, but left her filled with a hundred questions.

She never got the answers, as she was put to work ladling soup into disposable bowls, while others set out plates with sandwiches and cups of hot coffee. Daniel had been correct about the wide range of people who came for food. In her conversations with them, she observed that they represented all demographics and all walks of life. She enjoyed chatting with the people and couldn't remember a time she'd felt so useful and appreciated.

Just as the line began to wind down, Joe let out a whoop of happiness. "TV camera crews are coming down the steps. Everybody give me a big smile and think *donations.*"

In no time, Daniel appeared by her side. "We

can't stay. I don't want to be recognized, and I don't want them going after you,'' he murmured into her ear. The door where they'd entered was blocked by a group of people waiting to sit down. Daniel closed his hand around her arm. ''Follow me,'' he said, guiding her down a short hallway with three doors. He tried the first two doors, but they were locked. He finally found one that opened.

''Bingo,'' he said and scowled when he looked inside. ''It'll have to do. We shouldn't have to wait long.''

''Wait where?'' Erin asked, not liking the expression she saw on his face.

''In this closet.''

Five

"**W**hy on earth would we need to go into a closet?" Erin demanded.

"Hey, Daniel," a voice called from the main serving area. "Where's Daniel?"

"That's why," Daniel said, ushering her into the closet and closing the door. It was as black as pitch. More calls for Daniel echoed down the hall.

Erin felt Daniel's arm slide behind her waist and his hand gently covered her mouth. "Be quiet for the next few minutes," he whispered.

He touched her as if he'd known she might be uneasy in the dark with him, and she felt another stone fall from her defenses. She stood in silence and breathed in his scent and absorbed his strength.

He stood close enough for her to feel his chest brush hers. She could barely hear the sound of footsteps above her pounding heart.

She felt safe and breathless at the same time.

"I think they're gone, but we probably need to wait a few minutes before they leave the building," he finally said in a low voice after a door down the hall closed. "You okay?"

She nodded. "Yes," she whispered, reluctant to break the odd spell.

"After I dragged you in here, it occurred to me that you might have a fear of enclosed spaces. But it was too late."

The sound of his voice was low and intimate, the same voice he might use in bed with a lover. The knowledge warmed her from the inside out. She took a careful half breath. "Even as a child, I always liked small places," she confessed. "Something about them made me feel safer."

She felt his fingers sift through her hair. "Sometimes when I look at you, I wonder what you were like as a little girl."

Her stomach twisted at his remark. Although her childhood hadn't been miserable, she'd always wanted to belong, to be needed. She felt a strange knot of emotion form in her throat.

"Were you always so determined to be perfect?" he asked.

The darkness made it easier to talk. "I tried, but of course, I never was. I always thought that if I were perfect then someone would—'' Her throat swelled shut around the words.

''Someone would what?'' he prompted.

''Someone would want me with them all the time, and I wouldn't have to be alone,'' she said, and felt a tear burn a trail down her cheek. Shocked at the display of emotion, she blinked and thanked her lucky stars that Daniel couldn't see her. She tried to step back, but he tightened his hold on her.

He lifted his hand to her hair again, and she held her breath, terrified he would find her damp cheek. She was fully dressed, but she had never felt more naked. His hand grazed her cheek and abruptly stopped.

She heard and felt his sharp intake of breath. He lowered his fingers to her lips and chin and his mouth touched hers. It was a tender caress, reassuring and searching. She felt him wind his fingers through the back of her hair, tilting her mouth for better access. Everything about the way he kissed her told her she needn't be lonely. At least at this very moment, it was okay not to be perfect.

He brushed his lips back and forth against hers, and the very air in the closet seemed to change. His tongue swept over hers, making her heart jump. He made a low sound of approval and shifted slightly, urging her into the cradle of his hard thighs. His tongue dallied seductively with hers, making her warm.

She instinctively lifted her arms around his neck

and the position brought her breasts against his hard chest. He slid his hands just beneath her sweater. She felt the warmth of his fingers on the skin above her jeans and her breath hitched in her throat.

"What fool ever told you that you weren't perfect?" he muttered against her lips. He took her mouth with an edgy hunger that was echoed in the sensual thrust of his lower body against hers.

Light-headed, she drew back and gasped for air. She took several breaths before oxygen hit her brain and she realized she was kissing His Majesty. Panic rushed through her, and she felt the awful urge to hiccup. Erin covered her face and took a deep breath. "Oh, Lord, what am I doing?" she whispered to herself.

"Whatever it is, you're doing it damn well," he said.

Taking another breath, Erin bit her lip and thanked heaven for the darkness because she was certain she was a neon shade of red from head to toe. She cleared her throat and stepped backward, as much as she could in the tight closet, immediately struggling with a sense of loss. "Um, do you think we could maybe forget what we just did?"

Silence followed.

"No," Daniel finally said, and the single syllable oozed sexual suggestion.

Erin swallowed a groan. "Do you think we could pretend to forget?"

He leaned closer and she felt his fingers whisk through her hair like a ghost's touch. "No."

An anxious knot formed in her chest. "Then what are we going to do? I just kissed the incoming King of Altaria," she said, unable to keep her dismay from her voice.

"That's one way of looking at it," he said in a voice that managed to be both calm and sexy.

"And what's another way?" she asked.

"You kissed me—Daniel. And I kissed you," he said. "Next time it won't be in the dark."

After he and Erin successfully escaped the notice of the local TV news team and returned to his condo, Daniel dutifully held up his end of the bargain and endured his protocol lesson.

It was tough because he was distracted as hell by her mouth. Every time she spoke, he thought about how she had tasted and felt. Every time she moved her mouth, he thought about all the things he wanted to do to her.

He met her eyes and found her staring at him impatiently. "Do I need to repeat myself, sir?"

God forbid, Daniel thought and shook his head. "You said that I'm supposed to allow others to formally announce me before I approach people. In general, Altarian citizens will bow or curtsey, address me first as Your Majesty, then use sir. My question is, how much of a snit am I supposed to get into if someone forgets to bow?"

Erin blinked. ''That's entirely your prerogative, sir, but if you'd like to use King Thomas as an example, he simply ignored those who didn't show him proper courtesy or respect.''

''So I'm not expected to put them on the rack or throw them off the island if they don't curtsey correctly,'' he said.

Her lips twitched at his exaggeration. ''That would be correct, sir.''

''I suppose I could require any curtsey transgressors to give Jordan here a bath,'' Daniel said, nodding toward the dog snoring in front of the fire.

She looked at him in disbelief. ''You're planning to bring your dog to the palace with you, sir?''

''Sure am,'' he said. ''I can't bring my family and I have this funny premonition that I'm not going to have a lot of friends when I first arrive.'' He paused, watching her facial expressions shift. ''From your surprise, I'll guess that King Thomas didn't have a dog.''

''Correct, sir,'' she said, casting a doubtful glance at the dog.

''You look as though you're trying to figure out how to teach Jordan royal protocol,'' he said, and walked closer to her. ''Don't underestimate him. He might be easier to train than me.''

She pressed her lips together as if she didn't dare say what she was thinking.

''Say it aloud,'' he said.

''I suspect Jordan might very well be easier to

train as long as I kept an ample supply of pizza available, sir.''

"I need more than pizza," Daniel said, wondering how she would look naked on his bed.

Erin looked away. "I'm sure you do, sir."

Daniel stifled a sigh at her 'sir'. "I bet you're more of a cat person," he said.

"I actually always wanted a dog, sir, but the boarding schools didn't allow pets other than goldfish, and my father was too busy to care for a pet."

"Let me guess," Daniel said, teasing her out of her oh-so-proper mode. "A poodle."

She lifted her chin. "They are very intelligent, sir."

Daniel grinned. "And prissy."

"They don't shed or slobber," she returned and quickly added, "sir."

Daniel couldn't forget how her body had felt in his arms. "If you weren't so young, I'd kiss you again," he told her.

"I'm not too young," she retorted, then chagrin crossed her face. "But your instincts are entirely correct that kissing me would be inappropriate, sir."

"Why?"

"Because I am in your service, sir," she said.

"What if I fired you?"

Her eyes rounded. "You can't! You must not, sir. I mean—" She broke off as if she couldn't find the words.

Daniel dipped his head to catch her eyes. "Are you not attracted to me?"

She glanced at him, then away. "I didn't say that, sir."

"Then you *are* attracted to me."

She bit her lip. "I didn't say that either, but—"

"Then which is it?"

Erin gave a heavy sigh. "I'm sure I don't have to tell you that you're very attractive, sir."

That wasn't enough for Daniel. "But how do I affect you?"

Erin frowned at him. "It's not appropriate for you to affect me."

"The same way it wasn't appropriate for you to want a poodle? It didn't change the fact that you wanted one, did it?"

Her eyes were dark and full of forbidden secrets. "There is a very big difference between a poodle and you," she said.

He lifted a strand of her hair. "I can't disagree," he said and tugged her closer. He lowered his mouth a breath from hers. "I won't order you to kiss me. I won't use my position that way," he said.

Erin closed her eyes, lost in a swirl of contradicting emotions. "I shouldn't kiss you," she said desperately. "It's not right." Not right for many reasons, she thought, feeling as if she were twisting in the wind. She was supposed to have a professional relationship with Daniel. Plus there was the matter of her father. Kissing Daniel, even liking him, made her feel disloyal.

But her father didn't know him, she argued with herself. If her father knew Daniel, he would... Her stomach tightened with dread. If her father knew Daniel, he still wouldn't like him. Her father wanted a king who wouldn't upset the apple cart. Her father wanted a king he could keep under his thumb, and His Majesty or not, Daniel would never be kept under any man's thumb.

Frustration crowded her chest. She wondered if she could learn the same lesson of independence. She slowly opened her eyes and stared into his. So strong, so bold. He made her question everything that had come before him. He made her want to be as strong as he was. How in the world could she refuse him?

How could she not?

"It's time for me to go, sir," she finally managed, feeling his eyes burn through her.

Erin returned to her too-quiet hotel room and decided to go to bed early. Steeped in questions about her father, Daniel and herself, she pulled the covers over her head. The phone startled her. She glanced at the clock and knew it was her father calling. He would ask how she was progressing. He would ask if she had discouraged Daniel or reined him in. Not bloody likely.

The phone continued to ring, and she held her

breath. How could she help her father to see that Daniel was a man of honor and that he would genuinely care for the people of Altaria? How could she convince him that Daniel could bring a new combination of strength and compassion to the throne?

The phone stopped ringing, and Erin covered her face. She was bloody well in a pit of trouble. Convincing her father would be difficult enough. How could she convince Daniel that they shouldn't get involved when she was having trouble convincing herself?

Daniel insisted that Erin join him on Monday so she could gain a picture of the work environment he would be leaving. Erin took a cab to the Connelly corporate offices. She stared up at the modern glass-and-steel structure, reminded again of the Connelly family's wealth and success. Entering the mahogany-paneled reception area, she lingered over the pictures of the various Connelly family members who had created and built the company over the years. The more time she spent with Daniel, the more curious she grew about his father's side of his family.

Security allowed her to pass and she took the elevator to the floor that housed Daniel's office. Behind the receptionist's desk, she saw a beautiful watercolor of one of Altaria's beaches. Giving her name to the receptionist, she stared at the painting and tried to imagine Daniel in the setting. It wasn't difficult imagining him on the beach. In the palace, though, was a different matter.

Daniel rounded the corner wearing a dark wool suit that emphasized his broad shoulders and height. He waved her toward him. "Come on back. I'll show you my office, then I'm making an announcement."

She was amazed at how easily he shifted from casual sportsman to sophisticated businessman. Perhaps that was why he wasn't overly concerned about sliding into his new role as ruler. As she passed through a hall of offices and cubicles, she suspected he'd sharpened his leadership skills at Connelly Corporation.

"Is this entire floor devoted to marketing?"

"Actually two floors, and this is just corporate headquarters," he said. "We have marketing offices all over the world." He guided her past a young woman with honey-colored hair and blue-green eyes. "Erin Lawrence, this is Kimberly Lindgren, my assistant. Smart as a whip and quick."

Kimberly shot Daniel a fond, but skeptical glance. "Such flattery. Are you softening the blow that I'll have to work overtime tonight?"

Daniel chuckled. "Not this time."

"It's a pleasure to meet you," Erin said, admiring the woman's confidence and ease with Daniel.

"The pleasure's mine. Lovely accent," Kimberly said.

"Thank you," Erin said and followed Daniel into

his large, lush corner office. The view from his full-length glass windows took her breath. "It's beautiful," she said. "What a pleasure to work in these surroundings every day."

He came to the window just behind her. "Lake Michigan," he said. "I've always been partial to a great view." Glancing down at her, he stroked his finger under her chin and met her eyes. "Here's another great view," he murmured, clearly meaning her.

Erin's stomach dipped. She shouldn't care if he found her attractive, she told herself. But she did. Confused by her conflicting emotions, she laced her fingers together and looked out the window again. "It must be terribly difficult for you to give all of this up for Altaria, even to be king. Your family, your country and all of this," she said, waving her hand.

"Well, the Connellys might have a large slice of the pie, but we don't own all of Lake Michigan," he said lightly.

"Still, I wonder how you can give up all that is familiar to you for Altaria. Here, you're surrounded by supportive family, employees and friends. It will be very different in Altaria," she said, her father's hostility weighing heavy on her mind.

"I know I'm not entering a friendly situation. It won't be the first time I've had to win over the opposition. But I can make a difference in Altaria," he said with quiet but rock-solid confidence.

Something in his voice made her believe him.

"The end of my Connelly Corporation days is right around the corner," he said and glanced toward his doorway. "Which is why I'm taking Kimberly into my confidence today."

"Are you sure that's wise? I thought you didn't want to make an announcement yet," Erin said.

"I'm not making an announcement, but it's fair to let my closest employee know my plans. She won't have to keep the secret long." He punched the intercom button on his phone. "Kimberly, could you come into my office for a minute please?"

"Yes, Daniel," the woman said.

Erin bit her lip at the woman's familiarity. "Are all Americans as casual with their bosses?"

"I prefer it," Daniel said, then did a double take. "Are you jealous?" he asked in a low voice.

Erin felt her temperature climb ten degrees. "Absolutely not. I'm simply unaccustomed to the casual way employees address their superiors here."

"Kimberly's very attractive and intelligent, but I don't make a habit of getting romantically involved with my assistants," Daniel said as if Erin hadn't denied his accusation.

"The same way you've avoided romantic involvement with me," she said. Immediately appalled at her lack of propriety, she blurted, "Oh, my God, I can't believe I said that."

Daniel shot her a dangerous grin and moved toward her. "The thing you need to understand, Erin, is that you're different."

How? she wanted to ask, but managed to keep her mouth shut.

Daniel continued, "And we're not nearly as involved as I'd like to be."

Erin gulped at the way he made her knees dip.

"Daniel?" Kimberly said from the doorway. She glanced curiously from her boss to Erin.

Erin locked her knees and resisted the urge to fan her cheeks.

"Please close the door behind you," he said and leaned against his desk. "Have a seat."

Kimberly sat down and waited.

"This is strictly confidential, but I wanted you to know because there will be a period of transition during which you must limit your vacation days. I'm leaving Connelly Corporation in a couple of weeks," he said.

Kimberly's eyes widened. "Leaving? But you're a Connelly. What will you do?" she asked, shaking her head. "And I can't imagine who can replace you."

"My brother Justin," Daniel said.

Kimberly lowered her head. "Justin," she echoed. "He's so…" She appeared to search for the right words. "So…serious," she finally said.

"Exactly," Daniel agreed. "He'll work himself into an early grave if left to his own devices. I'd like you to make sure he chills out every now and then."

Kimberly blinked. "How?"

"I don't know. It'll take some creativity," he muttered.

Kimberly looked totally confused. "I don't know what to say. You've been a terrific boss. I've learned so much from you. May I ask why you're leaving?"

"I'm moving to Altaria," he said. "With the death of my grandfather and uncle, the throne goes to the eldest Altarian male."

It took a moment for his news to digest. She stood and lifted her hand to her open mouth. "Oh my goodness, you're going to be king!" She shook her head again. "King of Altaria. It's a small island, isn't it? Well, I suppose it's not that different than being a head honcho at Connelly Corporation. I don't know what to say." She looked at Erin. "You must be involved in some way," she said to Erin and walked toward her. "Will you be his new assistant?"

"Not in the same way," Erin began, mystified by the woman's reaction.

"But in some way," Kimberly said fervently. "You must know that Daniel is a terrific boss. I'm sure he'll be a wonderful king."

The woman's sincere admiration touched a chord inside Erin at the same time as it unsettled her. "Yes, of course, he—"

Kimberly turned to Daniel. "This is amazing. Congratulations. A king. I know a *king*. We are all going to miss you terribly," she said, her voice trembling.

Daniel closed his hands warmly around Kimberly's. "Thank you, but you must keep this confidential," he reminded her.

"I will," she promised solemnly.

"Don't forget to watch out for Justin," Daniel said.

Kimberly paused. "That's going to take some thought," she murmured and turned toward the door. "A king," she whispered. "And Justin..."

Erin watched the astonished woman leave and met Daniel's gaze. She could tell what was coming before he opened his mouth and spoke.

"Say it aloud," he said.

"Must I?"

He nodded.

Erin sighed. "You inspire great loyalty among your employees and family. How do you plan to operate when the political scheme is so different?"

"You mean because I have no one with the same loyalty to me right now in Altaria?"

She slowly nodded.

"Every once in a while you meet a person you know you can trust for life. By the time I get to Altaria, I plan to have at least one person that I can trust," he said and brushed his finger under her chin. "One person who is on my side."

He meant her. Erin's heart contracted. He wanted her trust and loyalty. He had no idea what he was asking.

Six

Erin sat across from Daniel at his favorite noisy downtown diner after a Bulls basketball game. Bloody tired of her conflicting feelings about Daniel, she'd parked her propriety in her hotel room and decided to enjoy the evening and the man. For once, she'd decided to pretend he wasn't the king. She had the uneasy sense that her relationship with him could change more quickly than the Chicago wind whirling outside. A half-consumed American beer sat on the table in front of her, and she was waiting to taste her first Chicago-style hot dog. When in Rome...

"What did you think of the game?" Daniel asked.

"The players were quite tall," she said in an attempt to be complimentary. "And they were very fast with the ball."

"But?" he prompted with his usual intuitiveness. How did he nearly always manage to read her like a book?

"It wasn't very exciting," she confessed. "There were only two fights and those were quickly over."

Daniel stared at her for a long moment, then laughed. "You bloodthirsty woman," he accused.

Erin lifted her chin. "I wouldn't call myself bloodthirsty. I just don't see the entertainment value of watching a bunch of men in baggy shorts running up and down a gym throwing a ball at a basket. There's nothing at stake. In rugby, someone nearly always breaks a bone or gets a tooth knocked out."

He took a long drink of his beer and appeared incredibly amused. "Is there rugby in Altaria?"

Erin winced. "Yes, but I can't say our teams are of a professional caliber." She paused. "In fact, the Brits call us sissies."

Daniel shook his head in disapproval. "That needs to be changed."

The waitress delivered their orders of hot dogs and French fries. "So this is the infamous Chicago hot dog," she said, tilting her head slightly to examine the ingredients. "I'm taking mental notes for the palace chef. It appears to be a beef sausage with mustard, relish, onions, a pickle spear and tomato wedges."

"And celery salt," Daniel added, lifting the hot dog and taking a bite.

"Celery salt," she echoed, watching in dismay as Daniel consumed the messy meal. She looked down at her hot dog and couldn't help wondering how Miss Emily Philpott, her most accomplished head-mistress, would recommend eating such a dish.

"It won't bite you," Daniel told her.

She shot him a dark look. "I know that."

"You don't eat a hot dog with a knife and fork. You're gonna have to get messy," he said. "I dare you."

She caught his green gaze and felt the ridiculous urge to meet his challenge. "Pardon?"

"I dare you to pick up that hot dog with your fingers and take a bite," he said. "A big bite. I bet you can't do it."

She saw through his dare. He was goading her. It would serve him right if she used a knife and fork to spite him. But she wouldn't. Erin deliberately picked up the hot dog and took a large bite. It was incredibly delicious. And incredibly messy. She licked her lips and took another bite, then another.

When she finished, she looked at him and licked her lips again. "I did it," she said, noticing that Daniel was staring at her mouth. She reached for a napkin. "Do I have something on my mouth?"

He shook his head and took a long drink of beer, still seeming fixated on her lips. "Did anyone ever tell you that you have an incredible mouth?"

She automatically licked her lips and heard him groan. "No. I can't say..." The sexual intensity she saw in his eyes snatched the words from her mouth. She felt herself grow warm. His forbidden invitation filled her with anticipation. She felt it in her blood, in her breasts...and lower.

She watched him take another drink of his beer and surreptitiously studied his mouth. She remembered the mind-blowing way he'd kissed her in the closet. Although she'd tried to forget it, the memory never left her alone. She took a careful breath. "That was quite splendid," she managed and took a long drink of beer in hopes of cooling herself off. It didn't work.

"Do you want your fries?" Daniel asked.

Erin shook her head. Her stomach dancing with butterflies, she couldn't imagine eating one more bite.

"Let's go, then," he said and tossed some bills on the table.

Daniel took her arm and led her out of the diner. No sooner had they walked one block toward his parked car than the rain began to pour down. He pulled her into a hotel doorway. "No sense in both of us getting wet. You wait here while I get the car."

Erin immediately shook her head. She didn't want him to think she was a prissy wuss, and besides, for some inexplicable reason, she'd rather get wet by Daniel's side than stay dry without him. "It's not that far. I won't melt," she insisted.

"You sure?" he asked doubtfully.

"Sure," she said and tugged him out into the rain. "Are you too old to run?" she teased.

"Not yet," he returned in a sexy, rough voice and they raced through the rain together. The cold wind whipped through her, and it occurred to Erin that even though she'd endured Switzerland's winters, Chicago's combination of wind and freezing rain chilled her to the bone. By the time Daniel ushered her into his sport utility vehicle, Erin's teeth were chattering.

He dashed inside the car and immediately turned the heat on high. He glanced at her and frowned. "You're shivering. I told you that you should have waited while I got the car."

"It's not that b-bad," she said, her teeth chattering.

"Uh-huh," he said, clearly unconvinced. Daniel quickly drove to his parking deck and hustled her up to his condo. Jordan greeted them with a loud bark at the front door.

Daniel gave the dog a quick pet, then began to peel Erin's jacket from her. "Got to get you warm," he said, rubbing her arms. He ditched his own jacket, led her to the sofa and immediately wrapped an afghan around her shoulders.

His tenderness left her speechless. He lit the gas logs in his fireplace, then sat next to her. "Better?"

She nodded, unable to tear her attention from his eyes. The firelight glowed in them, or perhaps it wasn't the firelight. Perhaps it was his power, more than physical, more than mental. All she knew was that he mesmerized her.

"I like the wet look on you," he said, lifting a damp strand of her hair.

Erin cringed at the thought of her appearance. "I'm sure you do," she said in complete disbelief.

"I'm serious," he said. "I like the way you look right now."

A swarm of emotions whipped through her. She looked anything but perfect, yet he was pleased with her. She glanced at him skeptically. "Why?"

"You look touchable," he said, rubbing her arms with his large hands again.

"I look like a train wreck," she corrected, feeling the same way. She wondered how he did that to her.

"No," he said, meeting her gaze and lifting his thumb to her cheek. "You look like you wouldn't mind being held," he told her. "Or kissed."

Her heart stuttered, and she couldn't look away from his green eyes. He was warm and strong, and he liked her even when she looked like a drowned rat.

She didn't know why or exactly how, but Daniel touched her in a secret place no one else had ever even seen. At that moment, all her defenses evaporated. He slowly leaned forward and closed his arms around her, and Erin had the awesome sense of finding home. The feeling was so strong it brought tears to her eyes. It couldn't be, she tried to tell herself, but as she inhaled his scent and sank into his embrace, heaven help her, but nothing in the world seemed to exist except Daniel.

She felt his heart beating against her and wanted closer. Erin sneaked her arms out from the afghan and slid them around him. They held each other for a long moment, then he nudged her chin upward.

He slowly lowered his mouth to hers. Just a brush of his lips, then he moved back, but Erin could tell he wasn't done.

Her heart hammered in her chest. "Are you sure this is wise?" she asked, clinging to a weak remnant of rational thought.

"Damn right it is," he said, brushing her mouth again, making her pulse skip again. "It's my fault you got cold, so it's my responsibility to get you warm."

She swallowed. "You already have."

"I can make you warmer," he told her and pulled her onto his lap so that she straddled him.

Erin barely had time to react to the impropriety before his mouth took hers and he slid his tongue past her lips. His was a lazy, yet purposeful invasion. He dallied with her sensitive inner lip and toyed with her tongue. She lost herself in the taste and texture of him. Tilting her head to the side to allow him better access, she heard him give a low murmur of approval. The pleasurable sound buzzed through her.

The kiss went on and on as if he couldn't get enough of tasting her. Erin wanted more, but didn't know how…. She felt a rumble of impatience build inside her. Opening her mouth wider, she drew his tongue deeper into her mouth.

Daniel immediately responded, and the tenor of the kiss changed from lazy to serious. She felt his hands slide beneath her sweater to the bare skin of her back.

"Your skin," he muttered. "So soft." His fingers wandered up her ribcage just beneath her bra, and she held her breath. Her breasts strained against the lacy material, but he moved his hands away. She swallowed the frustration nudging at her.

His fingers wandered again to the barrier just beneath her breasts and she held her breath. He slipped one finger beneath the lower band. Back and forth on the lower side of her breast, he moved his finger.

When he removed it, she nearly cried out.

Daniel began to move his tongue in a bold, decadent rhythm that mirrored sex. Erin couldn't withhold a moan.

He moved his hands over her back, and she felt her bra loosen. Then his hands were at last cupping her breasts. Heat pumped through her, making her restless. She shifted on his lap, and he pulled back slightly.

"Do you like this?" he asked, rubbing his fingers ever so lightly on the perimeter of her breasts.

"Yes, but—" She had to fight the urge to arch into his hands.

"Yes, but," he echoed, bringing his fingers closer and closer to her sensitive, erect nipples.

Erin bit her lip and closed her eyes. His thumbs glanced over her stiffened peaks and she moaned again.

He read her response and rubbed her nipples between his thumb and forefinger. A riot of electric sensation coursed through her, and she instinctively took his mouth with hers. She suckled on his bottom lip and dipped her tongue across his.

Daniel took over, French-kissing her until she felt liquid and edgy. Pulling back, he lifted her sweater over her head and pushed away her bra. His gaze greedily drank in the sight of her naked breasts. Tugging his own sweater over his head, he pulled her bare breasts against his bare chest. They both moaned at the sensation.

Firelight danced over the skin of his hard, muscular chest, and the sight of his chest hair arrowing down provocatively into his jeans unwrapped something basic and untapped inside her.

She moved her fingers over his shoulders and chest, luxuriating in the sensation of muscle beneath skin. He cupped her bottom and propped her upward. Dipping his head, he took the tip of her breast in his mouth. The delicious tug of his tongue pulled deep in her nether regions.

Consumed with a want she'd never experienced, Erin glanced down at the sight of his mouth on her breast. The wanton image filled her with shocking pleasure. She had never seen herself as sexy. The notion had been forbidden.

But Daniel's wicked mouth turned all that upside down. She felt him unfasten her belt and unzip her jeans. Her heart beat so hard she couldn't breathe. ''What are you doing?''

He dipped his finger beneath her waistband the same way he had touched her breasts just moments ago. ''Do you want me to stop?'' he asked, his voice easy but his eyes dangerous.

She couldn't honestly say she wanted him to stop.

He dipped his fingers lower then pulled them back. ''Do you?''

She would likely burn in hell for everything she was feeling right now, but Erin couldn't bring herself to stop him. She shook her head, and he immediately shifted her so he could push the lower half of her clothes down her legs.

Excitement and nervousness battled inside her. She watched Daniel's eyes devour her body and shivered.

''Cold?'' he asked, totally misreading her.

She shook her head as he cupped her bottom and drew her body against his. The denim of his jeans felt rough against her thighs, but his hands were strong and smooth.

''I've wanted to see you this way for a long time,'' he told her.

''You haven't known me that long,'' she managed over her hammering heart.

''I've wanted to see you this way since the day I met you. I wanted to do more than look.''

At the same time as he took her mouth, he slid his hand down her abdomen between her legs and touched her intimately.

Erin felt a shocking urge and panicked. She pulled her mouth from his and took desperate breaths, praying she wouldn't embarrass herself.

Daniel paused and looked down at her. "Problem?"

She shook her head, but her body gave her away. She hiccuped.

Erin closed her eyes at the nervous habit that had been the bane of her existence. *Why now?* She sucked in another breath and hiccuped again.

"Erin?"

"It's a terrible—" She hiccuped again. "—disability, but I can usually—" She hiccuped. "—make them go away."

"Do you want some water?"

She shook her head. "No. Water doesn't—" She broke off at another spasm. "—work. It must've been my knickers."

He looked at her incredulously. "Knickers?"

Filled with humiliation, she covered her face. "Could you please just give me a moment?"

Daniel did, moving her off his lap and offering her the afghan to cover herself. Erin gratefully covered her body and closed her eyes. It took a few extra seconds, but she conjured the image of a Swiss snowfall. The urge to hiccup subsided.

She reluctantly met Daniel's curious gaze. Her heart rate picked up again. His hair was mussed, his lips swollen from kissing her and his bare chest distracted her. "I can usually keep them under control. Ever since I was a little girl, when I become over-excited, I, uh—" She took a breath and miserably looked away. "I hiccup."

"So you're saying I just got you so overexcited

I made you hiccup?'' Daniel clarified, his voice a combination of astonishment and amusement.

Erin looked at him darkly. "It's not at all kind to make fun."

He immediately tugged her onto his lap. "Who's making fun? You just paid me the ultimate sexual compliment," he said. "But you said something about knickers."

Still uncertain about his response, Erin felt her cheeks heat. "Yes, well, I think it happened when you removed my knickers."

"Knickers," he echoed.

"Underdrawers," she clarified.

Recognition dawned on his face. "Ah, well, does this usually happen when your knickers are removed?"

"No," she said.

He studied her for a moment. "Just how often have your knickers been removed?"

"I remove my knickers every day," she hedged.

"By a man," he added.

She bit her lip and pulled the afghan around her more tightly. "I'm not sure that's any of your business."

"Oh, yes, it is," he told her. "Because I want to do a hell of a lot more than take off your knickers."

Seven

Daniel got a sinking feeling as he watched Erin bite her lip for the umpteenth time. "I knew you were inexperienced, but I didn't know you were…" He stopped, his words fading.

"I've been surrounded by women most of my life," she told him. "I've had a few opportunities with men, but—" She broke off and shrugged.

"But what?"

"I never really wanted—" She cleared her throat and her eyes darkened with a hundred feminine secrets he'd like to discover. "There's never really been someone I wanted to get this close to," she said.

Daniel felt his chest and groin tighten. Her revelation made him hard, but her vulnerability touched something deep inside him and made him want to be careful with her. "We haven't made any commitments, Erin," he reminded her as gently as he could.

"Of course not," she said as if the notion appalled her. "That would be foolish with all the changes you're facing."

"Then how do you justify—" He paused. "—letting me in your knickers?"

"I hadn't really tried to examine it too closely," she said. "It's far too complicated, and it's probably wisest not to get close to you, but—"

"But," he prompted.

She met his gaze. "But I want to," she said softly.

His groin and heart tightened further. He hated having to be the rational one when she was giving him an ache that wouldn't quit. He couldn't stop thinking about what she was wearing—or not wearing—underneath his afghan. "I'm much more experienced than you," he said, as much for himself as for her.

"Of course," she said. "I daresay I would have had to start my sexual experimentation at age two in order to match you."

Daniel shot her a dark look for her pointed reference to his age. "Two is an exaggeration," he said dryly.

She arched an eyebrow in disbelief and shifted slightly.

Shifted her naked bottom on his lap. Daniel groaned.

Her gaze holding his, Erin dropped the afghan from her shoulders, baring herself before him.

Daniel drank in the sight of her nakedness, her ivory skin, uptilted breasts, narrow waist and creamy thighs. Oh, how he wanted to slide between her thighs. The temptation was too much to totally resist. He allowed himself to dip his head and taste her. She allowed him access to the inner recesses of her mouth, and Daniel thought about the more intimate access he craved. She would be wet and tight. He shuddered at the thought.

His hands slid over her skin and touched her breasts. Her hardened nipples gratified the hell out of him. Lying back on the couch, he pulled her down with him. He slid his hand down between her legs and found her wet petals with his fingers.

She stiffened.

"I just want to touch you right now," he reassured her. "You feel so good, so wet. Open up for me, baby. Open your mouth," he coaxed her. "Open your legs."

He made love to her mouth while he played with her secrets. He felt her grow swollen, and she began to undulate against him. Her movements were so unconsciously sexy, Daniel began to sweat.

But the little sounds of pleasure she made threatened to make him burst the fly of his jeans. He slid his finger inside her and she nearly cooed. She was close. He could feel it in her small jerky movements. He slid another finger inside her and rubbed her with his thumb.

She gasped into his mouth and stiffened with pleasure. ''Oh, Daniel,'' she said, and the feeling of Erin coming undone sent him to another plane.

Despite the fact that he was so hard he hurt, he held her while she came down. Her breathing settled, and she lifted her eyes to look at him. Her blue eyes heavy with sensual satisfaction, she skimmed her hand down his chest and belly to the belt of his jeans.

Daniel swallowed a growl, and operating against every base instinct he possessed, he covered her hand with his.

''There's more,'' she said in a sultry voice that slid down his hardness the same way he imagined her mouth would.

''Not tonight,'' he said, seeing a freezing shower in his future instead of Erin's warm body. ''You're not ready,'' he said, answering her unasked question.

''Pardon me?''

''You're not ready. The rest of tonight would give you hiccups on top of hiccups.''

She pulled her hand from his. ''I'm not a child.''

''I never said you were, but facts are facts. You're small. I'm not. You're gonna feel it the first time.''

"Well, I would certainly hope so," she said in a voice bordering on prissy.

Daniel groaned and rose to a sitting position. "Time to get dressed. Time for you to go to your bed and me to go to mine," he said, although he knew he sure as hell wouldn't be sleeping. When she didn't move fast enough for him, he picked up her sweater and pulled it over her head.

She narrowed her eyes at him. "Are you one of those men who tease, then don't deliver?" she challenged.

Her accusation rendered him temporarily speechless. "No, I'm being rational and trying to be a gentleman, but you're making it damn hard. Now get dressed," he said through gritted teeth.

She made a muffled sound of outrage, gathered the rest of her clothes in her arms and flounced toward the bathroom, her delectable rear end taunting him with every step.

Daniel swore under his breath and rubbed a hand over his face. He was doing the right thing. Taking a woman's virginity shouldn't be done lightly. And it wasn't just any woman. It was Erin. Her combination of vulnerability and determination did something to him. He couldn't explain it, but more than anything, he wanted her to trust him and he wanted to be able to trust her.

He pulled his sweater back on and she returned to the room, her hair still a sexy mess, her eyes sparking with a combination of sensuality and anger. "I'll call a cab," she said.

"No," he said, pulling on his jacket and grabbing hers.

"There's no need—"

"There damn well is," he said, holding her jacket out for her.

Wearing a mutinous expression, she jammed her arms into the sleeves and strode with him to the car. During the brief, rainy drive to her hotel, she neither looked at him nor spoke to him.

Daniel suffered in silence until he pulled up to the door. "You were beautiful tonight," he said.

Her eyes looked hopeful, then she glanced away. "Obviously not beautiful enough," she murmured.

"What do you mean by that?"

"I mean, it's a bit humiliating being the only one who got—" She dipped her head. "—who got over-excited."

He stared at her, then glanced heavenward for help. Every swearword he'd ever heard raced through his mind. He counted to ten and turned to her. "Do you really think I wasn't turned on?"

She shrugged. "Not enough to—"

Muttering an oath, he pulled her close to him and kissed her. It was an outrageously carnal, sexual kiss that only revealed the tip of the iceberg of his need. He took her hand and brought it to his still-hard crotch. "Would you say that's excited or not?" he demanded in a low voice.

She met his gaze with surprised eyes.

"I want all the way inside you," he told her. "But I don't want to hurt you."

"How, then?" she whispered.

"We have to take it slow," he said and lifted his hand to stroke her hair. "I'm not walking you up to your room because if I get you anywhere near a bed, you won't walk for twenty-four hours." He pressed his mouth against hers. "Sweet dreams."

Two nights later, Erin folded her hands together to keep from fidgeting, but Daniel must have caught her.

"There's no need to be nervous," he told her, briefly reaching over to cover her hands with one of his as they waited in his SUV at a stoplight. "Most of my family members are friendly."

"I'm sure they are," Erin said. "It's just that I'm eating dinner with the former Princess Emma, and she is so loved by Altaria that she's nearly a legend."

"Why do I suddenly feel like mashed potatoes?" he muttered in a mock-offended tone.

Erin met his gaze and felt the connection between them vibrate from her head down to her toes. The unfinished intimacy they'd shared hovered between them like a steamy summer day. She could no longer deny to herself what an extraordinary man Daniel was, and she was having trouble denying her strong feelings for him in order to keep some sort of perspective.

"You don't need me to tell you that no one could ever think of you as mashed potatoes," she told him.

"No?" He pulled his hand away and turned onto a different road.

"What do you call it? Beef jerky, perhaps?" she suggested, tongue in cheek.

He shot her a dark look edged with amusement. "How far we've come from Your Majesty," he teased.

Chagrined, Erin bit her lip. "You're so right. Forgive me for not showing proper respect."

"Oh no, we're not going to start that again. I was joking with you," he said.

"But you make an important point," she said, and was compelled to add, "sir."

Daniel pulled the car onto the shoulder of the road, put it in park and pulled her against him. He lowered his mouth to hers and took her in a kiss that reminded her of everything they had shared and that intimated everything they hadn't.

He pulled back, and she drew a deep breath in search of her equilibrium.

"I'd say we're past the 'sir' stage, wouldn't you?" he said more than asked.

She nodded slowly. "I suppose, but what about when we go to Altaria? It will be expected—"

"We'll deal with that later," he told her and put the car in gear.

Erin could only nod. She felt a sharp jab of pain in her chest at how everything between them would be forced to change once Daniel made his permanent move to Altaria. She was certain he would take the throne, and he would do so in his own way. Her future wasn't nearly so certain. When her father learned that she hadn't accomplished his plans for Daniel, he would be severely disappointed. If he ever learned that Erin had fallen in— She broke off the terrifying thought. It was enough to bring on a fit of hiccups. Heaven help her, she would deal with all of this when the time came.

Daniel pulled into a long driveway leading to a large, beautiful redbrick Georgian manor home. "Home sweet home," he said.

"It's beautiful, and so large," Erin said.

"Both my parents wanted a big family, so they always knew they would need a large place to house them."

"How many children do they have?" Erin asked, fascinated by the idea of a large family.

"My parents have raised nine in all," he said, and stopped the car in front of the house. "Why?"

"I was just trying to imagine what it must have been like to have all those brothers and sisters. Never lonely," she said.

"Never alone," he corrected dryly. "But I wouldn't trade any of them for all the royal jewels in Europe and neither would my parents, even though each of us pushed them to the edge in one way or another.'' He paused and lifted his hand to touch her hair. ''Kinda like you've pushed me to the edge.''

Erin stared at him in surprise. ''Me? How have I pushed you to the edge? Until you berated me into dropping the appropriate form of address, I've been nothing but proper.''

He grinned and his eyes glinted with wickedness. ''Exactly. Erin, when will you learn I want you in ways that are anything but proper?'' he asked.

Before she had time to respond, he exited the car and rounded the vehicle to open her door. ''Ready?'' he asked, offering his hand.

''Yes,'' she said, although her stomach danced with nerves.

Daniel escorted her to the entrance and rang the bell. A housekeeper answered the door and immediately ushered them inside. The immense entryway featured a spiral staircase that floated up to a second story where a grand chandelier hung from the ceiling. The housekeeper took their coats, and it occurred to Erin that Daniel would likely feel comfortable with the grandeur of the palace.

Emma Rosemere Connelly entered the foyer with innate breeding and grace. She looked at her firstborn with love in her eyes. ''There you are,'' she said, and Daniel immediately embraced her. ''We haven't seen enough of you lately,'' she gently scolded.

"I've been busy preparing for my new job," Daniel told her.

"Of course," she said. "I just know I'm never going to see you once you leave for Altaria."

"Never is an exaggeration. Dad's jet has the capacity to cross the Atlantic," he said and gave Erin an insider wink. "Besides, from what Erin tells me, the people of Altaria would love a visit from the former Princess Emma."

Emma turned her attention to Erin. "Forgive me. I should have greeted you immediately. I can see my son is as incorrigible as ever. He gets that strictly from his father's side. I've been trying to civilize him for years, but there's only so much a mother can do," she said with gentle wit. "I commend you on your fortitude. I was afraid Daniel's stubbornness might send you back to Altaria on the first available plane."

Delightfully surprised by Emma's lack of reserve, Erin couldn't suppress a laugh. "Thank you for your kind greeting. I must confess this assignment has required a great deal of negotiation. Daniel is quite strong-minded."

Emma beamed. "His father often used the term *bullheaded,* but he's certainly one to talk. Strong-minded," his mother mused aloud and threw Daniel an arch glance. "A lovely description. You must have charmed her."

"And the source of all the charm is obviously my mother," Daniel told Erin dryly.

"Obviously," Emma said with a regal smile, then accompanied Erin and Daniel down the hall. "I'm delighted you both could come. I suspect Daniel won't be in Chicago much longer. Erin, I'm sorry you've had to endure one of our toughest months in terms of weather. I remember Altaria's mild climate and often long for those lovely temperatures in winter. Everyone is in the family room," she said as they rounded a corner into a large, comfortably furnished room with wooden paneling and cases of leather-bound books and trophies.

Daniel's father glanced up from his conversation with a young woman and lifted his glass. "Hail to the king," he said with serious eyes and a slight smile.

"Hail to the king," the others chorused, and descended on Daniel.

"When are you leaving?" one young woman asked.

"What are you going to do with Jordan?" a man asked.

Daniel raised his hands and laughed. "Hold on! I'm not sure when I'm leaving, but when I do, Jordan will go with me. In the meantime, I'd like you to meet Erin Lawrence. Erin, you've met Brett."

Erin nodded at Daniel's younger brother.

"That's my brother Drew," Daniel said, pointing to a tall man with Emma's blue eyes. "He's Vice President of Overseas Operations for Connelly and father of a six-year-old computer-whiz daughter."

"Pleased to meet you," Drew said, extending his hand.

"My pleasure," Erin murmured.

"This is my sister Maggie," Daniel continued, hugging a young woman with long brown hair. "She's a graduate student and she's the baby."

"Forever the baby," Maggie said with a moan and eyed Erin curiously. "Forgive my curiosity, but what is your role with his kingliness?"

"She's teaching him royal protocol and etiquette," Brett said, clearly amused.

Maggie winced. "Oh, my. Please accept my condolences."

"Maggie is also a brat," Daniel said.

Perhaps, but a perceptive brat, Erin thought. "I'm delighted to meet you. What are you studying?"

"Business and art," Maggie replied, as if the two fields were obviously related.

"I'm also interested in art," Erin said. "I'd love to hear more about your studies."

Maggie smiled with pleasure. "Maybe I can talk my mother into letting me sit next to you at the dinner table."

"Speaking of which," said a woman with short, chic black hair and sad violet eyes. "I can't stay. Previous dinner date with John Parker."

Daniel raised an eyebrow. "Isn't that one of Dad's business associates?"

"Yes it is," she said and stood on tiptoe to give Daniel a hug. "May you reign in truth, beauty and

safety. Don't work too hard in your new position."
She turned to Erin. "It's so nice to meet you. I'm
Daniel's sister Tara. I'm sorry I can't stay longer."

"I understand," Erin said. "I'm pleased to meet
you, and I hope you have an enjoyable evening."

Tara's eyes flickered with an emotion Erin
couldn't quite name, then Daniel's sister tightened
her mouth. "Thank you. I'll do my best," she said
and turned, waving to Daniel as she headed for the
door. "Take care of yourself, Your Majesty."

He gave her a two-fingered salute and glanced
thoughtfully after his sister. "Will we ever see Tara
the Terror again?" he murmured.

"Pardon?" Erin said.

His mother and father came up behind them.
"Tara lost her husband in a train wreck a couple of
years ago, and she's never quite been the same,"
Emma said, clearly grieved that her daughter hadn't
recovered.

Grant Connelly slid his arm around his wife in
support, but Erin could see a wisp of sadness in his
eyes too. "Someday the fire will return," he said to
Emma.

Erin felt her heart twist with longing at the obvious connection of love and history among the
Connellys. They had no idea how precious that special bond was.

Seeming to pull himself out of his thoughts, Grant
turned to Erin and extended his hand. "We're glad
you could come. Emma would have never forgiven

herself if she hadn't arranged for you to visit. She may have been born a princess, but she's a natural mother, and she couldn't stand the thought of not welcoming you when you're so far from home. She mothers everyone younger than her."

Emma's cheeks colored. "Oh, you're exaggerating."

Grant shook his head. "Didn't I hear you inviting Marc's daughter to visit?"

"Catherine said she would like to come visit once she gets Marc's affairs in order. Of course I invited her. Catherine is my niece, and I know that losing her father and grandfather has been devastating for her."

"As your own double loss has been, Mrs. Connelly," Erin said quietly.

Emma took her hand. "What a sensitive young woman. Thank you for your sympathy. Although I'll miss Daniel terribly, I take some solace in the fact that he is carrying on the Rosemere tradition. I'm grateful for any help you may give him in that respect."

Erin felt a sharp stab of guilt. If Emma only knew that Erin's father wished Daniel wouldn't become king.

"Can I get you something to drink?" Grant asked, while Erin continued to struggle with myriad feelings.

"You're very kind," Erin said, seeing in his father a resemblance of the strength and hospitality

Daniel also showed. "White wine would be lovely, thank you."

A woman appeared in the doorway to announce dinner, and the group filed into a long dining room beautifully decorated with mirrors and paintings.

Maggie sat beside Erin at dinner and they discussed art and Maggie's continuing education. Erin felt an immediate affinity with the youngest Connelly. Throughout the meal, however, she never forgot that Daniel was sitting right next to her. The way he talked and laughed with his family showed his ease with them and himself. Erin was beginning to see that Daniel seemed comfortable in every situation. A man for every man, she thought, watching him for a long moment.

"You're staring," he murmured for her ears only.

Embarrassed, Erin immediately glanced down at the peas on her plate. "I'm sorry," she whispered.

"That's okay. You can tell me what you were thinking after dinner."

She threw him a long-suffering glance.

He grinned. "Maggie might have told you about her art, but has she told you about her penchant for speed?"

Erin glanced at Daniel's sister. "Speed?"

Maggie rolled her eyes. "If I were male, we wouldn't be having this discussion. I drive a Lamborghini. My brothers would rather see me drive something with a little less power."

"It might have something to do with the speeding tickets," Grant interjected.

"I've talked my way out of most of them," she reminded him with a sigh. "I'm really a very safe driver. The car gives a terrific ride if you'd like to go some time," she said to Erin.

Delighted at the prospect, Erin smiled. "I'd love to."

Daniel made a growling sound. "We'll see. Dinner was great as usual. Please excuse Erin and me while I show her around."

The family murmured their temporary farewells and Daniel led her through the hallway and up the spiral staircase. Photos and portraits revealed the family history. Informal royal photos showed the pride of King Thomas and the quiet contentment of Queen Lucinda. Even as a child, Prince Marc's reckless charm glinted in his eyes. Princess Emma's fresh, exquisite beauty almost, but not quite, hid the determination in her gaze. That determination and adventuresome spirit had come in handy when she'd tossed her royal title the same way a bride tosses her bouquet. Erin couldn't help lingering over Grant and Emma's wedding portrait. Daniel told stories about his growing-up years as they walked through the grand house, and Erin could almost feel the love and passion of the Connelly family echoing through the walls. He led her into a small study to a floor-length window and cut the lights.

"Look," he said, pointing outside to a maze of boxwood shrubs lit with thousands of white lights.

To Erin, it looked like a wonderland. "I love it," she said. "How long has it been there? Did you play in it as a child?"

Daniel nodded. "It's been here as long as I have. When we were children, my brothers and sisters and I played hide-and-seek in there all the time. As I grew older, I sometimes went there for the solitude."

Erin felt an overwhelming impulse. "Can we go there right now?"

He looked at her doubtfully. "It's freezing."

"Are you afraid you'll catch a chill?" she goaded innocently.

Daniel's gaze darkened. "Absolutely not. I was thinking of you."

"But you were quite expert at warming me up," she ventured, following another bold impulse.

"Yes, I was," he said, and nudged her toward the door. "Let's get our coats."

Eight

Surrounded by the shrubs, tiny white lights and the cold night air, Erin stood with Daniel in the center of the maze. It was so cold their breaths made puffs of vapor, but the sky was like a black velvet blanket filled with diamonds.

"It's beautiful," Erin said, her voice hushed.

He nodded, putting both his arms around her to keep her warm. "Perfect night for wishing on a star, if you believe in that sort of thing."

Erin looked up at his firm jaw and chiseled features and felt a deep longing to know him. "Do you?"

"Experience has taught me that if you want something to happen, you usually have to make it happen, but I share my father's Irish roots, so I'm not opposed to a little good luck or magic.''

Erin glanced up at the sky and felt a flood of wishes race through her. Secret longings she buried every day. *I wish I'd known my mum longer. I wish my father and I were closer.* Erin's heart twisted. The prospect of her accomplishing what her father had asked grew less likely with each passing day. With Daniel's arms around her, however, she felt safer and less alone than she'd felt in her entire life. She wondered, though, what she could possibly bring to such a strong man. He hardly seemed to need anything, let alone her.

Erin closed her eyes. *I wish I were necessary for him.* She knew it was silly, but she made the secret, futile wish on the brightest star in the sky, thinking that for her entire life she had wanted to be necessary to someone.

''I'm making a wish,'' he told her in a low voice next to her ear.

She opened her eyes, and the glint of passion in his green gaze sizzled through her. ''What is your wish?''

''I want your lips on mine,'' he said.

Standing on tiptoe, Erin pressed her mouth to his and granted his wish, all the while thinking she wanted more with Daniel than this kiss, even if it meant that her father shut her out forever.

The knowledge ripped her reserve to shreds. She slid her hands inside his coat and dipped her tongue inside his mouth. He tightened his embrace around her, and, despite the cold night air, Erin felt warmth suffuse her. She gently sucked his tongue into her mouth and arched her breasts against his chest.

Daniel groaned and pulled his mouth slightly away. Resting his forehead against hers, he took a measured breath. ''You're making me wish for a lot more than a kiss.''

Erin's heart stuttered. She felt as if she faced a fork in the road, and, once she chose, she would never be able to turn back. She shivered, but the decision echoed inside her like a bass drum. It was so loud she almost wondered if Daniel could hear it. She could no longer deny how strongly she was drawn to him. Even though any woman in her right mind would know she had no future with him, she couldn't not be with him.

Trying to control her pounding heart, she rubbed her open mouth over his in invitation. ''You must be wishing on the right star.''

The next several moments passed in a blur. Daniel led her back through his family's home to say goodnight, then drove toward his condo. They spoke very little, but his every look was so sexually intense she felt branded. At each traffic light, he reached over and took her mouth in kisses that left her dizzy.

As soon as they entered his condo, he turned to her as if he couldn't bear not to touch her. He shoved her coat off her shoulders and unzipped her dress with mind-robbing speed. Before she could take a breath, he lifted her in his arms and carried her to his bedroom.

Erin felt as if she'd waited her entire life for this moment. He put her down on the bed, grabbed a couple of plastic packets of protection from his bedside-table drawer and shucked his clothes.

She admired his muscular body. When he removed his drawers and she saw the size of his masculinity, a sliver of trepidation scurried through her.

He looked at her through hooded eyes and propped himself on top of her, resting his weight on his elbows. "Are you sure about this?"

Loving the way he surrounded her, she fought a slice of panic. Heaven help her, she didn't want to hiccup. "Yes," she managed over the loud beating of her heart.

"You don't look sure," he said, nuzzling her neck and sending delicious sensations through her nerve endings.

"I'm sure," she insisted breathlessly, arching toward him.

"I wish you weren't wearing a bra," he said, running the tip of his tongue down her throat.

Erin bit her lip and fumbled with the clasp of her bra, freeing her breasts.

His gaze devoured her. "Your breasts drive me crazy," he said. "I can't decide whether to touch them with my hands or take them with my mouth."

Erin felt her nipples turn to stiff buds, and she deliberately shed her timidity. "With your mouth," she suggested, winning a look of aroused surprise from him.

He looked down at her breasts again and lowered his head to lazily lap at one of her nipples. He drew the tight peak into his mouth and she felt a tug all the way down to her blooming femininity.

Shifting restlessly beneath him, she lowered her hands to his head. At the same time he slid his hands down to her bottom, rotating her pelvis against his. The combination of sensations sent a roll of thunder through her.

"I wish I didn't want to go so fast," he muttered, lifting his head.

"I don't want to help you with that wish," she admitted, and he gave a low, sexy laugh that sent a rush of heat through her blood.

"I wish you weren't wearing any stockings," he said.

"Then help me take them off."

His eyes glittering with arousal, he helped her remove them, so that she was completely naked before him. His nostrils flared as he looked at her. He slid his fingers between her legs to where she was wet. "Soft as a rose," he said, toying with her, slipping his finger inside her. "So pretty," he murmured. "Everywhere." He met her eyes. "Touch me."

Her tight chest squeezed the oxygen from her lungs, and Erin lifted her hands to Daniel's chest. She ran her thumbs over his flat nipples, then lower to his belly, then lower still to his thigh.

Daniel watched her through dark, wanting eyes and stayed so very still, as if he were a lion preparing to pounce. She could sense his instinctual need to take her as he slid his finger inside her yet again. Erin felt herself grow swollen with need. With each stroke from his hand, she wanted more and more.

She skimmed her hand up his thigh to his hard masculinity and watched him exhale on a hissing breath. His passion fed hers; he guided her hand around him, gently pumping. A drop of honeyed arousal formed and she rubbed the tip of him with her thumb.

He closed his eyes as if her touch brought him to the point of pleasure/pain. He stilled her hand and shuddered.

He fondled and stroked her femininity until she was breathless, biting her lip to keep from begging him to take her. "I wish," she said, wrapping her fingers around his arms, "you were inside me."

Daniel swore under his breath and quickly put on the protection. Easing her legs apart, he pushed just inside her opening and stopped.

Feeling herself stretch to accommodate him, she wiggled to take in more.

Daniel swore again. "You're not making this easy for me. I want this to be good for you."

Her urgency for him making her restless, she moved again. "You are good for me, but I want—" She broke off when he pushed farther inside her. The stretching sensation intensified.

"Too much?" he asked through gritted teeth as his biceps strained with the force of his restraint.

Erin automatically shook her head. She could never get too much of Daniel.

He thrust past her resistance, taking her breath with his complete invasion. He felt too big, too hard, and it hurt.

For five seconds.

His nostrils flaring, he stared into her eyes. "Tell me when you're okay."

Erin bit her lip and felt her heart twist. "I haven't been okay since I met you," she confessed.

He closed his eyes for a second, then opened them and looked at her with such tenderness she could have wept. "You're such a sweetheart. You make me want to take care of you," he said, then slowly moved. "In every way."

Bending down, he took her mouth the same way he was taking her body. The combination was too erotic, too much for Erin, and a jolt of pleasure sent her over the edge. She felt as if she were free-falling from the sky and just as she started to land, he gave one final thrust and took his own pleasure in her.

Erin had never felt so fulfilled, so complete—almost necessary.

Daniel kept Erin with him the whole night, taking her again in the morning, then pulling her into the shower with him. He would have spent the entire day making love to her again and again, but he didn't want to make her sore. He was acutely sensitive to the fact that she had been a virgin and he was the man who had altered her status forever. He couldn't explain it, but he felt protective of her. She tried to hide her vulnerability, but now more than ever, he knew it was a front. Her trust wrapped around him like silken cord.

Underneath her prissy exterior she was a sensual woman just waiting to come into her own, and heaven help him, he wanted to be around for every discovery she made. Looking down at her naked body, he wanted to take her again. His body grew hard. He felt a possessiveness that surprised the hell out of him.

All along he'd sensed that Erin possessed a loyalty that a man would prize. Daniel wanted the prize, and she had just demonstrated that he had earned a part of it. He craved the rest.

"Why are you staring at me?" she asked.

"I was thinking how beautiful you are," he said, allowing his gaze to roam over her damp hair, lips swollen from his kisses and the rosy tips of her breasts.

"I'm not perfect," she told him.

"I thought we covered the perfection lesson. Even still, I have to disagree," he said, lowering his mouth to one of her nipples. He rolled his tongue over the tip, feeling himself grow hard at the same time she did. "Your nipples fit perfectly in my mouth,'' he said, and the arousal burned inside him. ''Damn, I want you again.''

She looked at him from beneath her eyelashes. ''Is that so horrid?''

He smiled at her British tone. ''No, but it would be horrid if I made you sore.''

''Does that mean you can't kiss me?'' she asked, wrapping her fingers around his arm and tugging.

Daniel groaned as he lowered his mouth. ''No,'' he muttered as she gave him a French kiss that belied her lack of experience. She slid her hands over his chest and down to his buttocks.

His mind teeming with swearwords, he fought the urge to devour her, to plunge inside her with nothing between them and spill his pleasure inside her. The very thought was so arousing it nearly sent him over the edge.

''How did you become such an incredible lover?'' she whispered into his mouth as she lowered her hands to the part of him that ached for her.

''Is it because you've had so much experience?'' she asked, and the combination of her words and hands taunted him mercilessly.

''Partly,'' he managed. ''But you motivate me.''

''It's not entirely fair that you have all this experience and I have none. I feel the need for more experience,'' she said, her hands driving him insane.

''You can get experience with me,'' he told her.

She moved her open mouth down his chest as she continued to caress him. She scorched him when she ran her tongue over one of his nipples, then kissed her way down his belly. Her cheek glanced his hardness, and he bit back a moan.

"Erin, what are you doing?" he asked.

She answered him by touching him intimately with her mouth. He looked down at the sight of her blond hair splayed over his abdomen and her lips on his masculinity.

He didn't know whether to pray or swear, but it didn't much matter. His vocal cords had ceased functioning.

She lifted her smoky gaze to his. "I want to do this right," she said, lowering her head again, "so tell me if I am."

She took him into her oh-so-proper mouth with such enthusiasm and untutored perfection that Daniel had to move her away while he spilled his pleasure. He pulled her head into the crook of his shoulder as he gasped for air.

"You never said if I was doing it right," she ventured.

Daniel could only groan.

Two days later after a call from his brother Brett, Erin watched as Daniel's world began its apple-cart turnover. The media had grown hungry and needed to be fed. It was time for Daniel's first interview as incoming King of Altaria. Her heart burst with pride at his immediate decision to show sensitivity to the citizens of Altaria by conducting an interview to be aired on Altarian television and radio before the American interview. Honoring the line of generational unity to a nation still grieving, his mother appeared with him, but gently demurred for the American interview.

The Altarian reporter was respectful and reserved, the American more hard-hitting, but Daniel appeared confident and in control.

"Why would a successful American businessman choose to accept a primarily superficial role as king of a small, exotic island country?" the American interviewer asked.

"This American chooses to accept the role based on some old-fashioned reasons: family honor and responsibility. I disagree with your view that the role of king is superficial. My understanding is that this job expands and contracts with the individual filling it."

The woman reporter looked surprised. "Is that so? Then do you have any plans for your reign, Your Majesty?" she asked with a great deal of skepticism. Erin felt an overwhelming urge to pinch the woman, but noticed Daniel didn't take the bait.

"It would be wrong for me to enter this role with the notion that I want to change everything. Altaria has succeeded just fine without my ideas for centuries. On the other hand, I would feel irresponsible if I didn't attempt to bring anything new to the table. I'm currently researching the possibility of expanding Altaria's airport. This would improve both tourist and business prospects. I want to explore some possibilities for initiating higher education on the island. I also intend to initiate an audit of all government agencies, including the Rosemere Institute, which my family has funded in the past.''

That reply might give her father indigestion, but Erin found it inspiring.

A Connelly PR person agreed, whispering to her, ''He's excellent. He handles the press as if he were born for the job.''

''He was,'' Erin reminded him, and at the same time, reminded herself that her relationship with Daniel would be changing all too quickly. Her stomach clenched at the thought.

''So you won't be the royal equivalent of an empty suit?'' the woman interviewer said.

Daniel smiled. ''Nothing could be less likely.''

''Tell me about the Rosemere Institute,'' she said.

''The Rosemere Institute was founded by my grandfather, the late King Thomas, to promote technical and medical research. In particular, after my grandmother died of cancer, significant research has been devoted to finding ways to fight cancer.''

Erin watched as Daniel used his everyman charm and intelligence to successfully field the interviewer's questions. His thoughtful sincerity would break down walls. By the end of the session, she had never been more certain that Daniel was the best man to become King of Altaria.

He disconnected his microphone, shook hands

with the interviewer and ran his searching gaze over the studio. "Erin?" he called, making her heart leap.

She waved and he spotted her. Shooting her a private half grin, he quickly joined her. "I'm hungry after that duel with the devil," he murmured for her ears only. "Chicago dogs or pizza?"

"What about security?"

"Tomorrow morning," he said, and she could feel the clock ticking inside her. "We have one more night without an army of Peeping Toms. I'm not wasting it," he promised.

Erin and Daniel filled every minute the rest of the day and into the night. They grabbed a take-out meal of Chicago hot dogs and Daniel fed Erin hers in the most audacious, provocative manner she could have imagined. She paid him back by using her tongue to lick a thin line of mustard all the way up the hot dog. The food was quickly forgotten and they devoured each other.

Rising early, Daniel hustled her in and out of the shower, and they took Jordan for a brisk walk.

"It's a sunny day," he said as he guided her down the sidewalk.

"A freezing sunny day," she said.

"I'll warm you up," he promised with an expression in his eyes that made her stomach dip and sway. He slowed and kissed her.

"You'll be too busy for warming me up," she gently told him. "Many meetings today."

"I'll never be too busy to warm you up, Erin. Don't forget that." He grabbed her hand and began to walk again.

Rounding the corner, Erin heard a loud sound as if a car were backfiring. The sound cracked through the air, and a window just above her shattered. Startled, she looked up.

"Get down!" Daniel cried, shoving her to the ground as another shot rang out. She heard the squeal of tires on the pavement and saw a black car disappear down the street.

Fear raced through her like ice water. She clung to Daniel. "Daniel? Daniel?" When he didn't immediately respond, her heart stopped. She turned his face to hers, and nearly fainted at the sight of his blood-splattered forehead.

Nine

Hours later after the Chicago Police Department had thoroughly questioned Daniel and Erin, and the Connelly men had joined ranks for a private meeting, an official Altarian security guard stood outside Daniel's condo. Erin began to breathe again.

Daniel met her gaze and flipped her hair behind her shoulder. "The bullet barely grazed my forehead."

Erin felt the bile rise in the back of her throat. "You were bleeding. You were hurt."

He pulled her into his arms. "You could have been too."

"You saved my life," she told him, tears welling up in her eyes. "I've never been so frightened in my life.'' What if he'd been hit? What if she'd truly lost him? Even though she knew he would never belong to her, Erin couldn't bear the thought of his death. She began to tremble.

Daniel pulled slightly away and frowned. ''You're shaking,'' he said. ''You must stop. You're okay and so am I.'' His expression shifted. ''And it's been decided that you and I will return to Altaria tomorrow.''

Erin searched his gaze. ''Who made the decision? Security?''

''Security, the Connelly men and me. It's time for me to take the next step in the transition. I might like to pretend that this was a random drive-by shooting, but...'' He drifted off, shaking his head.

''But it's entirely too coincidental that your interview was aired internationally last night and you were shot at in broad daylight this morning.''

He nodded slowly. ''For some reason, someone doesn't want me to be king.''

Her heart twisted. She thought of her father, but knew he wouldn't go to such lengths. ''Why?'' she wondered aloud.

''I don't know. I can't spend time thinking about detractors. There's too much else I need to be doing. Security will do their job,'' he said.

Erin shook her head. ''You could have lost your life. How can you shake this off so easily? Doesn't this give you second thoughts about becoming king?''

"No," he said with a determination in his eyes that could bend steel. "In fact, it makes me more certain than ever. Several people have been telling me this is a cream-puff job with the emphasis in my role on decorum. No real power to the position. No opportunity to make a difference. If there's no real power, then why does somebody want to kill me?"

Erin joined Daniel and several official security guards on a chartered jet bound for Altaria the following day. She had no idea what would happen once they arrived at the island. She only knew that things between her and Daniel were about to change in a drastic way.

They arrived late at night, as planned, with the goal of a low-key entrance. Word, however, must have gotten out, for a huge crowd of people and several official vehicles stood outside the airport waiting. The people waved welcome signs and cheered.

"You'll walk with me," Daniel said to Erin.

"Absolutely not," she said.

He blinked at her immediate disagreement. "Why not? Other than, 'It wouldn't be proper.'"

"That should be enough," she told him, her heart twisting in strange ways. "I don't want you facing any questions from the press regarding me."

"After that barracuda in Chicago, I can handle nosey questions from anyone."

"I insist," she said quietly.

He jammed his hand into his pocket impatiently. "You're going to be prissy about this, aren't you?"

"I prefer the word *firm*," she said and gently smiled. "You must meet your subjects. You represent their tie to the past and their hope in the future. Your very presence will be a tremendous source of comfort."

"Okay. But you have to come to the palace."

She shook her head.

"I'm not budging on this. If you need a job description, you are palace liaison, and your first duty is to escort Jordan to the palace and get him settled. I'm told he won't need to be quarantined."

Erin gaped at Daniel. "Jordan?"

Daniel nodded, pulling on a suit jacket. "That's appropriate. I want at least two on my side at the palace round the clock. That would be Jordan and you." He leaned toward her and kissed her. "Any last-minute protocol instructions? Is my tie straight?"

With numb fingers, Erin adjusted his tie. Daniel might fight it, but this was the beginning of the end for them. "Give them a chance to bow or curtsey. They want to show respect." A myriad of feelings tugged at her. "You are going to be a wonderful king," she told him.

His gaze grew serious. "I'll see you later at the palace."

Jordan wasn't particularly cooperative. Erin was forced to send a guard to secure a steak to bribe the beast to go along with her. She gave up trying to return him to the crate in which he'd made the transatlantic journey. Growling at every new human who crossed his path, Jordan finally settled down and stayed close to Erin as the limo left the airport and traveled toward the palace.

When he pawed at the window, she lowered it slightly.

The security guard frowned in disapproval.

"He's upset," she said. "He's had a rough couple of days."

Jordan spent the remainder of the ride panting and intermittently whining. He clearly wanted Daniel. Erin couldn't blame him. After they arrived at the palace, she took him for a short walk so he could take care of his business. By the time she was ready to take him inside, Daniel's motorcade had pulled into the private compound.

Jordan perked up his ears as the vehicles approached. When Daniel stepped from his vehicle, Erin nearly got whiplash holding Jordan in place. The animal began to whine and bark.

Daniel glanced up and spotted them. "Bring him over," he called.

Jordan dragged her along until they reached his master, when he began to whine and jump for joy. Daniel petted him and murmured words of reassurance. He nodded up at the medieval stone palace, then glanced at her. "Looks like we should be able to squeeze in a royal protocol expert and palace liaison."

"Sir," she said, all too aware of the watching eyes all around them.

"Don't start with that," Daniel said.

"I must," she whispered. "At least when others are around. It's expected."

He frowned, clearly not pleased. "I don't like it," he said.

"If you'll pardon me for saying so, sir, you don't have to like it."

"I'm not in the mood to pardon much of anything, so let's go ahead and get past the goons," he muttered, waiting for her to join him.

"You must precede, sir," she reminded him.

Daniel swallowed a half dozen swearwords. He would adjust to the changes. He'd long ago learned the power of the ability to adapt. After the events of the last few days, Erin had to play royal subject for the sake of prying eyes. It bothered the hell out of him that they had to hide their true relationship, even though he understood the wisdom behind it.

A doorman greeted him with a polite bow, and Daniel shook his hand, almost surprising the starch out of the man. A palace guide led him through the castle. Although he was weary, he took in the sight of the lavish decorations and medieval unicorn tapestries, the red-tiled floors carpeted with Oriental rugs.

Daniel waited for a bow or curtsey, then shook hands with the next fifteen palace personnel. When he was introduced to the senior housekeeper, he requested a room for Erin.

Reaching his private quarters, he sent the guards and palace personnel away, and insisted Erin bring Jordan with her into his private domain. Ditching his jacket and tie, he prowled his surroundings. The formal sitting room was decorated with fine period furniture. It needed light, he thought, then wandered into a study with shelves of leather-bound volumes and a beautiful large desk his grandfather must have used.

Daniel's gut twisted at the image of his grandfather and all the Rosemeres before him sitting at that desk. He felt the weight of his title settle on his shoulders. His grandfather descended from a long line of Rosemeres who had ruled with compassion. Daniel was determined to continue the tradition, to continue the honor.

Out of the corner of his eye, he noticed Jordan exploring his new surroundings, sniffing every inch of the place. He glanced up and saw Erin foraging in a small refrigerator. The sight of her eased the upheaval inside him.

"Would you like a sandwich?" she asked. "It appears someone stocked the refrigerator in anticipation of your arrival. Looks like ham, turkey, roast beef and cheese."

Thank God she'd ditched the sir. "I wish for a kiss," he said, and she turned to meet his gaze.

She looked soft and beautiful and like everything he'd never known he wanted but had needed.

She smiled and walked toward him, and Daniel felt the weight of the day grow lighter.

"A kiss. I can do that," she said, stretching on tiptoe to press her soft mouth to his.

Daniel closed his arms around her and savored the sensation of her body against his.

A knock sounded at the door, and he groaned. "I told them to go away."

Jordan barked at the door. "You should answer," she told him, nuzzling Daniel's cheek, then backing away. "I'll hold on to Jordan."

Daniel opened the door to a tall, reed-thin man with a receding hairline. "Your Majesty," he said. "My name is Gregor Paulus, Prince Marc's former assistant. I beg you to forgive the intrusion. I was unable to meet you earlier because I was ordering a tray for your arrival. May I come in, sir?"

Although the man was politeness personified, something about him seemed pushy. Daniel put the first impression down to weariness and set it aside. "Thank you very much, Gregor."

Gregor stepped inside the door. When Jordan barked at him, the man nearly dropped his tray. Daniel rescued it in time.

"Gregor Paulus, this is Erin Lawrence, my protocol expert and palace liaison, and my dog, Jordan.''

Gregor nodded at Erin and murmured a polite greeting. He glanced at Jordan and gingerly extended his hand to the dog's head. Daniel immediately concluded that Gregor was not a dog person.

Keeping one eye on Jordan, Gregor moved to the other side of the room. ''I wanted to greet you personally, Your Majesty,'' he said. ''I know you will be making many adjustments and I want you to know that I am at your service to help you in any way, day or night.''

Daniel considered asking the proper man to walk his dog, but he didn't want to put Jordan in misery. ''I appreciate your kind offer,'' Daniel said instead. ''If I should need you, I will call. It was very kind of you to prepare the food. Tonight I plan to retire as soon as possible.''

Gregor nodded, still glancing at Jordan. ''Very good, sir. You are most welcome. Again, if you should need anything, anything at all, please do not hesitate to call me,'' he said and backed out of the door.

As soon as the man left, Daniel turned to Erin. ''Is it just me or was that guy a little overboard?''

''He was extremely proper and respectful,'' she said and paused. ''Oh, all right. Something about him gave me the willies.''

''And he didn't like Jordan,'' Daniel added.

"You can tell a lot about a person by whether they like dogs."

"I technically don't own a dog," Erin pointed out.

"Yes, but you want one," Daniel said and grinned. "Poodles are prissy, but they're still dogs. And Jordan likes you."

"He likes me when I have food," she corrected.

"I want you to stay in my room tonight," Daniel said, expecting a disagreement as he moved toward her.

Erin shook her head. "It's not proper. It wouldn't be right. Heaven forbid the palace aides start talking right away," she said. "I cannot allow you to—"

Daniel pressed his mouth over hers, swallowing the rest of her protests. He kissed her with the passion and frustration from his day. He claimed her mouth in blatant possessiveness, and her objections finally died.

The phone rang the following morning just as Erin and Daniel finished eating breakfast in his private quarters.

Daniel frowned. "Damn, this better not be happening all the time, or I'm gonna have to make this number unlisted to everyone." He picked up the phone. "Hello."

"Daniel," It was his brother Brett.

"Right here," Daniel said, hearing a mixture of impatience and tension in his brother's tone.

"It's about time. This is my third try, but they wouldn't let me through because His Majesty was sleeping."

Daniel winced. "I'll have to tell them to allow calls from my family members," he said and mouthed Brett's name in response to Erin's look of inquiry. "What's up?"

"Nothing good, but we're working on it. We're beginning to think that King Thomas and Prince Marc may have been murdered."

Daniel's blood turned to ice. "What?"

"Yeah, we don't think the boating accident *was* an accident, so we're hiring an investigator. His name is Albert Dessage. He's based in France and he'll be coming to Altaria. We've also got a detective, Elena Delgado, in the Special Investigative Unit of the Chicago Police Department to look into that little drive-by that happened to you."

Daniel took a moment to allow his brother's announcement to sink in. He wondered why. Why would someone have wanted to kill King Thomas? Daniel had never been close to his maternal grandfather, but he'd always gotten the impression King Thomas had been a proper king with integrity to spare.

"You still there?"

Daniel rubbed a hand over his face. "Yeah, I'm just trying to figure out whom I can trust here."

"Watch your back," Brett said.

"I will," Daniel said. He might not have chosen

this situation, but he was determined to deal with it effectively. He suspected it wasn't the first trying situation he would face as monarch.

"And take pity on me," Brett added in a lighter tone. "I've been appointed to deal with the female detective."

Daniel grinned. "Why should I feel sorry for you, you dog? Something tells me you'll use that situation to your advantage."

"Ms. Delgado's probably a battle-ax. Besides, it's easy for you to say. You've got the pretty blonde with the sexy accent."

Daniel smiled at Erin. "I need some consolation."

"Yeah, right," Brett said in disbelief. "How's the palace?"

"Old, dark and the pipes rattle in the shower," he said. "But the temperature is seventy-three degrees and the view of the beach is great."

"It's fourteen degrees and snowing here."

Daniel laughed. "Come and visit."

"I can't. I've got to deal with the battle-ax. I better run. I meant what I said about you watching your back."

Daniel heard the heartfelt sincerity in his brother's voice and it warmed him. "I will. Thanks. Keep me posted."

Daniel hung up and met Erin's curious gaze. He crossed the room to her and took her in his arms. "I'm glad you're here with me," he said.

Her eyes widened. "Why?"

"Because the more I learn about things in Altaria, the less I think I can trust people. I know I can trust you."

Erin took a quick breath and looked downward. "Surely it can't be that bad. There must be others you can trust."

Daniel gave a laugh edged with gallows humor. "I'll be okay, but it's tricky right now. There's a strong possibility that King Thomas and Prince Marc were murdered. Add in the attempt on my life and it's not pretty."

She met his eyes again in disbelief. "King Thomas murdered?" She shook her head. "That's horrible. If it's true, then the same people might want you dead." The color drained from her cheeks and her eyes filled with fear. "Daniel, you must be very careful."

"I will be," he assured her, touched by the strength of her concern. When he had first met Erin, he never would have predicted that the prickly, proper woman could have such an impact on him. She was too young, too inexperienced. Now being with her felt nothing but right. He looked into her blue eyes and wondered if she knew she was becoming more and more important to him every day.

"King Thomas didn't get out among the people of Altaria frequently. He demonstrated the dignity and tradition of the throne in formal state appearances,'' the prime minister told Daniel during their first meeting in the palace's cabinet room. Daniel found himself surrounded by a dozen aides associated with either the PM or the palace.

''I agree that the state appearances are important for the people,'' Daniel said, thinking that if he heard the prime minister say ''King Thomas did it this way'' one more time, he was going to break a piece of the antique furniture. ''Because the citizens of Altaria are less familiar with me, I believe it would be wise to provide a greater degree of accessibility. They need to get to know me and I need to get to know them.''

Louis Gettel, the reserved, intelligent middle-aged prime minister, cleared his throat and adjusted his tie. ''May I inquire how you intend to get to know the citizens of Altaria, sir?''

''I'd like to visit some schools and farms. I'd like to invite some business owners to the palace to talk about their concerns,'' he said, and watched Louis's left eye twitch. Daniel considered joking about the fictional palace orgies he had planned to celebrate spring, but he bit back the audacious urge. ''In the meantime, I've asked a friend to study the possibility of expanding the landing strip at the airport, and I am requesting a full financial and security audit of all government agencies, including the Rosemere Institute.''

Louis nodded. ''Your request will be honored, sir. Your assigned aides will—''

"I'll be interviewing for my own aides," Daniel said.

Louis lifted his eyebrows. "As you wish, sir."

"Mr. Gettel, may I speak frankly?" Daniel asked.

Surprise crossed the man's face. "Of course, sir."

"By all accounts, you are a superb prime minister. Altaria is fortunate to have you in its service," Daniel said.

"Why, thank you, sir," he said, clearly pleased and relieved at Daniel's observation.

"I have no interest in being prime minister of Altaria, and I am not King Thomas, but I do want to be the best damn king I can be."

Gettel blinked, as if Daniel presented one surprise after another. Daniel saw a sliver of wariness leave the man's eyes. His mouth eased into the slightest smile. "We can ask for no more, sir."

Daniel extended his hand and Gettel's shake was strong and sincere. Daniel felt a flicker of hope that his transition wouldn't be a complete walk through hell after all.

After the meeting, Daniel wandered through the palace in search of Erin. He wanted to tell her about his first meeting with the prime minister. Rounding a corner, he thought he heard her talking to someone in a parlor near the entrance of the palace. As he drew closer, the voices became clearer.

"I'm glad you're back in Altaria, safe and sound," a man said. "It appears that you have been successful with your assignment."

Erin's father. Daniel's curiosity was piqued. He walked toward the parlor to meet the foreign minister.

"Father, I don't think—" Erin began.

"You needn't be modest, darling. It's clear you've made yourself indispensable. I'm sure you've rid his mind of any substantial changes he may have wanted to make."

Daniel slowed his steps, frowning.

"Father, I truly don't believe—"

"If you couldn't find a way for the American to refuse the throne, you've obviously done a smashing job of bringing him to heel," her father said. "Just as I instructed you."

Daniel absorbed the man's words. Had there been some kind of plan? Had Erin been scheming against him? The prospect of her betrayal burned like battery acid.

"Father, Daniel Connelly is—"

"I'm so proud of you," Erin's father said.

Daniel's stomach turned. Anger roaring inside him, he strode into the parlor and immediately locked his gaze with Erin's.

She gave a start and paled, her eyes shimmering with guilt.

Daniel's heart twisted to shreds. He glanced at her father, and bitterness backed up in his throat. "Foreign Minister Lawrence, we haven't met. My name is Daniel Connelly."

Erin's father, a thin, short, slightly balding man,

tried unsuccessfully to conceal his horror. He gave a deep bow. "Your Majesty."

"Damn right," Daniel said. "Just for the record, your daughter may have succeeded in making herself indispensable, but no one except my father has ever brought me to heel, and he would tell you he had a hell of a time doing it."

He flicked an icy gaze over Erin. "It appears I misplaced my trust," he said, then left the room.

Ten

Her heart crowding her throat, Erin raced after Daniel. She heard her father calling her as she left.

"Erin!" he said. "Come back here immediately."

She barely spared him a thought. She couldn't pretend to agree with her father one more second, even if it cost her the relationship with him she'd craved. Her heart and mind were with Daniel. The deep betrayal on his face had scored her soul. He had been bitterly disappointed, and she was responsible.

"Daniel," she called as she ran to catch up with him. He didn't pause as he neared his private quarters. "Daniel, *please*—let me explain."

He slowly turned and looked at her with such contempt it took her breath. The only sound between them was her harsh breathing from running.

"Two minutes. I have another appointment," he said and opened the door to his quarters.

Two minutes! Following him into his quarters, Erin panicked and felt the threat of hiccups. Not now, she told herself. Not now when she needed to explain everything to Daniel.

He turned to face her with a stony expression.

She took a deep breath. "I know the conversation with my father must've sounded quite damning, but you didn't hear everything."

"I'm not sure I want to," Daniel said, crossing his arms over his chest.

Erin bit her lip. "Well, you must. It's true that my father asked me to talk you out of taking the throne. He is afraid of change, and since you're American, he feared you wouldn't be at all suitable to be Altaria's king. It's also true that I very much wanted to please my father because we've never been as close as I'd like, so I intended to discourage you from the throne. Once I grew to know you, though, I disagreed with my father." Erin wrung her hands. "It was very distressing to me. I felt disloyal to him. Then I felt disloyal to you."

"You don't need to feel distressed anymore, Erin," he said in a voice so cold it reminded her of the winter weather in Chicago. "Your game is out in the open now. You're just like everyone else. I know I can't depend on you.''

Erin's heart cracked. She closed her eyes. He was so very wrong, but how in the world could she convince him? ''Do you wish me to leave the palace?'' she asked, fighting tears.

''That's up to you,'' he said as if he couldn't care less.

His attitude felt like a knife plunging into her. ''Since I'm more familiar with some of your tastes than most, I believe I should try to ease your transition as much as possible.''

''Your choice,'' he said, glancing at his watch. ''If you'll excuse me, I have an appointment.''

Erin felt her heart sink to her feet. Her two minutes were over, and so was her golden time with Daniel. Feeling lost, she left his quarters, returned to her room and sat down on the bed. She ran her fingers over the beautiful coverlet and felt her eyes well with tears.

How had everything gone so wrong? She had known all along that it wouldn't end well, she reminded herself. Even if Daniel hadn't overheard that terrible one-sided conversation with her father, he was king and he would be obligated to choose a different kind of woman for his bride.

But she had never felt so safe, so wanted, as she had with him. An image of his angry face flashed though her mind and she flinched. She wrapped her arms around herself for comfort, but the terrible emptiness inside her only grew wider and deeper.

Erin felt tears burn down her cheeks, and she couldn't stop a hiccup, then another. Sobbing, she gave in to the spasms until she was exhausted.

He would never hold her again. He would never look at her with light in his eyes again.

The reality brought fresh pain and tears. She rubbed her wet cheeks with the backs of her hands. The phone on her bedside table startled her with its ring. She hiccuped, wondering who it might be. Daniel? Wishful thinking. Her father? She hiccuped again and decided not to answer. Erin couldn't talk to her father. She was ashamed she had ever agreed to try to dissuade Daniel from the throne, and she couldn't pretend otherwise. Her father would be furious with her disloyalty.

Her throat tightened. She had lost both Daniel and her father. Strangely enough, the loss of her father bothered her far less than the fact that she had brought Daniel such pain.

Daniel was incredibly strong, but he was making a difficult transition in Altaria, and she had made it harder. He had been so angry, so cold. She could only imagine how betrayed he must feel.

Erin sighed, hiccuping again. The spasms irritated her, so she turned her attention to getting rid of them. She pictured a peaceful Swiss snowfall. She continued to hiccup and frowned.

Closing her eyes again, she allowed her mind to

drift to a different image. A cold, starlit night where she stood with Daniel in the middle of boxwoods lit with tiny white lights. Her heart hurt at the image, but she would never forget the magic they'd shared there that night.

Her hiccups faded and she opened her eyes.

Daniel would never love her. That would be a pain she would endure until she died. But she had the power to make life a little easier for him at this moment. She knew him as no one else in Altaria did. A seed of determination grew inside her.

After a long afternoon spent in meetings with a host of government officials, Daniel sought the solace of his private quarters. Loosening his tie, he entered and found Erin at his desk.

Suspicion immediately burned through him. "What are you doing?" he asked quietly.

Erin looked at him uncertainly. "Moving you in, Your Majesty," she said, lifting her hand to books she'd placed on a shelf.

Daniel gave the books a second look. They were the ones he'd brought with him from Chicago. He relaxed a millimeter.

"I knew you would immediately be plunged into meetings and royal duties, so I thought it best that I go ahead and unpack some of your things. You might not feel quite so out of place that way, sir," she said, arranging one of several photographs of his family. "Does this suit you, sir?"

Even now, when he was still bitter over her betrayal, her formal address grated on him. He glanced over the curves of her body and remembered how she had felt in his arms. Despite his anger, a forbidden flame of arousal flared through him. Disgusted with himself, Daniel looked away.

"It's fine," he said. "Thank you."

He heard her sigh and met her gaze. In her eyes, an expression of hurt and loss came and quickly went. Her hands fluttered nervously before she clasped them together. "I took the liberty of ordering a meal for you, sir," she said. "One of the aides projected the ending time for your meetings and I thought you might be hungry."

"Correct again," he murmured, spotting the covered silver tray behind her.

"Very good, sir," she said briskly. "I've left you Altaria's newspaper, *The Altarian Chronicle,* along with the *Wall Street Journal.* I've arranged for delivery of the Chicago newspaper, but you won't begin receiving that until next week. In the meantime, the palace is equipped with a television satellite with over two hundred channels and you'll be pleased to know one of them is a Chicago station. I've also arranged for some of the palace groundskeepers to build an outdoor run for Jordan. Now, if I may excuse myself, I'll leave you to enjoy your dinner while it's warm."

Daniel blinked at the list of all Erin had accomplished. Curiosity burned alongside his sense of betrayal. "Why?" he asked.

She met his gaze. "Why what, sir?"

"Why did you do all this?"

She shrugged. "As palace liaison, it's my job to make sure you are as comfortable as possible."

"It was also your job to persuade me not to take the throne, or at the least to have me accept that my position was one of decorum only," he said, to keep the edge from his voice.

She paled and took a careful breath as if she'd just been struck. "I obviously was not well-suited for that assignment, sir," she said. "Perhaps I was ineffective because I didn't remain in agreement with it. I hope I will be much more successful with my current assignment." She gave a small, perfect curtsey. "Enjoy your dinner, sir," she said and left.

His heart pounding with a terrible mix of emotions, Daniel closed his eyes. Her light flowery scent lingered in the air. He inhaled deeply and the image of her sweet and naked in his arms invaded his mind. He swore under his breath and opened his eyes.

Her touch lingered just like her scent. His family's photographs had never felt more valuable to him. Seeing his books on the shelf alongside his grandfather's made him feel less like an outsider. It was as if Erin had known exactly what would ease him. He wondered if she was trying to win back his trust.

Daniel immediately rejected the possibility and contemplated whether he should dismiss her. After all, he knew he would never trust her. He was appalled with himself that he'd allowed her to become so important to him.

His stomach churned with a combination of hunger and dissatisfaction. Determined to set thoughts of Erin Lawrence aside, he walked toward his dinner tray and lifted the heavy sterling top. A man's dream meal. Rare steak, new potatoes and green beans. He took a long drink from the cold bottle of beer on the tray and brought his plate with him to the sofa. He reached for the remote and noticed that the first channel on the television was a Chicago station. It was as if she'd been determined to provide him reassurance and comfort in every way.

His heart tightened at the thought, but Daniel would never forget her father's damning words. Never in a million years.

Daniel was in constant motion from the time he rose until late in the evening for the next two days. Each night he found a cold beer waiting for him along with an addition to his private quarters. The latest was a basketball hoop hooked over the wastebasket beside his desk.

Tonight he'd attended a private dinner party at the prime minister's home. Exhausted, all Daniel wanted was to sink into the comfort and privacy of his quarters. But as he entered his suite, he noticed

Jordan was missing. Frowning, he glanced out into the hallway.

Gregor Paulus approached him and bowed. Damn, if the man didn't always seem to be hovering nearby. "Good evening, Your Majesty. May I help you?"

"I'm looking for my dog."

Gregor twitched slightly. "I believe Miss Lawrence took him for a walk. She said he was barking and seemed lonely. Shall I collect them?" he asked, but didn't appear to relish the prospect.

"No, that's okay. I could use a walk myself," Daniel said and strode down the hall. He didn't want to see Erin, he told himself as he exited the palace through a side door. Even though he hadn't seen Erin during the last two days, he didn't miss her at all. He just wanted to see Jordan. He couldn't care less about seeing a certain shapely blonde with transparent blue eyes and warmth to spare beneath her cool English accent.

Daniel heard her before he saw her.

"You're going to be just fine," she said in a low, comforting voice. "You'll see. Your run will be ready in another day and you can play outside and dig holes and drive the palace groundskeepers crazy."

He couldn't stop a flicker of amusement at the sight of Erin sitting on the grass beside Jordan, petting him as she talked to him.

"The only thing is that you may need to mind

your manners a bit when His Majesty entertains special guests.'' She sniffed. ''And I do believe you could use a bath and some mint-scented doggy treats.''

''Royal dog walker too?'' Daniel asked, and watched both Erin and Jordan whip around to see him. Jordan barked and jumped to his feet, wagging his tail. He jolted forward, jerking Erin along with him.

Daniel bent down to rub his faithful pet. ''Rough day, big guy? Mine was jam-packed,'' he said, then found he was unable to delay looking at Erin one second longer. The incongruous sight of her dressed in a pink ultra-feminine dress with her hands wrapped around Jordan's leather leash in a death grip did something to his gut. Indigestion, he told himself. ''You can let him loose from his leash.''

Her blue gaze was full of doubt. ''Are you sure, sir? I've had difficulty retrieving him a few times.''

This was news to him. ''How many times have you taken him out?''

''Several, sir. He whines and barks when you're gone.''

He nodded slowly, not wanting to be moved by her attentiveness to his dog, of all things. ''You can let him go. He'll come when I whistle.''

''I should learn how to whistle,'' she murmured to herself and let Jordan free. The dog immediately raced across the lawn.

Watching Jordan gallop over the grass, Daniel

stood beside Erin. He was acutely aware of her presence and it irritated him. "Just out of curiosity, how have you been collaring him?"

"I've seduced him with steak, sir," she admitted.

The word *seduced* immediately conjured a slew of passionate images in his mind.

"It didn't take much," she continued. "Just a bite or two. The chef has been amenable so far, but I'd better not push it. If I didn't know better, I'd say Jordan laughs at me when I order him to return."

Daniel felt another sliver of amusement at the mental picture. He lifted his fingers to his lips and whistled sharply. Jordan immediately loped toward him and sat in front of him with his tongue hanging out, panting.

Erin stared at Daniel. "That's quite amazing, Dan—" Erin bit her lip at the slip. "Sir," she quickly corrected. "Would you mind showing me how you do that?"

Daniel repeated the whistle at a lower volume.

Jordan cocked his head.

Erin moved closer to study Daniel's mouth. "So you put your index fingers at each corner of your mouth." She lifted her fingers to her lips. "What do I do with my tongue?"

A blazing hot memory roared through Daniel and he bit back a groan. He could tell her several things she could do with her tongue. Tamping down his rampant arousal, he tried to focus on whistling.

"You make a V with your tongue and press it against your bottom lip, then blow."

Erin blew, but didn't produce a whistle. She frowned in consternation and tried again.

Daniel studied her pink mouth and lifted his hand to her jaw. "Try again," he coached. "And press your tongue against your bottom teeth."

Erin tried again and sighed in self-disgust. "I think I may need to practice."

"You didn't learn how to whistle in finishing school," Daniel said, unable to keep a chuckle from his voice.

"There were a lot of things I didn't learn in finishing school," she murmured, her gaze tangling with his.

Daniel's stomach twisted at the sensual awareness on her face. He had put that there, he realized. He had been the man to teach her what a woman couldn't learn in an all-girls finishing school. A primitive possessiveness snaked through his blood, taking him off guard. Lord help him, even though she'd betrayed him, he still wanted her.

The following day, Erin received a request to appear in one of the royal meeting rooms. She wondered if Daniel had instructed his chief of staff to fire her. The prospect filled her with a mixture of dread and relief. Although she hated the idea of losing her accessibility to him, she welcomed the possibility that she would no longer have to endure his anger or disdain.

Entering the room, she saw several palace aides, royal security, and Daniel's chief of staff already waiting. Erin approved Daniel's choice for his chief of staff, Anthony Muller. She'd thought Daniel might choose Gregor Paulus simply because the man was so ingratiating, but she should have known better. Daniel was his own man. He would choose the man he believed best for such a crucial position. Anthony Muller was slightly older than Daniel and had acquired his college education in the United States. To put it in crude terms, Anthony was no suck-up. When asked for the truth, he spoke it.

Anthony nodded toward her in greeting, then turned his attention to the crowd. "Okay, everyone. You'll be honored to know that you have been selected to join His Majesty on his first official outing this afternoon."

Low murmurs of excitement traveled through the room. Erin felt a ripple of surprise and wondered why she had been chosen. Perhaps Daniel planned to bring Jordan along and he wanted a companion for his dog, she thought wryly.

"Some of you have heard about the fires that recently destroyed several farms. His Majesty plans to visit the farmers in a show of moral support. We will depart promptly at thirteen hundred hours," Anthony said. "Meet here fifteen minutes prior to that for further instruction." As he dismissed the group, he gestured toward Erin, who met him in the door-way.

"His Majesty requires your services as protocol consultant on this visit," Anthony said.

Erin nodded, still surprised Daniel would want anything from her.

A couple of hours later she joined Daniel in his private quarters. He was stewing over his wardrobe. "It's ridiculous to wear a suit to a farm when the temperature is above eighty degrees."

"I agree, sir," Erin said. "Ridiculous, but nec-essary. After all, this is your first planned public appearance in Altaria, and it's best to project a royal image."

He frowned at her. "Don't tell me I'm supposed to wear a crown for this," he said.

"Of course not, sir. You won't receive your crown until the coronation. The press will be out in full force today."

"I plan to shake hands with everyone I meet," he warned her.

"That's fine. Just give them an opportunity to show their respect first," she said, then impulsively added, "I think you've made a splendid choice for your first outing, sir. The citizens you greet today will be quite honored by your presence."

"A new barn might be more welcome," he mut-tered, adjusting his tie. He glanced at his watch. "Time to go. By the way, the PM is sending along his niece. He said the two of you attended the same boarding school. Christina Whitestone.''

''Briefly,'' Erin said, recalling that Christina had been kicked out of boarding school for sneaking out at night to meet boys. Christina had been wilder than a March hare. She probably planned to seduce Daniel and have her wicked way with him. Or worse yet, marry him. Erin's stomach churned with jealousy.

''What do you know about her?'' Daniel asked, striding from his quarters.

That she's a slut, Erin thought. She bit her tongue, then sucked in a quick breath. ''I don't really know her well. We didn't attend the same boarding school very long, sir.''

Daniel stopped abruptly and studied Erin. ''What do you know about her? And I'd like the truth,'' he demanded. ''I have enough trouble knowing whom I can trust at the palace without wondering about the PM's niece.''

''I am truly not well acquainted with her. I only know her by reputation,'' Erin said, trying to take the high road.

Daniel arched an eyebrow. ''And her reputation is…?''

''Loose,'' Erin finally said.

His lips twitched, and his eyes glimmered with amusement. ''How refreshing,'' he said and continued down the hallway. ''I thought you were going to tell me she was interested in political espionage.''

"I'm quite sure political espionage is the last thing on Christina's mind," she said, and rounded the corner to the foyer. Erin immediately spotted Christina decked out in a dress that skimmed over every voluptuous curve. Seeing Daniel, the woman lifted her red lips into a sexually welcoming smile and gave a curtsey that gave His Majesty a perfect view of her enhanced cleavage.

Erin prayed her skin wasn't turning green as grass.

Eleven

With the exception of Christina's constant shrill laughter, Daniel's visit to the first farm couldn't have gone better. Erin noticed how he allowed the farmer to bow in respect, then Daniel was quick to show his own respect by shaking hands and asking questions as the entourage toured the damaged property.

Just as everyone prepared to leave, the farmer expressed his gratitude to his neighbors for donating materials and muscle for the barn-raising. As soon as the farmer mentioned it, Erin immediately knew what Daniel planned to do.

"Can I help?" Daniel asked.

The farmer gaped at him, embarrassed by the generous offer. "I can't—" The man shook his head in dismay. "Sir, I couldn't possibly—"

"My father made sure I could swing a hammer with the best of them. One more pair of hands will get the job done that much faster," he said and began removing his jacket.

Erin immediately went to his side. "Are you sure, sir?" she asked in a low voice, accepting his coat as he handed it to her.

"Very," he said, ditching his tie and unfastening a few of his shirt buttons. "I told you a suit was ridiculous."

Anthony Muller leaned closer. "Sir, we wouldn't want you to get hurt."

Daniel did a double take. "I realize that's your gentle way of telling me to avoid the embarrassment of hitting myself with the hammer. But I think I can manage. Tell the others if they want to join in and help, the palace will cover the dry-cleaning bills."

Christina and some of the aides watched in slack-jawed amazement as the new king joined the humble farmers in a barn-raising. Photographers snapped shot after shot. Erin joined a few of the farmers' wives in serving fruit juice and water.

The farmers were working on the roof while Daniel downed a glass of water. Sweat gleamed down his throat, and his white shirt was nearly transparent against his corded muscles.

Erin stared at him and felt her mouth go bone dry. She heard a cry and looked up in time to see a hammer falling from the roof and heading straight for Daniel. Still holding her tray, she clumsily lurched forward to push Daniel aside. Everything happened at once. She lifted one hand to deflect the falling hammer, while the other firmly clutched the tray. Her aim fell awry and the hammer's handle hit her on the head. Pain reverberated through her head.

"Erin!" Daniel said.

Her vision went black for a second. She felt her hands go slack. "The tray." Her head throbbed. She wobbled on her feet, then suddenly felt herself airborne.

Her vision slowly cleared, and she looked up to see Daniel frowning down at her and swearing.

"Did I drop the tray?" she whispered, wincing from the pain.

He rolled his eyes and swore again. Seconds passed and they were surrounded by farmers and aides. A palace security man pulled her from Daniel's arms and carried her to a limousine. Erin blinked at the dizzying effect of his movements.

Daniel appeared in the limo doorway, his gaze searching hers. "How are you?"

"I'm fine, sir," Erin said, hurting, but not enough to escape a feeling of total humiliation. "I suppose I'm not a very good catcher. Another one of those things I didn't learn in boarding school."

Daniel didn't smile. "What about your head?"

She gingerly touched her head and felt a goose

egg forming. "It's nothing," she lied. "Just a little bruise. Sorry for the fuss."

Daniel reached down to touch her head. "That feels like a knot to me. I'm sending you back to see the palace doctor."

Erin felt her cheeks heat with embarrassment. "That's totally unnecessary, sir," she insisted.

Daniel ignored her and turned his attention to the guard. "Take her back and make sure the doctor sees her."

"As you wish, sir," the guard said.

Daniel closed the door on her protests, and it occurred to her that he was enjoying his newfound ability to issue orders more quickly than she would have dreamed.

After the return drive to the palace, Erin endured an evaluation by the palace doctor. She was ordered to take her dinner in her room and rest. She was told she would be awakened every few hours. She groused to herself that she was being treated like a child, but fell asleep with the light on before eight o'clock.

Hours later a sound woke her from her sleep. She lifted her head and saw the outline of a man next to her bed. Fear raced through her, and she opened her mouth to scream, but panic froze her vocal cords.

"It's me. Daniel," the shadow said, moving closer so she could make out his face.

Her heart still hammering, Erin sagged with relief. "You scared me half to death."

"Fair is fair. You did the same to me this afternoon when you decided to have a head-on collision with a hammer," he told her, his voice softly chiding.

Erin sighed. "Well, I couldn't allow it to hit you," she said. "And I had nowhere to set the tray."

Daniel chuckled, and the sound evoked a ripple of pleasure over her nerve endings. "You have trouble letting things go."

She closed her eyes and covered her forehead with her hand. "It's that training I told you about. Though you would think they could have taught me to dodge a falling hammer or to whistle."

She felt his hand cover hers on her forehead, and the sensation was so comforting she held her breath. Oh, heavens, how she'd missed his touch.

"How's your head, really?"

"Fine," she said in a quiet voice. If she remained perfectly still, maybe he would stay a little longer.

"Thank you for catching the hammer," he said, sifting his fingers through her hair. "We're even now."

She peeked up at him through her fingers. "How are we even?"

"I helped you dodge a bullet. You helped me dodge a hammer."

Erin shook her head. "The hammer's head most likely wouldn't have killed you."

"Why didn't you tell me Christina had the most annoying laugh?"

Erin couldn't resist a smile. "I think most men don't listen to her as much as they look at her other...assets." Erin paused. "The prime minister is probably hoping you'll view her as a marriage prospect. Although she's—" Erin paused, searching for the most polite description "—extremely experienced, she has an excellent pedigree. You could do worse," she said dutifully and wondered why the whole discussion left a bad taste in her mouth.

Daniel lifted her hand to his lips. "Why are we talking about Christina?"

She slid him a sideways, accusing glance. "You brought her up."

He sank down on the bed beside her, searching her face. "I don't know what I'm going to do with you," he muttered. "You betray me, then save me from a hammer."

A knot formed in Erin's throat. "I didn't intend to betray you," she said, but he covered her lips with his finger and shook his head.

"Don't start," he said, his eyes moody and turbulent.

Erin's heart sank. She could see that he still struggled with his hurt and anger. "Will you ever be able to forgive me?" she whispered.

He looked at her for a long moment, rubbing his finger over her mouth. Finally, he nodded. "I'll be able to forgive you," he said. "But trust is another matter."

Erin knew she had lost something very very precious.

His gaze wrapped around her, and she felt a strange power surge between them. "Do you feel it?" she asked.

He nodded and lowered his mouth to hers. Erin closed her eyes and inhaled his scent, felt the texture of his lips against hers. She opened to his insistent pressure, wanting to please, to heal. She wondered if it was possible to love him so much on the outside that he felt it on the inside too.

His tongue tangled with hers and she lifted her hands to slide through his thick hair. His kiss grew more ardent. He slid his hands over the tiny straps of her nightgown, then rubbed his thumbs over the upper edge of her breasts.

Erin immediately felt her nipples tighten.

"I should stop," he said, pulling slightly away. "Your head must be hurting."

Erin bit her lip at the mix of arousal and passion plunging through her. "It's not," she said and pushed her hands through his open shirt to his muscular chest. "Are you aware that you drove all the women crazy with your broad shoulders and muscles today?"

His mouth lifted in a slight grin. "Can't say that thought crossed my mind. I didn't know you noticed my body."

Erin swallowed a groan. "That's the most ridiculous thing you've ever said."

"No, it's not," he said. "You've never said a word about my body."

Erin rolled her eyes. "Well, I suppose you could say I've revealed my opinion more by actions than words."

His lids lowered to a sexy half-mast. "What's your opinion right now?" he asked, his words both a challenge and an invitation.

Erin's heart pounded against her rib cage. "Come close and let me show you," she said, and she did.

She kissed her way down his chest, dragged her tongue over his belly and would have gone further, but he stopped her and took a little pleasure of his own. He suckled the tips of her breasts until she arched toward him, and slid his hand between her thighs to find her wet and swollen.

Murmuring his approval, he pushed her legs apart and thrust inside her. Erin sighed at the feeling of delicious fullness. He gave her seconds to grow accustomed to him, then began a rhythm that took away her mind and breath.

She craved every possible intimacy with him. He drove her higher and higher until she clenched around him. He shuddered, then pulled himself from her at the last moment before his release.

Erin immediately felt the loss. They'd been so close. Her breath was harsh with exertion, as was his. Confused, she stared up at him. "Why did you—"

"I didn't have any protection for you," he managed, his look as tumultuous as if he were fighting his own set of demons concerning her. He closed his eyes, then shifted away from her, pulling the sheet over her. "I shouldn't have done this," he muttered.

His words cut her. She understood his disappointment in her, his anger. She even understood his disenchantment. But she couldn't bear his regret. "You should go," she whispered, refusing to give in to tears. "You shouldn't be here."

She felt him look down at her, but she didn't meet his gaze. "Go to sleep, Erin."

She waited for him to leave, then buried her face in her pillow and sobbed. Overwhelming desperation shook her. She knew she couldn't look at him again. There was only one thing to do: she had to leave.

Daniel avoided Erin for the next two days. He was so busy it wasn't difficult to do. He resented his weakness for her. He shouldn't have made love to her the other night, but he'd been unable to resist his need for her. Even now, he struggled with the itchy need to see her. Three days was too long. He kept his eyes open for her throughout the day, but didn't see her.

During a formal business dinner, in a quiet voice,

he casually mentioned her to his chief of staff, Anthony Muller.

Anthony shrugged. "She resigned the day before yesterday, sir."

"Excuse me?"

Anthony must have perceived Daniel's displeasure. He frowned. "I apologize, sir. I thought you knew. She moved out and took a position with a local tour agency."

"Tour agency?" Daniel echoed. "Didn't she move in with her father?"

Anthony shook his head. "No. She took a small apartment at the far end of town. The tour agency is quite successful. They cater to businessmen, lead tours into the mountains and host beach parties."

Daniel felt his blood roar to his head. "Beach parties with businessmen? It sounds like a damn escort service to me"

Anthony shifted uncomfortably. "To my knowledge, sir, they're completely legitimate."

Daniel took a calming breath. "I'd like you to find out her schedule. I also want to know her new address," he said. "Immediately," he added and couldn't force down one more bite.

Immediately after Daniel finished the interminable meal one hour later, he received all his information and he didn't like most of it. Erin was apparently hosting a bonfire at the beach this evening. The very thought of her with all those men made him sick.

He wondered why she hadn't returned to her father, though he suspected Erin and her father were no longer on speaking terms. That probably hurt her to no end. It had been so obvious that she had wanted a close relationship with her father. She had wanted it badly, yet she'd given in to her feelings for Daniel.

The knowledge did strange things to his heart. Lord, what a mess. The truth of the matter was that if she'd been sent to him with a duplicitous scheme, she'd done a rotten job pulling it off. In fact, she hadn't pulled off what her father had apparently asked of her. Daniel wondered if that was why she wasn't living with the man and felt a surprising rush of protectiveness.

He thought of the sweet way she'd given him her innocence and her terror when the bullet grazed his forehead. He remembered the terrible hurt on her face when he'd rejected her, and recalled her determination to make his private quarters feel like a home.

He wanted her back.

He gave Anthony his instructions as the two men sat in the parked limo.

"Sir, I cannot recommend you making an unannounced appearance at the bonfire party tonight," the chief of staff said bluntly.

"Thank you for your recommendation. Have you informed security where I want to go?" Daniel asked, adjusting his tie and red sash.

"Yes, and the security chief is most displeased."

"He'll get over it," Daniel said.

Anthony sighed. "Sir, are you certain you want to do this?"

"Never more," Daniel said and knocked back some liquid courage from the limo's bar while security did their thing.

If Erin had to dance with one more man, she was going to scream. The bonfire blazed in the wind, and the sound of the ocean was muted behind the string quartet playing lively island music.

She bared her teeth in a smile as the music blessedly stopped, and stole a quick glance at her watch. Forty-five more minutes and she could return to her apartment and collapse.

Although thoughts of Daniel haunted her day and night, moving into her small apartment had been liberating. Now that she was employed, she was neither dependent nor obligated to anyone but herself. If she still ached with a terrible loss, she refused to dwell on it.

The music began again and another man approached her with a smile. "Dance?"

Swallowing a sigh, she allowed him to take her hand. Halfway through the song, the partying crowd began pointing down the beach. Erin looked over her shoulder, but her partner spun her around so she couldn't see.

Before she knew it, she looked beyond the customer and found Daniel staring at her. Her heart stuttering, she immediately fumbled and stepped on the customer's foot.

The man grunted.

Daniel tapped the man's shoulder, and the customer threw him a look of irritation. "This is my dance. I've been waiting all evening."

A palace guard stepped beside the man. "I would like to introduce His Majesty, Daniel Connelly, King of Altaria."

The customer's eyes nearly popped out of his head. "His Majesty!" He whirled around. "Are you the king?"

"I am," Daniel said, and extended his hand. "And you are?"

"Bob," the man said, clearly bowled over. "Bob Fuller."

"It's a pleasure to meet you, Bob. Are you enjoying Altaria?"

"Oh, yeah. It's great. The weather, the beach, the women," Bob slid his gaze toward Erin.

Daniel's cordial smile stiffened. "Would you mind if I finish this dance?"

Bob looked at Erin. "No. Go ahead. I'll catch her again later."

Daniel immediately took her into his arms. "Over my dead body," he muttered to himself. He looked at Erin. "What in hell are you doing?"

Erin's mind was spinning. "Working. This is my job."

"No, it isn't. Your job is at the palace," Daniel

said, his jaw as firm as granite.

"I quit," Erin said, her heart bumping against her rib cage.

He looked as if he were counting to ten to remain under control. "I'm talking about a different position."

"What?" she asked wryly. "Royal dog walker and pooper scooper?"

He sucked in a quick breath, and Erin got the uncomfortable sense that she had just crossed his line in the sand.

"We need to talk," he said. "You're coming with me."

"I can't," she protested. "I need this job."

"You're quitting this job," he told her.

"I don't think so."

"I know so," he said, and shocked the spit out of her by picking her up in his arms and carrying her. A roar of chuckles followed after them.

"What on earth are you doing?" she hissed as he trudged to a black limousine. "If the press gets wind of this, everyone will think you're crazy."

"Then there's only one solution," he said, dumping her into the back seat.

"What is that?" she demanded.

"I'll tell you when we get to the palace."

Erin crossed her arms mutinously over her chest during the short ride to the palace. He had gone entirely too far this time. She just knew she would get sacked for this, and it was all his fault.

As soon as the limo stopped, Daniel exited the car and came to her side to collect her. Erin refused to budge. "I want to return to my apartment. You have no right to force me into the palace," she told him.

He exhaled and softly swore. "Well, if you're going to be difficult," he said, and tossed her over his shoulder.

Erin's blood rushed to her head. "Put me down at once," she insisted, her voice rising. "Put me down. You're embarrassing both of us."

"I'm not embarrassed," he said, hauling her through the grand foyer.

"Put me down," she said, feeling her slim shred of control slipping through her fingers. "Put me—" She hiccuped. "Oh, look what you've—" she hiccuped "—done. You gave me the hiccups."

Still carrying her, he lowered her into a slightly more respectable position and looked down at her. "I want to give you hiccups for the rest of your life."

Confused and near tears, Erin hiccuped again. "What are you talking about?" she asked before another spasm shook her.

"I want to marry you."

Erin blinked. Her breath and heart seemed to stop. A second later, she hiccuped. "You can't marry me," she whispered. "You don't trust me."

"Change my mind," he dared her. "I'm almost there."

She bit her lip and felt another hiccup. "I can't imagine having any significant influence over a man as strong-minded as you."

"Then you need to do something about your imagination."

Erin fell silent. With the exception of her hiccups. She felt as if the world had been turned upside down. Or turned upright. She stared at Daniel and wondered if a person could burst from hope and love.

"I want you with me all the time, Erin," Daniel said. "Hell, I'll even get you a poodle."

She blinked. A poodle was the last thing on her mind.

His eyes were drop-dead serious. "When I look at you, I want things I've never wanted before. I want to love and protect you the rest of my life. I want to raise children with you. I want to lead Altaria into a great new age with you by my side. But most of all, Erin, I want to live every day of my life with you." His nostrils flared. "Damn it, Erin. Say something."

"Yes," she whispered and took her heart in her hands and gave it to Daniel's safekeeping. She wondered how she could have traveled her whole life and found her home in this man's eyes.

"Yes," he echoed as if he didn't quite trust her breathless response.

"Yes," she said with all the conviction flooding through her. "I will marry you. I will have your children. I will stand by your side." She lifted her hand to his strong jaw. "I will love you forever," she said and knew beyond the shadow of a doubt that she would.

Epilogue

A week later Erin and Daniel were married in an outdoor ceremony on the palace lawn. The royal advisors had protested the speed, but Daniel had been adamant. They would have to postpone an extended honeymoon until after Daniel's coronation, but Erin didn't mind. She knew the ongoing investigation into the deaths of King Thomas and Prince Marc weighed heavily on Daniel's mind and heart, and he wouldn't rest until the murderers were found and punished.

Despite her ambivalence, Daniel insisted that Erin's father attend the ceremony. He was determined that she would experience the feeling of family she'd missed her entire life. There'd been a moment or two of awkwardness, but Erin sensed her father wished for a genuine reconciliation as much as she did.

After the ceremony and reception, which was internationally televised, she and Daniel escaped to Dunemere, the Rosemere family's beach house. Erin was certain she and Daniel would take refuge in the two-story, shingled wood frame house on many future occasions. The hideaway overflowed with flowers from Daniel's family and the joy between she and Daniel. Erin had never dreamed she could be so completely cherished.

She looked down at her naked husband lying replete from their lovemaking. His urgency had taken her by surprise at the same time that it turned her on. It was as if he'd needed to claim her as his wife.

"I love you," he said, the power of his feelings glowing in his eyes.

Her heart swelled with emotion. "I feel like crying every time you tell me."

He gently smiled. "Better than hiccups?"

She laughed. "I suppose," she said, and traced his strong jaw. She thought about the vows they'd just made. "Sometimes I still don't understand, why me? Why would you want to marry me?"

He glanced away for a moment. "From the first moment I met you, something told me I could trust you."

Erin's stomach tightened, and she closed her eyes. She still hated to think of how hurt he had been.

"Look at me," he told her, kissing her lightly. "Even after I heard that awful conversation with your father, there was a part of me that still trusted you. That part was right," he told her. "I trust you with my life, with my future."

Her eyes welled with tears. "Do you realize you've made me the happiest woman in the world?"

"Erin," he said, with passion and promise in his eyes, "I'm just getting started."

* * * * *

Maternally Yours

KATHIE DeNOSKY

KATHIE DeNOSKY

lives in deep southern Illinois with her husband and three children. After reading and enjoying romances for many years, she is ecstatic about being able to share her stories with others as a Spotlight and Desire author. Kathie writes highly sensual stories with a generous amount of humour and her books have appeared on the Waldenbooks bestseller list. She enjoys going to rodeos, travelling to research settings for her books and listening to country music. She often starts her day at 2:00 am so she can write without interruption, before the rest of the family is up and about. You may write to Kathie at: PO Box 2064, Herrin, Il 62948-5264, USA.

One

Elena Delgado pressed a shaky hand to her stomach, took a deep breath and slowly got to her feet. She closed her eyes and leaned against the side of the rest room stall. The nausea wasn't supposed to last all day. If it was, they would have called it something besides morning sickness. But she'd been ill almost from the instant the test stick turned blue.

She didn't mind in the least. She'd gladly go through whatever it took to complete this pregnancy successfully. She bit her lower lip and took another deep breath. This was her last hope of having her own child, of holding it and loving it with every fiber of her being—she simply couldn't afford another trip to the sperm bank. Not financially. Not emotionally.

When her stomach finally settled down, she pulled the door open and walked over to the vanity. The click of her black medium-heeled pumps striking the tiled floor echoed through the empty room. She shivered at the hollow loneliness of the sound.

Tears filled her eyes as she looked at herself in the mirror above the bank of sinks. She'd been alone all of her life. So why was she feeling so lonely now?

Disgusted with herself, Elena jerked paper towels from the dispenser on the wall and held them under the faucet, then pressed the cool wetness to her flushed cheeks. Her unstable emotions had to be caused by the hormonal changes from her pregnancy. That was the only thing it could be.

Otherwise Elena Delgado never cried. Ever.

She finished wiping away the last of the tears, draped her coat over her arm, then checked her watch. Groaning, she quickly grabbed her shoulder bag, said a silent prayer that her queasy stomach would remain calm for the next hour and walked out into the stylish reception area of Connelly Tower.

Heading for the elevators, she shook her head. She hated to be late for anything. It was rude and inconsiderate to keep people waiting. She shifted from one foot to the other as she impatiently waited for an elevator. Just one more slowdown in a day that had been filled with a series of delays and frustrations.

She'd awakened this morning to find that sometime during the night the ancient furnace in her building had finally given up the fight against Chicago's cold, hard winters and died. It had taken her twice as long to get ready for work because she couldn't stop shivering. Then she'd gone out to find that her car wouldn't start, forcing her to walk six blocks in the frigid February temperature to catch the L.

The polished brass doors of the elevator finally swished open and Elena hurriedly stepped inside. She pressed the button to the seventeenth floor, and as it began to move, she closed her eyes against a wave of nausea. Express elevators should be outlawed, she decided as the rapid ascent played havoc with her already iffy stomach.

When it eased to a stop a few seconds later and the doors opened, she stepped out into the plushly carpeted corridor on shaky legs. After she met with Brett Connelly to arrange interviews with the rest of the Connelly family, she would spend the weekend trying to feel human again. But when she left, she would take the stairs.

Brett Connelly tapped the highly polished surface of his mahogany desk with his fountain pen. Glancing at his watch for the third time in as many minutes, he resumed staring out the window at the early-evening shadows covering Lake Michigan. He hated to be kept waiting. If the detective investigating the attempted murder of his older brother, Daniel, didn't show up damned quick, Brett was calling it a day. Babe didn't like him to be late getting home from work. In fact, he'd be lucky if she didn't destroy some of his things to get back at him. She'd done that several times already.

The intercom on the corner of his desk suddenly buzzed, interrupting his thoughts. "Yes, Fiona?"

"Your four o'clock appointment has finally arrived, Mr. Connelly."

"Thank you. Send her in." As an afterthought, he added, "If you'd like, you can leave now."

"Thank you, Mr. Connelly. I'll see you on Monday. Have a nice weekend."

"You, too, Fiona."

Seconds later his office door opened, and a young woman with shoulder-length, tawny-brown hair walked into the room. Brett couldn't keep from staring. This was the hotshot detective from the Special Investigative Unit of the Chicago Police Department?

Whoa, baby! He'd been expecting some middle-aged battle-ax who looked like a man and had a hard-as-nails attitude. Instead they'd sent a petite woman who had to be somewhere in her midtwenties and could put beauty queens to shame with her looks. He made a mental note to call and thank his father for assigning him the task of liaison between his family and the police.

Brett rose to his feet as his gaze zeroed in on her left hand to see if she wore a wedding band. She didn't.

Sending a silent thank-you to the powers that be, he rounded the desk, treated her to his most charming smile—the smile that had kept his social calendar filled since his sophomore year in high school—and extended his hand. "I'm Brett Connelly, Vice President of Public Relations. And you are?"

She quickly shook his hand but didn't return his smile. "I'm SIU Detective Elena Delgado. Sorry I'm late, Mr. Connelly."

She wasn't offering an explanation for her tardiness, and Brett wasn't asking for one. He was too preoccupied with the tingling sensation running from his palm, up his arm and warming his chest.

"Since we'll be working so closely together, please call me Brett, Ms. Delgado," he said, rubbing his thumb over the silky skin on the back of her hand.

She dropped his hand, and the look she gave him indicated that she hadn't been the least bit affected by his never-fail smile or his touch. At least not the way he'd been affected by hers.

"Shall we get down to business, Mr. Connelly?" she asked politely.

Her no-nonsense demeanor certainly went with her job. But it wasn't often that he encountered a female he couldn't charm. He took it as a personal challenge.

As she continued to gaze at him expectantly, he noticed something about her that had escaped him when she'd first entered the room. Elena Delgado looked tired. Very tired. Dark circles smudged the pale skin beneath her chocolate-brown eyes, and her voice sounded extremely weary. Maybe that had something to do with her no-nonsense attitude and refusal to use his first name.

Whatever the reason, something about her stoic demeanor urged him to take up the gauntlet and improve her mood. He checked his watch. It was dinnertime and he was already late getting home. Daniel and his wife, Erin, were safely hidden from any further attempts on Daniel's life in the tiny island country of Altaria, so there was no immediate threat to his brother on that front. And Babe would treat him to the cold shoulder now, anyway. In fact, she'd probably already started destroying the living room. Being an hour or two later wouldn't make much difference.

Besides, Elena looked as if she could use something to lift her spirits. What better way than spending an evening out on the town?

"I was just getting ready to leave for the day," he said, walking over to remove his suit jacket from the brass coat tree in the corner. Shrugging into it, he reached for his leather overcoat. "Why don't we discuss the details of the interviews over dinner?"

She shook her head, and if the expression on her lovely face was any indication, it wasn't going to be easy changing her mind. "I'd rather not, Mr. Connelly."

He wasn't about to let that deter him. "I skipped breakfast and worked through lunch," he said truthfully. "It's dinnertime and I'm hungry." He smiled. "And I'm betting you are, too."

Her stomach chose that moment to rumble, making any protest she might have had ineffective. Her cheeks colored a pretty pink. He hadn't seen a woman blush like that in years.

Brett chuckled. "Then it's settled." He pulled on his overcoat and placed his hand lightly at the small of her back to usher her to the door. "We'll talk over dinner."

She didn't look happy, but Brett took it as a positive sign when she allowed him to steer her to the elevators. The swift ride down to the basement parking garage was a silent one and he began to wonder if he was losing his touch. By the time the doors opened, she looked positively miserable about being in his company.

"I'll bring you back to pick up your car," he said as they stepped out into the parking area.

"My car wouldn't start this morning," she said, sounding even more tired than before. "I took the L."

"Well, you're not taking it home," he said emphatically. Police detective or not, he didn't like the idea of a woman riding the elevated train alone at night. It just wasn't safe. Before she could protest, he quickly led her to his black Jaguar and opened the passenger door. "Do you like Italian food?"

She practically collapsed into the bucket seat before she answered. ''Yes, I normally love Italian food, but I don't think it would be—''

''Good. Then Italian it is,'' he said, closing the door. When she glanced up at him, he thought her complexion looked a little green. But he dismissed the notion. The fluorescent lights, combined with the shadows of the underground garage, cast an unnatural glow on everything. Walking around to the driver's side, he opened the door and slid behind the wheel. ''I know a great little place not far from here.''

She looked as if she intended to protest again, but when he started the car and backed from his parking spot, she clamped her mouth into a tight line, closed her eyes and leaned her head back against the seat.

Brett felt a twinge of guilt that he'd insisted they have dinner, when it was plain to see she was dead on her feet. But reason won out. She had to eat. This way she wouldn't have to worry about cooking something for herself when she went home. Satisfied that he'd be doing her a favor by taking her to dinner, he steered the car out of the garage and into the flow of traffic on Michigan Avenue.

Ten minutes later he helped her out of her coat and held the chair while she settled herself at his usual table for two in a corner of the restaurant. Removing his overcoat, Brett hung both wraps on a nearby hook, then seated himself and stared at her over the flicker of a candle stuck in a Chianti bottle. She looked thoroughly exhausted.

''Why don't we save this discussion until Monday morning?'' he asked. ''You look like you're ready to drop.''

''I'm fine,'' she insisted. She extracted a notepad from her shoulder bag. ''I'd like to get the preliminaries out of the way so I can get started with the interviews Monday morning. Have you been filled in on what I'll need from you, Mr. Connelly?''

Brett leaned back in his chair and folded his arms across his chest as he tried to get his mind back down to business and off of the erotic scenario her innocent question evoked. He could think of several very exciting things he'd like for Elena Delgado to ''need'' from him, but scheduling meetings with his family wasn't among them.

Clearing his throat, he focused on the job his father had assigned him, which Brett had been eager to accept. He wanted nothing more than to get to the bottom of who had tried to kill his brother Daniel. ''When Dad called, he said you wanted to interview the rest of the family to help with your investigation.''

She nodded. ''That's right. Your father told me you'd take care of setting up the times and place.''

He grinned. Being efficient and anticipating others' needs were the very reasons he was considered one of the best PR men in the textile industry. ''I've already got the jump on it. I've arranged for you to speak privately with each of them in a conference room at Connelly Tower, starting Monday.''

''Good.''

''But it may take several days to get all of them rounded up,'' he warned her.

He propped his elbow on the table and cupped his chin in his hand as he watched her brush a strand of silky brown hair from her flawless cheek. He'd have liked nothing more than to touch her soft skin, to run his hands through her hair. The dancing candlelight cast a soft glow on her lovely face, and Brett wondered what it would be like to hold Elena close, to kiss her.

"I understand that it will take several days to speak with everyone," she said, bringing him out of his delightful musings. She glanced up from making notations on the notepad. "I'd also like to interview some of the employees at Connelly corporate headquarters. They may have information that will aid my investigation."

"That can be arranged. Anything else?"

"Not that I can think of." She glanced at her notes. "Of course, I'll need to interview you, too." She gave him a half smile. "I don't see any reason why we can't take care of that this evening."

Heartened by the small gesture, he decided he might not be losing his touch after all. Although it hadn't been the warmest of expressions, it was a start and gave him something to build on.

"Not tonight," he said, shaking his head. "I'm tired and so are you. Besides, I'm your first interview Monday." He grinned. "You wouldn't want to throw off my schedule before we even get started, would you?"

She frowned. "I doubt that my taking your statement now will make a difference."

"Oh, but it would," he said, trying not to smile. "We wouldn't be able to enjoy our dinner and I might get indigestion. If I did, it would probably keep me awake tonight and I wouldn't get anything done tomorrow because of being tired. Then on Sunday I'd have to catch up on all the things I missed doing on Saturday, and…" He tried to affect a pitiful expression. "Well, I think you see how it would throw off my schedule."

She stared at him for several long seconds before she slowly placed her pen on the table. "Let's get something straight right now, Mr. Connelly. This isn't a social—"

Their waiter chose that moment to place a basket of bread sticks on the table. "Good evening, Mr. Connelly. Would you like a wine list?"

When Brett gave her a questioning look, Elena shook her head and smiled up at the man. "No wine for me."

"A glass of wine will help you relax and take the edge off the day," Brett said. Turning to the waiter, he added, "Bring two goblets and a bottle of your best wine, Vinnie."

Elena did a slow burn. Brett obviously had the idea that because he was extraordinarily handsome, very successful and a member of the influential Connelly family, he could control any situation he pleased. Boy, oh boy, was he in for a rude awakening.

Any other woman would probably be down on her hands and knees, thanking the moon and stars that she was dining with the very eligible Brett Connelly. But Elena wasn't just any woman. Fortunately for her, she was immune to his movie star good looks, his bluer-than-blue eyes and his engaging smile. She'd been down that path before and learned her lesson well. The last thing she wanted to have to deal with was a playboy like her ex-husband.

She started to tell their waiter not to bother bringing a glass for her, but Brett chose that moment to speak to the young man hovering beside him. "And I think we'll both have a salad with the house dressing and the calamari, Vinnie."

"Very good choice, sir," Vinnie said, treating

Elena to a grin that said he'd watched Brett in action before.

As soon as the waiter walked away, Elena glared at Brett. "Don't you think that was a bit presumptuous of you?"

"You don't like calamari?" he asked, looking shocked. "I thought everyone liked it. If you'd prefer I order something else—"

When he raised his hand to hail Vinnie, she shook her head. "That's not the point, Mr. Connelly."

With a recalcitrant lock of wavy black hair hanging low on his forehead and confusion written all over his handsome face, he looked like a little boy who had no idea what he'd done wrong. She almost smiled. She'd bet he didn't wear that expression very often.

"What is the point, Elena?" He placed his hand on hers where it rested on the top of the table. "And please, call me Brett."

All thoughts of him looking like an innocent little boy were instantly erased. His warm palm caused the oddest sensation to course through her, and his rich, smooth baritone was releasing a herd of butterflies in her less-than-stable stomach. She quickly snatched her hand away and placed it in her lap. The man deserved every bit of the playboy reputation reported in the society columns. Too bad he was wasting all that charm on her. Thanks to her ex-husband, Michael, she was totally immune to that kind of tactic.

"I told you I didn't want wine," she said. The fluttering in her stomach changed to a churning sensation, and her palms turned cold and clammy. "I think it's time we set some ground rules, Mr. Connelly. I'm not interested in anything but the investigation of your brother's attempted murder, so you can stop this right here and now."

One dark brow rose in question as he stared at her. "What makes you think I'm trying to do anything but cooperate with your investigation, Elena?"

"Mr. Connelly—"

"Call me Brett."

"You steamrolled me into having dinner with you." She gathered her notepad and pen and jammed them into her shoulder bag. "*You* decided I could wait to interview you until Monday, then you even went so far as to decide that I'd have wine when I clearly stated that I didn't want it. Do you see a pattern here, Mr. Connelly?"

"Not really," he said, mesmerizing her with his guileless blue eyes and sexy-as-sin voice.

"I don't like being told what to do," she said, needing to put some distance between herself and Brett Connelly. She quickly rose to her feet, but the room swayed and she had to place her hand on the table to steady herself. "I'm used to being in control and calling the shots when I'm assigned to…an investigation."

"Are you all right?" he asked, jumping to his feet. To his credit, he looked genuinely concerned.

"I'm…fine." Elena closed her eyes in an effort to clear her vision. When she opened them again, Brett was standing at her side with his hand beneath her elbow. "It's been a long trying day, at the end of an exhausting week, Mr. Connelly. I think I'll skip dinner, catch a cab and go home."

"I'll drive you."

"No, it isn't necessary," Elena said, trying desperately to fight the increasing dizziness. "Please, stay…and enjoy your…dinner."

Brett studied her for several long moments. He wasn't sure what the problem was, but he knew for certain Elena suffered from more than just a simple case of exhaustion. Her breathing had become shallow and labored, and her face had become a ghostly white.

"Mario," Brett called, motioning for the maître d'. When the little man hurried over to them, Brett explained, "Ms. Delgado isn't feeling well and we've decided not to have dinner after all."

"Very well, Signore Connelly," Mario said, shooting Elena a worried look as Brett held her coat. "I'm sorry the *signorina* has fallen ill. I hope she will be all right."

Nodding, Brett took her by the elbow and started to guide her toward the door. But the moment she turned, her steps faltered and she stopped abruptly. She looked up at him, and he could see a mixture of fear and panic in her expressive brown eyes, and the desperation as she sagged against him.

"Please…help me…Brett," she whispered, a moment before her lashes fluttered shut and she lost her battle with consciousness.

Without a second thought, he swung her up into his arms, cradled her to his chest and shouldered his way through the exit. Fortunately, he'd been able to park in front of Mario's and it was only a few feet to his car.

He quickly placed her on the passenger seat of the Jag, fastened her seat belt, then trotted around the front of the car to slide into the driver's seat. Jamming the key into the ignition, he shifted into first and shot from the parking space.

"Hang on, Elena," he said, fighting an unfamiliar sense of panic as he wove his way around slower-moving vehicles. "I'll have you in Memorial's E.R. in less than two minutes."

Two

Brett loosened his tie, jammed his hands into the front pockets of his suit pants and paced outside of the examining room at Memorial Hospital's E.R. He was used to having women fall at his feet figuratively, but this was the first time it had ever happened literally. And the worst part of it was, he was to blame.

How could he have pulled such a stupid stunt? Elena had told him she didn't want to go to dinner, that she'd had a bad day and just wanted to go home. But he couldn't take no for an answer.

No, Brett Connelly, connoisseur of women, had taken her reluctance to spend time with him as provocation for turning on the charm—as if she was a challenge to be conquered. He'd noticed several times that she looked as if she wasn't feeling well, but he'd ignored it. He'd even gone so far as to convince himself that a little wining and dining was just what Elena needed to improve her mood. How could he have been so insensitive, so damned stupid?

"Brett Connelly, you're the last person I expected to see here," a female voice called.

He looked up to find Meg O'Reilly walking toward him. Great. What else could go wrong this evening? Not only was he responsible for a woman collapsing at dinner, now his past was coming back to haunt him.

Brett hadn't seen Meg in five years, not since the night the pretty blonde had told him she loved him and intended to marry him as soon as she finished medical school. It had only been a month after his twin brother, Drew's, wife, Talia, had died and the devastation his brother suffered had been too fresh in Brett's mind. As with most twins he'd felt Drew's pain almost as if it was his own. Brett had made a vow never to put himself in the position to experience that degree of guilt, of failure.

So he'd taken Meg home that evening and kindly, but firmly, explained to her that he wasn't the marrying kind. He'd tried to assure her that although there wasn't any possibility of a long-term relationship, they could still see each other. But she'd taken exception to his honesty and ended up throwing a lamp at him as he'd made a hasty escape.

Now, spotting in her hand some clear plastic tubing used for IV feedings, he figured she'd probably use it to lynch him right in the hospital corridor.

"Hello, Meg," he said cautiously. As a matter of habit, his gaze zeroed in on the ring finger of her left hand. Relief coursed through him at the sight of her shiny gold wedding band. "How have you been?"

She pointed to the M.D. after her name on the white lab coat she wore. "I finally made it through medical school." She gave him a wry grin. "And I see you're still checking out women's ring fingers."

Brett nodded absently. His mind had already returned to the petite police detective in the room across the corridor. It seemed as if she'd been in there for hours.

"Could you do me a favor, Meg? Could you check on a patient and find out what's going on?" he asked suddenly, pointing to the closed door in front of them.

"Sure." She glanced toward the crowded waiting area. "Is the patient a family member?"

He shook his head. "No. It's a woman I was having dinner with. She fainted."

Giving him a contemplative look, Meg turned toward the door he'd indicated. "I'll find out what I can."

He waited for what seemed an eternity before the door finally opened. "Is she going to be all right?" he asked, his guilt increasing as he faced Meg. Her expression gave nothing away and only served to heighten his anxiety.

If he'd caused whatever Elena had been suffering from earlier in the evening to worsen by insisting she go to dinner with him he'd never forgive himself.

"As long as she takes it easy she should be fine." Meg smiled knowingly. "They're getting ready to release her as soon as the attending physician prescribes medication for the nausea. But your job is going to be to see that she starts eating regular meals and getting more rest. It's important for everyone, but even more so for someone in Ms. Delgado's condition."

"Okay." He'd agree to anything, if it would make up for his colossal lack of sensitivity.

Meg's expression turned serious. "If she doesn't, she'll lose the baby, Brett."

"The baby," he repeated dumbly.

"Yes, the baby." Meg's beeper went off, and after checking the tiny screen, she smiled. "I've got to run." She touched his arm, her face filled with understanding. "Look, Brett, she's very upset and scared to death that she'll have a miscarriage. I can tell she and the baby mean a lot to you. Just take good care of them and everything should be fine."

"Me?" Brett opened and closed his mouth several times in an attempt to make his vocal chords work. "I didn't— I mean, I'm not—"

"Relax. You'll be a great father." Meg turned to walk away. "Good luck to the three of you."

Astounded, Brett watched the woman disappear around a corner, then looked at the closed door in front of him. Meg thought Elena's baby was his.

The assumption that he was the father was almost laughable. For that matter it held true of his being the father of anyone's baby.

He shook his head as he waited for Elena. If the truth came out, most of the society gossips would be shocked right down to the soles of their feet. Brett Connelly might have been seen dining or attending a social function with several different women, but he hadn't been seeing anyone steadily for the past six months. And beside being extremely careful to take the proper precautions when he was with a woman, it had been more than a year since he'd had sex.

Fear clawed at every fiber of Elena's being, and tears blurred her vision as she slowly got dressed. One thought kept running through her mind. She couldn't lose this baby. She just couldn't. Having already suffered two miscarriages during her disastrous marriage, this was her last hope for a child of her own.

She took a deep breath and forced herself to think positively. In seven months she'd have a beautiful child to love who would love her in return. This time she was *not* going to lose her baby.

Wiping the tears from her cheeks, she hoped with all her heart that Brett had gotten tired of waiting and left the hospital to pursue other interests for the evening. She took pride in her job and had worked very hard to earn her position as a special investigative detective. When she was on duty, as she had been this evening, she never allowed anyone to see her as anything but a consummate professional. Ever.

But Brett had witnessed her weakness, her vulnerability. It would be humiliating enough to face him on Monday morning when she began interviewing the Connelly family. Tonight it would be downright impossible.

Tucking the prescription and blister packs of medication the doctor had given her for nausea into her shoulder bag, she pushed open the door of the tiny examining room and walked out into the hall. She almost groaned out loud. There Brett stood looking as tall and handsome as ever.

He whirled around at the sound of her footsteps, and the look on his face surprised her. She would have expected a sullen impatience about him for the inconvenience she'd caused. Her ex-husband, Michael, had always worn that look whenever she'd done something to interrupt his plans. But Brett's expression held nothing but concern.

"Are you all right?" he asked, closing the space

between them to place his hands on her shoulders. She found the warmth from his palms oddly reassuring.

She nodded but couldn't meet his worried gaze. How could she? She was far too embarrassed. He'd witnessed her at one of the lowest moments of her life.

"Is there someone I should call?" he asked. "A husband or friend?"

Still unable to meet his gaze, she shook her head. "There's no one."

Placing his forefinger under her chin, he lifted her face until their gazes met. "I'm really sorry, Elena," he said, his voice soft and low. "I should have listened to you when you said you weren't up to having dinner with me. Do you think you can find it in your heart to forgive me for being an insensitive fool?"

His gentle touch, the sincerity in his words and the apologetic look he gave her caused tears to flood her eyes again and a huge lump to form in her throat. She couldn't remember the last time she'd heard a man apologize to her for anything, let alone ask for her forgiveness. In the entire four years of her marriage, Michael had only expressed regret a couple of times and he'd *never* asked for her forgiveness. Not the first time, when she'd discovered he was having an affair. Not the last time, when he'd told her he was moving out to live with the woman he'd been sleeping with for the previous six months of their marriage.

"Thank you for your help," she said, forcing words past the tightness clogging her throat. "But you shouldn't have waited. I'm sure you have more entertaining things to do with your evening than stand around the hospital."

"No problem," he said, smiling. He held her coat for her. "When we get to your place, I'll call and have some food delivered."

Elena shook her head. "Thank you, but you don't have to do that. I'll catch a cab and fix something for myself when I get back to my apartment."

"The doctor said you needed to start eating regular meals and getting more rest." Brett ushered her toward the exit at the end of the long corridor. "You can't possibly do that if you have to cook for yourself. Besides, it's late and you're tired. You need to put your feet up and take it easy."

"I'm used to fending for myself," she argued. Tears were threatening again, and she had to get away from him before she humiliated herself further with a crying binge.

"It's the least I can do. I feel responsible for you spending your evening in the E.R."

As they walked out into the bitterly cold night, he put his arm around her shoulders and tucked her to his side to shield her from the brisk wind blowing in from Lake Michigan and the snow that had begun to fall. Before she could find her voice to tell him that he owed her nothing, he had her settled in the plush leather passenger seat of the Jaguar and was sliding into the driver's seat.

"Do you think your stomach would be okay with soup?" he asked.

"I think so, but you don't have to—"

"Elena, I *do* have to," he interrupted. "I should have listened to you. But I didn't, and my lack of sensitivity put you and your baby in danger. I'm really sorry, and I want to make it up to you. Please allow me to do that."

That did it. The combination of his heartfelt apology, the self-reproach reflected in his blue eyes and her unstable hormones touched something deep inside of Elena that she'd thought long dead. Her eyes flooded with tears, and she quickly turned away before he noticed.

But it was too late. He had noticed.

He immediately pulled her into his arms. "Elena, honey, please don't cry." Brett held her close and caressed her cheek with his hand while she sobbed. "Everything is going to be all right. You and the baby will be just fine. The doctor told me that you need more rest, and I'm going to make sure you get it."

Her tears fell faster. Great! Not only was she crying because of her pregnancy hormones, she was also shedding tears of utter humiliation that he'd witnessed her collapse at the restaurant and her teary breakdown now.

His warm embrace, the feel of his arms tightening around her to draw her to his wide chest, almost made her believe he meant what he said. Almost. But having been married to a man just like Brett, she knew better. Men would say anything to get themselves off the hook or to manipulate a woman into doing what they wanted.

But at the moment she was too tired and emotionally drained to protest. All she wanted was to go home, crawl into bed and forget this day had ever happened.

When she finally felt in control enough to speak, she gave him the address of her apartment building. "Please, just take me home."

Nodding, he released her, started the car and shifted

it into gear. "That's not far from here. I'll have you home in no time."

Brett looked around as he pulled the Jag to a stop behind a waiting cab in front of a shabby four-story building. Although it was a respectable middle-class neighborhood, it was clear to see that her landlord hadn't seen fit to keep his property maintained.

"Thank you for the ride home, Mr. Connelly."

Brett's brow rose at the formal use of his name and the hand she offered for him to shake. So she was trying to turn back time and return to a business-only acquaintance.

Well, that was just too damned bad, he decided, ignoring her gesture. He'd spent a good two hours in the E.R. worrying about her, and that, in his opinion, took them well beyond a business association.

Besides, whether she admitted it or not, she was extremely fragile right now. She needed someone to be there for her, to lend her moral support. And since he was partly to blame for her problems this evening, Brett felt obligated to see that she was comfortably settled before he bade her good-night. The fact that he liked the way she felt in his arms had no bearing on his decision at all.

Getting out of the car, he opened the passenger door before she could do it herself. He'd told her that he'd make sure everything was fine for her and her baby, and he had every intention of carrying through on his promise.

"Mr. Connelly—"

"Brett." He smiled down at her. "I think we're well past the formalities, Elena. Now, let's get you inside where it's warm."

The cold February wind whipped the falling snow into their faces, and he placed his arm around her to hold her close. He told himself that it was just to keep her warm, to shield her from the frigid wind. But her small body pressed against his felt wonderful and he couldn't help but wonder how it would feel without the cumbersome layers of their coats.

As they reached the steps to Elena's building, a rotund lady in her fifties carrying a gym bag and resembling Nanook of the North, opened the door. "You'll have to find somewhere else to spend the night, Elena," she said, through the wool scarf covering her mouth and nose. "The furnace won't be fixed until tomorrow at the earliest and maybe not until sometime Monday. The super said it depended on when the parts he had to order got here."

Having made her announcement, Nanook hurried to the cab waiting by the curb, threw the gym bag inside, then hurled herself in after it.

"Wonderful," Elena muttered as they watched the cab drive away. "The perfect ending to a perfect day."

Brett held the door for her. "No problem. You can throw some clothes in an overnight case and stay at my place. I've got a nice large guest room and I guarantee it's warm."

He surprised himself with the invitation, but the more he thought about it, the more it made sense. Not only was it the decent thing to do, since he was partially responsible for her collapse, it was something his parents would expect of him, considering the circumstances. This woman was in charge of investigating the attempted assassination of his brother Daniel, the new king of Altaria. Brett had been assigned the task of assisting her in whatever way was needed. By having Elena stay at his place, he could follow through on his promise to see that she was all right, and if she felt like it later, they could go over the questions she intended to ask during the interviews with his family.

"No, I can't stay at your place," she said, entering the lobby of the building.

She turned to face him, and if the look on her pretty face was any indication, hell would freeze over before she agreed to his offer. Brett almost laughed. With the temperature hovering around zero, it wouldn't surprise him to hear that it had already started icing up.

"Don't be ridiculous, Elena. You and I both know you can't stay here."

"I'll…I'll stay at…"

When her voice trailed off, he nodded. "That's what I thought. You don't have any idea where to stay, do you?"

"I'll check into a hotel," she said stubbornly.

He shook his head. "That's not acceptable."

She treated him to an indignant look. "Oh, really? And why not?"

"Because you need someone to take care of you."

He immediately wished he'd used a little more diplomacy and phrased his statement differently. He could tell by the sudden straightening of her slender shoulders and the sparks of anger in her wide brown eyes, that he'd made a huge blunder.

"Mr. Connelly, I have never nor will I ever need someone to take care of me. I've been by myself for as long as I can remember and I've done just fine. I see no reason why that should change now."

He told himself he should just walk away, that she

didn't want his help. But whether she wanted it or not, it was clear she needed it. He had no idea where the man was who'd gotten her pregnant, but it appeared as if he was out of the picture and she was on her own. For some reason that bothered him more than it should.

Brett didn't fully understand what he was about to do, or why, but he'd made her and her unborn child a promise. It was time to play his trump card. ''Elena, you don't want to lose your baby because of some misguided belief that you'll relinquish your independence. Think of what's best for your child. If that means staying at my place tonight, then swallow your pride and accept my offer.''

Her expression instantly changed from fiercely indignant to anxious and frightened. He felt like an absolute jerk.

Reaching out, he drew her into his arms. ''I'm sorry. I shouldn't have said that.''

Elena nodded her head. ''Yes, you should. You're right. I should be thinking how this will affect the baby. But it would be best if I went...''

Where would she go if not to a hotel? She certainly couldn't go to a relative's. She didn't have any. Her last foster mother—the only person who had cared enough to try to get close to her, and who'd made an effort to stay in touch after Elena left the foster care system—would be more than happy to help her. But Marie Waters lived over three hundred miles downstate in the tiny little town of Johnston City. No help there. She could go to a friend's house, but she really hadn't become close to anyone since her divorce last year. And it seemed that Michael had won custody of the few friends they'd made during their turbulent marriage.

As Brett continued to hold her, she felt her resolve to refuse his offer start to melt. They were really no more than strangers, yet he was offering to take her into his home.

A warmth began to steal into her soul that she hadn't felt in a long, long time. She tried to ignore it. She didn't want to think of Brett Connelly as anything more than a shallow self-centered playboy like her ex-husband. It was the only way she could keep things in perspective and maintain their professional relationship.

He rubbed his hands up and down her back in a soothing manner as he held her close. "Can't think of anyone to stay with?"

She reluctantly shook her head. "Not really."

He held her a moment longer, then set her away from him. "It's settled, then." He gave her one of his charming smiles, blew on his hands, then rubbed them together. "Now, let's go upstairs to your apartment, throw some things in a bag and get going. It's freezing in here."

Three

Twenty minutes later Brett parked his car in his assigned space in the basement garage of his building and escorted Elena to the elevator. It was all she could do to keep from groaning when he punched in the security code to open the door. What was it with Brett and elevators, anyway? Why couldn't he live and work on the ground level? Or at the very least, take the stairs up to his condo?

She held her breath and said a silent prayer that the medication the E.R. doctor had given her had had time to take effect as the door swished open and they stepped inside. To her immense relief, the ride wasn't nearly as upsetting as she'd feared it might be, and when they stepped out into the hall on the twelfth floor, her stomach was only mildly queasy.

Brett guided her to the far end of the building where the more expensive penthouses were located, unlocked and opened the door. "Don't be surprised if the place is a wreck," he warned her. "Babe destroys something every time I'm late coming home from work."

"Babe?" He was living with someone?

He nodded and turned on the light in the foyer just in time for Elena to see a small ball of long black hair come racing around the corner. The little dog yipped and bounced around happily at her feet, but when Brett bent down to pick up the animal, it skittered out of his reach, turned around and glared at him.

"So that's the way it's going to be, huh?" He laughed and guided Elena into the spacious living room. "She'll be ultrafriendly with you, but I'll get the cold shoulder for the rest of the evening."

When he turned on the lamp by the end of the couch, he let loose a muttered curse. "Well, it looks like I'll be shopping for throw pillows again."

Elena couldn't help but laugh as she looked around at the stuffing strewn across the thick beige carpet. "I take it you've been down this path before?"

Nodding, he helped her out of her coat. "Every time I'm late coming home from work."

"She only does this when you're late? What about during the day?" Elena asked, bending down to pick up a hunter-green satin remnant and several chunks of stuffing.

"Don't do that," he said, sounding alarmed. He motioned toward a comfortable-looking, overstuffed brown armchair with a matching ottoman. "Sit down and put your feet up while I get this cleaned up."

"I'll help."

"No, you won't." He took the destroyed fabric

from her and led her to the chair he'd indicated. ''Just sit back and take it easy. I got off lucky. She only took out two of the pillows this time. Normally she tears up three or four, then shreds a magazine or two for good measure.''

Elena barely had time to settle herself in the chair before the little dog jumped into her lap. Two black eyes peered up at her from beneath a tuft of black hair a moment before the friendly animal pushed her head under Elena's hand to be petted.

''What breed is she?'' Elena asked, rubbing Babe's small head.

He shrugged as he bent to collect chunks of stuffing. ''The vet said she's mostly Shih-Tzu with maybe a little Pekingese mixed in somewhere a generation or two back.'' Straightening, he grinned. ''But I'm pretty sure she has a bit of Tasmanian devil in her too.''

Cuddling the furry little body, Elena smiled. ''Whatever she is, she's adorable. How old is she?''

''The vet estimated she was about six months old when I found her wandering around outside of Connelly Tower. She was starving, scared of her shadow and extremely grateful.'' He laughed. ''That was a little more than a year ago. Now she's well fed, arrogant as hell and thinks she owns me, instead of the other way around.''

He left the room to dispose of the tattered pillows. When he returned a few minutes later carrying a leash, Elena noticed that he'd changed into jeans and a sweatshirt. ''I hope you like Chinese food.'' When she nodded, he looked relieved. ''Good. I just called in an order for chicken noodle soup, rice and stir-fried vegetables. It should be here in about twenty minutes.''

He walked over to snap the leash onto Babe's collar. His hand brushed hers as he fastened the snap, and heat streaked up her arm. Elena quickly pulled back.

She wasn't sure why, but every time Brett touched her—no matter how brief the contact—warm tingles radiated from the spot. ''Do you have someone to take her out while you're at work?'' she asked, hoping he hadn't noticed her breathless tone.

Nodding, he lifted the dog from her lap and set it on the floor. ''I have a dog-walking service that comes by twice a day.'' He looked down at Babe. ''Ready to go out?''

Elena laughed when the dog glanced up at him, then aloofly turned her head and, ignoring him, started for the door. ''You weren't joking when you said she'd give you the cold shoulder, were you?''

The long-suffering look on his handsome face was ruined by the grin he couldn't quite hide. ''I get no respect around here. No respect at all.'' His expression turning serious, he added, ''Just sit there and relax. I'll only be a few minutes.''

After he pulled on his coat and allowed Babe to lead him out the door, Elena propped her feet on the ottoman and thought about the many complexities of Brett Connelly. Her first impression of him had been that he was exactly like her hedonistic ex-husband. A man who lived for the moment and ran from anything that interfered with his good time or required that he take on any kind of responsibility.

She shook her head. Normally she could gauge someone's personality with complete accuracy within the first five minutes of talking to them. She had to. It was her job to assess people and decide whether they were as they appeared.

But she had to admit she might have been a bit hasty with her first impression of Brett. Not only had he shocked her with his heartfelt apology in the E.R. and later at her apartment, he'd proven his compassion and generosity by insisting that she stay at his place while the furnace in her building was being repaired.

Elena looked around at his condo, at the expensive furniture and original paintings. What self-respecting playboy rescued stray dogs then good-naturedly allowed them to destroy his things as if it were nothing more than a minor annoyance? Or promised to help a pregnant cop with no one to turn to and nowhere else to go?

When Babe jumped onto the middle of his stomach and started doing a tap dance, Brett opened one eye. "Don't tell me you have to go out now," he muttered. "It's barely daylight."

In answer, the little dog yipped, scampered up his chest and licked his cheek.

He scratched behind her ears. "Oh, so with one doggy kiss I'm supposed to forgive and forget the way you treated me last night?"

Babe curled up on his bare chest, rested her head on her front paws and stared at him with two guileless black eyes as she whined an apology.

He groaned. "Okay, you're forgiven. I'll take you for a walk. Just don't start with the sad puppy eyes."

Brett plucked the little dog from his chest, rolled to the side of the bed and placed her on the floor. As he pulled on his sweat suit, Babe danced impatiently at his feet. He just hoped she didn't start barking to hurry him along. Elena was in the bedroom just across the hall, and he didn't want to wake her. She needed rest.

He quickly tied his running shoes, picked up Babe and walked out into the hall. The door to the guest room was still closed, and he didn't hear sounds of Elena moving around. Good. They hadn't disturbed her.

Last evening, when he and Babe had returned from their walk, he'd found Elena curled up in the chair where he'd left her. He smiled, remembering the scene.

She'd looked so relaxed, sleeping like a baby, that he hadn't had the heart to wake her. She probably wouldn't be happy with him, but after he'd moved her overnight case to the guest room, he'd picked her up and carried her to bed. So sound asleep, she'd barely stirred when he'd removed her shoes and pulled the comforter over her.

But he'd been left with two very distinct impressions from having her small body pressed to his chest. The first was how soft and feminine she'd felt, and the second was how shocked he'd been by the degree of heat that had coursed through him. His body stirred at the memory, and his pithy curse made Babe turn around to give him a curious look.

Forcing himself to focus on his other impression of Elena's body, he frowned. He didn't have any experience with pregnant women, but he was pretty sure they were supposed to be a little sturdier than Elena. He'd been disturbed by how light she was and how fragile she'd felt in his arms. She couldn't weigh much more than a hundred pounds.

The doctor's orders had been for her to start eating more regular meals, and it bothered him that she'd missed dinner last night. But he would see that she made up for it this morning. As soon as he returned to the condo, he would prepare a big breakfast and make sure she ate every bite.

Half an hour later Brett opened the door of his condo to the scrumptious smell of bacon frying. "Elena?"

"In here," she called.

He quickly shed his coat and unsnapped the leash from Babe's collar. "What the hell do you think you're doing?" he demanded, walking into the kitchen. "You're supposed to be taking it easy."

"Good morning to you, too," she said, removing several strips of crisp bacon from the skillet. She looked around his feet. "Where's Babe?"

Brett jerked his thumb in the direction of the living room. "Burrowed under what's left of the pillows on the couch." He noticed that Elena had showered and changed into jeans and a gray sweatshirt with Chicago Police Academy silk-screened across the front.

"Why did she do that?" she asked, removing a carton of eggs from the refrigerator.

"She always does that to warm up after she's been out." He took the carton from Elena and placed it on the counter.

"I don't blame her," she said, smiling. "February in Chicago can be miserably cold." She reached for an egg. "How do you like your eggs? Sunny-side up, over easy or scrambled?"

"Over easy." He took the spatula from her hand

and guided her to the table in the breakfast nook. "But I'll take care of it. You sit down."

"I'm perfectly capable of cooking." Her eyes narrowed. "Just as I would have been capable of putting myself to bed last night if someone had bothered to wake me."

He'd figured on her having something to say about that. "You were tired."

"That's beside the point," she said stubbornly.

"No, Elena. That *is* the point."

He watched the color heighten on her cheeks as the sparkle of anger grew in her beautiful brown eyes. Propping his fists on his hips, Brett glared down at her from his much taller height. He hated using intimidation with anyone, and especially with a woman. But if it kept her from overdoing things, he'd do whatever it took.

"You're supposed to take it easy, and I'm going to make sure you do," he said sternly. "Besides, you're my guest. So sit down."

She glared at him as if she intended to argue further, then finally relented and seated herself at the table. "Brett, I…"

To his horror her eyes filled with tears and her perfect lips trembled. His gut twisted into a tight knot. He hadn't thought her feelings would be hurt over something as trivial as his insistence that she relax, while he finished cooking breakfast.

"Elena, honey, I'm sorry," he said, kneeling in front of her. He took her hands in his. "Please don't cry."

"I hate this," she said, pulling away. She covered her face and cried harder.

He felt like a world-class jerk as he wrapped his

arms around her and pulled her to him. "I don't blame you for hating me, honey. I was out of line. I shouldn't have spoken so harshly."

She shook her head and sobbed into his shoulder. "It's not you. It's me."

"You?"

She nodded and Brett had no idea what she meant. But at the moment he didn't care. Her small body pressed to his, the feel of her arms wrapped around him and her warm breath teasing the sensitive skin of his neck were wreaking havoc with his good intentions.

"It's...hormonal," she sobbed. "I can't...control it."

So that was it. Her uncontrollable crying was due to her pregnancy.

Thinking back several years, Brett remembered his twin brother, Drew, mentioning that his wife had experienced all kinds of emotions while she was pregnant with their daughter, Amanda. In fact, he and Drew had jokingly referred to Talia's sudden mood swings as the Nine-Month Nutsies.

Of course, they hadn't dared mention that to Talia or any other woman. They'd had better sense than that.

"Feeling better?" he asked when Elena's sobs tapered off and her shoulders stopped shaking.

She nodded and pushed away from his embrace. "I'm so embarrassed," she said, her voice nothing more than a whisper as she stared down at her clasped hands.

He retrieved a handful of tissues from the box on the counter, then gently touched her damp cheek to wipe away her tears. "Don't be embarrassed. It goes along with being pregnant."

Elena looked up at him with one perfect brow raised questioningly. "You've had experience with pregnant women before?"

"No, but my twin brother's late wife had a lot of trouble with her emotions when she was pregnant," Brett explained. "That was back when Drew and I still confided in each other."

The look on his handsome face, the sadness in his deep baritone made Elena wonder what had happened. "You're no longer close?"

"Not as close as we were." He shrugged, but she could tell it still bothered him. "After Talia died, Drew pretty much shut himself off emotionally from the rest of the family."

"Why did he do that?" she asked, unable to understand why anyone would distance themselves from their family at the very time they needed them most. If she'd ever had a family, she knew for certain she would have turned to them innumerable times for their love and support. It would have made coping with her two miscarriages and the breakup of her marriage so much easier.

Brett stood and walked over to the stove. He broke a couple of eggs into the skillet before he spoke again. "I think Drew pulled back from the family emotionally because he blames himself for Talia's death. She died of a drug overdose when their daughter was little." Brett turned to face her. "The rest of the family knew there was something wrong with her, that she was taking way too much prescription medication, and we tried to tell him. But Drew was in denial about her problems. When he finally found the evidence and faced facts that his society bride was addicted to drugs, it was too late. He came home from work one day to find her dead.''

"I remember reading about that. That must have been awful for him."

He nodded. "And the media just added to it. Since she was a Van Dorn, married to a Connelly, the newspapers were like sharks in a feeding frenzy. Every publication from here to Milwaukee carried the story, and most of the television and radio stations gave it more than average attention."

Having dealt with reporters at crime scenes, she was well aware of the tactics used by some reporters to slant the facts or to create a story where none existed. But when two of Chicago's most prominent families were touched by the same scandal, it was noteworthy. Factor in Brett's mother, Emma, being the former princess of Altaria and it would naturally become front-page news.

"There are times I've despised dealing with the media," Elena said sympathetically. "More than once they've complicated and, at times, even jeopardized investigations."

"That doesn't surprise me." Brett removed two plates from the cabinet and scooped the eggs onto them. Turning back to the stove, he broke an egg into a bowl, beat it, then poured it into another, smaller skillet. "How long have you been a policewoman?" he asked.

"I've worked for the Chicago P.D. ever since I left the foster care system eight years ago—first as a file clerk in records, then as soon as I turned twenty-one, I applied and was accepted into the academy." She frowned. "Are you expecting someone else for breakfast?"

"Nope." Grinning, he shrugged. "I like over easy, but Babe prefers her egg scrambled."

Elena smiled back at him. "I've been meaning to ask, why did you name her 'Babe'?"

A flush rose on his lean cheeks. "I, uh, don't think you'll care much for my answer."

"Try me."

He cleared his throat, then took a deep breath. "Not long after I found her, I discovered that women were drawn to cute little dogs."

"Oh, please. Tell me you didn't."

Nodding, the color on his cheeks deepened. "Her full name is Babe Magnet."

Brett placed the last plate in the dishwasher, then walked into the living room to find Elena curled up on the couch with Babe. He watched Elena dig into her shoulder bag and extract her notepad. She scribbled something on the top page before looking up at him.

"Would you mind my asking you a few questions about your family?" she asked.

"I'd rather wait until Monday, if you don't mind."

She gave him a suspicious look. "Why? Don't you want whoever made the attempt on your brother's life caught immediately?"

"Don't get me wrong. I want the S.O.B. caught as soon as possible. But not at the expense of your health." He sat down beside her. "Daniel is safe now, and I'd rather wait until Monday when you've had more rest."

"I'm fine," she said, her cheeks coloring a pretty pink.

He knew she was still embarrassed that he'd witnessed her collapse and the crying jags. She viewed it as weakness and a loss of control—something he was quickly learning that she found intolerable.

"The doctor said—"

"Oh, brother." She rolled her eyes. "Will you get over that? You sound like a broken record."

"I told you I'd make sure you took it easy and didn't overdo." He removed the notepad from her hands and placed it on the coffee table.

She glared at him a moment before she reached out and picked it up again. "Don't worry about it, Connelly. Sitting here on my buns isn't all that taxing."

He pried the paper from her fingers and tossed it into the chair across from them. "What are your regular days off?"

The sound of her throaty laughter sent a streak of heat straight up his spine. "There's no such thing as a set schedule with regular days off for an SIU detective," she explained. "If we're assigned to an investigation, we may be off duty, but we're always on call."

"Always?" He didn't like the sound of that at all.

"Day and night," she said, nodding.

She rose to her feet to retrieve the notepad, but when he caught her hand to stop her, she stumbled and wound up on his lap. They stared at each other for several long seconds before he finally spoke. "Why don't you give me a break here, Delgado?" He ran his index finger down the soft skin of her cheek. "I'm trying to keep my promise to see that you take it easy."

A myriad of emotions flashed in her chocolate brown eyes, but the strongest, most identifiable was awareness. Satisfaction and male pride coursed through him. So, the lady wasn't as immune to him as she'd tried to let on.

"You have no idea how beautiful you are, do you?" he asked, tracing the perfect cupid's bow of her upper lip with the tip of his finger.

"I've never given it much thought."

"Why not, Elena?" He watched her tongue dart out to moisten the spot he'd just touched.

She shrugged. "Probably because I don't care."

Brett was astounded. He'd never met a woman quite like her. Most of the women he knew were overly concerned with their beauty, some of them to the point of obsession. But he could tell that it truly didn't matter to Elena. Amazing.

The pager in her shoulder bag suddenly went off, causing her to jerk away from him. "You're off duty," he reminded her. "Ignore it."

"I told you, I'm on call," she said, scrambling from his lap. She pulled the offending beeper and a cell phone from her purse, glanced at the tiny screen, then started to make a call. "Rats! The battery on my phone is dead. May I use yours?"

Brett stared at her for endless seconds before he finally nodded and pointed toward the kitchen. "I left the cordless unit on the counter by the coffeemaker."

Two hours after he'd taken Elena home, Brett and Babe took turns prowling the condo like a pair of caged tigers. The page Elena had answered had been from one of her neighbors, advising her that the furnace had been repaired and that it was warm enough in their building for her to go home. He'd tried to talk her into staying for another night, but she'd insisted that she would rest better at her own apartment. He'd finally given up and driven her home.

He looked around the living room and couldn't believe how empty and abandoned it felt. Which, he decided, was completely ridiculous.

He'd lived alone since college and preferred it that way. While some of his friends had shared apartments after graduation, Brett had moved into his own place. He liked living alone, and until last night he hadn't even had a woman spend the entire night with him in the six years he'd lived there.

Brett stared out at Belmont Harbor as he tried to figure out why he felt the way he did. It wasn't like he and Elena had shared great sex, or anything beyond companionable conversation. He could better understand his wanting to be with her if they had. And although he certainly wouldn't object to their making love, it wasn't foremost on his mind.

He swallowed hard. He'd never in his life had the hots for a pregnant woman and he wasn't at all comfortable thinking about it now.

No. It was more that he felt a need to protect her. Which, he was certain she'd be quick to tell him, was absolutely ridiculous. She was a cop—a veteran of at least five years experience on the streets of Chicago— and perfectly capable of taking care of herself. Besides being an intelligent, independent woman, she carried a gun, and he had no doubt she knew how to use the weapon quite well. He would also lay odds on the fact that she was *very* good at her job. She wouldn't have been promoted to the position of an SIU detective if she wasn't. And even though the thought of her facing a meaner-than-hell criminal made anger and apprehension burn at his gut, it wasn't physical harm that he wanted to shelter her from.

He'd recognized a vulnerability about her that she valiantly tried, but couldn't quite hide. At least not from him. He'd glimpsed a flash of deep loneliness in her eyes last night at the hospital when she'd told him there was no one to call. Then he'd seen it again at her apartment when she'd reluctantly admitted there was nowhere she could go for the night.

Coming from a large, loving family, he couldn't imagine not having their emotional support. But she'd mentioned being a child of the foster care system, and it seemed she had no one to turn to for help of any kind. And that bothered him. A lot.

He left the floor-to-ceiling window at the end of his living room to pace into the kitchen. He met Babe coming out as he walked in.

"It's not right for anyone to be *that* alone," he told the little mutt.

In answer, Babe's plume of a tail drooped and she let loose a low, mournful whine.

Brett nodded. "My sentiments exactly."

Four

Tucking a strand of hair behind her ear, Elena tried to concentrate on what Drew Connelly was saying. The man looked exactly like Brett, which was distracting enough. But to her dismay she found herself comparing the differences between the two men— their personalities, their mannerisms.

She'd always heard that with a set of twins, one tended to be an extrovert and the other more introverted. And that certainly seemed to hold true with the Connelly brothers. Brett was the outgoing charmer, while Drew seemed to be more serious and withdrawn. Of course, Brett had told her Drew changed after the tragic death of his young wife. That might have something to do with the differences between the two men.

Without warning, the door to the conference room suddenly opened and Brett strolled into the room as

if he had every right to be there. Elena wasn't the
least bit surprised. He'd had an excuse for interrupting
every interview she'd conducted so far. Why would
this one be any different?

"What is it this time, Mr. Connelly?" she asked,
allowing her impatience to color her tone.

"Just checking to see if things are going well." He
flashed her an unrepentant grin—the same one she
was quickly coming to realize always made her insides tingle and her heart skip a beat.

"Everything was fine until about ten seconds ago,"
she answered wryly.

Elena tried to ignore the way his blue oxford cloth
shirt hugged his wide shoulders and complemented
his deep-azure eyes. Or how an errant lock of his
raven hair, hanging low on his forehead, made him
look like a mischievous little boy.

But there was nothing childlike about the look he
was sending her way. It felt as if he caressed her with
his eyes. She swallowed hard and tried to ignore the
heat warmimg her. She didn't want or need a man in
her life.

"I think you're making a nuisance of yourself, little
brother," Drew said, a ghost of a smile playing at the
corners of his mouth.

"You think so?" Brett asked, laughing. "I guess
because you're fifteen minutes older than me, you
think you're a lot wiser?"

Drew nodded. "Wise enough to see that you're annoying Detective Delgado."

Elena watched the exchange with interest, relieved
that Brett had turned his attention to his twin and from
her. She'd never had a sibling—never had anyone—
with whom to share the same type of easy banter. A

twinge of loneliness tightened her chest and she quickly turned her attention to her notes, away from all that she'd missed in life.

"Is there anything else you need from me, Ms. Delgado?" Drew asked, glancing at his watch. He rose from his seat at the conference table. "My daughter is home from school today with a cold and I need to call the nanny to see how she's feeling."

Elena shook her head. "No. I think we've covered everything."

Drew hadn't been present when the attempt was made on his brother's life and, therefore, was unable to add anything pertinent to the investigation. And his answers had been consistent with what Brett had told her over the weekend. Drew's wife, Talia, had died several years ago of a prescription drug overdose, leaving him with a young daughter.

At first, Elena had followed procedure and treated his recount of his wife's death as if there might be a connection. But after reviewing the facts, she determined that the two cases were completely unrelated. With his inheritance of the Altarian throne, Daniel had become the target of an assassin, while Talia had been the unfortunate victim of her own indulgence and self-destructive lifestyle.

Elena smiled. "If I have more questions, I'll contact you."

"Be sure you do," Drew said, nodding. "I'd like to see the person responsible for trying to kill Daniel caught and put away for good."

"We're doing our best to accomplish just that," Elena assured him, standing to shake his hand. "Thank you for your time, Mr. Connelly. I hope your daughter is feeling better soon."

Drew nodded, then walked to the door. Turning back, he pointed to his twin. "A word of advice, Brett," he said, his eyes twinkling with humor. "You'd better stop being your usual pesky self."

"What makes you say that?" Brett asked, innocently. "I'm just trying to be helpful."

"You're forgetting that the lady carries a gun," Drew answered. "She just might decide to use it on you if you don't leave her alone and let her do her job."

When Drew closed the door behind him, Elena turned her attention on Brett. "I also have the power to arrest you for hindering an investigation. Which I'll do in a heartbeat, if you don't stop interrupting my interviews."

Brett walked over to where she stood at the head of the big mahogany table. "Why would you want to arrest me, when all I'm trying to do is look out for your welfare?" he asked, his voice sounding so sensual that her toes curled.

He was too darned sexy for her peace of mind and way too close for comfort. What on earth was he up to?

"Mr. Connelly—"

"Brett."

"All right, Brett," she said, emphasizing his name. She pushed against his chest to back him away. She might as well have been trying to move a brick wall. The man was as solid as a chunk of granite. "There's a code of conduct concerning fraternization with—"

"Am I the victim of a crime you're investigating?" he interrupted.

"No. But—"

She pushed against him again, but this time she'd

used more force and stumbled backward when he remained immovable. He placed his arms around her waist to keep her from falling, and his nearness made her heart skip a beat.

"Am I a suspect?" he asked, resting his forehead against hers.

"N-no." He drew her even closer, aligning her body with his. How was she supposed to concentrate with him so close, with his lips hovering only a fraction of an inch above hers?

"Then it sounds to me like I'm exempt from these rules you're so concerned with," he said, his mouth brushing hers. "Correct?"

She nodded, then shook her head as she tried to make her suddenly fuzzy brain work. "It…it's a gray area."

"No, Elena," he murmured against her lips. "It couldn't be more clear."

A split second later his lips settled gently on hers, and Elena immediately forgot all about following rules or why she'd vowed over a year ago to steer clear of men, and especially ones like Brett Connelly. She didn't even give a second thought to where they were or that someone could walk into the conference room at any moment. All she could think of was how wonderful Brett's mouth felt moving over hers, how his arms were pulling her closer to his strong, muscular body.

Reason faded as Brett used his tongue to coax her to open for him, wordlessly asking for access to the sensitive recesses within. She didn't even hesitate. When she allowed him entry, he deepened the kiss, slipping inside to stroke, tease and taste her with a tenderness that took her breath away. A groan of pleasure rumbled up from deep in his chest, causing her legs to turn to rubber.

When she clutched at his shirt for support, he pulled her more firmly against him, allowing her to feel his arousal, the desire he wasn't even trying to hide. A coil of need pooled deep in her lower belly, and her sensitive breasts tingled, the nipples hardening as heat shot through every fiber of her being.

She'd been kissed before, but never like this. Never with such mastery. Not even in the early days of her marriage, when love was new and the fire of passion burned bright, had she experienced sensations so intense that she lost control of her ability to think clearly.

The sound of the conference room door opening, a quiet gasp, then the swish as it was quickly pulled shut, brought her back to her senses. What on earth was she doing? She was on duty.

Pushing against Brett's chest, she tore her mouth from his. "St-stop."

Brett allowed her to put space between them, but continued to hold her. "That was incredible," he said, his breathing labored. "You're so damned sweet. So—"

"Incredibly stupid," she finished for him. She backed away from his embrace, but Brett caught her hands in his to keep her from getting away. "I'm not interested in becoming involved with you or anyone else," she said, wishing she'd sounded more adamant.

He gazed at her for several long seconds before he spoke. "I won't deny that I liked kissing you, and that I'm going to kiss you again. But next time we'll find somewhere more private."

"There won't be a next time," she said emphatically.

His sudden grin surprised her. "Oh, there'll be a next time, sweet Elena. But only when you're ready for it."

She moved away from him and sat down in the leather chair at the conference table. She had to. Otherwise she might have fallen on the floor from the way his sexy voice made her knees wobble.

"Don't hold your breath waiting for it, Connelly." She took a deep breath. "I'm not interested in you or any other man. Period."

Brett bent down, placed his hands on the arms of the chair and leaned forward, bringing them nose to nose. "I don't know who the guy was, or what he did to hurt you, but I'm not that man, Elena." He lifted his hand to caress her cheek. "I know we could be good together. But I don't want you to feel pressured. It's not good for you or the baby."

He brushed her lips with his, then straightening to his full height, turned and left the conference room.

"This isn't good," she muttered. "Not at all."

Reaching for her appointment book, her hand shook so badly she could barely read the schedule. She breathed a sigh of relief when she discovered she'd be able to call it an early day. As soon as she spoke with the head of the accounting department, she'd go home, put her feet up and concentrate on forgetting that kiss. She didn't want to remember how it made her feel, or that it made her want things that she knew in her heart she'd never have.

Brett propped his feet on the corner of his desk, crossed his ankles, then absently checked his watch

as he went through the motions of listening to his
team make their report and outline what they had
planned for the rest of the week. His mind wasn't on
the projected reaction to the upcoming ad campaign
or the latest stats concerning customer satisfaction.

One thought dominated his mind, distracting him
with its disturbing implications. Nothing in his experience with women could have prepared him for the
way he'd felt when he kissed Elena. From the moment their lips met, it seemed as if the world came
to a screeching halt and that nothing would ever be
the same again.

Now more than ever he had the overwhelming desire to get to know her better, to kiss her again
and…more.

Brett suddenly had to force himself to breathe. If
that didn't raise a red flag the size of Vermont in his
obviously demented brain, nothing would. He didn't
want to become involved in a relationship.

A sliver of panic skipped up his spine. He wasn't
even comfortable with the *R* word popping into his
thoughts. To him it represented being responsible for
another's happiness, placing his own happiness into
a woman's hands and risking the possibility of one
of them failing. And *failure* was the one word Brett
never allowed to enter his vocabulary. Ever.

Brought out of his disturbing introspection by the
buzz of his intercom, he frowned. He'd told Fiona to
hold all calls during the meeting.

"What is it, Fiona?" he asked, irritated.

"I'm sorry to bother you, Mr. Connelly," his secretary said, sounding nonplussed. "But you told me
to let you know when Detective Delgado finished for
the day."

Brett's feet hit the floor with a thud as he straightened in the chair. "Thank you, Fiona." To the three men and one woman sitting in front of his desk, giving him curious looks, he apologized, "I'm sorry, but we'll have to delay going over the rest of these figures until tomorrow."

Frowning, Henry Sadowski held up a folder. "But what about the—"

"It can wait," Brett said firmly. He watched the four exchange looks, then stand and silently file out of his office.

He barely had enough patience to wait for them to close the door before he pressed the page button on his intercom. "Fiona, please come in here."

When the woman entered the room, he motioned her over to the desk. "I'm sorry for being short with you, Fiona. I was a bit…preoccupied."

"It's all right, Mr. Connelly. Was there something else you needed?"

Nodding, he smiled. "Could you go down to the conference room and tell Ms. Delgado that I'll be ready to leave in a few minutes?"

"Detective Delgado has already left."

In the process of clearing his desk, he snapped his briefcase shut, then glared at his unflappable secretary. "When did she leave?" he demanded.

"I'm not sure," Fiona said calmly. "I took a late lunch. When I returned, she'd left a note on my desk saying she'd be here again tomorrow."

Frustrated, Brett barely managed to keep his oath to himself. Crossing the room, he jerked his overcoat from the coat tree. Had Elena overdone it with too many interviews and become ill? Was she experiencing problems like she'd had the other night at the restaurant?

"I'm leaving for the day," he said, stuffing his arms into his coat sleeves. He walked to the door, then turned back suddenly. He really did owe the woman an apology for being so abrupt. "Have the switchboard forward my calls to voice mail and take the rest of the afternoon off with pay."

Nodding, Fiona smiled. "Thank you, Mr. Connelly. I'll do that. Have a nice evening."

Heading for the elevators, he slowed his pace. He knew exactly why Elena had left early, and it had nothing to do with her overworking herself or feeling ill. He'd seen the apprehension, the wariness in her beautiful brown eyes right after he'd kissed her. She was putting distance between them, running from him.

And if he was smart, he'd take off in the opposite direction himself. Hadn't he spent the past half hour reminding himself of all the reasons he didn't want to become involved with Elena, or any other woman?

When the elevator doors finally opened, he walked inside and pressed the button for the parking garage. It would probably be wise to take a step back from the situation and put distance between them.

Deciding that it would be best for all concerned, he stepped off the elevator and slowly walked to his car. Throwing his briefcase into the passenger seat of the Jag, he got in behind the wheel. He'd go by her apartment later and see that she was all right, then check on her occasionally while she worked on Daniel's case. But after that, he fully intended to back off and allow her to go her way and he'd go his.

* * *

Elena covered her head with a pillow and tried to ignore the knocking on her apartment door. Maybe whoever it was would get tired and go away, then she could resume her nap.

Since the building had an intercom security lock at the entrance that required visitors to page someone inside to gain entry, the persistent person on the other side of her apartment door had to be one of her neighbors. Probably Martha McNeery again. Once she'd learned that Elena was a cop, she'd called at least twice a week to have Elena check her apartment for intruders.

"Mrs. McNeery, we've been through this before," Elena muttered, dragging herself off the couch. "There's nobody hiding in your closet, under your bed or outside on the fire escape."

Before she could get to the door, the knocking turned to pounding. "I'm coming, Mrs. McNeery," Elena shouted, shoving her feet into her slippers. She didn't know why she bothered saying anything. The woman never had her hearing aid turned up enough to hear anything unless it was loud enough to wake the dead.

Flinging the door wide, Elena opened her mouth to ask Mrs. McNeery what the problem was this time, but to her surprise she found Babe bouncing around her feet. "What are you doing here, sweetie?" she asked, bending down to scoop the little dog into her arms.

When she straightened, Brett stood in front of her, holding a large sack. "Looks like somebody just woke up," he said, his blue eyes twinkling.

Elena blinked, then glanced down at her oversize

sweatshirt, baggy sweatpants and moccasin slippers. She must look a mess.

She'd come home right after leaving Connelly Tower, changed clothes and curled up on the couch with the intention of reading through her notes. She glanced at the clock on the VCR. She'd been sleeping for the past three hours.

"Are you going to let me in, or do I have to stand out here in the hall while our dinner gets cold?" Brett asked good-naturedly.

Stepping back, she silently watched him carry the sack into the kitchen, remove his coat and start pulling out containers of food. The delicious smells of something Italian wafted throughout the room, making her suddenly ravenous.

Brett walked over to the cabinets and started opening doors as if he belonged there. He removed a couple of plates and glasses, then glanced over his shoulder. "Where do you keep the silverware?"

"Make yourself at home, Connelly," she said, closing the door.

He gave her an unrepentant grin. "Silverware?"

"First drawer on the left." She set Babe on the floor, then asked the little dog, "Is he always this pushy?"

Babe wagged her tail and yipped as if to say yes, then headed straight for the couch to burrow under the afghan.

"Don't listen to her," he said, setting the table. "Sometimes Babe exaggerates."

"I have a feeling she's telling the truth this time," Elena said dryly. She watched him move around her kitchen a moment longer before she asked, "What are you doing here, Brett? And how did you get into the building?"

"Your neighbor, Nanook of the North, was coming out as I—"

"Mrs. Simpkins," Elena corrected.

"Okay. Mrs. Simpkins let me in as she was leaving." He smiled. "And I'm here to make sure you eat right." He started removing lids from the containers of food. "By the way, Mario says hello and he's glad to hear you're feeling better."

"Brett, you don't have to keep checking up on me."

He ignored her and pulled a bottle from the sack. "I figured wine is out because of the baby, but I thought sparkling grape juice would be okay." He held it out for her perusal. "It is, isn't it?"

She nodded. "Yes, but—"

"Great." He opened the bottle and filled the glasses he'd placed beside the plates. "I hope you like vegetable lasagna. I thought it would be more healthy for you than regular lasagna."

"You didn't have to do this," she said, wondering what she was going to do with him. He was the most infuriating and at the same time endearing man she'd ever met.

"I know I didn't have to do it." He grinned. "But when I stopped by Mario's on my way home from work, I remembered that on Friday night you missed trying some of the best Italian food in Chicago. Besides, I didn't feel like eating alone." He grinned. "Babe doesn't talk much during dinner."

Elena couldn't keep from laughing. "So you think she talks to you at other times?"

He nodded. "Maybe not in the conventional way,

but she definitely lets me know what she's thinking and what she wants.''

"Ah, yes. I almost forgot about the throw pillows,'' Elena said, settling in the chair he held.

"Is your car out of the repair shop?'' he asked, opening another container.

"Not yet.'' Sighing she shook her head. "The mechanic said it would be sometime next week before it's fixed.''

Nodding, Brett removed several meatballs and placed them in a small bowl he'd pulled from the bag, then, setting it on the floor, he seated himself. "Come and get it,'' he called to the dog. To Elena he said, "I'll pick you up tomorrow morning.''

"That's not necessary,'' she insisted, shaking her head. "I can get there on my own.''

"Maybe so, but I'll be by around eight to pick you up.'' Before she could protest further, he pointed to her plate. "Go ahead and eat before it gets cold.''

Brett kept a close eye on Elena's plate and was satisfied that he'd done the right thing when she finished all of the lasagna. He still wasn't sure why he'd made the decision to pick up food on his way over to check on her, but he was glad that he had. It was clear she hadn't eaten since lunch.

"Thank you. That was heavenly,'' she said, when she'd finished the last of two soft breadsticks. "I'm stuffed.''

"I'm glad you liked it,'' he said, rising to take their plates to the sink. When he looked for, but couldn't find, a dishwasher, he ran water into the sink to wash the dishes.

"You don't have to clean up,'' she said, carrying

their glasses to the counter. She stood at his elbow. "I'll take care of it."

He shook his head. "Nope. You need to rest. Why don't you join Babe on the couch?"

"I can't do that. You're my guest."

She tried to shoo him away from the sink, but he wasn't about to budge. "I invited myself over for dinner, so technically, I don't think I could be considered a guest," he said, adding dishwashing liquid to the water.

"Look, Connelly, I'm not going to stand here and debate the issue." She reached for the sponge, but he held it out of her reach. "You furnished dinner. I'll take care of cleaning up."

He shot her a stubborn look. "What do you say we compromise? I'll wash and you dry?"

She gave him an odd look. "You really don't mind?"

"What gave you the idea I would?" he asked, wondering at the confused expression on her pretty face.

"Probably because Michael would have died before he offered to help." She shrugged. "And if he had, he wouldn't have meant it."

"Who's Michael?" Brett asked, careful to keep his voice casual, despite the fact that every nerve ending in his body was drawn up tighter than a violin string.

"My husband." She shook her head. "Make that my ex-husband."

Brett nearly dropped the plate he held as he connected the name. "You were married to Michael Delgado?"

Grimacing, she nodded. "Afraid so. I can't say it's the smartest thing I've ever done. Even my foster mother, Marie, thought he was a snake. And she always managed to find something good about everyone.'' Elena looked chagrined. ''But I didn't listen to her and lived to regret it.''

Brett certainly wasn't going to argue with her on that one. Michael Delgado was an assistant district attorney, reputed to be one of the biggest skirt chasers in Chicago and as slippery as an eel.

''I didn't know he'd ever been married,'' Brett said truthfully. ''How long were you together?''

She dried the plate he handed her, then placed it on a stack in the cabinet. Just when he decided she was going to ignore his question, she answered.

''I don't think he knew he was married, either,'' she said, her tone reflecting her disgust. ''I was married for four years, but I don't think he ever was. He never seemed to remember that little detail about himself. The ink hadn't much more than dried on the marriage license before he started going out with other women.''

It suddenly occurred to Brett that the man had to be her baby's father. ''How does he feel about the baby?''

Frowning, Elena asked, ''It didn't seem to matter to him the two times I was pregnant with his babies. Why would he care about this one?''

Brett stared at her. ''This is your third child?''

The sudden look of sadness crossing her expressive features caused his stomach to twist into a tight knot. ''No, I miscarried both times,'' she said quietly.

Every muscle in his body tensed. He had a feeling he knew, but he had to ask. ''How far along were you?''

''Two months.''

Aside from the obvious reasons, it was no wonder Elena was terrified by the problems she'd been experiencing. She couldn't be more than a couple of months along with this baby. "Do the doctors know what was wrong?" he asked gently.

She shrugged. "Stress mostly. I was trying to work full-time, become a mother and hold together a marriage that never was."

"So Michael isn't the father of this baby?"

"No," she said, sounding relieved. "He walked out on Valentine's Day last year, I filed for divorce a week later and I haven't seen him since."

"Then who…?" Brett let his voice trail off, afraid she might tell him to mind his own business.

But instead of the outrage he expected, she laughed. "You're probably never going to believe this. I have no idea who the father is."

That did it. Brett did drop the second plate. Fortunately, the dishwater slowed its descent and kept the heavy ironstone from breaking on the bottom of the sink. The water splashed onto them but neither noticed.

"Don't look so shocked." She shrugged. "All I know about the father is he's six feet two inches tall, has blue eyes and black hair." Her gaze raked him from head to toe, then laughing, she added, "For all I know, he could be you."

Brett's heart slammed against his ribs so hard it felt like he might have cracked a couple. When he finally found enough breath to speak, all he could manage to get out was a strangled, "Me?"

Laughing harder, she reached out to touch him, and on contact a current coursed up his arm, then headed straight for the region below his belt.

"Relax, Connelly." Her chocolate-colored eyes twinkled with humor. "You don't have anything to worry about. Unless, of course, you've ever made a deposit at the Partners in Fertility sperm bank."

Brett shook his head. "Never even considered it."

"I didn't think so." She dried the last plate, put it in the cabinet, then closed the door. "My donor was an intern from one of the hospitals."

"Why?" Brett couldn't stop the single word from escaping.

"They pay for donations and I've heard that medical students sometimes supplement their schooling by being donors," she answered.

"No. I mean why—"

"Go to a sperm bank?" she asked. When he nodded, she explained. "It was the only logical solution. I get the baby I want, without the complications of a relationship I don't. And I won't have to share custody with anyone." She took the sponge from him to wipe off the kitchen table. "The baby will be mine alone."

Sweat popped out on Brett's forehead and upper lip as a feeling so strong it almost brought him to his knees raged through him. It quickly passed, but for a moment he'd felt a keen disappointment that Elena hadn't waited for him to father her child.

Brett suddenly felt the need to run like hell.

"I need to be going," he said, making a show of glancing at his watch. He grabbed his coat and Babe, then headed for the door. "I just remembered I have another appointment this evening."

Five

Waiting for her last morning interview to show up, Elena propped her elbow on the mahogany conference table, rested her chin on her hand and stared out of the floor-to-ceiling windows at Lake Michigan. As had been the case so many times over the past five days, Brett Connelly filled her thoughts. Since Friday evening she hadn't been able to keep her mind off him. Of course, that probably had a lot to do with the fact that he hadn't allowed her to think of much else.

She'd rarely, if ever, allowed anyone to bowl her over the way he had. And she never opened up to anyone the way she had with him last night.

It bothered her that she'd been so forthcoming with information about herself—things she normally considered nobody's business but her own. But Brett had been extremely easy to talk to and more than a little understanding.

Of course, her ex-husband had been that way in the beginning. When she'd first met Michael, he'd showered her with attention, pretended to listen to what she had to say and appeared to care about the same things that mattered to her. But all too soon she'd discovered it was nothing but a ploy, a way to learn where she was the most vulnerable and to use it to his advantage.

When they met, Michael had needed a wife in order to obtain the promotions within the district attorney's office that the family-oriented D.A. thought to be essential for his assistants. Once Michael had discovered that she'd grown up alone and desperately wanted to have a family of her own, he'd used that to entice her into marrying him. But just a matter of weeks after the wedding, the D.A. had suffered a fatal heart attack, and his replacement didn't see the need to base promotions on his assistants' marital status. So Michael Delgado had been saddled with a by-then pregnant wife, he didn't want.

Shaking off the disturbing memories, Elena checked her watch. Apparently, her eleven-o'clock interview was going to be a no-show. The man had probably gotten busy with something and couldn't break away. Understandable, considering the many duties of the executives working for a company the size of Connelly Corporation.

It was just as well, she decided, rising from her chair to walk down the hall to speak with Brett's secretary. She had a doctor's appointment right after lunch, and with her car still in the shop for repairs, she'd have to catch the L.

"Fiona, will you please call and reschedule my in-

terview with Robert Marsh?'' Elena asked when the
secretary looked up at her approach.

"Of course." The woman picked up the phone.
"Would you like to meet with him later this afternoon?"

Elena shook her head. "I have a doctor's appointment and won't be conducting interviews again until
tomorrow morning. Could you see if he's available
sometime within the next couple of days?"

"Certainly," Fiona said, already dialing the man's
extension.

Walking back to the conference room, Elena collected her things and had just put on her coat when
Brett burst into the room. "What's wrong?" he demanded, rushing over to her. He placed his hands on
her upper arms and eased her down into the nearest
chair. "Are you feeling dizzy? Nauseated? What?
Why didn't you have Fiona page me?"

The concern on his handsome face rendered her
temporarily speechless. When she finally found her
voice, she shook her head. "I'm all right. What made
you think otherwise?"

"Fiona said you're on your way to the doctor." He
released her but didn't move away. "If you're feeling
fine, why do you need to see a doctor?" he demanded.

She couldn't believe how worried Brett looked. Her
ex-husband hadn't shown that degree of concern either time she'd miscarried. She smiled reassuringly.
"I'm going to the obstetrician because I have regular
prenatal checkups. Today's appointment is one of
them."

"Oh."

Brett straightened and rubbed the tense muscles at

the base of his neck with a less-than-steady hand. He felt foolish as hell. But as soon as Fiona told him Elena was leaving to see a doctor, fear had knifed through him with an intensity that was staggering.

So much for his decision to back off and only be around her when it was an absolute necessity. "What time is your appointment?"

"One o'clock, but since Robert Marsh was unable to make it for our scheduled interview, I thought I'd take an early lunch, then go on to the doctor's office." She rose and began gathering her purse and briefcase. "I'll see you tomorrow."

He took hold of her arm when she started past him. "Wait a minute. I thought you told me last night that your car is still in the repair shop."

She nodded. "It is. And the guy called this morning to tell me he has to order another part that will probably cost me a small fortune."

"I'll drive you," Brett said, guiding her toward the door and out into the hall.

"Thank you for the offer, but I'll catch the L."

"No way," he said, steering her toward his office. "I don't like you riding the L."

She stopped to glare at him. "It doesn't really matter whether you like it or not. Back off, Connelly. It's not your call."

The thought of her riding the elevated train alone made his stomach hurt. "It's not safe."

"I think I can handle myself well enough to survive," she said dryly.

Telling himself she carried a gun, knew how to use it and probably had enough self-defense training to take down a full-grown gorilla didn't alleviate Brett's concerns. He didn't like having to use the trump card again, but dammit the woman was as stubborn as anyone he'd ever met.

"Given your past history of miscarriages, I doubt the excitement would be good for you or the baby in the event that someone tried to accost you."

He hated the haunted look that flashed in her big brown eyes, the worry lines that suddenly creased her forehead. But she had to see reason.

"That was a low blow, Connelly," she said, her voice nothing more than a whisper. "You're not playing fair."

Brett felt like the biggest jerk in the tri-state area, but sometimes the woman let that independent streak of hers override common sense. "I'm sorry, Elena," he said, pulling her into his arms. "But you have to think of the baby."

Conscious that they were standing in front of Fiona's desk and that the woman was openly gaping at the scene in front of her, Brett led Elena into his office. Once the door was closed behind them, he framed her face with his hands. "I know you've been trained to take care of yourself, but the circumstances are different now. It's not just you anymore. It's Peanut, too."

"Who is Peanut?"

"The baby." He had to make her understand. "You have to consider the potential risks these things pose for him, too."

"Her," she said, frowning. "You know, Connelly, I really hate when you're right."

"I do, too, honey."

He lightly kissed her forehead, then set her away from him. If he hadn't put distance between them, he wasn't sure he could stop himself from taking her into his arms and kissing her until they both collapsed from a lack of oxygen.

"Let me cancel my meeting for this afternoon," he said, walking over to his desk. "We'll stop for something to eat, then I'll drive you to your doctor's appointment."

"You don't have to do that," she said, shaking her head. "You stay here and take care of whatever you need to do. I'll get a cab."

He snorted. "That's not much better than the L. The last thing you need is to be in a car accident."

She glared at him. "You don't drive any better than cabbies. You zip that Jag in and out of traffic like you're jockeying for position in the Grand Prix."

He laughed. "Yes, but I know what I'm doing."

"And you think they don't?" she asked incredulously. "Oh, brother! You've got an ego that just won't quit."

Grinning, he nodded. "And you know what they say about the male ego."

"What would that be?" she asked, one perfect brow rising in question.

"It's fragile," he said simply.

That got a good laugh out of her. "Where did you hear that?"

"All the talk shows have devoted at least one program to the topic, and the women's magazine are constantly printing articles about how to do this or that without shattering a man's ego," he answered as he collected a stack of papers to shove into his briefcase.

"You read a lot of those, do you?"

Smiling at the laughter he detected in her voice, he shook his head. "Not in this lifetime. But I have sisters who read them."

He pressed the button on his intercom, quickly instructed Fiona to reschedule his appointments for the afternoon, then shrugged into his coat and took Elena by the elbow. "Where's your doctor's office?"

When she gave him the address, he grinned. "I know this great little mom and pop joint not far from there. They have the best cheddar-baked potato soup in the city."

An hour later, as they drove away from the little Irish pub, Elena had to agree with Brett about the soup. Served in sour dough bread bowls, it was delicious and without a doubt the best she'd ever eaten.

"How are the interviews coming along?" he asked, steering the Jag into the flow of traffic.

"Everything is progressing nicely." She settled back in the leather seat. "I've interviewed all of your brothers and sisters, except for Seth."

"Seth had to be in court this week," Brett said, downshifting the powerful car in order to make a turn. "He should be available by Friday. If not, he'll definitely be freed up by the first of next week."

"Isn't he the attorney?" She couldn't help but wonder what it would be like to have so many siblings, or what it would be like trying not to confuse what they did for a living. "Are you close?"

"We weren't when he first came to live with us," Brett said, weaving the Jag through the midday traffic. "Back then Seth was too angry to become close to anyone. But in the last few years I'd say we've become pretty good friends."

Elena frowned. "I'm confused. If Seth didn't live with your parents, where—"

"Seth is my half brother," Brett interrupted. He

looked straight ahead, but she could tell he was deciding just how much he should tell her. Finally, as if coming to a decision, he shrugged. "You might as well know, my parents separated for a time right after my brother Rafe was born. That was thirty-three years ago. Seth's mother, Angie Donahue, was Dad's secretary at the time."

Elena noticed that Brett's hands tightened on the steering wheel. "Let me guess. She was more than ready to console him?"

Brett nodded. "After Mom and Dad got back together, Angie quit Connelly Corporation and dropped out of sight. Dad made sure that he provided support for Seth, but apparently the woman didn't have a clue about raising kids. By the time Seth was twelve, he was so out of control, she packed him up and signed over custody to my dad."

"That must have been a very difficult time for all of you," Elena said. Having been in foster homes with troubled youths, she was well aware of the disruption one angry child could cause a family.

"Drew and I were only seven at the time, but I can still remember a lot of it." Brett turned into the parking garage of her obstetrician's office building. "It didn't take long for Mom and Dad to see that if they didn't do something pretty quick, Seth was headed for big trouble. Dad checked around to see where he could get Seth the best possible help, then pulled some strings to get him admitted into one of the best military schools in the country. That's where Seth straightened up his act."

"He's lucky they found the right place for him," Elena said, remembering several children from her past who weren't as fortunate. "Does he see his bi-ological mother very often?"

Brett got out of the car and came around to open the passenger door. "Nobody's seen Angie Donahue since the night she dropped Seth off on our door-step."

"That's odd," Elena said thoughtfully. "Why wouldn't she want to at least check on Seth from time to time?"

"You'll have to ask her about that," Brett said, guiding her into the covered walkway bridging the garage and the office building. "If you can find her."

"I think it might be a good idea if I check on her whereabouts just to be on the safe side," Elena said as they rode the elevator to the third floor.

When they stepped out into a waiting room, Brett removed his coat and found them a place to sit while Elena registered with the receptionist. He was more than a little surprised to see that he wasn't the only man in the waiting area. He had no idea why the others would be there, unless they'd come along to lend moral support for someone like he'd done for Elena.

"They should be calling me in just a few minutes," Elena said, handing him a magazine. "I thought you might like something to read while you wait. I'm sorry, but they don't seem to have a big selection, and this was about all that was left."

He read the title aloud. *"Pregnancy and Birth."*

Laughing, she removed her coat. "It was either that or a pamphlet titled, Your Uterus and You."

He chuckled. "I don't think I have much need for that."

"I didn't think so, either." She hesitated, then

asked, "Would you mind watching my coat while I'm in seeing the doctor?"

"No problem," he said, taking it from her and placing it across the empty chair on the other side of him.

"Elena Delgado," a nurse called at the doorway of several long corridors branching off from the waiting area.

"I shouldn't be long," Elena said, following the woman.

Settling back in the chair, Brett had just opened the magazine when the same nurse walked up to him. "Are you with Ms. Delgado?"

"Yes. Is something wrong?" He was halfway out of the chair when her smile stopped him.

"No, everything's fine," the woman assured him. "I just thought you might want to be with Ms. Delgado. This is something I don't think you'll want to miss."

"Okay," he said, confused. He wasn't sure what the woman wanted him to see, and he was positive Elena wouldn't like his being there, but curiosity had him rising to his feet. Collecting their coats, he followed the nurse down the corridor Elena had gone down only minutes before.

When he opened the door to the room the nurse indicated, he found Elena lying flat on a examining table, staring at the ceiling. She turned her head at the sound of his entrance, and her friendly expression vanished immediately.

"What are *you* doing here?" she demanded. She obviously wasn't of the same opinion as the nurse about his not missing whatever was about to take place.

"I was told I'd want to see this," he explained, noticing that she'd changed into a hospital gown. The fact that she probably didn't have on a stitch of clothing beneath the ugly garment sent his blood pressure up several points.

She glared at him as she pulled at the sheet that draped her from the waist down. "Trust me, you don't. Now get out."

He ignored her protest and walked over to the examining table. "Don't get upset. It's not good for you or the baby."

"This isn't any of your concern, Connelly."

Tossing their coats over the chair at the side of the table, he placed his hands on her shoulders to keep her from rising to a sitting position. "Calm down."

"No."

Her cheeks had colored a pretty pink, and her brown eyes glittered with anger. He didn't think he'd ever seen a woman look more beautiful.

Brett wasn't sure why it had suddenly become important to him that he witness whatever mystery event was about to take place, but it had. Knowing only one way to silence her adamant protests, he leaned down and firmly placed his lips over hers.

At first Elena pushed against his chest with her hands, but as he moved his mouth over hers, he felt her relax a moment before she slipped her arms around his neck. Primitive male satisfaction filled him at her acceptance, and he forgot all about where they were or the reason for the kiss.

When her lips parted on a sigh, Brett seized the opportunity and slipped his tongue inside. Her tiny moan of pleasure encouraged him and he boldly explored her soft mouth, tasted the sweetness that was

Elena. The tentative touch of her tongue to his sent heat coursing through his veins and made his heart thump hard against his rib cage.

Lifting her to a sitting position, he wrapped his arms around her and slid his hand into the split at the back of her gown. The silky feel of her skin beneath his palm made breathing difficult and his arousal not only predictable but inevitable. He wanted her, and he could tell by her response that she wanted him.

The door opened suddenly, reminding him that he'd once again forgotten his vow to restrict their contact to business only. Lightly brushing his lips over Elena's one last time, he loosened his hold and laid her back onto the examining table.

When he turned, a woman in a white lab coat smiled as she pulled a folder out of a pocket on the door. "Good afternoon, I'm Dr. Simmons."

He shook the hand she extended. "Brett Connelly."

"I see you had a few problems this past weekend," the doctor said, turning her attention to an uncharacteristically quiet Elena.

Sensing that she needed the support, Brett took her hand in his.

"Besides the usual nausea, I've had some problems with dizziness," Elena answered.

"She fainted Friday evening," he added.

Brett felt her hand flex in his, and he gently returned the pressure, lending her his strength. He glanced at her to gauge how she was holding up, and his heart twisted at the vulnerable look on her pretty face.

"I've spoken with the staff at Memorial and they've filled me in on the details," Dr. Simmons said, reviewing the chart. Snapping the folder shut, she smiled. "I don't think we have anything to worry about, but I want you to continue to get plenty of rest and eat well-balanced meals."

"Okay," Elena said, her voice reflecting how relieved she was at the news.

"Is there anything else she should do or avoid doing?" Brett asked, drawing a stormy look from Elena. He ignored it as he waited for the doctor's answer.

"Given Elena's history of miscarriages, I wouldn't advise her running a marathon or lifting anything over ten pounds," Dr. Simmons said. Apparently thinking that he and Elena had an intimate relationship, she smiled. "But I see no reason to avoid less strenuous activities, including lovemaking."

Elena shook her head. "We haven't—"

"I'm sure the doctor understands, honey," Brett interrupted, barely able to keep a straight face.

Dr. Simmons nodded. "You should be able to enjoy normal relations until a month or so before delivery." She grinned. "Now, what do you say we take your baby's first picture?"

Brett wasn't sure what the woman meant, but it seemed to please Elena immensely. He'd never seen her look this excited and happy.

"Can we tell anything at this point?" she asked.

"It's a possibility. You're close enough to your third month that we may be able to see something," Dr. Simmons said, pulling down the sheet to just below Elena's waist and pulling the bottom of the gown up to expose her gently rounded stomach.

Fascinated, Brett watched the doctor squeeze a generous amount of a clear lubricant just below Elena's navel, then remove what looked like a microphone from the side of a monitor to press it into the thin gel. She moved it around in a circular pattern on Elena's lower abdomen until a fuzzy picture popped up on the monitor.

"There's your baby, Elena," Dr. Simmons said, grinning.

He watched tears fill Elena's eyes. "Oh, she's beautiful," she whispered, her lips trembling.

"It's a girl?" he asked, staring intently at the screen. "How can you tell? I don't see anything that even resembles a baby."

"It's a little too early to determine the sex," Dr. Simmons answered. "I think Elena's hoping for a girl." She pointed to the screen. "See, there's an arm and a leg."

What the hell did they see that he didn't? All he could decipher from the fuzzy black and gray image was that something in the middle of it twitched rhythmically. Then, as if by magic, the picture cleared. Or maybe he'd concentrated on it long enough to understand what Elena and Dr. Simmons had seen all along. He wasn't sure, but Brett suddenly felt as if the breath had been knocked out of him. A tiny hand, complete with a thumb and four fingers, became discernible as it moved on the screen.

"My God! That's awesome." Without a second thought he leaned down and kissed Elena with all the awe and wonder that the moment held for him.

Tears of happiness slid silently from the corners of Elena's eyes as Brett's lips moved gently over hers. When he lifted his head, he smiled down at her. "Thank you for allowing me to see this, Elena."

"Thank you for being here with me," she whispered, surprised that she really was happy to have him there to share the moment.

She'd never made it far enough in her other two pregnancies to have a sonogram, to see the tiny life within her. But she knew that if she had, her ex-husband wouldn't have bothered to make it to the doctor's office for the first look at their child. The only interest Michael had had in the miracles they'd created together had been how it would affect his career or cramp his style. Beyond that, he simply hadn't cared whether they had a baby or how much of an emotional toll losing it had taken on her.

As she gazed up at Brett, she wondered how she could have come to the conclusion that he and Michael were cut from the same cloth. In the past week Brett had shown more concern and offered more in the way of moral support than Michael had in the entire four years of their marriage. And not once had Brett complained about being inconvenienced in any way.

"Here's your baby's first portrait," Dr. Simmons said, handing Elena a printed copy of the sonogram.

"Would you make another copy of that?" Brett asked.

Clearly amused, Dr. Simmons smiled. "Of course."

She quickly made adjustments, and the machine spit out another picture. "Now, do you have any questions or complaints that I should know about before we do the rest of the examination?"

Elena thought for a moment. "I don't think so. I'm taking my vitamins, and with the medication the nausea is bearable."

"I'm making sure she doesn't overwork herself,"

Brett volunteered. He sat down in the chair beside the table as if he intended to stay.

"Could you excuse us a moment, Dr. Simmons?" Elena asked.

Dr. Simmons nodded. "I'll be back in a few minutes. I have to get a couple of brochures to give you."

"Thank you," Elena said as the woman quietly closed the door behind her. Turning her head to look at Brett, she tried to keep from laughing. He obviously didn't have a clue what was going to happen next. For some reason she found that fact quite endearing. "I think you'll be more comfortable out in the waiting room, Brett."

"Don't worry about me," he said, staring at the picture of the sonogram. "I'm fine."

"This isn't about you. I'm more worried about *my* comfort level." When his head snapped up, she almost laughed at his confused expression. "The doctor is going to be doing a routine examination on other parts than just my stomach."

His brows shot up as understanding dawned. "Ohh…one of those." Rising to his feet, he gathered their coats and walked to the door. "I'll, uh, be in the waiting room if you need me."

Brett sat with his forearms propped on his knees, staring at the picture he held in his hands. He was completely unaware of the other occupants in the waiting area. One thing kept running through his mind—he'd never in his life felt more humbled or privileged than when the image of Elena's baby had popped up on the sonogram screen. And although she hadn't invited him to witness the first glimpse of the child growing within her, Elena had been easily persuaded to allow him to stay.

He sat back in the chair and thought about the apprehension he'd seen in her expressive brown eyes, the fear, when the doctor had first walked into the room. Whether she admitted it or not, Elena needed someone to be with her, to hold her hand and lend her emotional support.

Brett leaned his head back against the wall and stared at the ceiling. So much for his decision of keeping his distance from her, he thought, feeling more than a little uneasy. To his dismay he was quickly discovering he wanted to be the one she turned to. And that scared the hell out of him.

For the first time in his life, he wanted to be needed, wanted to take care of someone other than himself. And that was where the problem arose. He wasn't sure he could do that without giving more of himself than he was willing to invest.

Six

When Brett arrived at Connelly Tower the next morning, he was furious and itching for a fight. Bypassing his office, he walked straight into the conference room. He found Elena there, nibbling on a bagel as if she didn't have a care in the world.

"I went by your apartment to pick you up this morning." He removed his overcoat and threw it at one of the chairs, not caring if it hit the mark. "Imagine my surprise to find you'd already left."

Glancing up at him, she smiled. "I'll bet that was a surprise."

"Did you get your car out of the repair shop?"

She scribbled something on the notepad in front of her, then finished the last of the bagel before she answered. "Nope."

"How did you get to work this morning, Elena?" he asked, trying to stay calm despite the churning in his stomach. He dreaded to hear what he knew she was going to say.

"I took the L."

"I thought we discussed the dangers of you taking the train alone," he said, careful to keep his tone even. What he really wanted to do was shout that she'd taken an unnecessary risk and in the process scared the living hell out of him. It hadn't been until he walked into the conference room that he'd known for sure she was all right.

When she looked up at him, she shrugged. "You discussed it. I didn't."

"But you agreed—"

"No. I didn't agree to anything." She slowly placed her pencil on the table, then rose to her feet. "You told me about all the dangers riding on the L could pose to my pregnancy. You even insisted that riding in a cab wasn't the answer." Poking his chest with her finger, she glared up at him. "Do *you* see a pattern here, Connelly?"

Elena was gaining steam as she went, and Brett didn't think he'd ever seen her look more beautiful. Reaching out, he loosely wrapped his arms around her waist. "I sure do, Delgado." He dropped a kiss on her forehead. "I see you being too stubborn to see that Chicago's transit system isn't safe for you and the baby."

"That's bull and we both know it." She sounded a lot more breathless now than angry.

Brushing her lips with his, Brett marveled at how perfect she felt in his arms even though there was a good eight-to-ten inch difference in their heights. "Elena, I don't like you using public transportation."

"Tens of thousands of people do it every day and nothing happens."

"I don't know those people," he said stubbornly.

He knew he was being unreasonable, but he didn't care. He wasn't at all comfortable with the thought of Elena alone on the train or a bus. And it didn't make him feel any better to think of her taking a cab ride with the driver weaving in and out of traffic at breakneck speeds on the overly crowded Chicago streets.

"Then how do you suggest I get to work, or anywhere else, for that matter?" she asked.

He rested his forehead on hers. "I'll drive you."

"I can't ask you to do that."

"You're not asking," he said, placing a kiss on the tip of her nose. "I'm volunteering."

Lowering his mouth to hers, he reveled in the feel of her perfect lips beneath his, the softness that was uniquely Elena's. When she slipped her arms from between them, he expected her to push him away, but to his satisfaction, she encircled his neck, welcoming his embrace.

Encouraged by her gesture of acceptance, he deepened the kiss to reacquaint himself with the sweet taste of her. At the first tentative touch of her tongue meeting his, heat shot through every fiber of his being and his body responded with a tightening that made him light-headed.

He slid his hands down her back to pull her into the cradle of his hips, to allow her to feel his hardness, to let her know what she did to him. But her breasts against his chest, her tiny moan of pleasure, caused his insides to feel as if they'd been set on fire and the only way to extinguish the flames would be to make love to her.

His throbbing body reminded him of just how long it had been since he'd been with a woman. He tried to tell himself that was the reason for his immediate reaction and that thinking about making love to Elena wasn't going to help calm his libido. But he had a feeling the intensity of his arousal had very little to do with his lack of sex in the past year and more to do with the woman he held.

Kissing Elena was quickly becoming an addiction—a habit he wasn't sure he'd ever be able to break—and one he wasn't sure he ever wanted to. In that moment he knew beyond a shadow of a doubt that he was getting in way over his head.

Slowly lightening the pressure of his mouth, he lifted his head to stare down at her. Her eyes had darkened to a deep, rich chocolate and the pink blush of desire colored her smooth cheeks.

Brett took a step back in order to calm his aching body. He didn't want to walk out into the reception area in a state of arousal and traumatize his straitlaced secretary.

"What's your schedule like for today?" he asked, placing his hands on Elena's shoulders to keep from drawing her to him again.

"I...have to meet with...Robert Marsh this morning," she answered, her breathing shallow.

He picked up his coat from the chair he'd thrown it over earlier. "How about after lunch?"

"I'll be going to Lake Shore Manor at two o'clock to set up an interview with your mother's secretary, Jennifer Anderson, and to give your parents an update on your brother's case."

Confident now that he could walk out into the reception area without shocking Fiona down to the roots of her bleached-blond hair, he started for the door. "Good. We'll go out for a leisurely lunch, then drive up to Mom and Dad's." When she looked as if she intended to protest, he shook his head. He wasn't about to take no for an answer. "This isn't negotiable, Delgado. Get used to it. I'm your chauffeur until your car is repaired."

After setting up the time for her interview with Jennifer Anderson, Elena found herself sitting with the Connellys in the sun room at Lake Shore Manor. Naturally they wanted an update on the case. Elena just wished she had something more to tell them.

"I've interviewed most of your children and several of the Connelly Corporation employees," Elena said, carefully placing her china teacup on the saucer. She wasn't at all comfortable handling something so elegant and obviously expensive.

Setting them on the glass surface of the coffee table in front of her, she breathed a sigh of relief. If she chipped the delicate pieces, it would no doubt cost a small fortune to replace them.

"Did you learn anything new?" Brett's mother asked, the remnants of her European accent more pronounced due to her obvious worry.

At the age of sixty, Emma Connelly was a strikingly beautiful woman with an air of elegance that only the royals possessed. But the events of the past month were beginning to take their toll. Sadness and worry marred her otherwise flawless features, and her blue eyes reflected the anxiety that still haunted her. The former princess of Altaria, Emma had not only experienced the terror of having an assassination attempt made on her eldest son, she'd also lost her father, King Thomas, and her brother, Prince Marc, in a tragic boating accident.

Elena regretted not having news to help relieve the woman's stress. "Unfortunately, Mrs. Connelly, I haven't been able to turn up anything we don't already know."

"That's not acceptable." Grant Connelly's steel-gray eyes and granite jaw indicated that he was a man used to demanding answers and having those demands met. "Someone came damned close to killing our son. We want the SOB caught."

"We all do, Dad," Brett spoke up. He left his spot by the French doors leading out to the patio to sit with Elena on the white wicker love seat. "But these things take time." He put his arm around her shoulders, causing Emma and Grant to exchange a bemused look. "Elena's been working very hard to sort through all the facts, even at a risk to her own health."

"That's not an issue here," Elena said quickly, shrugging out of his embrace.

She gave Brett a look she hoped would keep him quiet. She wasn't comfortable sharing the intimate details of her life with just anyone, nor was she happy about the speculative expressions the Connellys wore at the familiarity their son displayed toward her. Glancing at her notes to regain her composure, she tried to find a way to turn the focus of the meeting back to the investigation.

"Mr. Connelly, since your son inherited the Altarian throne, and there were no attempts made on his life prior to his being named King Thomas's successor, we've already established that the attempt on his life had to be political in nature,'' she said, choosing her words carefully.

She felt confident that her tact had worked when Grant nodded. ''But what we don't know is why,'' he said, running a hand over his face.

Emma Connelly wasn't the only one feeling the strain of the recent upheaval in their lives. The chiseled lines in Grant's distinguished face had deepened with worry over the past month, and Elena would swear that his black hair carried a few more strands of white, especially at his temples.

''No, we don't know why,'' she agreed. ''But we do know whoever pulled the trigger was a professional. He deliberately chose a public place with the express purpose of blending into the crowd after he'd carried out the hit. That tells us there's a definite reason behind the attempt and that it's not just some crackpot seizing the first opportunity that comes along. Once we figure out exactly what that reason is, it should lead us to whoever hired the gunman.''

''Excuse me, Mr. Connelly,'' a maid said, standing poised at the entrance of the sun room. ''You have a phone call.''

''Tell whoever it is that I'm tied up in a meeting,'' Grant said dismissively.

''You're going to want to take this,'' the woman insisted with all the confidence of one who'd worked for the Connellys for many years. ''It's that Albert Dessage fellow you hired from overseas. He said to tell you it's urgent.''

Elena immediately recognized the name of the European-based P.I. the Connellys had hired to look into the case on the Altarian end of the investigation.

When Grant rose from his chair to take the call,

the maid handed him a cordless unit. "He's on line two."

"Thank you, Ruby," Grant said, taking the phone. He waited until she'd left the room before he punched a button to take the phone off hold. "What have you discovered, Dessage?" Grant demanded, dispensing with a polite greeting.

Elena watched Grant's eyes shift immediately to Emma, then a frown crease his forehead. He listened for several more seconds, before saying, "Yes, she's here. Just a moment." Holding the phone out to Elena, he said, "Dessage wants to talk to you, Ms. Delgado."

From the look on Grant Connelly's face, she had no doubt that the case had just taken a relevant turn. Taking the phone from him, she placed it to her ear. "This is Detective Delgado, Mr. Dessage."

"As we suspected to be the case, I've just received confirmation through Interpol that King Thomas and Prince Marc were murdered," Dessage said, his voice crackling into her ear. "The boat had been rigged with plastic explosives and a timing device. It was set to explode once they were several miles out in open water. They never had a chance. They were doomed from the moment they stepped on board."

"Any leads indicating who's responsible?" she asked.

"Not at this time," the man said. "But please assure the Connellys that King Daniel and his wife are safe and have the Royal Guard's protection at all times."

"I'll do that," she said, feeling Brett's reassuring hand on her shoulder.

She heard Emma's sharp gasp and glanced up to see the woman quietly sobbing into her mono-grammed linen hankie. Apparently, Grant had given her the news that her father and brother had been murdered.

"Anything else?" Elena asked Dessage.

"Yes." Dessage's voice began to cut out, forcing her total concentration on what he was saying. "Tell the Connellys that...family should be safe. The assassinations...directly related to the throne."

With a crackling pop, the connection was lost before Elena could respond.

When she turned her attention back to the Connellys, Grant was trying to comfort a grieving Emma. "Mr. Dessage said, and I have to agree, that it's almost a forgone conclusion that the attempt on your son's life is directly tied to the Altarian throne."

"What about my other sons?" Emma asked through her tears. She glanced at Brett, then pinned Elena with a beseeching look. "Are they in danger, too?"

"Don't worry about the rest of us, Mom," Brett said. "We'll be fine."

Elena nodded, carefully placing the cordless phone on the coffee table. "I have to agree, Mrs. Connelly. As long as King Daniel is safely hidden away in Altaria, I don't think we have to be concerned about the others. He's the king now, and unless something happens to him, there would be no reason for the assassin to go after your other children." She glanced at Brett, thankful that he was too far down the royal lineage to be in much of any danger. "But I would encourage them to be extremely cautious. If they do see anything suspicious or feel threatened in any way, please advise them to call the police immediately," she said, rising to leave.

"I have a security detail here at Lake Shore Manor," Grant said, "and I'll speak with the head of security at Connelly Tower about tightening things there. Would it be advisable to have the other boys placed under surveillance?''

''No, Mr. Connelly,'' Elena said honestly. ''I don't think that's necessary. But I do believe they should be on the alert, since the men of the family are the only ones eligible to inherit the throne.''

''All right.'' Grant stood to shake her hand. ''Thank you for dropping by to give us an update.''

''No problem, Mr. Connelly,'' she said, putting her arms into the coat Brett held for her.

''Brett, please be watchful,'' Emma pleaded.

''I will, Mom,'' he said, walking over to place a kiss on his mother's cheek.

Elena couldn't make any promises concerning the woman's other sons, but she could with the youngest. ''Mrs. Connelly, Brett and I have been working very closely together, setting up the interviews and coordinating the investigation of Connelly Corporation's higher level employees. Let me assure you that I've seen nothing unusual, and as long as we're working together, you have nothing to worry about. I'll personally see to Brett's safety.''

Lost in thought, Brett silently steered the Jag through the gates of Lake Shore Manor and out onto Lake Shore Drive. He wasn't sure whether to be amused or insulted by Elena's promise to his mother.

On one hand, he found the idea of a woman as petite as Elena vowing to keep him safe almost laughable. He was at least ten inches taller and outweighed her by a good seventy-five pounds. What chance would a woman of her stature have against anyone posing a threat to him?

On the other hand, his ego had taken a glancing blow. He didn't like that she might have the opinion he couldn't take care of himself or her. Did she see him as nothing more than a desk jockey with the self-defense skills of a slug?

"Before you sit there and build my statement to your mother into a personal insult, remember this," Elena said quietly. "I'm trained to observe situations and analyze any and all potential danger." She reached over and placed her hand on his leg just a few inches above his knee. On contact a shaft of heat snaked up his spine and quickly spread through the rest of his body. "I wasn't saying you couldn't protect yourself, only that I would be there to alert you if I felt there was a threat." She gave his thigh a playful pat, sending his blood pressure skyrocketing. "Besides, I carry a gun. You don't."

Startled that she'd read him correctly, he jerked his head around to look at her. "I wasn't thinking anything like that," he lied. He wasn't about to admit that her assessment had been accurate. After all, a man had his pride.

She gave him a smile that said she saw right through him. "Whatever you say, Connelly."

How did she do that? How did she know what he was thinking? Was he that transparent?

Deciding it was time to change the subject before he opened his mouth and proved her right, he asked, "What have you got planned for this evening?"

She removed her hand from his leg and placed it in her lap. He reached over, took hold of it and placed it back on his thigh, then covered it with his own. He liked having her touch him.

"I really don't have anything planned besides a hot

bath, putting on my sweats and moccasins and vegging out in front of the TV with a toasted cheese
sandwich and a can of soup," she answered, her voice
sounding a little shaky.

Satisfied that he got to her as much as she did him,
he grinned. "Why don't we go by my condo so I can
change clothes and get Babe, then we can pick up something more nutritious than soup and veg out together?"

She gave him a long look and for several seconds
he thought she was going to turn his idea down. "I
have to warn you, I don't have a remote control to
my TV," she finally said, grinning.

"My God, woman, this is the twenty-first century,
not the Stone Age." Relieved, he gave an exaggerated
shake of his head. "A TV without a remote? What's
the world coming to?"

She laughed. "It had one, but I lost it when I
moved after the divorce last year."

"Okay, that's more like it." He turned off Lake
Shore Drive and, driving several blocks to the west,
pulled to a stop in front of an electronics store in a
strip mall.

"What are we stopping here for?"

"Two words—universal remote."

She laughed. "You're kidding, right?"

"Nope." He grinned as he prepared to get out of
the car. "A man has to have a remote in his hand if
he's going to do this right. It's a huge part of the
vegging process."

Three hours later Brett sat on the couch with his
arm around Elena. She leaned against him while Babe
snoozed lazily in her lap.

After ten minutes of watching the most mindless

show he'd ever had the misfortune to tune into, he
picked up the remote he'd purchased. "This is the
biggest waste of film I've ever seen," he said, channel
surfing for something more interesting.

"That's what vegging is all about," Elena said,
sounding sleepy. "It's sitting on the couch, watching
television shows that don't inform you of something
or make you think about anything."

When he paused on one of the network news pro-
grams, she shook her head. "If you don't mind, I'd
rather not watch this."

"Why not?" he asked. The anchor had just announced a special report on Valentine's Day rituals
around the world.

She sat up straight. "I don't much care for this
particular holiday."

As Brett sat there wondering what her reasons
were, understanding suddenly dawned. How could he
have forgotten? A few days ago she'd told him about
her husband leaving her.

"Don't think about what happened last year," he
said, tightening his arm around her. "I'm sure you
have more pleasant memories of other Valentine's
Days."

"Not really." She placed Babe on the couch and
rose to her feet. Gathering their empty popcorn bowl
and soda cans, she walked into the kitchen.

Brett followed her. "You haven't had one memorable Valentine's Day?"

She gave him a wry smile as she placed the bowls
on the counter. "Last year was pretty memorable."

"I don't mean that and you know it," he said,
walking up to stand in front of her. "What about the

years before? Didn't Delgado buy you flowers or at least take you out for dinner?''

"No," she said, shaking her head. "The closest thing I ever got from him that could even remotely be considered romantic was a call telling me we had a political fund-raiser to attend and that he wanted me to go out and buy a new dress for the occasion. That was on Valentine's Day."

"That's it?" Brett couldn't believe anyone was that insensitive.

Laughing, she nodded. "Then he went to a happy hour with some of his co-workers and conveniently forgot to come home to pick me up."

"He went to the dinner without you?"

"Don't look so shocked," she said, running water into the sink to wash the few dishes they'd used. "He ended up taking his secretary to the dinner."

Brett was outraged that the man would treat Elena so shabbily. "How long had you been married?"

"Six months." She shrugged as if it didn't matter. "I really wasn't all that surprised. By that time the honeymoon was over, and I knew exactly what I'd gotten myself into."

"Why did you stay with him?"

Turning to face him, she smiled sadly. "Partly because I wanted our marriage to work, and partly because I didn't have anywhere else to go."

"But—"

She placed her finger to his lips to stop him. "I didn't know right away that I'd married such a jerk," she explained. "Michael was quite good at covering up his infidelity, and I was eager to accept his excuses."

Brett reached out to take her into his arms. "You really didn't know what was going on?"

"I knew," she admitted, resting her head against his chest. "I just didn't want to admit that I'd been so desperate to have a family that I'd made the biggest mistake of my life."

"How did you manage to stay with it for four years?" he asked, holding her close. Brett ached for the loneliness she must have felt throughout most of her life—first as a foster child and then as the wife of a philandering husband.

"It wasn't so bad." She shook her head. "Michael wasn't abusive or anything like that. For the most part we led separate lives. He went his way, and I went mine." Glancing up at Brett, her eyes begged for his understanding. "But as long as I was married, I was still part of something. I still belonged."

Brett didn't know what to say. He'd never experienced that kind of loneliness, never known what it was like not to have anyone who really loved him. He'd always been secure in the knowledge that whether it was his parents, grandparents or siblings, he belonged to someone, he meant something to.

Knowing that anything he said would be grossly inadequate, he did the only thing he could think of to convey what he was feeling—he kissed her.

Careful to keep the kiss light at first, he gently moved his mouth over hers. He wanted to let her know how much her trusting him with the secrets of her past meant to him, wanted to apologize for the inconsiderate actions of the lowest of his gender. But the feel of her breasts pressed to his chest, the electrified impulses that skipped over every nerve in his body from the tentative touch of her tongue to his lips, sent his good intentions right out the window.

Gathering her more firmly against him, he brought

his hand up to cup her breast, to tease the tip with his thumb. But the barrier of fleece between them proved to be more frustration than he was willing to put up with. Groaning, Brett slid his hand beneath the tail of her sweatshirt. Her satiny skin filling his palm and the discovery that she hadn't bothered with a bra when she changed clothes caused heat to shoot through his body with an intensity that threatened to buckle his knees.

At that moment Brett knew he wanted her more than he'd ever wanted anything in his life. And it scared the hell out of him.

Forcing himself to release her, he straightened her shirt, then stepped back. "I have to go."

Elena nodded. "I think it would be best."

"I'll be by tomorrow morning around eight to pick you up," he said, putting on his jacket.

"I won't be going to Connelly Tower tomorrow," she said, shaking her head. "I have to spend the day in my office at SIU headquarters, transcribing my notes and filing reports."

"What time should I be by to drive you over there?" he asked.

"You're off the hook for tomorrow, Connelly," she said, sounding almost relieved. "I'll be riding into work with a colleague of mine."

He stared at her for endless seconds, wondering why the thought of her not being down the hall from him tomorrow on the seventeenth floor of Connelly Tower bothered him so much. Deciding he was better off not knowing, he picked up Babe and walked out the door before he turned back and made a complete fool of himself by asking her to let him spend the night.

Seven

The next day stretched out interminably for Brett, and it was all he could do to force himself to wait until he was sure Elena had returned home from work before he called to check on her. Expecting to hear her usual clear, concise greeting, he knew as soon as she picked up the phone that something was wrong. Her voice quavered when she answered and he could tell she was sniffling back tears.

"What's happened?" he demanded, sitting up from his slouched position in the armchair. The silence on the other end of the line was killing him—second by slow, agonizing second. "Talk to me, honey. Are you all right?"

"No." Her voice was little more than a whisper when she finally answered, and he had to strain to hear her. But that one word caused icy fingers of fear to wrap around his heart and his lungs to feel as if he couldn't draw in air.

"I'll be right over," he said, punching the off button on the cordless phone. He pitched it at the couch and ran into the bedroom for his shoes. His heart pounded against his rib cage like a jungle drum and his graphic curses as he struggled into his coat sent Babe diving for cover under the couch pillows.

Driving at speeds that would probably have gotten him thrown in jail had a patrolman tried to stop him, Brett made it to Elena's in record time. Thankfully, one of the other tenants in her building was leaving as he arrived, and he dashed through the entrance without having to wait for her to buzz him in.

Taking the stairs two at a time, he ran down the hall to pound on her door. "Elena, open up!"

It seemed it took forever for her to release the locks and open the door. When she did, his heart felt as if it dropped to his feet. Tears streaked down her porcelain-pale cheeks, and her hand shook as she wiped at them with a tissue.

"What's wrong?" he demanded, pulling her into his arms. "Is it the baby?"

She shook her head as she wrapped her arms around his waist and pressed her cheek to his chest. "No."

Relieved that she still had Peanut tucked safely inside of her, he moved them farther into the apartment in order to close the door, then led her over to the couch. Sitting down, he pulled her onto his lap and held her while she sobbed against his shoulder. Unsure of what else to do, he stroked her silky brown hair and murmured what he hoped were words of comfort as her tears ran their course.

When she finally quieted, he asked, "What happened, honey?"

"I...saw Michael today at SIU headquarters." She sounded defeated.

Brett felt his gut burn at the mention of the man's name. Did she still harbor feelings for the jerk?

"And?" he prompted.

She dabbed at her eyes. "He took great delight in telling me...his new wife is scheduled for a C-section a week from today...to deliver their son."

Valentine's Day. It took a moment for Brett to remember why that day was significant. Then it hit him. It was the one-year anniversary of the man walking out on her.

Brett wasn't sure he wanted to know the answer, but he had to ask. "Does it bother you that Delgado remarried?"

"No." Her lack of hesitation made him feel a little better.

"Then what's wrong, honey?" he asked, soothing the tight muscles at the base of her neck.

She took a deep breath, then sat up to look at him. "It's ridiculous."

"That's okay," he said, giving her a smile he hoped was encouraging. "It's a big deal to you. That's all that matters."

Glancing down at her hands, she shook her head. "It just hurts that Michael's wife is able to do what I don't seem capable of doing."

"You mean have a baby?" he asked gently.

She nodded. "Why is it so easy for some women, but not me? What's wrong with me?"

"Look at me, Elena," Brett said. When she raised her eyes to meet his, he placed his hand on her stomach. "There's nothing wrong with you. You're pregnant and the doctor said you and the baby are both doing fine."

She bit her lower lip to keep it from trembling as she nodded.

"Considering the problems you had in the past, it's only natural for you to be concerned." He cupped her cheek with his hand. "But you don't have the stress of a shaky marriage to deal with this time, and you're already further along than you've ever been before. Right?"

"Right."

He hugged her close. "Then I'd say a celebration is in order, wouldn't you?"

For the first time since he'd entered the apartment, she smiled, making him feel like the sun had come out on a rainy day. "I guess so."

"Go wash your face and change clothes," he said. "I'm taking you out."

"Where are we going?"

"You'll see," he said, grinning.

"What are we doing *here?*" Elena asked, when he parked the Jag in front of Baby World.

"We're going to make this baby thing more real for you," he said, opening the driver's door. He gave her the grin that always made her stomach flutter. "Besides, Peanut is going to need a bed."

"But I'm—" She waited for him to come around the front of the car to open her door. "I'm not ready for baby furniture. I have to clear out the spare bedroom, paint—"

"Forget painting." He took her by the elbow and led her to the entrance of the brightly lit store. "It's not good for the baby. We'll pick out wallpaper while we're here.''

Elena dug in her heels, forcing him to stop just inside the double doors of the store. ''How do you know what's good for a baby and what isn't, Connelly?''

''I read all about it in the magazine you gave me the other day in the doctor's office,'' he said, his grin smug. He turned to look at the huge display room. ''Now, what colors do you want for the nursery?''

She laughed and shook her head. ''You read one magazine article and you think you're an expert. You're impossible.''

''Impossibly amazing,'' he said, sounding quite confident and more than a little pleased with himself. ''Now, let's see what this place has to offer in the way of baby stuff.''

''I'm not buying anything tonight,'' she warned him.

''That's okay.'' He took her by the hand and led her toward the furniture department on the far side of the store. ''We'll just look and see what they have.''

Elena shook her head as she followed Brett through several full nursery displays. How could she be angry with the man? He'd come running when he thought there was something seriously wrong, had seemingly understood her ridiculous reasons for feeling lower than dirt, then kept her laughing with outrageous questions and comments about what purpose the different items of baby furniture served.

''Did you see anything you liked?'' he asked as they stood looking at the last color-coordinated set.

Pointing several displays over, she nodded. ''The yellow-and-white ensemble was my favorite. It's bright and cheerful and the light oak furniture is beautiful.''

"Then yellow-and-white are your nursery colors,'' he said, leading her out of the furniture department and into an area filled with shelves of stuffed animals. He let go of her hand to examine some of the toys. "What do you think Peanut will like more, bears or bunnies?''

"I don't know,'' she said, laughing as he rubbed several of the toys against his lean cheek. "What are you doing?''

"Checking for softness.'' He sneezed. "That one sheds.'' He placed the furry rabbit back on the shelf, then picked up a large white bear with a yellow gingham ribbon around its neck. Apparently satisfied by the feel of its fur against his skin, he grinned. "I like this one.''

"Babe is going to be jealous,'' she warned.

He held the bear in the crook of one arm, took Elena by the hand and headed for the checkout. "This isn't for me. It's for you until Peanut arrives.'' He stopped suddenly to put his finger under her chin and tilt her face until their gazes met. "Every time you look at this bear, I want you to remember that you have Peanut inside of you and that your dream of being a mother will come true. That he—''

"She,'' Elena corrected him.

He grinned. "Or *she* will be here very soon.''

Touched by his thoughtfulness, Elena swallowed around the lump in her throat. "Thank you, Brett.'' A tear slowly trickled down her cheek.

"Don't cry, honey,'' he said, wiping it away with the pad of his thumb. "It's just a teddy bear.''

"It's not the bear, silly. It's the gesture. This is one

of the sweetest, most thoughtful things anyone's ever done for me." Reaching up, she placed a kiss on his cheek. "Thank you."

On Valentine's Day afternoon, Brett sat at his desk, staring out the window at Lake Michigan. He wanted to do something for Elena, but couldn't figure out what that something should be.

All she had were difficult memories to represent the day, and this one didn't seem to be shaping up any better. Not only did it mark the anniversary of the breakup of her marriage, her ex-husband's child was scheduled to be born today.

How could he take the focus off the past and make the day something she'd remember fondly? How could he go about doing that without getting more emotionally involved than he already was?

Deciding that taking her out for dinner was about the best he could do, Brett paged Fiona and told her to make reservations at one of Chicago's most exclusive restaurants.

But fifteen minutes later he pressed the off button on his intercom with a curse. Every place Fiona had called was booked solid, and some even had a waiting list.

Frustrated, he glanced around the room, his gaze coming to rest on the collage of family pictures hanging on the far wall. As he stared at the photo of himself and Drew taken the summer they built their cabin on the family property up at Lake Geneva, an idea began to form.

Satisfied that he'd found the perfect solution, Brett picked up the phone and made the arrangements, then walked down the hall to the conference room. He knew exactly how to get Elena to accompany him without tipping her off that he had something up his sleeve.

When he entered the room, he found her alone. "I need to talk to you."

"Do you even know how to knock, Connelly?" she asked, looking up from her notes. The smile she wore took the sting out of her words. "You're lucky my last interview just left, or I'd be forced to arrest you for obstructing an investigation."

He barely resisted the urge to hold out his wrists for her to cuff him. Instead, he adopted what he hoped was a worried expression. "I just got a call that my cabin up on Lake Geneva may have been broken into. I'm headed up there to check it out. Would you like to go along in case it has something to do with your investigation?"

Her smile vanished. "Of course." She stood and quickly gathered her notes. "How did you find out about the break-in?"

He hated lying to her. "The caretaker didn't say it was a break-in exactly, just that it looked like someone had been inside."

"Have you notified the authorities up there?"

"No."

She gave him a suspicious look. "Why not?"

He blinked. What reason could he give her? Naturally, if there had been the possibility of a real break-in that was the first thing he'd have done.

Think, Connelly.

"I, uh, thought you might want to check it out first," he said, hoping his excuse made sense. "You know, on the outside chance there's evidence that someone unfamiliar with the case would overlook."

"Or inadvertently destroy while checking things out," she said, agreeing with him. "That's happened more times than I care to count."

Brett glanced at his watch. "If we leave now, we should get up there with plenty of daylight left to look around." He took her coat from the brass coat tree by the door and holding it for her, added, "It might not be a bad idea if we change clothes before we head up that way."

She turned to face him. "Why?"

Giving himself a mental pat on the back for having a logical answer this time, he said, "It's cold and there's a lot of snow on those rural roads. If we get stuck, I'd rather we have on heavier clothing than what we wear to the office."

"Good point." She glanced down at her black suit coat and matching skirt. "Jeans and a sweatshirt would definitely be more practical."

Guiding her out of the conference room, Brett congratulated himself on his plan and the skillful way he'd executed it. Everything was going off without a hitch.

Elena hoped Brett's visibility was better from the driver's side of the car than from where she sat in the passenger seat. The snow flurries that had started falling as they left Chicago had turned into a full-fledged blizzard by the time they'd reached the Wisconsin state line.

"Can you see where you're going?" she asked.

"Barely," he said, shifting the car into a lower gear and steering it off the main road onto a narrow lane. "The weather report said this storm front wouldn't move through for days."

When Babe whined from her spot between Elena's feet, Elena reached down to give the little dog a reassuring pat on the head. "Somebody at the weather service missed this forecast."

"Obviously," Brett muttered, navigating the tree-lined road.

The snow slacked off a bit, and in the approaching twilight of late afternoon, Elena could see the shape of a large house through the branches of the leafless trees. "Is that the cabin?" she asked incredulously.

"That's it." When the low-slung car came to an abrupt stop, he muttered an oath. "We're stuck in a snowdrift. We'll have to walk the rest of the way."

"Some cabin," she said, staring at the impressive structure. "I've seen smaller apartment buildings."

"I never really thought about it," he said, shrugging. "You don't like it?"

She shook her head. "I didn't say that. It's just not as small or as rustic as I expected it to be."

He grinned as he reached for the door handle. "Well, it's made out of logs."

She stared at the two-and-a-half-story house. "So this is where your family vacations?"

"Nope." Getting out of the car, he waded through the drift to open the passenger door. "My mom and dad's cottage is on the other side of the property. This belongs to me and Drew. After his wife died, we spent the following summer up here putting it together."

"You two built it?"

Nodding, he admitted, "We had a crew helping us position the logs and put up the trusses, but we worked right along with them. And we did the majority of the interior work ourselves."

"I'm impressed," she said, truly meaning it.

He looked puzzled. "Why? Log homes come as precut kits and all we had to do was put it together."

"Yes, but that took a lot of work for something this big," she said, handing him Babe. "I don't guess I thought of you as the type to enjoy physical labor."

As he took the dog from her, he leaned forward to whisper close to her ear. "Don't tell anyone, but I enjoy a lot of physical activities. And I'm *very* good at most of them."

Tingles of excitement raced through her at the feel of his warm breath on her skin and the insinuation of what else he was good at doing. "I'll take your word on that," she said, feeling her cheeks color.

Get your mind back to business, Delgado. Thinking about Brett in any way other than being a friend could prove disastrous.

She reached into her handbag to remove her service revolver, but when she stepped out of the car into the snow, Brett blocked her path. He set Babe down, then stood with his fists planted on his lean hips.

"What do you think you're doing?" he asked.

"I'm preparing to investigate a potential crime scene." She pushed at his chest to get him to move. It didn't do a bit of good. The man was built rock solid and wasn't about to budge. "What's wrong with you, Brett? We came up here to check out—"

"Put the gun away," he demanded.

She shook her head. "If there's been a break-in—"

"There hasn't been." Before she realized what he was doing, Brett reached out and took the gun from her, then shoved it into his jacket pocket. "But if there had been, there's no way I'd let you go in there ahead of me.'' He turned around and bent down. ''Climb on my back.''

''I can walk.''

''No, you can't.'' He reached behind him to place his hands behind her thighs and pulled her up and onto his back.

Surprised by his sudden move, she had to link her arms around his neck in order to steady herself. ''Put me down.''

''No.''

''What's going on here, Connelly?''

''I'm giving you a piggyback ride.''

She tried not to enjoy the feel of her breasts pressed to his strong back. ''If someone is in there—''

He started walking toward the cabin. ''Trust me. There isn't.''

''You don't know for sure, unless—'' She gasped. ''This is a setup, isn't it?''

Brett stopped trudging through the snow and turned his head to glance over his shoulder at her. ''It sure is.''

He walked the few short yards to the wraparound deck and bent down to lower her to her feet. Unlocking the door, he turned to cup her cheek with his palm. The look in his blue eyes took her breath. ''I wanted you to have something good to remember about Valentine's Day.''

Struck speechless, Elena followed when he took her by the hand and led her through the house and into the huge great room. Distracted by Babe racing by them to dive under the pillows on the leather sofa in front of the big stone fireplace, she needed a moment to notice the table set for two in front of the wall of windows overlooking the lake.

Tears filled her eyes. A single white taper in a silver holder sat in the center of the table, the ring of red roses surrounding its base adding a splash of color to the white linen tablecloth.

"Oh, Brett," she said, turning to look at him. He held his arms out, and she didn't think twice about walking into his embrace. "No one has ever done anything this nice for me."

"Please tell me these are happy tears," he said, holding her close.

"They are." She leaned back to look up at him. "Why did you do it?"

His smile warmed her insides and caused her toes to curl. "Because you deserve it." He wiped the tears from her cheeks. "And because I wanted to do something that you could look back on with fond memories."

"Thank you, Brett," she said, wondering how she could ever have thought him to be anything like Michael.

She reached up on tiptoe to give him a brief kiss, but the moment their lips met, he pulled her to him and took control. His firm lips moved over hers with such exquisite thoroughness that heat streaked to every cell in her body. His tongue traced her mouth, asking her permission, letting her know that he wanted to take the caress further. Without hesitation she opened for him. She wanted the feel of his tongue mating with hers, wanted to savor the taste that was uniquely Brett.

As soon as he slipped inside to tease and stroke, her knees felt as if they'd turned to jelly, and she had to wrap her arms around his neck to keep from melting into a puddle at his feet. She moaned when he pressed himself to her, allowing her to feel the hard ridge of his arousal, his growing need for her.

Holding her close, he slowly slid one hand beneath the tail of her sweater, then brought it up to gently cup her breast. The heat of his strong palm holding her, the pad of his thumb teasing her sensitive nipple through the lace of her bra, created an aching need deep inside, and Elena gasped at the strength of the feeling.

"It's all right, honey," he said, trailing kisses from her mouth to the column of her throat. "Nothing is going to happen that you don't want to happen."

Momentarily incapable of speech, she could only nod.

He removed his hand and smoothed her sweater back into place, then gazed down at her with slumberous navy eyes. "I want you to sit down and relax while I go check on our dinner."

"Is there anything I can do to help?" she asked finally, making her vocal chords work.

He shook his head. "No. I'm going to take care of everything. This evening is just for you. All you have to do is enjoy it."

When he kissed the tip of her nose and turned to light the logs in the fireplace, Elena bit her lower lip as reality began to invade her thoughts. They were in a remote area of the Connelly property on Lake Geneva. It was still snowing, and the car was stuck in a drift. Their chances of returning to the city before sometime tomorrow were down to zero and sinking. And they wanted each other.

A shiver of intense longing coursed through her at the thought. Not even in the four years of her marriage had the desire to be intimate with a man been this intense.

She wrapped her arms around herself and turned to stare at the table for two, the candle's dancing flame reflected in the windows overlooking the lake. They were stranded, the setting couldn't be more romantic and there was an attraction between them that bordered on explosive.

If that wasn't a recipe for destroying her peace of mind and breaking her heart, she didn't know what was.

Eight

Brett watched Elena over the flicker of candlelight and wondered how he was ever going to keep his hands to himself. She was absolutely gorgeous and the most desirable woman he'd ever known. And the irony of it all was that she didn't even realize it.

She had no way of knowing that the soft glow of the candle's flame made him want to see her lying gloriously nude in his bed, her satiny skin glistening with perspiration from their lovemaking. Nor did she realize how watching her sweet, perfect mouth sip sparkling white grape juice from a champagne glass made him want her lips kissing him, tasting him as he wanted to taste her.

When she picked up a chocolate-covered strawberry, bit into it, then licked the juice from her fingers with the tip of her tongue, he swallowed hard and barely suppressed a groan. What had he been thinking when he'd called Sam, the Connelly's Lake Geneva caretaker, and asked if the man's wife, Rosie, could prepare a Valentine's dinner for two? What made him think that he could remain detached from the situation? And how the hell was he going to survive when the second phase of his plan was executed?

Brett had no doubt that Elena would love it. But he'd already suffered heart palpitations from the kiss they'd shared earlier. If she kissed him like that again, he wasn't sure he'd be able to stop himself from throwing her over his shoulder, carrying her upstairs and ravishing her lovely body for the rest of the night.

Of course, her reaction—the surprise and happiness he'd seen in her beautiful brown eyes—when they'd first walked into the cabin had been worth it. He'd known for sure that he'd accomplished his mission. He'd given her a Valentine's Day memory that she could look back on without sadness or regret. That alone was well worth whatever hell he had to go through.

Glancing out the windows at the lake, he noticed that the flurries had stopped and the clouds had cleared, allowing the moon and stars to cast a soft-blue glow over the newly fallen snow. Sam should be arriving any minute to pick them up.

As if on cue the doorbell rang.

"You weren't expecting anyone, were you?" Elena asked, frowning.

Brett couldn't help but smile at her cautious expression. "Always the suspicious detective, aren't you?" He rose, then held out his hand. "Come with me."

"What have you got up your sleeve this time, Connelly?" she asked. But she trustingly placed her hand in his, and the touch of her soft palm sent his blood pressure soaring. He might just have to strip down and roll around in the snow in order to cool his libido.

Taking their coats from the closet beside the door, he held hers out for her. "Close your eyes."

"What are you—"

"Hush," he said, placing his finger to her lips. "Trust me. You'll like this last surprise."

When she looked up at him, Brett swallowed hard. She did trust him. He could tell. But if she only knew what deliciously wicked scenario had been running through his mind just moments ago as he gazed at her over the flicker of the candle, she would probably use her gun on him.

He quickly placed his hand over her eyes before she had a chance to read the desire he was sure blazed in his. Putting his arm around her shoulder, he led her outside and down the steps.

As they passed Sam and Rosie, the middle-aged man nodded and gave Brett a grin. "Nice night, isn't it?"

"Who's that?" Elena asked, turning her head in the man's direction.

"Elena, I'd like you to meet Sam and Rosie," Brett said, removing his hand from her eyes. "Sam takes care of the houses and grounds for us here at Lake Geneva, and Rosie is the best cook in southern Wisconsin."

"It's nice to meet you, Sam," Elena said, shaking the hand of the man in front of her. Turning to Rosie, she asked, "Are you the one responsible for that delicious dinner?"

"Yes, ma'am," Rosie said, beaming. "Did you find it to your liking?"

Elena smiled and placed her hand over her stomach. "It was heavenly and I'm positively stuffed."

She wondered why Brett had made meeting the couple such a big secret, until Sam took a step back. "Ready to go for your ride?"

Elena's gaze followed the sweeping gesture of his hand to the horse-drawn sleigh behind him. "Oh, my Lord!" she gasped, covering her mouth with both hands.

"Do you like the rest of my surprise?" Brett whispered close to her ear.

Throwing her arms around his neck, she kissed his cheek. "I love it. It's so…so wonderful."

"Don't cry," he said quickly. "In this temperature your tears will turn to little ice cubes." He placed a kiss on her forehead and helped her climb into the antique black sleigh. Seating himself beside her, he pulled several heavy blankets over their laps, then took up the reins. "We won't be too long," he said to Sam.

The man nodded as he slapped the chestnut-colored horse on the rump. "Take your time and have a nice ride. Rosie and I will take care of cleaning up while you're gone."

Elena watched the couple start up the steps to the deck. "They seem so nice."

Brett nodded. "They are. They've worked for us since before Drew and I were born."

As he guided the horse onto the lane, Elena's attention was captured by the sights and sounds of the wintry night. Moonlight shining through the naked tree branches cast an ethereal glow over the landscape. The swish of the sleigh runners sliding over the snow and the horse's muffled hoofbeats were the only sounds interrupting the otherwise silent night.

"It's like something out of a fairy tale," Elena whispered. "It's magical."

"You deserve magic," Brett said, turning his head to smile at her. The expression on his handsome face told her that he meant every word of what he'd said, and she lost a little bit more of her heart to the man who had given her the Valentine's Day memory of a lifetime.

They rode in easy silence for some time before he turned the horse onto a path that led off through the woods. The darker shadows of the thick trees blotted out the moonlight and lent an intimacy to the quiet night that made Elena feel as if the world had been reduced to just the two of them.

"Where does this lead?" she asked, snuggling closer to him.

"Down to a little cove," he answered, his deep baritone sending a shiver up her spine that had nothing to do with the chilly air. As the sleigh emerged from the tree-lined trail, Brett drew the horse to a stop and pointed toward the lake ahead. "I thought you might like to see this."

Stars twinkled above, and the moon shone brightly over the frozen surface of Lake Geneva. The powdery white snow covering the shoreline glistened in the moonlight, making it look as if diamond dust had been cast over everything.

Elena's breath caught at the sight. "Brett, it's beautiful!"

"I thought you'd like it," he said, putting his arm around her to draw her closer.

They stared at the picture-perfect landscape for several long minutes before she kissed his lean cheek. "I love it. I don't think I've ever seen anything more breathtaking. Thank you for sharing it with me."

"I've seen something more breathtaking," he said, lowering his head to hers. "You."

Holding the reins in one gloved hand, he cupped her face with the other, then brought his mouth down on hers. Excitement instantly tingled every nerve in her body as he gently traced the outline of her lips, then slipped his tongue inside to stroke her with a featherlight touch. The kiss was so sweet, yet so provocative that Elena felt deep need begin to coil in the pit of her stomach.

Brett secured the leather reins to the front of the sleigh, then took her into his arms. Holding her close, he kissed his way from her cheek down to the sensitive hollow behind her ear.

"You're so soft, so sweet," he murmured against her skin.

Unbuttoning her coat, he slipped his hand inside. But when he cupped her breast, they both groaned in frustration at the barriers of her heavy sweater and his leather glove.

"We need to be getting back," he finally said, leaning back to draw her coat together. "I don't want you to get chilled."

She nodded as she tried to get her breathing to return to normal. "It would probably be best. But I don't think you have to worry about my getting cold. At the moment, I'm feeling quite warm."

He chuckled as he dropped a kiss on the tip of her nose. "Me, too." Taking up the reins again, he steered the horse onto the path leading back to the lane. Brett was quiet for several long moments before he said, "You do realize we'll have to spend the night here."

"I had that much figured out," she admitted. "It's probably going to take quite a bit of digging to get your car out of that drift."

He shrugged. "Sam can bring the tractor over and pull it out in the morning. I'd ask him to do it tonight, but it's getting late. Besides, by tomorrow morning the road crews should have everything plowed." She heard him inhale deeply, then as if coming to a decision, he added, "I want you to know that I didn't bring you up here with seduction in mind."

"I never thought you did," she said, meaning it. Brett had never tried to hide his attraction to her, but he'd never taken it any further than a few heated kisses.

He nodded. "I meant what I said earlier, Elena. I won't do anything you don't want me to. You're safe with me." He paused for a moment, then continued. "But I think it's only fair to warn you that when we get back to the cabin, I'm going to have a hell of a time keeping my hands off you." He turned his head to look at her, and the desire she saw in his dark blue eyes took her breath away. "I want you, Elena."

She thought about what he said for the rest of the ride back to his house. A mental image of Brett's hands on her body, caressing, teasing, coaxing, sent a delicious heat racing straight to the pit of her stomach.

Did she want to continue keeping Brett at arm's length? Or did she want him to take her into his arms and show her how deeply his passion ran. Did she want to allow herself to revel in making love with the man she'd fallen in love with?

Time seemed to stand still at the knowledge that she'd fallen in love with Brett Connelly. How could she have let that happen? Hadn't she sworn never to give another man that kind of power over her—the ability to devastate her emotionally?

She glanced over at him as he skillfully steered the horse along the snow-packed lane. She'd tried her best to keep her distance from him. But he'd made that an impossible task.

From the moment they met, he'd gone out of his way to lend her the support and encouragement that she'd never known. He'd stayed with her at the hospital when she'd feared losing her baby, then later opened his home to her when he learned she had nowhere else to go. He'd gone out of his way to make sure she took care of herself and didn't overdo things. He expressed a genuine concern for her safety and had taken it upon himself to squire her around the city as if he had nothing better to do.

He'd even been with her for the first glimpse of the life growing inside of her. And although she was sure he hadn't fully understood why it bothered her, Brett had helped her overcome the self-doubt that she'd suffered at the news of her ex-husband and his new wife having a child.

How could a woman not fall head over heels for a man who had appointed himself her own personal white knight? A man who went out of his way to replace bad Valentine's memories with good ones?

When Brett pulled the horse to a stop by the steps of the deck, Elena looked around. She'd been so lost in thought, they'd arrived back at his cabin without her even realizing it.

"Did Brett show you the cove?" Rosie asked as she and Sam stepped out of the house onto the deck.

"Yes, he did," Elena answered. She placed her hands on Brett's shoulders as he helped her down from the sleigh. "It was quite beautiful."

"I always love taking a ride down there right after it snows," the woman said, looking expectantly at Sam.

Chuckling, Sam shook Brett's hand. "Looks like we'll be taking the long way back to the lodge."

Brett grinned mischievously. "You two kids have fun."

Sam laughed as he helped Rosie into the sleigh. "We will."

"I put the leftovers in the fridge, and Sam walked your dog, Brett," Rosie said, holding the blankets so Sam could climb in beside her.

"Thanks for helping me this evening on such short notice," Brett said.

Settling himself on the seat beside his wife, Sam nodded. "I'll be over here in the morning to pull your car out with the tractor."

Elena felt warmed all over when Brett looked at her for several long moments. The question in his eyes was undeniable and with a slight nod of her head, she gave him her answer.

Brett turned back to Sam. "Make it around noon."

"Will do," the man said, slapping the horse's rump with the reins. "Good night."

"'Night," Rosie called, waving as she and Sam started down the lane.

"Let's go inside the house and get warm," Brett said, taking Elena by the hand.

As soon as they walked into the cabin, he helped

her out of her coat, took off his own, then motioned her toward the great room. "Why don't you warm yourself by the fire, while I hang these up and make some hot cocoa?"

"Do you want me to help?" she asked.

"No." Touching her cheek with his index finger, he drew it down the line of her jaw, his gentle touch causing her breath to come out in shallow little puffs. "This evening is all for you, honey. I'm going to take care of everything."

Elena watched him hang their coats in the closet, then turn and walk toward the kitchen. He was giving her time to think about her decision, giving her time to change her mind. But that wasn't going to happen.

"Brett?"

"Yes?"

"I don't want cocoa."

The light in his eyes as he turned to face her caused heat to pool between her legs. "What do you want, Elena?" he asked, his voice deeper than it had been only seconds before.

"I want you," she said simply.

He walked up to her and drew her into his arms. "Once we go upstairs, there won't be any turning back," he warned. "I want you too much." His gaze caressed her face. "When we close the bedroom door I'm going to take off our clothes and make love to you until we're both exhausted."

"I'm going to hold you to that," she said, hardly recognizing her own voice. What else could she say? She wanted him in every way a woman could want a man.

Without another word, Brett stepped back, took her by the hand and led her up the planked staircase and into a huge bedroom. Closing the door behind them, he guided her over to stand in front of a pair of French doors on the far side of the room. He brushed her lips with his, then he opened the drapes to allow moonlight to flood the room with the same ethereal glow that it had cast on the snow at the cove.

"I want to see you bathed in moonbeams," he said, coming back to stand in front of her. "And I want you to see me."

Capturing her gaze with his, he reached for the end of her burgundy cable-knit sweater. "Hold your arms up for me, honey," he said as he slowly, carefully drew the garment up and over her head. He tossed it on a chair to one side of the doors, then unbuttoned her shirt.

When she placed her hands on the band of his sweatshirt, he shook his head. "Remember, you don't have to do anything but let me love you," he said, quickly pulling the shirt off to toss it on the chair with hers.

Elena's eyes widened at the sight of his sculptured physique. Reaching out, she reverently touched his smooth skin, the hard muscle beneath her fingers flexing and bunching as she lightly traced the ridges and plains of his chest and flat stomach. "You're beautiful."

"Not me," he said, parting her shirt to push it from her shoulders. His sharp intake of breath made her glad that she hadn't bothered with a bra. "You're the one who's beautiful."

He brought his hands up to cup her breasts, to tease her with his thumbs. Her nipples immediately hardened into pebbles of pure sensation and Brett leaned down to kiss each one with such tenderness it brought tears to her eyes.

He stepped back to shed the rest of his clothing, and she knew he was revealing himself to her first, in order to make her feel less vulnerable. Her heart swelled with love at his concession.

Turning to face her, he smiled, and the butterflies in her stomach went wild. Heat, combined with a delicious fluttering, pooled in the pit of her stomach, and her knees felt as if they might not support her. He was absolutely gorgeous.

Wide shoulders tapered down to lean flanks and narrow hips. Her gaze dropped lower. The strength of his thick arousal rising proudly from the patch of black curls at his groin caused her heart to stall. He wasn't a small man.

He must have read the sudden hesitance in her eyes. "You aren't frightened of me, are you, Elena?"

She shook her head. "It's not that I'm afraid exactly. It's just been a long time since—"

"It's going to be all right, honey." He stepped forward to thread his fingers in her shoulder-length hair. Tilting her head up, he smiled when their gazes met. "We'll take this slow and easy. I'm going to make sure everything is perfect for you. Trust me?"

When she nodded, he stepped back and knelt before her to pull off her boots and socks. Straightening, he brought his index finger up to touch the valley between her breasts, then trail it down her body to the snap on her jeans. He unfastened and unzipped the denim, then, catching her gaze with his, he slowly, carefully pushed them and her cotton panties from her hips.

Elena shivered at the heated look he gave her when

she stepped out of them. "You're perfect," he said, taking her into his arms.

He gently drew her forward until their bodies met, and she could feel her breasts pressed against his hard chest. The touch of skin to skin sent tiny sparks of pleasure skipping along every nerve in her body. She circled his neck with her arms and marveled at the man holding her.

The warm strength of his much larger body, the smell of his spicy cologne and the sound of his harsh breathing all combined to tighten the coil of desire deep inside of her. His hands caressed her back as he ran them the length of her spine to cup her bottom and pull her forward. She couldn't stop a tiny moan from escaping when his heated arousal came into contact with her soft belly.

Brett's answering groan let her know he was experiencing the same intense pleasure, feeling the same exquisite need. "You're so warm, so soft…" His lips brushed hers. "So sweet."

Closing his eyes, Brett took several deep breaths. He wanted Elena more than he'd ever wanted any woman, and it was going to take every ounce of control he'd ever possessed in order to take things slowly.

Incapable of speech, he brought his mouth down on hers to show her what he was feeling, to let her know how beautiful he thought she was and how much her trust meant to him. Her soft lips molded to his almost desperately, firing his blood and sending it surging through his veins with the speed of a raging river.

Her soft sigh allowed him entry to her sweetness, and he thought the top of his head might just come off when her small tongue boldly met his. She was answering him, letting him know that she felt the passion as keenly as he did.

Breaking the kiss, he led her to the bed and turned down the covers. She stared at him wordlessly for one long moment, then slid between the pristine sheets. His heart stalled, then slammed against his ribs with brutal force when she raised her arms in an age-old welcome.

It was then that his lack of planning hit him between the eyes. He hadn't anticipated making love with Elena and therefore hadn't planned for protection. But as he looked down at the woman inviting him into her arms, her very body, he realized there was no possibility of his making her pregnant. And it wouldn't matter to him if she wasn't already pregnant.

For the first time in his life, the thought of fathering a child somehow appealed to something deep inside him. It was something he didn't entirely understand and, at the moment, didn't want to.

Without another second's hesitation, he slid into bed beside her and gathered her into his arms. Desire thrummed through his veins, and he had to fight the urge to cover her with his body, to sink himself deep within her sweet depths. This was Elena's night, and if it killed him, he wasn't going to rush things, no matter what his body demanded.

When Brett pulled her to him, he pulsed with desire. He'd never felt anything so intense, so urgent as the need to claim her.

He trailed kisses down to the base of her throat, then past her collarbone to the slope of her breast. She threaded her fingers in his thick hair and held him to her when he took the hardened peak into his mouth. Sparkles of light much like the stars in the

inky night sky outside flashed behind his closed lids
when she arched her back to give him easier access
to her sensitive flesh.

"Please," she whimpered.

Her body heated with a need that stole her breath.
If Brett didn't make love to her soon and end the
sweet torture, Elena knew for sure she'd go mad.

"Not yet, honey," he said, lifting his head to look
at her. "I want you to remember this night for the
rest of your life."

She could have told him that he'd already given
her a night she'd never forget, but words failed her.
He was trailing his hand down her side to her hip and
beyond. He cupped her mound of curls, parting her
to stroke the tight nub of pleasure, then dip his finger
inside.

Tears filled her eyes from the pleasure of his intimate touch. "I need you, Brett," she said, her voice
little more than a whisper. "Now."

His breathing was as ragged as hers as he nudged
her knees apart and levered himself over her. He
kissed her tenderly and moved his lower body into
position. At the first touch of his blunt tip, the coil
inside her tightened unbearably.

"Look at me, Elena," he said, his voice sounding
like a rusty hinge.

He held her gaze with his and slowly, carefully
pushed himself forward. Her body seemed to melt
around him as he sank deeper and deeper into her.
Never had she felt so filled, so exquisitely stretched.
She raised her hips for more of him and when he was
buried completely, she sighed at the pleasure of being
one with him.

"So tight," he said between clenched teeth.

He eased his hips back then forward, thrusting into her again and again, increasing the rhythm with each stroke. She wrapped her legs around his lean waist in an effort to get closer, and the pressure of his body pressed so intimately with hers had her poised at the edge of fulfillment.

Brett must have recognized her readiness because he thrust deeply into her one last time, causing her body to be swept up in wave upon wave of satisfaction.

A groan rumbled up from deep in his chest and his big body shuddered as he poured himself into her, then collapsed from the force of his own climax.

Reality slowly descended on Brett, and it was several minutes before he found the strength to move to Elena's side. Gathering her protectively against him, he knew for certain he'd just experienced the most powerful lovemaking of his life. Never had his pleasure been more intense, more debilitating than with Elena. And although it scared the hell out of him, it also made him feel complete in a way he'd never felt before.

"Are you all right?" he asked, gently touching the soft roundness of her stomach.

"Yes," she said, her breath feathering his chest as she spoke. "That was incredible."

Chuckling, he nodded. "I couldn't agree more."

She yawned, and he realized that she had to be exhausted. The magazine he'd read in the doctor's office had said that expectant mothers required more sleep in the first and last months of a pregnancy.

Brett kissed the top of her head, then pulled the sheet and comforter over them. "Rest now, honey."

He'd no sooner said the words than he realized Elena had already drifted off into a peaceful sleep.

Staring at the ceiling, Brett held her close and thought about the feelings that coursed through him. He'd never before felt this way after making love to a woman. The degree of possessiveness coursing through him was so strong it was almost palpable.

Absently stroking the soft skin of her lower belly, he thought about the emotional attachment that he'd let form for Elena and Peanut. He tried to remind himself that relationships were dangerous, that unless he wanted to risk suffering the same hell his twin brother had suffered, he'd do well to distance himself now. But the thought of not being with Elena, of taking her back to Chicago and asking his father to assign one of his other siblings to the task of helping her with the interviews, was unthinkable.

It was a completely new and alien concept to him, and one he wasn't at all comfortable with. But he wanted to be with her, wanted to be a part of her and Peanut's lives.

He just wished he knew how to go about doing that without risking his heart in a relationship that he knew for certain would destroy him if Elena ever walked away.

Nine

The sun was turning the early-morning sky to pearl gray when Elena opened her eyes to look over at the man sleeping beside her. Brett had awakened her during the night to make love to her again, and her feelings for him increased tenfold each time they came together. She'd never known a man who put her pleasure before his, who was more concerned with pleasing her than satisfying himself.

Of course, there had only been Michael before Brett, and even though she'd first thought they were exactly alike, she'd quickly learned there was no comparison between the two men. Michael was a shallow, self-centered playboy with nothing on his mind but his own selfish pleasure, while Brett had depth and character and went out of his way to see to her welfare and happiness.

From the moment they met, Brett had been there

for her in a way she wasn't used to. He'd taken care
of her when she'd pushed herself too hard with work,
been there with her to share the happiness at the doctor's office and comforted her when she'd let her fears
get the best of her. Brett had seen her at her most
vulnerable, yet it hadn't caused him to run in the opposite direction as it would have with Michael.

No, Brett and Michael were worlds apart, and it
was past time to admit that she loved Brett in a way
that she'd never loved Michael.

Easing from beneath Brett's arm where it draped
her stomach, Elena got out of bed, gathered her
clothes and went into the master bathroom for a quick
shower. It was going to take time to get used to the
idea of loving again, of putting her faith and trust in
another man.

She'd just stepped beneath the refreshing spray
when the shower door opened and Brett stepped inside. "What are you doing here?" she demanded,
suddenly feeling self-conscious. She wasn't sure, but
she had a good idea that moonlight streaming through
a bedroom window was much more flattering than the
bright lights of a bathroom.

"I missed you," he said.

He must have noticed her apprehension, because
he took her into his arms and kissed her until the
world spun dizzily around her. When he raised his
head, he smiled that charming smile that never failed
to set the butterflies fluttering wildly in her stomach.

"You're beautiful."

"So are you," she said breathlessly, deciding there
was no lighting, natural or artificial, that could make
Brett look anything less than perfect.

Without a word he released her to pick up the soap

from the built-in holder in the shower wall and, rubbing it into a rich lather, he ran it over her back then
around to her chest. He placed the soap back in the
soap dish, then cupped her breasts with his soapy
hands. His gaze caught hers, and the desire in his
eyes, his heart-stopping grin as he tenderly circled her
nipples with his slick thumbs caused her pulse to race.

As Brett leisurely smoothed his hands over her
body, Elena's head fell back and she let the exquisite
sensations overtake her. She'd never realized how
erotic the simple act of taking a shower could be. But
then she'd never had a man bathe her before.

He massaged and soothed, caressed and teased everywhere he touched, and by the time he reached the
apex of her thighs, she thought she'd go mad from
the need he had created. Pure, electrified desire raced
over every nerve in her body as his hands skimmed
from her inner thighs to the sensitive folds of her
feminine flesh. He placed one arm around her back
to steady her, then parted her with his other hand to
stroke her intimately.

His mouth came down on hers almost desperately,
and she returned his kiss with the same degree of
urgency. When his tongue sought and found entry to
the inner recesses of her mouth, there was nothing
soft or tender about the invasion. He demanded her
uninhibited response and she gladly gave it, meeting
his advance with a boldness of her own, wordlessly
telling him what she wanted.

Unwilling to be denied the pleasure of touching his
body as he touched hers, she reached out to encircle
his engorged flesh, to measure his length and the
strength of his need for her. He shuddered against her

as she stroked him, and feminine power, pure and sweet, swept through her.

"We've got to get out of here," he said suddenly. He turned off the shower, then, pulling her with him, he opened the shower door to lower them both to the thick throw rug on the bathroom floor. "I can't wait," he said, his breathing ragged. "I want you now."

"Then take me," she said, positioning herself to cradle him to her.

Brett took hold of her hips and lifting her to him, knelt before her to join their bodies in one smooth stroke. The feel of her body surrounding him, the passion filling her eyes as he made them one sent his blood pressure to an all-time high and made his heart pound against his ribs in a primitive cadence. Her readiness for him, her unbridled response, took him to new heights of arousal and made setting a leisurely pace impossible.

Thrusting into her, he watched passion paint her cheeks a rosy glow, saw her brown eyes darken to deep pools of chocolate as he moved inside her. Never had lovemaking been so urgent, never had it felt so elemental and wild.

Moments later he felt her body tighten around his, saw her squeeze her eyes shut as she reached the peak. Grinding himself against her, he heard her cry of ecstasy a moment before her spasms of release gripped him and pulled him into the same tumultuous storm.

Throwing his head back, he felt as though her body drained him of his essence. With a groan that he barely recognized as his own, he fell forward and, gathering her to him in order to keep from crushing her, rolled to her side.

As they slowly floated back down to the realm of reality, the only sound in the bathroom for several long minutes was that of their labored breathing.

"Are you all right?" he finally managed to ask. "I didn't hurt you, did I?"

"I'm wonderful." She snuggled against him to press her lips to his chest. "That was incredible."

"You're incredible," he said, pulling her up to lie on top of him.

As he gazed into her soft-brown eyes, he realized that he could make love to Elena every day for the rest of his life and never get enough of her, never sate the passion that threatened to consume him every time they came together. And it scared him senseless.

"Let's get off this floor before you get chilled," he said suddenly.

He rose to his feet and pulled her up with him, then took two thick towels from the linen closet. Wrapping one around his waist, he draped the other around her shoulders and gently rubbed the terry cloth along the goose bumps on her upper arms and across her shoulders.

Even touching her through the thick towel wasn't preventing his body from reacting to her nearness. "I'm going to get dressed and take Babe for a walk," he said, needing the chill of the outside air to help cool the heat that was rapidly building within him once again.

Elena smiled, and his knees threatened to buckle. "I think I'll finish the shower that someone so delightfully interrupted," she said, opening the glass door to turn on the faucet.

If she kept looking at him like that, he'd wind up joining her again and Babe would never forgive him.

"I won't be long," he promised, dropping a kiss on her forehead and hurrying from the bathroom before he changed his mind.

Three hours later Elena absently patted Babe's small head as Brett pulled the Jag out of the lane and onto the main road. She hated leaving the winter wonderland of Lake Geneva. It reminded her of her native southern Illinois with its many lakes and lush trees.

Thinking of where she'd grown up reminded her that she hadn't been back to see her foster mother, Marie, in several months. Elena missed the woman who had been the closest thing to a mother that she'd ever known. If not for Marie Waters, Elena knew for certain she wouldn't be the person she was today. Having been abandoned when she was two years old, she'd been shuttled from one foster home to another until, at the age of fourteen, she'd finally been placed with Marie.

Elena smiled fondly at the thought of the woman who had an uncanny knack for accurately judging a person's character in the first few minutes of meeting them. She'd taken one look at Elena and had seen right through the tough exterior and false bravado to the hurting, uncertain teenager within.

Glancing at Brett, Elena wondered what Marie would think of him. She'd certainly been correct in her assessment of Michael Delgado. After meeting him only once, she'd proclaimed him nothing but a shifty-eyed womanizer with few, if any, redeeming qualities.

"What's so funny?" Brett asked, smiling at her.

Unaware that she'd laughed out loud at Marie's

description of her ex-husband, Elena gave him an embarrassed shrug. "Just thinking about Marie."

"That's your foster mother, right?"

She nodded. "She's a real character, and I miss getting to see her as much as I'd like."

"How far away does she live?" he asked, merging onto the interstate highway. He set the cruise control, then switched on the radio to a soft classical station.

"About 325 miles south of Chicago, in Johnston City."

"How often do you get to see her?" he asked, sounding genuinely interested.

"I try to get down there two or three times a year," she said, placing Babe on the floor between her feet. "That's usually the way I spend my vacation time." Leaning back against the seat, she yawned. "I've been thinking about making a trip home after the weather clears up a little more."

He reached over to take her hand in his. "You sound pretty tired."

She smiled. "That's because someone woke me up in the middle of the night and I missed out on a full night's sleep."

"Something came up," he said, his voice sounding so sexy that it made her stomach flutter wildly and her toes curl inside her boots. He brought her hand up to his lips. "We've got another hour's drive. Why don't you try to get a little sleep?"

"I think I will take a nap," she said, removing her hand from his. How could she sleep with him kissing her palm like that, reminding her of how his talented lips had felt on other parts of her body?

Deciding she'd do well not to think about last night, she closed her eyes and settled back against the

seat, certain there was no way she'd be able to rest
because of the man sitting next to her. But the soft
sounds of a harp solo on the radio lulled her with its
beauty, and she felt herself start to drift off. Her last
thoughts were of Brett and the most memorable Valentine's Day—and night—of her life.

Brett sat in his car in the parking garage at Connelly Tower on Monday morning, his apprehension
growing with each passing second. Elena should have
arrived twenty minutes ago. He'd tried calling her,
both at her apartment and on her cell phone. But the
answering machine had picked up at her home number, and he'd gotten voice mail when he dialed her
cellular. He hadn't bothered leaving a message on either.

Where could she be? More important, was she all
right?

When they returned Friday afternoon from Lake
Geneva, there had been a message on Elena's answering machine telling her that her car had been repaired and was ready to be picked up. He'd driven
her to the shop. Even though he didn't fully understand why, he didn't like the idea of her driving
around the city by herself. The thought of her job
taking her into some of the worst neighborhoods in
Chicago made his blood run cold.

He'd tried to convince her that car pooling made
more sense than both of them driving separately. But
she'd laughed and pointed out that he'd have to drive
ten minutes in the opposite direction to pick her up.
After that, he hadn't been able to come up with another plausible argument why it would be wise to
continue letting him drive her. He knew better than

to mention the real issue—his concern for her safety. They'd already covered that innumerable times, and she refused to listen to reason.

He checked his watch again. Thirty minutes late. Where could she be? Had she been in an accident? Were she and Peanut all right?

As he sat there trying to decide whether to go looking for her or call the police to report her as missing, her car pulled into an empty visitor's spot on the other side of the garage. Relieved that she hadn't been in an accident, he quickly got out of the car and marched over to her driver's door.

"It's about time," he muttered, his relief quickly turning to anger as he yanked the car door open. "Where the hell were you? You should have been here half an hour ago."

To his further irritation, she leisurely gathered her purse and briefcase before turning to face him. "My, aren't we in a good mood this morning," she said, smiling congenially.

She pushed at his chest to back him up, then got out of the car, locked it and started toward the elevator.

"Well?" he said, shortening his strides to match hers.

"'Well' what?" she asked, punching the call button. While she waited, she stood there humming a tune as if she didn't have a care in the world.

Brett couldn't believe he was letting her bait him, but try as he might, he couldn't seem to stop himself. "I was worried that you might have been in an accident...or worse."

"I wasn't," she said, smiling at him. She was purposely ignoring his bad mood.

When she didn't offer an explanation, he tried to stay calm but found his voice rising with each word. "I tried calling you, but got your answering—"

"So that was you." The elevator doors swished open and she walked inside. "You should have left a message."

Gritting his teeth, he stepped into the car beside her. "You were home and didn't pick up?"

"I was pulling on my panty hose."

"And I don't suppose it occurred to you to stop and pick up the phone," he said, lowering his voice as the elevator opened on the seventeenth floor.

"Actually, it did," she said, stepping out into the corridor. She started walking toward the conference room without elaborating on why she hadn't answered.

"And?" he prompted.

"I didn't want to run the risk of pushing my thumb through my hose or snagging them just to find out it was a telemarketer." She opened the conference room door and strolled over to place her briefcase on the table.

"It never occurred to you that it might be me?" he asked, slamming his briefcase on the polished mahogany surface. He knew he was being unreasonable, but at the moment he didn't care. She'd scared the hell out of him.

"It did occur to me that it might be you." She pulled off her coat to drape it over one of the chairs. "But I thought if it was, you'd leave a message."

He caught her around the waist and pulled her to him. He wasn't sure whether to yell at her for worrying him to the point of distraction or kiss her senseless.

"What the hell," he muttered, bringing his mouth down on hers.

When their lips met, she let loose a startled squeak, and Brett seized the opportunity to plunge his tongue inside. He wanted to punish her for making him worry, wanted to assure himself that she was all right. But the taste of her passion, the smell that was uniquely Elena's sent a jolt of need down his spine to swirl around and explode in his gut. Softening the kiss, he leisurely explored her mouth until they were both gasping for air.

"God, you scared me to death," he said. "Please don't do that again."

"I thought you knew my appointment with Jennifer Anderson wasn't until later this morning," she said, sounding breathless.

Brett thought for a moment, then shook his head. "When you talked to Jennifer, I was in the sunroom with Mom and Dad."

"I'm sorry you were worried, but I was just fine," she said, stepping back to straighten her navy linen suit.

A light tap on the door prevented him from answering, as Fiona stuck her head inside. "Mr. Connelly, Ms. Anderson is here to speak with Ms. Delgado. Would you like me to send her in?"

Before he could answer, Elena stepped around him. "Please give me about five minutes, then send her in, Fiona." Turning back to Brett, she smiled and straightened his tie. Her small hands touched the underside of his chin, causing him to swallow hard. "Just so you don't suffer another anxiety attack, this is my last interview. Unless there's a significant development in the case, I won't be coming back here to Connelly Tower.''

Brett's stomach twisted into a painful knot, and he felt as if the floor had dropped from beneath him. He'd purposely avoided thinking about her finishing the interviews, had refused to contemplate what his day would be like without the knowledge that she was right down the hall from him.

Finding the situation totally unacceptable, he picked up his briefcase from the conference table. ''We'll talk later.'' He needed time to think. ''Do you have plans for dinner?'' he asked suddenly.

''Not really.''

''Good.'' He placed a kiss on the tip of her nose. ''Why don't you come by my place around seven? I'll fix some of my famous vegetable lasagna.''

''You mean you'll go by Mario's for takeout,'' she said, laughing.

He grinned. ''I'll tell him you said hello.''

Elena watched him exchange a pleasant greeting with Jennifer Anderson as he held the door for the young woman to enter the room. Then, winking at Elena behind Jennifer's back, he disappeared down the hall.

Smiling, Elena turned her attention from the man she loved to the young woman walking toward her. ''I'm glad you were able to make it,'' Elena said, extending her hand to the pretty blonde. ''I hope you don't mind my asking to meet with you here at Connelly Tower instead of Lake Shore Manor.''

''Not at all,'' Jennifer said, shaking Elena's hand. ''It gave me the chance to spend a little more time with my daughter before I had to take her to the day-care center this morning.''

"How old is she?" Elena asked, motioning for Jennifer to take a seat at the table.

"Eighteen months," the young woman said proudly. Smiling, she asked, "When is your baby due?"

"I'm due in August. How did you know?" Elena hadn't told anyone connected to the Connellys except Brett.

Before Elena could decide on the method of execution she intended to use on him, Jennifer smiled. "You have that pregnant glow about you."

"Oh," Elena said, feeling her cheeks heat. "That's how you knew?"

Jennifer nodded. "What are you hoping for? A boy or a girl?"

Smiling, Elena placed her hand over her stomach. "I'm hoping for a girl."

"That's what I was hoping for when I found out I was pregnant with Sarah." She glanced down at her hands. "Naturally, my husband wanted a boy."

Elena knew the story of Jennifer's police officer husband and how he'd been killed during a drug bust gone sour. Although Elena had never met the man, she'd attended his funeral to show support for a fallen comrade, as had most of Chicago's police force.

"Have you been doing okay?" she asked, reaching out to touch Jennifer's tightly clenched hands.

The pretty young woman took a deep breath, then met Elena's concerned gaze head on. "It's not easy raising a child alone," she said carefully. "There's no one there to share the worries and fears or to help with the 1001 things that taking care of an infant entails."

Elena didn't know what to say. It sounded as

though the woman was warning her of the difficult time she had ahead of her. "I'm sure it isn't easy."

Deep regret shadowed Jennifer's wide green eyes. "But the worst part is having to be away from Sarah while I work." She hurried on to explain. "Please don't get me wrong. I love working for Mrs. Connelly and she's very good about letting me have time off when Sarah is ill. But I really hate missing most of my baby's firsts."

"You mean her first steps?" Elena asked, feeling the woman's pain.

Jennifer nodded. "That and her first word. The first time she pulled herself up to stand. The first time she crawled."

Elena really hadn't considered how she would feel when she had to leave her baby with someone while she worked. She had decided that she'd eventually take a desk job at SIU because of the more regular hours. But she'd thought it would be a few years down the line.

"I'm sorry if I've upset you," Jennifer apologized. "It's really tough taking care of a baby on your own, but I'm sure you'll do fine."

Nodding, Elena admitted, "I'm really looking forward to being a mother, but I still have a few things to work out."

Deciding that she needed to give it a lot more thought once she got home and had the time to give the matter her undivided attention, Elena opened her notebook and picked up her pencil. "Now, what can you tell me about the day someone tried to assassinate King Daniel?"

Ten

Brett glanced at the clock on the microwave. Time to light the candles. Elena should be there in a few minutes, and he wanted everything to be perfect when she arrived.

Touching the flame from the lighter to the wick, he surveyed his efforts. The candles were lit, the sparkling grape juice sat chilling in the silver ice bucket to one side of his chair, and the red rose in the crystal bud vase emitted just the right amount of fragrance.

Satisfied that he'd done everything he could in preparation for her arrival, he walked over to the windows to stare out at the quiet night. Surely Elena would see the wisdom in his proposition. She had to. He'd spent the entire day reviewing options and working out the details, and it had been the only acceptable solution.

When the doorbell rang, he smiled. Time to put his plan into action.

"Good evening, gorgeous," he said, opening the door to sweep her into his arms.

He brought his mouth down on hers but made sure he kept the kiss brief. He didn't want to be distracted from his mission.

"Good evening to you, too, handsome," she said, sounding breathless. Babe bounced around their feet, vying for attention, and Elena bent down to scratch behind the dog's ears.

"I missed you after you left Connelly Tower this afternoon," he said. When she straightened to look at him, he helped her out of her coat.

"I missed you, too," she said. Her soft voice sent his pulse into overdrive.

Brett quickly put his arm around her shoulders and his hand over her eyes. He not only wanted to surprise her, he needed to block her mesmerizing gaze before he forgot about his mission, picked her up and sprinted for the bedroom to make love to her until they both passed out from exhaustion.

She laughed as he led her toward the dining room. "You certainly have a flare for the dramatic, Connelly. What are you up to now?"

"Trust me, you'll like it," he whispered close to her ear. To his immense satisfaction, she shivered against him, and his confidence in his well-thought-out plan grew.

Stopping by her chair, he removed his hand and directed her attention to the table for two with a sweep of his arm. "Welcome to Café Brett."

"Brett, you didn't have to—"

He placed his index finger to her soft lips. ''I know I didn't have to do all this. I wanted to.''

''Thank you,'' she said, kissing the tip of his finger.

Seating her, he walked into the kitchen, took their salad plates from the refrigerator, then returned to the dining room. Once he'd set their places, he opened the grape juice, poured them each a goblet and took his seat on the opposite side of the table.

He stared at her for endless seconds. Why the hell was he so nervous? He was one of the best PR men in the business. He was good at selling ideas and negotiating deals. Besides, his plan was foolproof.

''So tell me about your day,'' he said, picking up his salad fork. His first bite of the leafy mixed greens might as well have been a mouthful of weeds, for all he could taste of them.

She took a sip of her grape juice before she answered. ''Let's see, after you left the conference room this morning I had a very interesting talk with Jennifer Anderson.'' Elena stared at her plate for a moment. When she looked up, Brett saw a good amount of worry clouding her eyes. ''I really feel sorry for Jennifer.''

''Why?''

''She's having a tough time right now,'' Elena answered. She placed her fork across the top of her salad plate. ''Life hasn't been very fair to her.''

''How do you mean?'' he asked, collecting their plates to take them to the kitchen.

She waited to answer him until he'd returned with plates of vegetable lasagna and slices of crusty garlic bread. ''She's just too young to be carrying so much responsibility.''

''I know she has a child,'' he said, biting off a

piece of the warm garlic bread. He wisely refrained from pointing out that Jennifer was only three years younger than Elena, and that in a few months she'd be in the same position as Jennifer—a working mother, trying to raise her child alone. "Are things really that hard for her?" he asked.

Elena nodded. "After her husband was killed in the line of duty, she not only had to deal with his death, she was pregnant and faced with the responsibility of raising her child alone. Not to mention having to find a job to support herself and the baby."

"To my knowledge Jennifer is paid pretty well for organizing my mom's social schedule," he said thoughtfully. "But if you think it would help, I'll talk to Mom about giving her a raise."

"It's not a money issue." He watched Elena push lasagna around her plate before putting her fork down and leaning back in her chair.

"Then what is it?" he coaxed when she remained silent.

She looked him square in the eye, and he could see that Elena wasn't just talking about Jennifer anymore. She was expressing her own fears as well. "Jennifer has missed out on so much. She wasn't there for her baby's first words, first steps."

Brett set his goblet on the table and reached for Elena's hand. It tore him apart to see the apprehension marring her lovely features, to see her worried about a problem for which he'd already found a solution.

"Come here," he said, scooting his chair back. He tugged on her hand, and she rose to step around to his side of the small table. Settling her on his lap, he wrapped his arms around her and pulled her to his chest. "Don't worry. You and Peanut are going to be just fine."

She sat up to look at him. "Do you really think so?"

"Trust me on this—I know so," he said, nodding.

She put her arms around his neck. "So you've looked into your crystal ball and know what the future holds for me?"

"Something like that."

He couldn't keep from smiling. His plan was going to work without a hitch. Time to make his proposal.

Elena leaned forward, and his pulse took off. So did all of his thoughts. Her soft lips on his were distracting enough, but when she used her tongue to part his mouth and slip inside, he thought he'd have a coronary.

Elena wasn't the least bit shy about letting him know what she wanted. And Brett loved it.

Her tongue stroked and teased his, and her delightful little bottom wiggled against the part of him that was changing so rapidly, making him glad that he'd chosen tailored slacks instead of jeans. He was harder than he'd ever been, and the confines of denim would have been painful.

Restlessness built inside of him and he tried to shift positions, but the dining room chair proved to be extremely restrictive. He wanted them both to have the freedom to once again explore each other with total abandon.

Breaking the kiss, he cradled her to him and stood up. "Let's take this where we can be more comfortable," he said, heading for his bedroom.

She didn't protest, but instead wrapped her arms around his shoulders and pressed her lips to the pulse pounding at the base of his throat. Raining tiny kisses all the way to his ear, she nipped at the lobe, and he thought his knees might give way right then and there.

When he reached the bedroom, Brett shouldered the door closed behind them, then set Elena on her feet at the side of the bed. "You're driving me crazy," he said, hardly recognizing his own voice.

The smile she gave him sent the blood racing through his veins. "It's only fair." She reached up to touch his face. "You drove me out of my mind at the cabin, now it's my turn to send you over the edge."

When she trailed her fingers down the middle of his chest, stopping just above his belt, his heart thumped against his ribs and his stomach muscles tightened. Tugging his shirt free from his trousers, she started at the bottom and slowly, painstakingly slipped each button through its hole. Her hands brushed his abdomen and chest, and by the time she reached the top, Brett found it hard to draw a breath. But when she pushed his shirt from his shoulders, then leaned forward to kiss his chest, he felt as if he might never breathe again.

He reached for her, but she shooed his hands away. "I'm running this show, Connelly. All you have to do is enjoy yourself."

He'd never harbored a lot of sexual fantasies. But he knew for sure that if he had, one of them was about to come true. He'd never been with a woman who took the part of the aggressor, and he found it excited the hell out of him that Elena wanted to do that.

Finding it hard to stand still, Brett placed his hands on her shoulders and rested his forehead against hers. "You're killing me, honey."

"You don't like what I'm doing?" she asked,

bending to remove his shoes and socks, then hers. Straightening, she unbuckled his belt.

He chuckled and shook his head. "I didn't say that."

"What are you saying, Brett?" She kissed his chest again, and a jolt of need shot straight to his groin.

"It...doesn't matter," he finally managed. How was he supposed to think when she was playing with the tab of his zipper?

When she finally unzipped his slacks, then pushed them down his thighs, he took a deep breath to steady himself and stepped out of them. But the air became lodged in his lungs as her soft palms skimmed his legs from ankle to hip and she brought her hands back to the bulge straining the white cotton of his briefs.

His head fell back and he gritted his teeth so hard his jaw ached when she reached out and ran her fingers along the hard ridge of his erection. In all of his twenty-seven years, he never would have believed that a man could be debilitated with one touch of a woman's hand. But then, this wasn't just any woman. This was Elena.

"This...isn't fair," he said through gritted teeth. "I'd like...to return the favor."

She stepped back, shook her head and gave him a smile that sent his blood pressure into the danger zone. "Not yet."

Reaching for the hem of her sweater, she held his gaze with hers, pulled the sweater over her head and tossed it on top of his clothes. He swallowed hard at the sight of her red lace bra. She unhooked the front closure, then slowly slipped if off her arms. His pulse pounded so hard in his ears, he thought he might go deaf. Her breasts seemed to be a little fuller than he remembered, the nipples a bit darker. He wanted to fill his hands with them, wanted to kiss and taste her until she begged for him to take her.

She popped the snap on her jeans, lowered the zipper and revealed the top of a pair of red lace panties to match her bra. Red had never looked so good to him. By the time she slid the denim down her thighs, sweat beaded his forehead and Brett felt as if he'd been set on fire.

"You're beautiful," he said, reaching for her.

She took his hands in hers and placed them on her shoulders. "Not yet, darling." She ran her fingers along the elastic waistband of his briefs. "I want you to remember tonight."

If he could have found his voice, he would have told her there was no danger he'd ever forget. But she was dipping her fingers below the band to slide his briefs off. He couldn't have strung a sentence together if his life depended on it.

Once she had the cotton tossed on top of the growing pile of his and her clothing, she took him in her small hands. Brett wasn't sure how much longer his legs would support him.

Her warm palms gently caressed and stroked him until he thought he might just start Chicago's next big fire. Taking her hands in his, he squeezed his eyes shut and fought for control. "I think...we'd better lie down," he choked out.

Treating him to the sexiest smile he'd ever hoped to see, she nodded and turned down the comforter. Brett stretched out and watched as Elena removed the scrap of red lace covering her, then joined him.

He immediately pulled her into his arms, and her soft body pressed to his sent desire sweeping through him with the force of a tidal wave. Unable to find the words to express how she made him feel, he worshipped her with his lips and hands.

Her full breasts filled his palms perfectly, the nipples beading in anticipation of his attention. Kissing his way down the slope of one creamy breast, he flicked his tongue across the tightly beaded peak, then drew it into his mouth. She moaned and tangled her fingers in his hair to hold him to her.

"Feel good?" he asked, raising his head to smile down at her.

"Yes."

He gave the same attention to her other breast. "Want me to stop?"

"If you do, I swear I'll arrest you for committing a criminal act," she said breathlessly.

He ran his hand down the smooth skin of her torso, then cupped the dark brown curls at the apex of her thighs. "And what crime would that be, sweet Elena?" he asked, parting her with one finger to stroke the tiny nub hidden within.

Her head pressed back against the pillow and she arched her lower body upward against his hand. "Failure to cooperate…with a police officer."

Brett tested her readiness with one finger. "Is the officer in need of assistance?" he murmured against her lips.

"Yes…she is."

Grinning, he nudged her knees apart and settled himself between her thighs. "Considering it's my civic duty, I'll be happy to do what I can. Could the officer tell me exactly what that might be?"

Her brown eyes sparkled with a hunger than made his body throb. "Make love to me, Brett."

"Honey, I thought you'd never ask," he said, pushing the blunt tip of his erection forward to slowly penetrate her warm, moist heat.

When she tilted her hips to take all of him, her slick body absorbed him into her until he wasn't sure where he ended and she began. So intense were the feelings coursing through him that he had to remind himself to breathe.

He pulled back, then once again pushed forward, setting a slow, easy pace that gained momentum and depth with each stroke. Every fiber of his being was tightening with the need to empty himself into her, but he fought to hang on to what slender thread of sanity he had left.

Her cry of need, the pleasured pain of her nails scoring his back, urged him to deepen his thrusts, to quicken the pace. He answered her demands and felt the waves of fulfillment ripple around him as she gave in to the storm raging within her.

Unable to hold back any longer, Brett's control snapped and he plunged into her, his body joining hers with the quaking spasms of released passion. His body pumped rhythmically, draining him of his essence, his strength. Losing the ability to support himself, he collapsed on top of her and buried his face in the pillow beside her head.

Several long moments later, reality finally returned and he quickly levered himself to Elena's side. Her eyes were closed and she lay so quiet, so still that his heart nearly stopped. If he'd hurt her...

"Elena, honey, are you all right?"

Her smile sent relief coursing through him. "I couldn't be better." She opened her eyes and wrapped her arms around his neck. "Unless, of course, you make love to me again."

He felt like beating his chest and yelling like Tarzan. "I think that can be arranged," he said, kissing her with all of the emotion he had welling up inside of him.

When he broke the kiss to nuzzle the sensitive hollow behind her ear, he felt her chest rise and fall as she took a deep breath. "I love you," she said quietly.

Brett went perfectly still. Had he heard her correctly? "What did you say?" he asked, propping himself on his forearms to stare down at her.

"I said—" She paused as if she weren't sure she should repeat it. "I said I love you."

The uncertainty reflected in her eyes tore at his insides. He had to tell her what he knew in his heart to be true. "I love you too, sweet Elena."

Several hours later, their arms twined around each other, they sat on the couch with Babe, watching the late-night news. Elena yawned and started to get up. "I really need to get home."

Brett shook his head. "Don't go."

She looked at the man she loved. She'd tried so hard not to care for him, but from the moment they met, Brett had made it impossible to resist him. "I can't. I don't have my clothes for work tomorrow and I—"

He placed his index finger to her lips. "Call in tomorrow and tell them—"

"I really can't stay." She placed a quick kiss on his lips, then, lifting Babe from her lap, Elena rose to her feet.

"I don't mean for you to tell them you're sick."

Brett stood up and took her into his arms. "I mean call and turn in your two-weeks' notice."

"I can't do that," she said, laughing. Surely he had to be joking.

"Sure you can. I've got it all worked out," he said, sounding quite pleased with himself.

It seemed as if her world came to a halt, and a tight knot formed in her stomach. "What do you mean you have it worked out?"

"The head of security at Connelly Corporation will be retiring this summer and I've arranged for you to take the job." Naming a ridiculously high sum of money that would be her salary he added, "And I want you to move in here with me and Babe."

Elena felt her heart shatter into a million pieces. "I have to go," she said, needing to get away from him.

She felt sick inside. How could Brett tell her he loved her and know so little about her? About what was important to her?

"What's wrong, honey?" he asked, sounding truly puzzled. He reached for her. "Do you want more money?"

She stopped to look at the hand he'd placed on her arm, then up at his confused expression. "You just don't get it, do you, Connelly?"

"Get what?"

"Me." She shook free of his grasp. "You don't have a clue how hard I've worked to be promoted to the SIU, or how important my career is to me."

"But—"

"But nothing." She poked his chest with her finger. "I'll bet *you* take pride in what you do as vice president of public relations."

He nodded, folded his arms and stared down at her. "Of course I do."

"Well, I'm no different." She paced the room. "I'm proud of the job I do and the fact that I'm good at it. And I'm also proud that I beat the odds and made something of myself when everything was stacked against me."

"I never doubted that you worked hard to get where you are," he said, sounding as if his patience was wearing thin. "But you're pregnant now and your job is dangerous. You've got to think of Peanut."

She stopped pacing to turn around and stare at him. "I am thinking of my child."

"But this will solve all your problems," he argued. "You can set your own hours at Connelly." He came to stand in front of her and, reaching out, placed his hands on her shoulders. "You won't miss out on all of Peanut's firsts." He pulled her into his arms. "And when you move in here with me and Babe, *I'll* be here to see all the firsts, too."

"I'm not taking the job, Brett." She pushed away from him. "And I'm not moving in with you."

He looked as if he couldn't quite grasp that she was turning down his offer. Propping his fists on his hips, he asked, "Why not?"

Tears blurred her vision. "You don't understand how much value I place on my independence or how much real commitment means to me."

"Yes, I do."

"No, you don't." She walked to the closet to get her coat. "If you did, you'd never have taken it upon yourself to arrange a job for me, nor would you have asked me to play house. Call me selfish, but I want it all." She stuffed her arms into her coat, then turned back to face him. "I want the freedom and respect to make my own career choices. And I want the fairy tale. I want to belong to a family where love and commitment go hand in hand, where there's a happily-ever-after."

"I do love you and Peanut," he insisted. "And we can have those things."

"No, Brett," she said sadly. "It's not love if I'm the one making all the concessions. You need to learn that love isn't a matter of money or a job offer or playing house. It's far too valuable for that. I know that's a novel concept, and one that you've obviously never considered, but love is an emotional investment. To find real love and happiness, you have to invest the most valuable asset you have—yourself. You have to invest your heart and your soul."

"I have." He ran his hand over the back of his neck as if to relieve the tension. "I've never told another woman that I loved her, nor have I asked one to live with me."

She sadly shook her head. "You only think you love me, Brett."

"How can you say that?" he demanded. "I'm doing everything in my power to show you."

The tears flowed unchecked down her cheeks, but she didn't care. "When love is real, you accept the person for who they are and what they value in life. You don't try to get them to change the career they've chosen or to ask them to accept an imitation of what they truly want in life." Her voice caught and she had to swallow hard before she could force words past the lump in her throat. "I will always love you, Brett. But I'm not the woman for you."

"Yes, you are, Elena." He looked as miserable as she felt, but she couldn't let it sway her. If he couldn't accept her for who she was, they had no future together.

Reaching down, she picked up the little dog whining at her feet. "Take care of him, Babe," she whispered.

Setting the animal back on the floor, Elena stared at him for several long moments. Her heart felt as if it were being torn from her body.

"Goodbye, Brett."

Eleven

Elena pulled the quilt up to her chin, curled into a ball and took a deep breath. She wouldn't shed another tear over Brett Connelly. She wouldn't.

But as she lay in bed, listening to the sounds of Chicago's early-morning traffic, moisture filled her eyes and ran down her cheeks. Why did she always fall for the wrong man?

With Michael she'd been young and had naively believed his empty promises. But she couldn't use that excuse with Brett. He hadn't promised anything. And it wasn't as though she hadn't tried to keep her distance with him.

But he'd been too strong a force to resist. He'd come into her life like a whirlwind and overwhelmed her with the sheer force of his personality. He'd taken it upon himself to befriend her when she'd needed someone the most. He'd been kind and caring, romantic and sentimental. How could she not fall in love with him?

She bit her lower lip to hold back the sobs. How was she going to be able to continue working on his brother's investigation? Brett was the Connelly family liaison, and she would have to meet with him occasionally to update them on her findings. How could she do that and not have her heart break each time she saw him?

And what would happen when she picked up the newspaper and read about him and another woman in the society columns? The first time she'd seen Michael's name mentioned as the escort of a well-known socialite to a charity ball, it hadn't bothered her one bit. But she knew for certain it would devastate her to see Brett's name linked with another woman's.

A wave of deep emotional pain swept through her at the mere thought of him with another woman, and Elena had to catch her breath to keep from crying out. She'd never loved Michael as completely as she'd loved Brett.

Squeezing her eyes shut, she willed herself to think. She had several very difficult decisions to make.

The walls suddenly seemed to close in, and unable to stay in bed another second, she threw back the covers and stumbled to her feet. She needed to get out of the apartment, out of Chicago.

Picking up the phone, she dialed her supervisor and arranged to take a few days off. That done, she grabbed a suitcase and began shoving clothes into it. She knew exactly where she needed to go and whom she needed to talk to in order to put her life back into perspective.

* * *

Fiona glared at him as he walked past her desk, and if looks could kill, Brett figured he'd be a dead man in short order. The woman had even stopped speaking to him by midmorning. His PR team wasn't any happier, either. They were ready to mutiny over his criticism of their latest proposal. And in the past two days Babe had torn up three more throw pillows and refused to acknowledge he even existed until it was time for him to take her for a walk.

Truth to tell, he couldn't blame them. Lately he didn't even like himself. In the two days since Elena walked out of his condo, he'd been in the worst mood of his life.

Staring at the papers on his desk, he tried for the thousandth time to figure out how he could have been such a fool. Instead of asking Elena if she'd be interested in taking the job with Connelly Corporation, he'd just thrown it at her. He'd been so damned arrogant and sure that she'd jump at the opportunity that he hadn't even considered how it would sound. He rubbed the tension knotting the back of his neck. He'd come across as if he thought her career was insignificant and worthless. It was no wonder she'd refused.

If that wasn't bad enough, he'd asked her to move in with him, instead of offering her the permanence of a commitment. And he'd known full well how important that was to her.

Hell, he couldn't have handled it worse if he'd tried.

Brett propped his elbows on the desk and rested his head in his hands. He'd never been this miserable in his entire life. He hadn't slept worth a damn the past two nights, and his appetite had disappeared completely. But those were easy to deal with compared to the ache in his chest. It felt as though someone had reached in and ripped his heart out.

He took a deep breath. Now he understood how Drew had felt when Talia died. Although they hadn't been madly in love, Drew had suffered terribly from her loss. And that was what Brett had tried to avoid by not getting too close to Elena.

But from the moment they met, he'd been drawn to her. He'd tried hard to convince himself that he just wanted to help her, to lend her moral support because she had no one else. But that had been an excuse, and a damned flimsy one. He'd never seen a more capable woman than Elena. She knew exactly what she wanted in life and she wasn't afraid to go after it.

No, the truth was that he was the one incapable of dealing with things. He'd fallen in love with her the moment he'd laid eyes on her, but he'd done everything in his power to try to deny it. He was the one who needed her, not the other way around.

So what are you going to do about it, Connelly?

He glanced at the phone. He'd tried calling her last night, but her machine had picked up and he'd figured she was screening calls to keep from having to talk to him. But if he called her at work, she'd have to talk to him.

Before he could think twice about what he would say to her, Brett picked up the phone and dialed SIU headquarters. When the switchboard operator put his call through, his palms started sweating and his mouth went dry.

''Detective Johnson,'' a man barked into Brett's ear.

''I'm trying to reach Detective Delgado,'' he said,

his impatience mounting now that he knew exactly what he wanted to do.

"Sorry, she's not in. Want to leave a message?"

Disappointment stabbed at Brett's gut. "This is Brett Connelly. Would you have her call me when she gets back?"

"Does this have something to do with the Daniel Connelly case?" the man asked.

"Yes, it does," Brett lied. He figured if Elena thought his call had something to do with the investigation, he'd have a better chance of setting up a meeting with her.

"I can take the information," Detective Johnson said.

"No, I'd rather speak with Detective Delgado," Brett insisted, making sure his voice carried a no-nonsense edge to it.

"She took some time off and won't be back until sometime next week," Johnson said.

Brett felt as if the floor dropped from beneath him. "Is she all right?" Had their arguing caused her to have problems with Peanut?

"Far as I know, she's fine. She said something about visiting a relative or friend or something." The man's blasé attitude grated on Brett's nerves.

"Do you know if she left town?" Brett demanded, knowing of only one person she might be going to see.

"Look, buddy, I don't get paid to keep track of who leaves town and who doesn't." Detective Johnson sounded more than a little annoyed. "All I know is she had vacation days built up and decided to take some time off. Now, if you have something to add to the Connelly case, I can take the information. Otherwise, she'll call you when she gets back next week.''

"Thanks," Brett said when the man hung up on him. There was no way he'd wait that long to talk to Elena.

Dialing Lake Shore Manor, he asked Ruby to put him through to one of his parents. He wanted to make sure they knew how to get hold of him in case there was another development.

When his mother came on the line, she sounded as if she'd been crying. What the hell else could have happened? he wondered.

"What's wrong, Mom?"

"Brett, it's good to hear from you. How are you, darling?" his mother asked, her manners as impeccable as always.

"I'm fine." He took a deep breath to keep from sounding as impatient as he felt. He wanted to get on the road. "Why are you crying, Mom?"

"Your cousin, Princess Catherine, called to say she's delaying her visit," Emma said, sniffling.

"Did she say why?" Brett asked as he started clearing his desk.

"She mentioned something about finding questionable papers in her father's belongings." Emma's voice caught. "This is all so upsetting."

Brett understood how hard it was for his mother. Having one of her sons be the target in an assassination attempt was bad enough, but learning that her father and brother were quite possibly the victims of the same assassin had to be devastating.

"Did she say what kind of papers they were?" Brett asked.

"No, darling. Just that they were somehow tied to Sheikh Kaj al bin Russard."

"Who's he?" Brett asked, snapping his briefcase closed.

He heard his mother sniff back more tears before she went on. "He's the new prince of Walburaq. He's on his way to Altaria for a state visit and asked to speak to Catherine privately. She's hoping he might have answers about the papers."

"Be sure to let me know if she finds out anything," Brett said, thinking that what his cousin learned might help Elena with Daniel's case.

"I will."

Before his mother could start speculating on what the sheikh knew about the mysterious papers, Brett said, "Listen, Mom, I'm going out of town for a few days. If you need me for anything, I can be reached on my cell phone."

"Of course, darling," Emma said. "Do be careful, Brett. With everything that's taken place—"

"I will, Mom," he promised. "I'll call when I get back in town."

Hanging up the phone, Brett gathered his coat and briefcase, his mind already on Elena and his plan of action. He'd have to go by her apartment to be sure, but he had a hunch that he'd be headed down state before the day was over.

"Elena, honey, it sounds like somebody's at the door," Marie Waters said, kneading a large ball of bread dough. "Would you see who it is?"

"Sure." Elena put down the knife she'd been using to chop carrots and wiped her hands on a towel. "It's probably your friend Mr. Quimby."

"If it is, tell the old goat to pack his papers else-where." Marie pounded the dough. "I'm not lookin' for him or any other man to fill my time."

Elena smiled as she walked to the front door and turned on the porch light. Some things never changed. Mr. Quimby had been trying to get Marie to go out with him for as long as Elena had known them, and Marie still wouldn't give the poor old gentleman the time of day. When Elena asked her why, Marie had pointed out that she'd been married to her late hus-band for forty years and she wasn't about to settle for second best now that the love of her life was gone.

Looking out the peephole, Elena didn't see anyone on the other side. "Are you sure you heard some-one?" she called to Marie.

Before her foster mother could respond, Elena heard a light tap, then a definite thump. It sounded as if it came from the side of the house instead of the other side of the door. Probably one of the neighbors' children bouncing a ball against the side of the ga-rage, she decided. But she opened the door just to make sure.

Blinking, she couldn't believe her eyes. A small black ball of hair danced and yipped happily at her feet. "Babe?" Elena said incredulously. She picked up the wiggling little dog. "How did you—" She stopped abruptly and looked around. "Where's Brett?"

"Right here," he said, stepping from the twilight shadows to climb the porch steps. He held one hand behind him.

"Why are you here?" she demanded, hugging Babe close.

She'd traveled over three hundred miles in order to

put things in perspective, to get away from him so she could decide what she had to do to survive life without him. Now here he stood looking so handsome and sexy he stole her breath.

"Could I come inside?" he asked, pulling a bouquet of red roses from behind his back.

Elena shook her head. "I don't think that would be a good idea, Brett."

He stepped closer. "Why not?" Touching her cheek with his finger, he traced a line down to her chin. "I think we need to settle a few things between us."

She set Babe on her feet, then took a step backward. "We said all there was to say the other night at your condo."

Brett shook his head. "You might have, but I didn't."

"Who's at the door, Elena?" Marie asked, coming from the kitchen to stand at Elena's shoulder. Her curious gaze raked Brett from head to toe. "You look a little too old to be sellin' candy to raise money for the high school band, so I assume you're the young man who put the shadows under Elena's eyes."

"I'm afraid you're right," Brett said. "And I'm sorry about that. But I've driven all the way from Chicago to try to make things right."

"I would hope so," the little woman said, nodding her head until her short white curls bobbed. She glanced down at Babe. "And who is this little sweetie?"

"My dog." One glance at Elena's disapproving look and he decided not to elaborate. "I call her Babe."

"She's a real cutie," the woman said, bending down to pick up his dog.

Brett liked Marie Waters immediately. "With your

permission, Mrs. Waters, I'd like to come in and speak with Elena.''

The woman nodded her approval as she patted the top of Babe's head. ''That would be up to her, young man.'' Turning to Elena, Marie asked, ''How do you feel about him joinin' us for supper?''

Elena didn't look happy about it, but she finally shrugged. ''I don't mind if you don't, Marie.''

''Then it's settled.'' The woman took the bouquet of roses he still held, then, holding both the flowers and his dog, turned to go back into the house. ''Me and Babe are goin' to the kitchen to find her a treat and put these pretty flowers in a vase while you two young folks settle your differences.''

Taking a deep breath, Brett followed the two women inside and closed the door. He'd made it over the first hurdle. He at least had the chance to talk to Elena.

While Marie and Babe disappeared down a hall, Elena walked over to the couch and sat down. Her body language shouted that she was on the defensive, and he knew for certain he'd have a hard time convincing her of his sincerity.

He purposely remained standing. He had too much pent-up energy to sit still. This was the most important moment of his life, and he didn't want to blow it.

''Before you say anything, I want you to promise me you'll hear me out.''

She stared at him for several long seconds, and the hurt he saw reflected in her big brown eyes twisted his gut and made him want to rush his appeal. ''Brett, I can't do this,'' she said, her voice shaky. ''Please make your apologies to Marie, take Babe and leave.''

He shook his head. "No. I can't just walk away and let go of what we have."

"We don't have anything," she said, shaking her head.

"Yes, we do." He wasn't about to let her deny the best thing that had ever happen to either of them. "We love each other."

"Brett—"

He watched tears fill her eyes, and the thought that he'd caused her such pain tightened the knot in his stomach. "Just give me five minutes, Elena. If I can't convince you to give us another chance, then I promise I'll leave."

She stared at him for endless seconds, and just when he thought she was going to refuse his request, she nodded. "Five minutes, Connelly. That's it."

His relief was almost staggering. Unable to stand still any longer, he began to pace. "There's something you need to understand, Elena. I've never felt like this before." He stopped in front of her. "I've never found myself in the position of being so consumed by wanting to make another person happy that—" He took a deep breath. It wasn't easy for him to admit there was an area where he was unsure of himself, but this was too important to mince words. "I'm not real sure of what to do. Or how to go about doing it."

When she remained silent, he went on. "I want you to know right up front that I do respect your career even though it scares the hell out of me to think of you having to investigate criminals."

"I can take care of myself."

He nodded. "I know that. But it doesn't keep me from worrying about you."

"Most of my job consists of taking statements and

filing reports,'' she said, staring down at her tightly clasped hands. ''We're usually called after a crime has been committed.''

Her small reassurance gave him hope. At least she was listening to him. ''That makes me feel a little better. And I promise from now on to discuss things with you instead of trying to take matters into my own hands.''

''How do you know there will be a next time?'' she asked.

''That's why I'm here, Elena,'' he said, swallowing his pride. ''I'm begging you to give us—give me— another chance.''

''But do you think you could ever accept that I'm going to keep my job with SIU? Respect the fact that it's my career? My choice?''

''It will always be a source of worry for me,'' he said honestly. ''But, yes, I promise to trust your judgment and training.''

''You wouldn't try to pressure me into taking the job with Connelly Corporation?'' she asked.

''No. No more pressure.''

She looked up at him and he knew what was running through her mind. He hadn't mentioned anything about their relationship. He took a deep breath. He felt as if he was about to leap off a cliff.

''I want you to understand something about me, Elena. Until now I haven't had any experience with the give and take of a relationship, of talking things over and coming to a compromise.'' He shook his head. ''And, I have to admit, until I met you, I really hadn't cared to gain any.''

''Why not?''

Rubbing the knot of tension at the back of his neck,

Brett searched for the right words. How could he explain how he'd felt without sounding like a coward? Would she understand that he hadn't wanted to hand over his heart and risk being hurt? Or worse yet, end up hurting the woman he loved?

"Until now, I wasn't interested in learning about commitment because the Connellys don't exactly have an exemplary track record when it comes to relationships," he said honestly. "Even my mom and dad had problems and almost divorced after my brother Rafe was born."

"I remember that coming out during the interviews," Elena said.

Brett nodded. "My half brother Seth, was born during that time, and although my mother came to love him, it was really hard for her to get over my father being with another woman." He knelt down in front of Elena and took her hands in his. "I know this is going to sound crazy, but I never want to hurt the woman I love that way."

"I don't think you would, Brett," she said, her voice little more than a whisper. "You're too kind, too caring for that."

Her words gave him hope that she understood what he was trying to tell her. But would she understand that he'd also avoided involvement because he didn't want to suffer the same kind of hurt that Drew had when Talia died?

"There's something else," he said.

"What's that?" she asked softly.

"When I realized your job held even a hint of danger, all I could think about was the hell Drew went through when his wife died." Brett took a deep breath. "Drew survived, but I know as surely as I breathe air that if something happened to you, I couldn't go on. You're my heart, Elena. My soul." His voice shook with emotion, but he didn't care. "Can you find it in your heart to forgive me and give us another chance?"

Tears ran down her cheeks. "You're not the only one who's afraid, Brett."

Wrapping his arms around her, he held her close. "I know, honey. But I'm willing to take the chance if you are. I can't live without you. I want us to get married and spend the rest of our lives together."

She pulled back, looking uncertain. "You won't have a problem with the fact that the baby I'm carrying—"

He placed his finger against her lips to stop what she was about to ask. "I love Peanut. I already think of him—"

"Her," Elena corrected, giving him a smile that warmed his soul. "I keep telling you, this baby is a girl."

Brett grinned. "I already think of *her* as mine. I want to be there with you when you give birth to Peanut. I want to be the man she calls Daddy. And years from now if she can ever find a boy I think is worthy of my daughter, I want to walk her down the aisle at her wedding."

"Really, Brett? Do you mean it?"

"Honey, I love you. You're my everything and I want to be yours," he said, feeling he'd been set free with the admission. "Will you marry me?"

"Yes," she said, laughing and crying at the same time. "But only on one condition."

He didn't think the stipulation would be too bad, since she was laughing. "What's that, honey?"

"You have to change the dog's name from Babe Magnet to just Babe."

"Not a problem," he said, laughing. Her tears continued and he had to ask, "These are some of those happy tears, right?"

She nodded. "Why?"

"Just checking." Taking her hand in his, he rose to his feet and pulled her up with him. "Let's go see if Marie puts her stamp of approval on all this."

Elena gave him a kiss that made his body tighten and his heart hammer against his ribs. "You already have it. Otherwise, she would have never let you in the house."

He looked thoughtful. "You know that's something we'd better consider."

She looked thoroughly confused. "What are you talking about?"

"A house." He smiled and place his hand on the gentle roundness of her stomach. "We're going to need a big house with lots of bedrooms and a big yard for Peanut and the rest of the kids to play in."

"Uh, Brett, how many children are we talking about?" she asked. "Morning sickness isn't exactly a picnic in the park."

"Six or eight." He loved the idea of being a husband and father. "You choose."

"I'd be pregnant all the time," she said, laughing.

"Maternally mine," he said, kissing the tip of her nose.

Elena wrapped her arms around him and, nodding, gave him a smile that lit the darkest corners of his soul. "Maternally yours."

* * * * *

The Sheikh
Takes a Bride

CAROLINE CROSS

CAROLINE CROSS

always loved to read, but it wasn't until she discovered romance that she felt compelled to write, fascinated by the chance to explore the positive power of love in people's lives. She grew up in Yakima, Washington, the "Apple Capital of the World," attended the University of Puget Sound and now lives outside Seattle, where she works (or tries to) at home despite the chaos created by two telephone-addicted teenage daughters and a husband with a fondness for home-improvement projects. Pleased to have recently been No.1 on a national bestseller list, she was thrilled to win the 1999 Romance Writers of America's RITA® Award for Best Short Contemporary Novel and to have been called "one of the best" writers of romance today by *Romantic Times*. Caroline believes in writing from the heart – and having a good brainstorming partner. She loves hearing from readers, and can be reached at PO Box 47375, Seattle, Washington 98146, USA. Please include an SAE (with return postage) for a reply.

Special thanks to Ann Leslie Tuttle for
suggesting me for this story, Shannon Degen
for patience above and beyond the call of duty
and Joan Marlow Golan for believing in me.
The company is lucky to have you,
and so am I.

One

"You're absolutely right, Kaj," Joffrey Dunstan, Earl of Alston, said in his usual thoughtful way. "She's even lovelier than I remembered."

Glancing away from the slim, auburn-haired young woman who was the subject of his observation, the earl retreated a step from the balcony railing overlooking the grand ballroom of Altaria Palace. Though more than two hundred members of Europe's elite milled down below in their most elegant evening wear, they might not have existed for all the attention he gave them.

Instead, with a bemused expression on his face, he turned to stare at his companion, who stood in a pocket of shadow, hidden from casual observance. "But marriage? You can't be serious."

Sheikh Kaj al bin Russard raised an ink-black eyebrow in question. "And why is that?"

"Because... That is..." Always the diplomat, Joffrey cleared his throat and tried again. "Surely you're aware that Princess Catherine has a certain... reputation. And Sheikh Tarik's will was quite specific—"

"That I marry a virgin of royal blood." Kaj grimaced. "Have a little faith, cousin. I haven't forgotten my father's unfortunate directive. I'd simply remind you that for all Catherine's reputedly wild ways, there's a reason she's known as the ice princess."

"I suppose you have a point. Still..."

Kaj took one last look at the woman he intended to marry, his hooded gray gaze admiring her auburn hair and slim white shoulders before he turned his full attention to his favorite relative.

He was quite aware that, despite the fact their mothers were sisters, there was no physical resemblance between himself and Joffrey. His cousin was five-ten, with a slim build, blue eyes, cropped blond hair and a fair, exceedingly English face. In contrast, he was a trio of inches over six feet, with a distinct copper cast to his skin and ink-black hair long enough to necessitate pulling it back for formal affairs like tonight's.

Yet for all their outward differences, he valued Joffrey's opinion above all others.

It had, after all, been his cousin's matter-of-fact friendship that had eased Kaj's crushing homesickness for his homeland of Walburaq when he'd been sent away at age eight to attend English boarding school. Just as it had been Joffrey's steadying presence and astute counsel that had allowed Kaj to get successfully through Ludgrove and Eton, where he'd stood out like a hawk among pigeons. In all the ways that mattered, Joffrey was the brother Kaj had never had.

The reminder softened the chiseled angles of his face. "If it will ease your mind, Joff, I've made certain inquiries. The princess may be a tease, but she's no trollop. On the contrary. I have it on excellent authority that her virtue is very much intact. Her pleasure seems to come from keeping her admirers at arm's length."

Joffrey's eyes widened in sudden comprehension. "You see her as a challenge!"

Kaj shrugged slightly, his broad shoulders lifting. "If I have to marry, I might at least enjoy the courtship, don't you think?"

"No, I most certainly do not," the other man retorted. "At least not to the exclusion of more important considerations."

Kaj crossed his arms. "And those would be what, exactly?"

"Compatibility. Mutual respect and understanding. Similar values. And…and love." A faint flush of embarrassed color tinted the earl's cheeks at that last, but his gaze was steady as he plowed stubbornly on. "This isn't a prize to be won, Kaj. This is your life, your future. Your happiness."

"Do you think I don't know that?" the sheikh inquired softly. "Trust me. I have no intention of making my parents' mistakes."

Joffrey looked instantly stricken, as well he should since he was one of the few people who understood the price Kaj had paid for Lady Helena Spenser's and Sheikh Tarik al bin Russard's disastrous marriage, bitter divorce and subsequent flurry of heated affairs. "Of course not. I didn't mean to imply you did. It's just that this hardly seems the answer."

"And what is?" Kaj's voice was studiously polite. "Given the need for my bride to be pristine, what are my choices? Should I marry one of those tremulous debutantes your mother keeps throwing into my path? Or should I make an offer for some Walburaqui chieftain's daughter, a sheltered innocent who'll build her whole life around me?" He sighed. "I don't want that, Joff. I want a woman who's pragmatic enough to see a union with me as a mutually beneficial partnership. Not some starry-eyed romantic who'll fall desperately in love with me and expect me to fulfill her every wish and need."

"Ah, yes, adoration can be so trying," Joffrey murmured.

Kaj felt a lick of annoyance, only to have it vanish as his gaze locked with his cousin's and he saw the affection and concern in the other man's eyes. His sense of humor abruptly resurfaced. "More than you'll ever know," he said dryly.

For an instant Joffrey looked surprised, and then his own expression turned wry. "Well, if it's any consolation, I doubt excess worship of you will be a problem with Princess Catherine," he said, matching Kaj's tone.

Kaj cocked his head in feigned interest. "Do tell."

The earl shrugged. "It's simply that the more I think about it, the more I understand your choice. Unlike every other female on the planet, the princess has never shown the slightest tendency to swoon when you walk into the room. And though she may

indeed be a virgin—I bow to your superior sources—
she doesn't strike me as the kind of woman who'll
ever fall at your feet in girlish devotion. As a matter
of fact—'' he glanced down at the ballroom spread
out below them ''—you'll probably be lucky to get a
date.''

Kaj followed his gaze. He quickly noted that Altaria's new king, Daniel Connelly, was about to kick
off the dancing with his queen, Erin. Of more immediate interest to him, however, was the discovery
that the group of young men vying for Princess Catherine's attention had grown even larger than before.
He felt an unexpected pinch of irritation as one
would-be swain said something that made her laugh.
Vowing to put an end to such familiarity—and
soon—he nevertheless refused to rise to his cousin's
bait.

Catherine *would* be his. He'd given a great deal of
thought to her selection, and one way or another he
always got what he wanted. ''I appreciate your concern, Joffrey, but I assure you I'll do just fine.''

''Yes, of course.'' The other man's words were
perfectly agreeable, but there was a note of skepticism
in his voice that was distinctly annoying. ''I merely
hope you're not counting on a quick courtship. Because from the look of things, it may take some time
just to breach the crowd around her, much less win
her heart.''

''Oh, I think not,'' Kaj said firmly. ''One month
should do the trick.''

Joffrey turned to look at him, brows raised.
''You're having me on, right?''

"One month and I'll have Catherine of Altaria in my bed, my ring on her finger. Guaranteed."

Joffrey rocked back on his heels. "*Really*. Doesn't that first part rather violate your father's purity directive?"

Kaj rolled his eyes. "I think not. My intended is supposed to be chaste for me—not *with* me."

"I suppose you have a point."

"I suppose I do."

"In that case... Care to chance a small wager as regards to your success—or lack thereof—in this venture?"

"By all means. Simply name your terms."

"Well, I have always fancied Tezhari..."

Kaj nodded. His cousin had long coveted the exquisite Arabian brood mare. "Very well. As for me, I think the Renoir that graces your drawing room at Alston will make Catherine a lovely wedding present."

Joffrey winced but didn't back down. "It's a deal, then. And may I say good luck. Because in my opinion, you're going to need it."

For the first time all evening, Kaj smiled, regarding the other man with cool confidence. "That's very kind of you, Joff, but unnecessary. This hasn't a thing to do with luck. It's all about skill. Trust me."

At that his cousin laughed. "Why do I suddenly feel as if I should pen the princess a note of condolence?"

The sheikh nonchalantly flicked a nonexistent speck from his impeccably tailored Armani tux. "I can't imagine. But I do hope you'll excuse me." His gaze once more located Catherine down below, and he felt a distinct spark of anticipation. "I suddenly find I'm in the mood to dance."

"Oh, by all means." Joffrey stepped back, clearing the way with a flourish.

A twist of amusement curving his mouth, Kaj strolled away.

"Please, Highness." The handsome young Frenchman at Catherine's side gripped her hand and drew it toward his lips. "You are so very exquisite, with your Titian hair and your *yeux emerauds*. Take pity and say you'll dance with me."

Fighting an urge to roll her "emerald eyes," Catherine told herself to be patient. After all, the ball, for which she'd done the bulk of the planning, was going well. Overhead the thousand tiny lights in the mammoth chandeliers twinkled like iridescent butterflies. The lilting strains of the orchestra were neither too loud nor too soft, and the scent of blooming flowers drifting through the score of French doors thrown open to the mild March night was refreshing rather than overpowering.

Add the men in their sleek black tuxedos, the women draped in silk and satin and a glittering array of jewels, and it was perfect, a storybook scene. Most important to Catherine, the guests of honor—her cousin Daniel and his wife, Erin, Altaria's new king and queen—appeared to be enjoying themselves.

She watched for a moment as they danced, smiling at each other. There was such happiness in the looks they exchanged, such perfect understanding. Out of nowhere she felt an unexpected pang of envy.

What must it be like to share such closeness with

another person? Catherine couldn't imagine. She might be only twenty-four, but she'd long ago concluded that such intimacy wasn't for her.

Her conviction had its roots far in the past, when her nouveau-riche mother had happily surrendered Catherine to the royal family, making it clear in the years since that she regarded her illegitimate daughter as a stepping-stone to high society, nothing more.

It had been further shaped by Catherine's father, Prince Marc, who had always treated her like a unique trinket to be displayed when he wanted, then promptly forgotten once his need to impress others had passed.

Only her grandmother, Queen Lucinda, had ever truly cared for her. But that wonderful lady had passed away five years ago, and her loss had only underscored to Catherine how truly alone she was.

Oh, she had an abundance of suitors, but none of them had ever bothered to get to know the real her, the person beneath the public facade. They were too afraid of making a misstep and losing the chance to win her favor—and with it her money, her connections and, she supposed, her body.

Usually she didn't care. But every once in a while she caught a glimpse of what her life might have been if she'd been born plain Catherine Rosemere, instead of Her Highness Catherine Elizabeth Augusta. And she would suddenly feel unutterably weary of fawning admirers, frivolous soirees and always feeling alone no matter how big the crowd that surrounded her.

Oh, poor, pitiful princess, said a mocking voice in her head. *What a trial to be required to spend time in such a lovely setting, surrounded by the cream of high society. How unfair that you have to wear pretty clothes and listen to a few hours of lovely music and some meaningless chatter. What a tragedy that you're minus your very own Prince Charming.*

One hates to think how you'd stand up to a real problem, like being hungry or homeless. Or wait, how about this—you could be dead, like your father and grandfather, their lives snuffed out in an accident that now appears to have been no accident at all, but rather a deliberate act of murder.

Appalled at the direction her thoughts had taken her, Catherine cut them off. But she was too late to stop the anguish that shuddered through her. Or the guilt that came hard on its heels as she recalled the report by the Connelly family's investigator concluding that the speedboat involved in the disaster had been sabotaged. A speedboat meant to be manned by her, not her father.

"S'il vous plaît, belle princesse." The Frenchman stepped closer, demanding her attention. She looked up to find him gazing limpidly at her, looking for all the world like an oversize, tuxedo-clad flounder. "Do say yes to just one dance. Then I can die a happy man." Practically quivering with anticipation, he pressed his wet mouth to the back of her hand.

The tight rein Catherine had on her emotions snapped. She snatched her hand away, just barely suppressing the urge to scrub it against the delicate chiffon of her midnight-blue dress. "I told you before, Michel, I'm not in the mood. What's more, I'd appreciate it immensely if you'd hold off expiring for at least the next forty-eight hours. Your absence

would throw a decided wrench into the seating ar-
rangement for Monday night's banquet.''

The young man blinked. Then, as her words sank
in, his smile abruptly vanished. ''But, of course,'' he
said, pouting in a way that made him look more fish-
like than ever. ''A thousand pardons, Highness.''
Stiff-backed with affront, he turned on his heel and
marched off.

Catherine felt a prick of remorse, but quickly dismissed it. After all, she'd been exceedingly polite to
Michel the first three times she'd refused his requests
to dance. She could hardly be held responsible that
he refused to take no for an answer.

Sighing, she glanced at the miniature face of her
diamond-encrusted watch. It was barely half past ten,
which meant it would be at least another two hours
before she could hope to make an unremarked-upon
escape. She wondered a little desperately what she
could do to make the time go faster.

She was saved from having to come up with an
answer as a small murmur ran through the throng surrounding her. A second later everyone in front of her
appeared to take a collective step back, clearing a path
for the tall, ebony-haired man who strode toward her
with a palpable air of leashed power.

Catherine tensed, the way she always did when she
encountered Kaj al bin Russard. Although most of the
women she knew found the enigmatic Walburaqui
chieftain irresistible, she personally didn't care for
him. Granted, his chiseled features, heavily lashed
gray eyes and beautifully accented English had a certain exotic charm, but there was simply something
about him—an innate reserve, the assured, almost ar-

rogant way he carried himself, his indisputable masculinity—that she found off-putting.

She watched as he cut a swath through the crowd like some Regency rake from a bygone age, her edginess increasing as she realized his gaze was locked on her face.

He came to a halt and swept her a slight bow. "Your Highness."

She gathered her composure and inclined her head. "Sheikh."

"I don't believe I've had the chance to tell you in person how sorry I am for your loss."

"Thank you," she replied dutifully. "The flowers you sent were lovely."

He made a dismissive gesture. "It was nothing." He moved a fraction closer, making her intensely aware of how big he was. "Would you care to dance? The orchestra is about to play a waltz. Strauss's Opus No. 354, if I'm not mistaken."

Common sense urged her to simply say no and be done with it. But curiosity, always her curse, got the better of her. "How would you know that?"

"Because I requested it. I believe you once mentioned it was your favorite."

"I see." Ridiculously, she felt a stab of disappointment. In the past two months everything had changed: her father was gone; her position as court hostess was coming to an end; her entire future was uncertain. Now here was Kaj al bin Russard, apparently deciding to join her band of admirers. Though she hadn't liked him before, he'd at least been unique. "How resourceful of you," she said coolly. "Unfortunately, my favorite has changed."

"Then this will give you a chance to tell me what has supplanted it." Without warning he reached out and clasped her right wrist with his long fingers.

His touch gave her a jolt, and for a moment she felt anchored in place by the sheer unexpectedness of it. Then she instinctively tried to pull away, only to find that though he was careful not to hurt her, his grip was as unyielding as a steel manacle.

Her temper flared at the same time her stomach fluttered with unexpected excitement. "Let go of me," she ordered tersely, mindful of the interested stares suddenly directed their way.

"Oh, I think not." Matching her clipped tone, he stepped to her side, planted his hand in the small of her back and propelled her toward the dance floor. "It would be a shame to waste such enchanting music. Plus it just so happens—" he swung her around to face him, waited a beat as the orchestra launched into the waltz, then pulled her close and led off "—I'm curious to see how you'll feel in my arms."

Catherine couldn't believe it. Speechless, she stared up at him. She was shocked at having her wishes ignored, shocked by his statement—and more shocked still by the startling discovery that his hand felt deliciously warm against her cool, bare back.

She shivered as his fingers slid lower, unable to stanch her reaction. Only the sight of the faint smile that tugged at the corners of his mouth saved her from making a complete fool of herself by whimpering or doing something else equally mortifying. "How dare you!" she managed instead, finally finding her voice.

"How dare I not, princess." Never missing a beat, he guided her deeper into the phalanx of whirling dancers. "I could never forgive myself if I let the most beautiful woman in the room remain all alone during her former favorite waltz."

His outrageous flattery, coupled with the realization that he'd noticed her solitary state, brought her chin up. "Is there some reason you're toying with me?" she asked abruptly.

His gaze dropped to her mouth and lingered for an endless second. When he finally raised his eyes, they had a lazy, knowing quality that caused an unexpected clenching in the pit of her stomach. "You really must pay more attention. Toying is hardly my style."

"Just what do you hope to gain from this?" She managed to keep her voice steady, but just barely.

"Surely it's obvious. The pleasure of your company."

"And you believe *this* is the best way to attain it?"

One black eyebrow rose in question. "Isn't it?"

"No," she said flatly. "I don't like being commandeered."

"Ah." His expression lightened. "Does it happen often?"

"Of course not!"

He shrugged, and she felt the steely strength of his body beneath her fingertips. "How unfortunate. Perhaps you simply need to give yourself over to the experience. You might find you enjoy it."

Oh, what nerve! She opened her mouth to reply, then stubbornly shut it again. She would not let him provoke her into causing a scene. She would *not*. Besides, it was time he realized he didn't get to have everything his way. Pursing her lips, she deliberately shifted her gaze to the weave of his impeccably tailored jacket and tried to pretend the rest of him didn't exist.

To her surprise, rather than making another outrageous comment, he actually fell silent. At first she was grateful…until it dawned on her that with the cessation of conversation between them, she was growing increasingly conscious of other things.

Like the hardness of the thigh brushing hers. And the size of the hand now pressed firmly to the base of her spine. Then there was his scent, all dark starry nights and cool desert breezes. Not to mention the warmth that radiated seductively from his powerful body.

Suddenly, she felt…funny. Hot, cold, short of breath and shivery. Alarmed, she tried to pull away, but it was not to be. Instead of letting her go, the sheikh gathered her even closer.

"Princess?"

She felt his heartbeat against her breast, and the funny feeling grew worse. "What?"

"Relax. You're far too lovely to be so unyielding. And far too intelligent not to accept that sometimes the best things in life are those we initially resist."

It was too much. She jerked her head up to stare at him. "I suppose you include yourself in the category of 'best things'?"

He smiled. "Since you see fit to mention it, yes."

"Oh, my. And here I've always believed conceit wasn't a virtue but a vice."

He made a tsking sound. "Such a sharp tongue, little one. But then, the past weeks can't have been easy. Tell me, does it bother you that much to be passed over as Altaria's ruler?''

Well, really! ''Of course not. I've known all my life that women are excluded from inheriting the throne. What's more, Daniel will be an excellent king. He has a very American sense of responsibility and a fresh way of thinking that should be good for the country.''

To her surprise, he actually appeared to consider her words. ''I agree.''

''You do?''

''Yes. I've had occasion to do business with the Connelly Corporation in the past, and found your cousin to be a very resourceful man. Still, it's not Daniel who concerns me, but you. It's never easy to lose a parent. Even a disappointing one.''

Wonderful. And just when she thought he might have some redeeming qualities after all. ''That's hardly any of your business.'' Particularly in light of the second part of the Connelly investigator's report, which had revealed that her father died owing considerable amounts of money due to extensive gambling. The now familiar shame pressed her, but she thrust it away. She had no intention of discussing her father's shortcomings with the sheikh, never mind her failures as a daughter.

He didn't seem to notice the chill in her voice, however. ''My own father passed away some seven months ago. I was never the son he wanted, just as he was never the father I needed. Yet it was still hard to lose him.''

''Oh.'' Suddenly confused, she set her own concerns aside, wondering again if she'd misjudged him—and why he would say something so revealing. "I'm sorry."

"Don't be. Typically, he's managed to complicate my life even now."

"In what way?"

"It seems if I'm to inherit, I must marry."

She was so startled by the disclosure that for a moment she couldn't think what to say. "How...how unpleasant for you."

"Not really. It's been a challenge, but I've finally settled on a wife."

Her budding sympathy evaporated at the complacency in his voice. "I'm certain she's thrilled," she said tartly.

Incredibly, he laughed, a low, husky chuckle that turned several female heads their way and had an odd effect on the strength of her knees. "Perhaps not yet, but she will be." He looked down at her, his eyes gleaming with good humor...and something else.

It took her a moment to identify what she was seeing. And then it hit her.

Possessiveness.

Her breath lodged in her throat as she was struck by a terrible suspicion. In the next instant she found herself reviewing everything that had just passed between them—his sudden attention, his insistence they dance, that surprising revelation about his father. And for the first time she let herself wonder just what was prompting his uncharacteristic behavior. It couldn't possibly be because *she* was the future wife he'd "settled" on. Could it?

Of course not. The very idea was ludicrous. Not only didn't she care for him, she barely knew him, any more than he knew her. And yet, why else would he be looking at her as if she were a prime piece of real estate he'd decided to acquire?

The waltz ended. Determined to make an escape, she looked around, relief flooding her as she spied her cousin, the king, standing alone a few feet away.

"Daniel!" Forcing a smile to her lips, she took a step back the instant Kaj loosened his grip and hastened to her cousin's side, linking her arm with his. "What luck to find you!"

Clearly startled, Daniel tore his attention from his wife, who was threading her way through the crowd, apparently headed for the powder room, and turned to look at her. "Catherine. Is everything all right?" Concern lit his jade-green eyes.

"Yes, yes, of course. It's simply that I was dancing, and then I saw you and realized I'd forgotten to tell you I talked to your mother earlier and she'd like me to visit Chicago soon since Alexandra has asked me to be one of her bridesmaids."

A frown knit her relation's sandy eyebrows. Catherine felt an embarrassed flush rise to her cheeks since she was fairly certain his distress was caused by her rapid-fire statement, rather than the reminder of his sister's recent engagement to Connelly Corporation executive Robert Marsh.

But all he said was, "I see." Before he could comment further, he caught sight of Kaj, his frown disappearing as a welcoming smile lit his face. "Al bin Russard. How nice to see you again."

"Your Majesty."

"I take it you're the one responsible for my cousin's rather breathless state?"

"I believe I am," Kaj said easily.

To Catherine's disbelief, the two exchanged one of those men-of-the-world looks she always found totally irritating. She drew herself up, gathering what was left of her dignity around her like a cloak. "I really do need to talk to you, Daniel."

"Right." With an apologetic smile for the other man, he said, "If you'll excuse us, then?"

Just as Catherine had hoped, Kaj had no choice but to take his leave. With impeccable manners, he tendered the pair of them a bow. "Of course, Your Highness." He shifted his gaze to Catherine. "Princess, thank you for the dance. I look forward to seeing you again."

Not if she could help it, Catherine vowed. With a flick of her head, she turned her back, dismissing him. Sheikh Kaj al bin Russard might not know it yet, but as of this moment she had every intention of excluding him from her life like the unwelcome intruder he was.

Two

"What are *you* doing here?" Catherine demanded from the doorway of the palace's family dining room.

For all its elegant spaciousness, the room suddenly seemed far smaller than normal, due to the presence of Kaj al bin Russard. The sheikh sat at the far side of the gleaming satinwood table, his suit coat discarded, the sleeves of his white dress shirt folded back, a newspaper in his powerful hands. At the sound of her voice, he looked up. "Princess. How nice to see you."

Catherine stared at him, clenching her teeth against a sudden urge to scream. Taken aback by her reaction, she struggled to rein in her emotions, assuring herself her extreme response to him was merely the result of surprise, frustration and a poor night's sleep. Add to that her worry about her favorite gelding who'd turned up lame this morning, a meeting with her secretary that had run long so that she needed to hurry to avoid being late for an engagement in town, and it was no wonder the unexpected sight of the sheikh made her feel a little crazy.

"That's a matter of opinion," she retorted, watching warily as he pushed back his chair and rose politely to his feet.

"I suppose it is," he said calmly.

She refused to acknowledge the way her pulse stuttered as he stood gilded by the sunlight that filled the room or how she once again felt the force of his masculinity. She'd made her decision about him, and the long hours she'd spent in bed last night tossing and turning, bedeviled by an unfamiliar restlessness, had only strengthened her conviction that he was best avoided.

"I believe I asked you a question," Catherine said. "What are you doing here?" Last night circumstances had compelled her to be on her best behavior, but she saw no reason for false pleasantry today.

His gaze swept over her and a faint frown marred his handsome features. "Are you always this tense?"

Oh! She struggled for self-control. "Sheikh al bin Russard, this area of the palace is off-limits to everyone but family. I would suggest that you leave. Now. Before I'm forced to call security."

A faint, chiding smile curved his sensual mouth but otherwise he didn't move so much as an inch. "You really must work on your temper, *chaton.* And not be so quick to jump to conclusions. As it happens, I had a meeting with the king this morning. When it concluded, he was kind enough to invite me to lunch.

Regretfully, something came up and he had to leave, but not before he assured me there was no reason for me to rush through my meal.''

An embarrassed flush rose in her cheeks. Stubbornly she ignored it. Daniel wasn't here now and she was. As for the sheikh, he might be fooling everyone else with his designer suits and civilized manner, but she hadn't forgotten the way he'd looked at her last night. Beneath that polished exterior she sensed something intense and formidable, and she wasn't about to lower her guard.

She glanced pointedly at the table, which was bare except for the paper and an empty cup and saucer. ''I see. Well, it appears you've finished, so don't let me keep you.''

''Actually, I was about to have some more coffee.'' He moseyed over to the sideboard and lifted the heavy silver coffeepot off the warming plate, then turned to her, his expression the picture of politeness. ''May I get you a cup?''

For half a second, she considered simply turning on her heel and walking away. Except that she was hungry, since she'd skipped last night's midnight buffet in order to avoid a certain interloper and she'd long since burned off the tea and croissant she'd had in her room at dawn.

She was also certain that if she left now, the sheikh would no doubt conclude it was because of him—and her pride wouldn't allow that. He was already too arrogant by half.

Squaring her shoulders, she strode around the table to the opposite end of the sideboard. ''No. Thank you.''

''As you wish.'' He poured a stream of steaming

brew into his cup and set down the pot. He turned, but instead of returning to the table, he stayed where he was.

She felt his gaze touch her like a warm breeze. And for a moment everything around her—the ivory silk brocade wallpaper, the richly patterned rug beneath her feet, the soothing gurgle of the garden fountain beyond the open windows—seemed to fade as her skin prickled and an unfamiliar warmth blossomed low in her stomach. Appalled, she gave herself a mental shake and tried to convince herself that her response was merely the result of extreme dislike.

It was a delusion that lasted no longer than it took her to snatch up a plate, fill it with cold cuts, fresh fruit and cheese from the buffet, carry her food to the table and set it down.

Because suddenly he was right behind her. ''Allow me,'' he murmured, his bare forearm brushing her shoulder as he reached to pull out her chair before she could seat herself.

The heat from his body penetrated her every nerve ending; she might as well have been naked for all the protection provided by her cream linen slacks and sleeveless yellow silk sweater. Nor could she control the sudden weakness of her knees as his fingers closed around her upper arm and he guided her onto the chair. Or the way the warmth in her middle spread when his palm lingered far longer than was necessary.

Not until he stepped back and released her could she breathe again.

Shaken, she sat motionless on the chair, asking herself what on earth was the matter with her. She'd dealt with a variety of men's advances from the time she'd become a teenager, yet she'd never experienced this sort of acute, paralyzing awareness. It was unnerving.

Worse, it made her feel uncertain and out of control, and that made her angry. "Don't you have an oil deal or a camel auction or something that needs your attention?" she demanded as he picked up his cup, moved around the table and slid into the seat across from her.

"No." He cocked an eyebrow at her and took a sip of his coffee. "All of Walburaq's oil comes from offshore reserves, and its distribution is controlled by the royal family. As for camels, we don't have any since, like Altaria, we're an island nation."

Her annoyance shifted from his presence to his presumption that she was actually that ignorant. "Yes, I know. Just as I know Walburaq is located in the Arabian Sea, was a British protectorate until 1963, declined to join the United Arab Emirates and is currently ruled by your cousin, King Khalid." Doing her best to look bored, she picked up a small, perfect strawberry from the royal hothouse and popped it into her mouth.

"My, my princess, that's very good. I'm gratified that you've taken time to study my country."

She touched her heavy linen napkin to her mouth. "Don't be. It's nothing to do with you." Which was nothing but the truth. Not that she'd ever reveal that her knowledge sprang from a futile attempt when she was younger to impress her father by learning about Altaria's various trading partners. "I've always been good at history."

"Apparently." He took another swallow of coffee.

"It makes me wonder what other hidden talents you possess."

In the process of reaching for another berry, Catherine stilled, her gaze locking with his. She had an uneasy feeling that they'd just moved onto dangerous ground.

It was a sensation that increased as he added softly, "I look forward to finding out."

Alarm shot through her. She parted her lips to tell him in no uncertain terms that wasn't ever going to happen. But before she could say a word, Erin, Altaria's new queen, walked into the room.

Kaj came instantly to his feet. "Your Majesty."

Catherine, schooled in the strict protocol her late grandfather had insisted on, started to rise, too, only to sink back into her chair as her cousin-in-law sent her a remonstrative look. Although Daniel's wife possessed an air of reserve that sometimes made her seem rather distant, one of her first acts upon moving into the palace had been to insist that, among the family, royal etiquette was to be relaxed. It was a necessity, she'd wryly informed Catherine later, since there was little chance that Daniel's very American brothers and sisters would ever consent to bow down and call him Your Majesty.

"Catherine, Sheikh." Erin smiled. "Please, be seated." Letting the footman who'd suddenly appeared pull back her chair, she sat down herself and promptly reached out to touch her hand to Catherine's. "I'm so glad to see you. I haven't had the chance to tell you how much I enjoyed the ball last night. It was simply wonderful. Thank you for showing me how such an affair should be done."

"It was my pleasure," Catherine said sincerely.

The regal young queen gave her arm a squeeze and then turned her attention to Kaj. She sent him a warm and gracious smile. "My husband informs me you've agreed to be our guest."

"I beg your pardon?" Caught by surprise, Catherine couldn't keep the dismay out of her voice.

Kaj shot her a quick glance, and she could have sworn that his hooded gray eyes, so pale in contrast to his inky lashes and olive complexion, held a glint of triumph. Yet as he turned to Erin, his voice was nothing but polite. "It's very kind of you and the king to offer to put me up."

"I assure you, it's no problem. We have more than adequate room."

Catherine had heard quite enough. Setting her napkin next to her plate, she pushed back her chair. "I'm sorry, but I have an appointment in town. If you'll excuse me?" The last was directed toward Erin.

"Why, yes, of course."

She stood, but before she could take so much as a single step, the sheikh was on his feet as well. "Pardon me, ma'am." He bowed to the queen, then immediately turned his attention to Catherine. "Might I beg a favor, princess, and get a ride with you?" His smile—part apology, part entreaty—was charm itself. "I'm afraid I'm without a car today."

Catherine couldn't help herself. "Then how did you get here? Walk?" Erin shot her a startled look and she abruptly realized how she must sound to someone unaware that the sheikh had an agenda all his own. She swallowed. "It's only…I'm running late and I'd hate to cut short your conversation with Her

Majesty. I'm sure one of the servants can drive you later.''

''You mustn't concern yourself with me, Catherine,'' Erin interjected. ''It just so happens I have a meeting in a few minutes.''

''Yes, but I really need to go straight to my appointment—''

''I wouldn't dream of inconveniencing you,'' the sheikh said smoothly. ''I'd be honored to accompany you to your appointment. Afterward, if you wouldn't mind, we can go to my hotel and collect my things.''

''Good, that's settled, then,'' Erin said decisively, coming to her feet and heading for the door. ''I'll look forward to seeing both of you at dinner.''

Catherine simply stood, her face carefully composed so as not to show her horror.

Yet there was no getting around it. Her day had just gone from intense-but-survivable annoyance to major disaster.

Long legs angled sideways, Kaj sat in the passenger seat of the sleek silver Mercedes, watching Catherine put the powerful sports car through its paces.

Pointedly ignoring the ever present security detail following in their wake, she drove as she did everything else. With grace, confidence and—at least where he was concerned—a deliberate air of aloofness. The attitude might have succeeded in putting him off, if not for her breathless reaction to his touch at lunch or the way she'd trembled in his arms when they'd danced last night.

Try as she might to pretend otherwise, she clearly

wasn't indifferent to him. But it was also obvious she had no intention of giving in to her attraction to him.

That alone made her an irresistible challenge, he mused, since he couldn't remember a time when women hadn't thrown themselves at him. And though he'd be the first to concede that some of those women had been drawn by his power and money, he also knew that the majority had been attracted by *him*—his personality, his looks, his unapologetic masculinity.

But not Princess Catherine. To his fascination, she seemed intent on not merely keeping him at arm's length but on driving him away. Not that she had a chance of succeeding…

"Quit staring at me," she said abruptly, slicing into his thoughts.

He settled a little deeper into the dove-gray leather seat. "Now why would I want to do that?"

"Because I don't like it."

"But you're very nice to look at, *chaton*."

Her grip on the steering wheel tightened. "Do *not* call me kitten," she snapped. "I have a name. And whatever your opinion of my appearance, I dislike being studied like some sort of museum exhibit."

"Very well. If it makes you uncomfortable… Catherine."

Her jaw tightened and he smothered a smile even as he dutifully turned his head and pretended to examine the view.

It was magnificent, he conceded. In between the small groves of palm trees that lined the narrow, serpentine road they were traveling on, aquamarine expanses of the Tyrrhenian Sea could be seen. Red-roofed, Mediterranean-style villas hugged the craggy-coastline, while a dozen yachts were anchored in the main harbor, looking like elegant white swans amidst the smaller, more colorful Altarian fishing boats.

Yet as attractive as the surroundings were, they didn't interest him the way Catherine did, and it wasn't long before he found himself surreptitiously studying her once again.

He felt a stirring of desire at the contradiction of her, her air of cool containment so at odds with the banked fire of her hair and the baby smoothness of her skin, which practically begged to be touched. She wasn't a classic beauty by any means—her mouth was a little too full, her nose a little too short, and the way her dark-green eyes tilted up at the corners gave her a face a faintly exotic cast. Yet, looking at her pleased him. And made him hunger to do more.

The realization brought a faint frown to his face. Catherine, after all, was going to be his wife. He expected theirs to be a lifelong commitment, and if he'd learned anything from the debacle of his parents' marriage, it was that excessive emotions were not to be trusted. It was all right to find his future bride desirable. Just as long as he didn't want her too much.

Of course, given Catherine's current attitude toward him—and he'd known enemies of the state who'd been treated more warmly—being overcome by uncontrollable lust was probably the least of his worries.

With that in mind, he couldn't resist reaching out and resting his hand on the top of her seat as he turned to face her more fully. "Where, exactly, are we going?"

For a moment he wasn't sure she would answer. But then she sliced a quick glance at him. "If you must know, I like to drop in from time to time on the various charitable organizations supported by my family." She took advantage of a straight stretch of road to accelerate.

"Ah." He pictured her striding down a hospital corridor, doctors and administrators trailing like so much confetti in her wake as she looked in on patients. Or asking pertinent questions of the scientists at the Rosemere Institute, the cancer research facility founded by her grandfather.

Pleased by her sense of responsibility, he shifted a fraction more in her direction, just far enough to slide his fingers beneath the silken tumble of her hair.

A slight shiver went through her, and her lips tightened. "Today—" without warning she hit the brakes and made a sharp left turn, dislodging his hand "—I'm visiting an orphanage."

The explanation was unnecessary since by then they were sweeping past a high stone wall marked with a brass plaque that read "Hope House—where every child is wanted." Beneath that, in letters so small he almost missed them, were the words, "Founded 1999 by Her Highness, Princess Catherine of Altaria." He shot her a startled glance that she ignored.

Seconds later she slowed the car as they approached a rambling two-story house wrapped by a wide, covered veranda. Pulling into an adjacent parking area, she switched off the engine, opened her door and exited the car, all without another word to him.

With a slight shake of his head, Kaj reached for

the door handle. But before he could exit, an explosion of sound had him twisting around. He watched, bemused, as a small army of children burst out of Hope House's front doors, swarmed across the veranda and down the steps, all chattering at once as they ran toward the car.

"Princess, you came!"

"Amalie was ascared you forgot."

"I told her she shouldn't worry. I told her you'd be here soon!"

"Did you bring her a present?"

"Nicco said maybe the new king wouldn't let you visit. He said maybe the new king doesn't like kids like—"

"Children, stop!" To Kaj's surprise, Catherine laughed. It was a husky, musical sound that tickled his nerves like velvet against bare skin. "Of course King Daniel likes you." As she looked down at the dozen small people all vying for her attention, her remoteness melted away. "As a matter of fact, I've told him and Queen Erin all about you, and they've asked if they might come visit you themselves."

"They have?"

"Really?"

"Wait till Nicco hears that."

"Does that mean *you* won't come anymore?" This last was asked by the smallest of the children, a petite black-haired girl with big brown eyes in a too-serious face.

"No, of course not, Amalie," Catherine said gently. "We're friends, no matter what. Yes?"

The child nodded.

"What's more, today is your birthday. I couldn't possibly forget that."

A bashful smile crept across the little girl's face. She sidled closer and leaned against Catherine's hip, rewarded as the princess laid a reassuring hand on her thin shoulder.

Kaj felt a surge of approval. It was good to know the future mother of his children had a maternal side.

Yet even as he told himself he'd made the right choice, that Catherine of Altaria was going to make him a fine wife, he also felt the faintest flicker of uneasiness.

Because just for a second, as he'd watched Catherine's face soften and heard her affection for the children in her voice, he'd experienced an unfamiliar hunger, a desire to have her laugh at something *he* said, a need to have her reach out and touch *him*.

Which was ridiculous, given that he had every confidence that sooner, rather than later, he would be on the receiving end of her affection. All he had to do was stay close and he'd find a way to get past her reserve.

As for this nagging little itch of need she seemed to inspire... It was nothing he couldn't handle.

Three

Catherine sat on the padded chaise longue on her bedroom balcony. She stretched her tired muscles, then huddled a little deeper beneath the ice-green satin comforter she'd dragged from her bed. A golden glow pierced the gunmetal-gray horizon, announcing the sun's imminent arrival and the start of a new day.

For the second night in a row, she'd barely slept. And as much as it rankled to admit it, she knew exactly who was to blame for her second bout of insomnia.

The sheikh. Kaj al bin Russard. Or, as she was beginning to think of him: he-who-refused-to-go-away.

Perhaps she wouldn't be so disturbed if she could write him off as simply another pretty face. Or just a magnificent body. Or even an incredibly willful personality. But the truth was he was all of those things and more.

He was presumptuous, but also perceptive. He was arrogant, yet intuitive. And unlike most of the men she knew, his ego was disgustingly healthy; sarcasm, indifference, even outright hostility all rolled off him like rain off a rock.

Most disturbing of all, his lightest touch was all it took to ignite an unfamiliar fire inside her.

She shivered, not wanting to think about that last bit. Instead she did her best to concentrate on the chorus of birds tuning up to welcome the sunrise— only to make the unfortunate mistake of closing her eyes. The scene at Hope House when Kaj had climbed out of the car yesterday promptly popped into her mind.

Without exception, all the children's eyes had widened at the sight of him. "Who's he?" Christian had asked.

Marko had sucked in a breath. "Is that the king?"

Catherine had been tempted to make a sharp reply—until Kaj had come to stand at her side. The same faint breeze that tugged at his gleaming black hair had carried his clean, masculine scent to her, and suddenly he'd seemed much too close. To her disgust, she'd found she had to swallow hard in order to locate her voice.

"Children, I'd like to introduce Sheikh al bin Russard." Not wanting anyone to get the wrong idea, she'd added, "The sheikh is a friend of my family's."

There were several nods and an "Oh."

And then Christian burst out, "Is he a real sheikh?

Does he live in a tent? How come he doesn't have one of those sheet things on his head?''

Catherine had hesitated a mere instant, and Kaj had stepped into the breach. "Those sheet things are called ghotras," he'd said easily. "I wear one when I'm in my country, as is the custom. But when I'm here, I try to follow your fashions. And much like you, I live in a home made of mortar and stone. Though I do own several tents. For the times—" he displayed a quick flash of white teeth "—when I feel a need to escape and sleep under the stars."

Whether it was the sentiment or the brief, impish grin that accompanied it, the children all nodded in understanding and several of the boys murmured, "Yeah!"

Isabelle, one of the older girls, looked earnestly up at him. "Do you have a camel?"

He shook his head. "I'm sorry to say, no." Although his expression was suitably apologetic, his eyes gleamed with humor as he glanced briefly at Catherine. "That seems to be a common misconception. What I do have is horses. Beautiful Arabian horses. Oh, and I'm also the keeper of a truly magnificent tiger."

"You have a tiger?" Christian, Isabelle and Marko all exclaimed at once. "A real, live tiger?"

"Mmm-hmm. His name is Sahbak and he was a gift to my father. He's quite a wonderful fellow. Do you know, if you scratch him behind the ears, he purrs?"

"Wow," Marko murmured.

That seemed to be the general sentiment. Eyes rounded, the children had stared up at him with a

combination of awe and admiration. And though un-
impressed by his status as a big-cat owner, Catherine
had found that, as the afternoon went along, she
couldn't fault his manner. He was wonderful with the
children, relaxed, down-to-earth, friendly without
seeming too eager. Even little Amalie, who was usually standoffish with strangers, had eventually lowered her guard.

Catherine wanted in the worst way to blame the
latter on the exquisite gold coin Kaj had given the
child as a birthday present. But honesty forced her to
admit it probably had more to do with the coin's pre-
sentation. Who would have suspected a Walburaqui
chieftain could, with a flick of his long, elegant hands
and a widening of his eyes, make a coin vanish once,
twice, thrice? Or that, with a subsequent snap of his
fingers, he could make it reappear—much to the
delight of a giggling little girl—from its hiding place
behind one of her shell-like ears?

Certainly not Catherine.

She pulled the comforter up a little higher and
sighed. Perhaps it was the earliness of the hour, but
for the first time she admitted that keeping the sheikh
out of her life was turning out to be more difficult
than she'd imagined. And not just because he'd managed to finagle an invitation to stay at the palace,
either. But because no matter how hard she pretended
otherwise, when she was with him his presence took
center stage. A part of her seemed always to be holding its breath, waiting to see what he would do or say
next.

Which was annoying but not totally surprising,
given the dominant force of his personality.

Far harder to accept was his ability to invade her thoughts. To her horror, every time she let down her guard even the slightest bit he seemed to be there, making her wonder all manner of things.

Like why was he pursuing her when he already had money, power and connections of his own? And what would happen if, in a moment of temporary insanity, she allowed him to get close? How would it feel if she let him kiss her? Or if she let him draw her into the strength of his embrace and touch her? And what would it be like to touch him back, to let her hands roam over his smooth, bronze skin…?

She scrambled off the chaise. Enough, she chastised herself, doing her best to ignore the way her heart was pounding. Clearly two nights of inadequate sleep were addling her brain. A condition that lying around brooding wasn't doing a thing to help.

Her time would be far better spent if she got moving, got some exercise, found a focus for her untrustworthy mind. And the time to start was now.

Impatiently she tossed back the tangled skein of her hair and marched into her room. Fifteen minutes later she was washed and dressed in a white shirt, slim beige twill pants and her favorite knee-high riding boots. She gathered her hair into a high ponytail, snatched up a thin navy vest to guard against the morning chill and slipped out her door.

Kristos, one of her bodyguards, sprang to attention. "Your Highness. Good morning."

She motioned for him to relax. "I'm going for a ride. I promise I'll keep to the palace grounds, so why don't you take a break."

He was clearly not thrilled, but after a moment he

nodded. "I'll let the stable detail know you're on your way."

"If you must." Swallowing a sigh, she started down the corridor, knowing the heightened security was necessary in light of what had happened to her father and grandfather, yet still disliking the increased loss of privacy.

Thanks to the thick, intricately patterned runner that covered the stone floor, the sound of her footsteps was muffled as she began the long, familiar walk toward the west stairway, which was closest to the stables. She reached the intersecting hall that led to the king and queen's apartments, nodded to the pair of guards standing sentinel there, and continued on, moving briskly until she reached a solitary door set midway down the remaining stretch of corridor.

And there she faltered.

She wasn't sure why. After all, she'd passed the entrance to her father's quarters numerous times since his death. And though she'd experienced any number of emotions—disbelief, grief, guilt—not once had she been tempted to step inside.

Until now.

Yet suddenly she wanted to know if Prince Marc had read the note she'd sent him the last day of his life. The note thanking him for going boating in her place with King Thomas and apologizing for disrupting his schedule. The note asking if they might meet later that day so she might explain the real reason she'd begged off at the last minute.

Whether her need sprang from simple curiosity, a belated need to reconnect with her father or some sort of subconscious attempt to occupy her mind with a subject other than the sheikh, she didn't care. She simply had to know. She opened the black-wreathed door and stepped inside.

The elegant sitting room looked the way it always had, as if it was waiting for the prince's imminent return. The carved mahogany furniture was freshly polished, the plush gold, maroon and navy carpet recently vacuumed. Her father's favorite smoking jacket lay folded over the arm of the Queen Anne chair next to the fireplace, and the cut crystal decanter on the wet bar in the corner was three-quarters full.

A lump rose in her throat, but she swallowed it. This was no time for self-indulgence; she'd already given in to enough rampant emotion this morning. Clinging to her composure, she dragged her gaze from her surroundings, crossed the room and let herself into her father's study. She walked to the desk that held his computer and switched the machine on.

Waiting as it hummed to life, she reflected on the contradictions of her father's personality. In so many ways—his belief in the superiority of nobility, his attitude toward women, his resistance to societal change—he'd been a nineteenth-century man. Yet he'd also been fascinated by new technology and had fully embraced the instant access of e-mail. Most likely, Catherine suspected, because without a paper trail he could ignore whomever he chose. In any event, during the past year it had become the best way to communicate with him.

She brought up his on-line server and clicked on the mail-waiting-to-be-read icon. Two entries appeared, and her heart sank as she saw that one of them was indeed hers.

Regret, sadness and a familiar sense of inadequacy washed over her. Well, really. What had she been thinking to harbor even the slightest hope that the prince would have considered anything she had to say of interest? She'd always known she was low on her father's list of priorities.

The only thing that was unexpected was that for once she didn't appear to be alone. Like hers, the other e-mail was timed and dated hours before the prince had left for the marina. Unlike hers, however, the subject line read "urgent."

She frowned, wondering what that could be about even as she clicked the read button and the entire message popped into view.

Your Highness,
The powers that be have agreed to your request, and everything is now in order. As long as the operation continues smoothly, your loan will be reduced as previously discussed.
Your servant,
The Duke

What on earth? Perplexed, she started to read the e-mail again when a faint sound behind her and a sudden prickle at the back of her neck warned she was no longer alone. Unwilling to explain what she was doing—not entirely certain herself—she instinctively clicked off the program before swiveling around.

Gregor Paulus, her father's aide and most trusted servant, stood in the doorway, his usual polite mask firmly in place. ''Your Highness. What are you doing in here?''

Although his manner was perfectly civil, there was something in his tone that made Catherine feel like the hapless child she'd been, the one whom Gregor had excelled at discovering at her worst possible moments. Like the time she'd beheaded all her grandfather's prize hothouse orchids to make a bouquet for her nanny. Or the night she'd hidden in her father's closet to surprise him with a good-night kiss only to be trapped when he brought Lady Merton home with him.

She didn't think she'd ever forget the fury in her father's eyes—or the disdain in Gregor's—when the servant had hauled her out of her hiding place the next morning. It most certainly hadn't been one of her more shining hours.

But she wasn't six anymore. She had every right to be here. And even if Gregor didn't agree, it was hardly his place to question her. She drew herself up and stared haughtily at him. ''I felt like it. What about you? Isn't it early for you to be on duty?''

He assumed an expression of wounded dignity. ''I beg your pardon, but Prince Marc liked having me here first thing in the morning. Carrying on, doing my best to get his affairs in order, is the least I can do to honor his memory.'' He sounded so sincere that Catherine felt a prick of remorse—until he added piously, ''Someone must.''

The verbal slap hit its mark. Try as she might to tell herself that Gregor wasn't worth it, that with her father's death he'd lost his power to harm her, his words hurt. Only her pride kept her chin up. The one thing worse than how she felt would be for him to know he'd succeeded in getting to her. "And who better to honor Father than you, Gregor?" To her relief, her voice sounded steady. "No one. So I'll leave you to it."

She could have sworn she saw a flicker of triumph in his pale blue eyes. Yet it vanished as she took a step toward the door and his gaze flicked to the workstation behind her. He stiffened. "Why is the computer on?" he asked sharply.

She shrugged. "I haven't the slightest idea. It was running when I came into the room." She doubted he believed her, but she didn't care. It suddenly felt as if the palace were pressing in on her and all she wanted was to escape. "If you'll excuse me, I'm due elsewhere." She brushed past him, not waiting to hear his response.

Just as she'd intended earlier, she'd go to the stables. By now a groom would have a horse saddled and warmed up for her. Except for the usual exchange with the stable master, she wouldn't have to talk to anyone, much less answer questions or explain herself. She would be able to simply climb into the saddle, take up the reins and head out. She could clear her mind, try one more time to put her feelings about her father into some kind of perspective and drive a stake through any lingering, inappropriate thoughts about the sheikh.

For a little while she'd be free.

Catherine swept into the short end of the L-shaped stable block, her boot heels clattering on the well-swept cobblestones. Blinking as her eyes adjusted from the sunlight to the shadowed corridor, she felt some of the tension drain out of her at the familiar scene.

A dozen roomy box stalls, six to a side, lined each wall, and were occupied by a dozen horses of varying sizes and colors. Some of the animals were still enjoying their morning meals, some were dozing, some stood alertly with their heads thrust out the upper halves of their stall doors. Although there was no sign of another human being, she knew that could be deceiving. "Chalmers?" she called.

There was a sudden movement in the stall to her left and a groom appeared, tipping his head shyly when he saw it was her. "Mr. Chalmers is in the long block, ma'am."

"Thank you, Carlo."

He nodded and she headed briskly down the passageway, swept around the corner—and plowed straight into what felt like a warm steel wall.

Her body knew instantly who it was. Her skin flushed, her nipples puckered, her heart thumped as a pair of strong hands reached out to steady her.

A second later her mind caught up with the rest of her, and she jerked her head up. Just as she feared, she found herself confronted by a pair of bold gray eyes in a familiar face. Her stomach flip-flopped. "You!"

Kaj looked down at her with a wry smile, a faint pair of grooves scoring his lean cheeks. "Good morning, princess."

She parted her lips to ask what he was doing here, then abruptly clamped her mouth shut. She'd asked that question far too often lately, and there was no way she was going to ask it again. Besides, a quick glance at his attire pretty much told the story. Like her he was dressed in a white shirt, breeches and a gleaming pair of tall boots. All he needed to complete his ensemble was a horse.

The discovery was as alarming as his presence. Or would be, she amended, if she gave a whit about how he spent his time. Which she didn't, as long as it wasn't with her.

She pulled free of his hold. "Pardon me," she said sharply, stepping around him. "Chalmers!" She lasered a gaze at the stable master, who stood no more than ten feet away, holding the reins of a compact blood bay as well as a rangy gray. "I assume Cashell is ready?" Not waiting for an affirmative—why else would he be standing there?—she strode forward and snatched the bay's reins from his hands. She glanced at the gray, automatically sliding a reassuring palm down her mount's neck when he pranced sideways. "Why is Keystone saddled?"

Chalmers looked uneasily from her to the sheikh and back again. "Mr. al bin Russard requested him, Your Highness."

Kaj moved to her side. "I thought we might go for a ride."

"Oh, did you?" Once again she moved away from him. Even so, he was still so close that with a sideways glance she could see the faint shadow of beard beneath his bronze skin and a faint scar that bisected his left eyebrow. Out of nowhere, an urge to reach out and touch him—to lay her palm against his cheek, run her fingertips over that inky eyebrow—swept her. Appalled, she wrenched her gaze away and slid the nearest stirrup iron down the saddle leather. "I don't think so."

There was a moment's silence, and then he inquired softly, "Are you all right, Catherine?"

She heard the concern in his voice and looked down to see her hands were shaking. Mortified, she bunched them into fists and rounded on him. "No! Yes! That is, I would be if you'd just leave me alone!"

"Ah." He nodded, his expression almost sympathetic. "I'm sorry, *chaton,* but that's not going to happen."

"Why? Because you have some ludicrous notion that if you hang around long enough I'll marry you?" She regretted the words as soon as she said them. After all, she had no basis for the accusation other than her suspicions. And even if it were true, he'd hardly admit it.

Which was why it was such a shock when he calmly nodded his head and said, "Yes. Precisely."

She stared at him in stupefaction. "You can't be serious! In case it's escaped your notice, this is the new millennium, the twenty-first century! I don't care who you are, you don't get to select a bride the way you would a piece of candy."

"I assure you I put far more thought into this than I would choosing a bonbon," he answered gravely.

"Oh! You're impossible!" She whirled away from him and, before he could make a move to stop her, swung herself lightly into the saddle. Instinctively adjusting her seat as the bay sidled nervously beneath her, she gathered the reins, freed the far stirrup and slid her foot into place. "In the event you still haven't gotten the message, the answer is no. No, I won't go riding with you. No, I won't marry you. Not now. Not ever. For the last time, I want you to leave me alone!'' She urged Cashell forward, not caring as the bay responded with an eager lunge that forced the sheikh to jump out of the way or be run over.

Somehow she found the control to keep the bay at a trot until they were clear of the stable and courtyard. But the minute they reached the path that led to the cliffs above Lucinda Bay, she gave the high-strung gelding his head. With a toss of his silky black mane, the animal leaped into a ground-eating canter that became a flat-out gallop as they turned onto the wide track that skimmed the edge of the headland.

The reckless flight perfectly matched her mood. She'd had enough of reining herself in, of behaving like some witless pushover. She was done allowing Kaj to alternately outrage and sweet-talk her. She was done with him, period. Marriage? What incredible nerve! She didn't even know the man—or him, her.

As for the inexplicable ribbon of loss curling through her, it had nothing to do with the sheikh. Yes, he was charming. Yes, he was attractive, in a purely physical, hormonal sort of way. And yes, she supposed that deep down a tiny, juvenile part of her may have been somewhat flattered by his attention. But that was all it had been; she didn't *care* about him. She didn't.

Cashell stumbled, startling her. He quickly regained his footing, but his misstep was enough to bring her back to the moment. Realizing the bay was tiring, she reined him in, bringing him first to a canter and then to a walk.

That was when she finally heard the sound of hoof-beats, coming on strong. She twisted around in the saddle, incredulous as she saw the sheikh atop Keystone bearing down on her. So what if the Walburaqui chieftain rode divinely, so flawlessly balanced in the saddle that he and the big gray might have been one body? How dare he follow her? How dare he disregard her direct order that he leave her alone?

Catherine couldn't remember the last time she'd completely given in to her temper. But now anger, hot and unfamiliar, bubbled through her. She reined in and waited, and when Kaj caught up with her moments later, bringing the gray to a sliding halt, she let go. "This is the outside of enough, sheikh! I want you to leave this instant—"

He cut her off, saying something in Arabic that sounded as fierce as it did profane. Then he vaulted to the ground, closed the space between them in two big strides, reached up and clamped his hands around her waist.

Catherine stared at him in shock, a funny feeling blossoming in the pit of her stomach. At some point during his ride his rich black hair had come loose and now brushed his open white collar. The bronzed vee of his chest rose and fell with his every agitated breath, while his gray eyes glittered like shards of silver. He looked achingly beautiful, more than a little uncivilized—and every bit as furious as she was.

She told herself that was his problem and vowed not to let him intimidate her, regardless of how formidable he might appear. "How dare you! Let go of me this instant or I swear I'll have you deported!"

"*Bes.*" Enough. He yanked her out of the saddle,

her feet barely touching ground before he gave her a hard shake. "What do you think you're doing, riding so recklessly?" he demanded through his teeth. "You could have broken your neck!"

She blinked. She'd expected him to berate her for her treatment of him, not care about her welfare. Not that it mattered. "Well, I didn't! And even if I had, what I do is none of your business!"

"The devil it's not." He pressed forward, looming over her. "Everything about you concerns me."

"Oh!" She shoved at his broad shoulders, but she might as well have tried to move the promontory they stood on. "Either you're profoundly hard of hearing or simply the most conceited man to ever walk the earth! Whichever it is, I don't give a damn. Just go away!"

"No. And don't swear."

"Or what?" she said scathingly. "You'll say something else I'll choose to ignore?"

She knew she'd made a mistake even before his jaw tightened. Still she wasn't prepared when he abruptly pulled her so close she could feel his heart thudding against her breasts. She parted her lips to protest, but that too proved unwise. With a savage murmur he lowered his head and sealed her mouth with his own.

Her mind reeled. She couldn't believe his sheer audacity. Or that rather than struggling to escape, she was standing statue still, allowing him to take such a liberty. But then, nothing in her life had prepared her for the pleasure suddenly pouring through her in a scalding tide.

The world around her vanished. There was only

Kaj, his heat enveloping her, his scent filling her head, his big, hard angular body the perfect fit for her smaller, softer one.

Far away, she heard someone start to moan. Vaguely she recognized her own voice, but it didn't seem to matter. What was important was the firm, knowledgeable mouth fixed to hers, the tongue breaching her lips, the heat spinning downward to pool in the tips of her breasts and the juncture of her thighs.

She couldn't seem to get enough. Not of the drugging warmth of his kiss, the hands clamped possessively to her hips, the tantalizing friction as their bodies pressed against each other.

He tugged her shirt out of her breeches and slid his hand over her bare abdomen. His thumb swept the lower curve of her breast. She sucked in her breath at the foreign sensation and willed his hand to move higher. When it did, she squeezed her eyes shut, unable to contain a whimper when his fingers closed around her distended nipple.

Her whole body flushed. She arched her back, pressing closer until she felt him, thick and hot against her. Startled and uncertain, damning her lack of experience, she hesitated, not sure what to do next.

Kaj had no such reservation. Reaching down, he slid one powerful arm under the curve of her bottom and lifted her up, bringing her to rest against the bulge of his erection. He pressed her against him, and all the hot, liquid sensation thrumming through her seemed to converge in one aching, sensitive spot.

It was way too much and not nearly enough. Guided purely by instinct, she wrapped her legs around his waist and rocked her hips, rewarded as a groan escaped his lips. He tore his mouth from hers and she started to protest, but the words caught in her throat as he shifted her upper body away from his and his lips found the underside of her jaw. He began to string a chain of kisses downward, into the open vee of her shirt. When he ran out of bare skin, he lifted his head. In the next second his mouth settled greedily over the swollen tip of her cotton-covered breast.

Hot. Wet. Urgent bliss. Sensations flooded her. Who would have thought that being with a man could be like this? That she—justifiably referred to as the ice princess by a legion of spurned suitors—could feel dizzy with desire? Not her.

The idea that she'd finally found a place where she belonged whispered through her mind.

And then it vanished, forgotten as a throbbing, unfamiliar need began to build in her, growing and growing until she couldn't think, couldn't breathe, couldn't stand it a second longer. "Kaj." She pressed her face into the silk of his hair. "Please. Make love to me."

For a moment he didn't seem to hear her. Then he went very still. A violent shudder racked him and the delicious pressure of his mouth at her breast ceased, replaced by the ragged wash of his breath. He slowly raised his head. "Catherine. *Min fadlak fehempt—*"

She might not know the exact meaning of his words but she recognized *no* when she heard it. Even so, for the space of several heartbeats she still didn't understand. And then it struck her. He didn't want her.

An icy fist seemed to close around her heart. As if emerging from a dream, she realized she was clinging to him like a starfish plastered to a rock at high tide. And that despite his obvious arousal, he was still very much in control of himself.

Her desire drained away, replaced by stinging humiliation. For the first time in her life she'd actually wanted a man to make love to her—and he'd said no. Her face burned and it was hard to breathe over the mixture of shame and embarrassment suddenly clogging her throat.

"Catherine?"

She pushed hard against him, and this time he let her go, which she took as a further sign of his rejection. "I...I beg your pardon." Unable to meet his gaze, she addressed the vicinity of his right ear. "This was clearly a mistake."

"No," he said roughly. "You don't understand—"

"Oh, yes, I do." She lifted her chin and forced herself to speak clearly, although she still couldn't bring herself to look directly at him. "I don't know what game you're playing, sheikh, but this never should have happened. Stay away from me. Just... stay away."

To her horror tears suddenly filled her eyes. Not about to break down in front of him, she swiveled on her heel, located Cashell and crossed to him. Her body felt leaden, but somehow she still managed to climb into the saddle where, without so much as a backward glance, she put her heels to the bay's barrel and urged him away.

Back ramrod straight, she pretended not to notice the tears running down her face. After all, there was no reason for them: it was her pride Kaj had bruised, not her heart.

She paid no attention to the small, inner voice that called her a liar.

Four

—

"Ah, there you are."

At the sound of his cousin's voice, Kaj looked up to see Joffrey step through the wide glass doors that opened onto the palace's west balcony. Backlit by the warm light that spilled from the first-floor drawing room, the Englishman looked dapper as always, his evening clothes impeccably tailored, his pale hair gleaming as he strolled across the exquisitely patterned tiles that comprised the floor.

Reaching a spot just short of where Kaj stood, his back to the balustrade, Joffrey came to a halt. "Getting some air?" he inquired.

Kaj inclined his head. "Yes."

"I must say, it is a lovely night out. Not too warm, not too cold. Full moon, beautiful sky. And while I'm a little disappointed in you, I suppose your aversion to being inside with the rest of us is perfectly understandable under the circumstances.''

"I beg your pardon?"

"I'm referring to Princess Catherine's choice of company this evening, of course. One can hardly blame you for conceding the field. Although personally I've always found that Italian bloke to be a tad cheeky. Then again, if the princess looked at me that way, I'd no doubt feel a bit brazen myself.''

Unable to help himself, Kaj glanced toward the drawing room. Catherine, exquisite in a black lace gown, stood inside next to the grand piano. She was listening intently to something Ricco Andriotti, the internationally known race car driver, was saying to her.

The two had had their heads together all through dinner. By the time the company had quit the table to stretch their legs and mingle, the brash young playboy had even grown bold enough to occasionally touch her. Which he did now, first gesturing ebulliently as he spoke, then reaching out to run a finger down her cheek to underscore his point.

Kaj forced himself to look away, afraid if he watched one second longer he might do something he'd regret. Of course, he wouldn't regret it nearly as much as Andriotti.

"She really does have incredible eyes, doesn't she?" Joffrey mused. "And those lashes. They're as thick as the imported paintbrushes Great-Aunt Marietta was so fond of. Add in all that lovely alabaster skin and one can hardly blame Signor Andriotti for wanting to leave his handprints all over—"

"*Shut up, Joff.*"

There was a brief silence. Then Joffrey delicately cleared his throat. "No need to inquire how the courtship's going, I see. So do be a dear boy and remind me to call home tomorrow. It appears I need to instruct my people to hurry putting the finishing touches on the stall I'm having readied for Tezhari."

Kaj sliced him a look as sharp as a razor blade. "Tell me, cousin, are you simply feeling reckless tonight, or are you deliberately courting a death wish?"

Joffrey had the brass to chuckle. "Oh, dear. As bad as all that, is it? Would it help if you told me all about it?"

Kaj smiled humorlessly. "I think I'll pass."

"Now, don't be hasty. You know what they say—confession is good for the soul."

"Yes, and silence is golden." Too bad he was the only one who seemed to know it, Kaj thought as he glanced back at the drawing room in time to see Catherine smile at something Andriotti was whispering in her ear. To his disgust, the race car driver's hand seemed to have taken up permanent residence on her forearm. He had a brief fantasy of snapping the man's fingers one by one.

Unfortunately, it didn't help that Catherine seemed to be hanging on the Italian's every word. She'd never looked at *him* that way. But then, he might as well be invisible for all the attention she'd paid him tonight. Hell, for the past two days she'd barricaded herself in her room, refusing to take his phone calls or accept either the notes or flowers he'd sent her. And the one and only time their gazes had met this evening she'd looked right through him.

Not that he didn't deserve her scorn. It was bad

enough that he'd lost his temper the last time they'd been together. But to also lose command of the situation, to first lay hands on her and then give in to the temptation to kiss her...

But that wasn't the worst. Oh, no. That designation was solely reserved for how close he'd come to mindlessly stripping Catherine of her breeches and taking her right then and there, out in the open, on the hard ground with nothing but gorse for a bed, where anyone could have seen them.

With no thought for her pleasure, but only his own.

A nerve jumped to life in his jaw. Never, ever, had he experienced such a monumental failure of control, not even when he'd been a raw, inexperienced youth and his father had arranged for a courtesan to instruct him in the art of love.

A part of him still couldn't believe what he'd almost done. And he certainly couldn't excuse it. Any more than he could excuse the clumsy way he'd handled things when he'd belatedly come to his senses. Thanks to his self-absorption, his shock at his behavior, he'd unwittingly hurt Catherine's feelings.

Not that she seemed to be suffering unduly, he noted grimly, his gaze never leaving her.

Nevertheless... For one of the few times in his life, he wasn't sure what to do. He was a man accustomed to taking command; sitting on his hands was no more his style than being on the outside looking in. But what could he possibly say to her? That she made him a little crazy? But not so much that he'd been willing to do what she'd asked and make love to her? He swallowed a sigh. Perhaps, if he gave it enough time, she'd come around all by herself...

"You know," Joffrey said suddenly, "I must say I'm surprised. It's not like you to so readily concede defeat. You still have three weeks remaining, after all."

"I haven't conceded anything."

"Really? You could have fooled me. Hiding out here in the dark, brooding and licking your wounds—"

Kaj frowned, beginning to feel irritated. "I am not brooding."

His cousin regarded him with raised eyebrows. "Then you're doing a bang-up imitation. And may I add, it doesn't suit you."

"What would you have me do? Go in there, grab the princess and cart her off to my room?"

"If that's what it would take to get that pathetic look off your face, yes."

"Pathetic?" Kaj repeated in a dangerously low voice. He drew himself up to his full height. "I'm never pathetic—" He broke off as he saw Andriotti sidle even closer to Catherine. Something primitive took hold of him, and his displeasure with his cousin shifted solidly to the Italian.

Joffrey was right, he decided abruptly. Standing around waiting for the perfect moment to approach Catherine wasn't accomplishing anything. It was time to take action. "Excuse me," he ground out, shoving away from the railing and heading for the drawing room.

"Does this mean I should hold off on phoning home?" Joffrey called after him.

Kaj ignored him and stepped inside. Whether it was his grim expression or the purposeful set of his shoulders, the other guests took one look at him and scurried out of his way, clearing a path as he strode toward Catherine.

She and the Italian seemed to be the only two people in the room oblivious to his presence. Though that made him feel grimmer still, he made a conscious effort to unclench his teeth when he reached them. "Catherine. Andriotti." He zeroed in on the smaller man, whom he topped by more than a head, and managed the facsimile of a smile. "Would you be so kind as to excuse us? There's something I need to discuss with the princess."

"Don't be ridiculous," Catherine contradicted immediately, laying a hand on the Italian's arm. "The sheikh is mistaken, Ricco. He and I have nothing to talk about. Nothing at all."

Kaj's gaze flicked from her hand to Andriotti's face. "I would suggest that you go, Ricco. *Now.*"

Whatever the Italian saw in his expression, it was enough to make the other man take a hurried step back. "Yes, of course," he said hastily, sending Catherine an apologetic look. "*Arrivederci, bella principessa.* For now." With that, he went.

Catherine shifted her attention to Kaj, her exotic green eyes glittering with anger. "You simply don't know when to quit, do you?"

"Let's take a stroll through the gardens," he countered, reaching out to clasp her elbow.

She jerked her arm away. "No. I'm not going anywhere with you." Her voice was frigid enough to cause frostbite.

"Yes," he said, "you are. Your only choice is

whether you prefer to do so under your own power or over my shoulder.''

She stared at him. ''You wouldn't dare.''

He didn't deign to answer but simply raised an eyebrow.

Furious color touched her cheeks. She glared at him for the space of several heartbeats, then with a little ''hmph'' averted her gaze and flounced toward the French doors. He fell in behind her, doing his best not to stare at the lissome line of her exposed back or the enticing sway of her hips.

She crossed the terrace, marched down the wide, shallow steps that led to the gardens, then turned to face him, her slender arms crossed over her breasts. ''Now,'' she said. ''What is it you want?''

Such an interesting choice of words. For an instant he actually considered telling her the truth. *You. I want you. Under me, on top of me, around me. Hot, wet, willing. For however long it takes to sate this exceptionally bothersome hunger you induce in me.*

Yet even without the protectiveness of her posture or the wariness in her eyes, it didn't take a genius to guess how that declaration would be received. Like it or not—and he didn't like it one bit—he was going to have to take a different, far more humbling, tack. ''I'd like to apologize.''

''For what?''

''For what happened between us on the bluff.''

Although he wouldn't have thought it possible, her expression grew even more remote. ''There's absolutely no need for that. You made your regret crystal clear at the time. So now if you'll excuse me—'' She started to step around him, intent on gaining the stairs.

"Catherine, don't." He moved into her path and reached for her.

She jerked back. "Don't you touch me!"

He raised his hands. "Very well. As long as you stand still and listen."

Once again she crossed her arms. "I'll give you exactly one minute. Then I'm calling the palace guard."

He took a calming breath and marshaled his thoughts. "As I said, I'm sorry about what happened. There's no excuse for my behavior, but if you only had more experience—"

"Oh! If you think I'm going to stand here and let you insult me on top of everything else, you're sadly mistaken. Get out of my way. Now!"

"*No.* Not until you hear me out. What I'm trying to say is that you deserve better—"

"Finally something we agree on!"

"—than for the first time we make love to be some quick, mindless encounter. My only defense is that I lost my head. I've known a number of exceptional women, but I've never desired anyone the way I do you. Which, I can assure you, you'd know if you had more experience."

For what felt like an eternity she said nothing. And then he heard her utter a faint, "Oh."

"Make no mistake, Catherine," he said, picking his words with care. "I want you. And I intend to have you. But not until the time is right. Not until you trust me and know that I want you for who you are, not just for the physical pleasure you make me feel."

"But…why bother?" The chilly note had left her

voice, replaced by defensiveness—and a faint note of uncertainty. "Why not just take what you can when it's offered? After all, you've already decided we should marry."

"Because you deserve better. You have a right to expect candlelight and tenderness, to have a man take his time with you. You deserve a lover who makes you feel cherished, not just drunk with desire. You shouldn't have to settle for a quick toss in the grass with someone you don't trust."

Again she was silent. Then, after what felt like a very long time, a sigh escaped her lips. "I don't understand you, Kaj," she said softly. "I don't understand you at all."

"All I want is a chance, *chaton*. A chance for us to get to know each other, to spend some time together. Perhaps we'll find we don't suit. But then again, perhaps we'll find we do. What can it hurt to find out?"

The question seemed to hang in the moonlit air between them. "I'm not sure," Catherine answered finally. "But you may not feel that way when you learn that I decided a long time ago that I'd never marry. You or anyone else."

"So perhaps I'll have to settle for our being friends."

"Do you mean that?"

"I always mean what I say." It wasn't a lie. He did want to be her friend, just as he wanted to be her lover. That he still intended to marry her despite her naive and unrealistic, if rather touching, intention to remain unwed, was a mere detail. One he had every confidence she'd come to view the way he did, as a practical necessity, once they spent more time together.

After all, she had no place here in Altaria now that Prince Marc was dead, while as the wife of Sheikh al bin Russard she'd have a position in society, unlimited wealth and the personal freedom to do whatever she liked. She was an intelligent woman; given a little time and the proper attention, she was certain to see the advantages of a union between them.

"All right," she said a trifle breathlessly. "As long as you understand how I feel."

"I believe I do. Now, what do you say to the proposition that we get away from the palace tomorrow?"

"To do what?"

He smiled. "I can't tell you that, Catherine. It would ruin the surprise. Simply say you'll meet me at the south portico at noon." By then he'd have figured it out himself, he thought wryly.

"All right. I'll be there."

"Good. Then there's just one more thing." Eliminating the space between them, he cupped her face in his hand. Her cheek felt baby smooth against his fingers, her jawbone light and delicate.

Apprehension flared in her eyes. "Kaj... I don't think—"

"Hush." He pressed his thumb to her lips; he knew he was taking a chance, but the need to erase every trace of Andriotti's touch on her was riding him hard. "Trust me." He slid his thumb to the base of her chin and lowered his head, ignoring the heady rush of need that deluged him as he settled his lips against hers.

Damn, she was sweet. Her scent, her taste, the tex-

ture of her skin...all of it pleased him. For a few
seconds he let his hunger off its leash, sliding his arm
around her, finding the bare valley of her spine with
his hand, allowing himself the sheer sensual luxury
of exploring that warm satin hollow with his fingertips.

Yet he had no intention of jeopardizing their newfound understanding. Just as quickly as he'd let himself go, he reined himself in, shifting his hand to the
lace-covered indentation of her waist and easing his
mouth away from hers.

"Ah, you're such a temptation," he murmured,
pressing a kiss first to one corner of her lips, then her
cheek and finally her temple. He rested his forehead
against hers, allowed himself a moment to catch his
breath, then eased back. He looked down at her with
a rueful smile. "But I swear to you that the next time
we kiss—if there is a next time—it will be only at
your invitation. Now, we'd best go in, before you
succeed in unmanning me completely."

Even in the moonlight he could see the look of
satisfaction that crossed her face, and he congratulated himself. Admitting to a temporary weakness
couldn't be all bad if it succeeded in restoring her
self-esteem.

"Come." He held out his hand and after the briefest hesitation, she took it. Try as he might, he couldn't
entirely contain a sense of triumph. Or quiet the
deadly serious little voice that whispered, "Mine,"
as, side by side, they headed inside.

Five

"Amazing," Catherine murmured, still trying to take in the sight before her: the glistening blue-white ice filling the temporary skating arena, the bubble dome enclosing it, the stereo speakers issuing pop music.

It would have been a surprise even without the presence of the children from the orphanage. But they were very much in attendance, dotting the ice like sprinkles atop an ice-cream cone. Some clung to the tubular rail that encircled the rink, some stood wind-milling their arms in desperate bids for balance, some were actually gliding around the mirrorlike surface. All together they were as noisy as a convocation of crows, expressing their delight in their surroundings with a mixture of shrieks and laughter.

Catherine turned to look at Kaj, unable to keep the

wonder out of her voice. "Whatever made you think of this?"

He shrugged. "Your cousin Daniel deserves some credit. He and I were enjoying a game of chess the other night when he mentioned you'd visited his family one winter in Chicago, learned to skate and had seemed quite taken with it."

"But that was a decade ago, at least. I can't believe—" She broke off as she realized she was about to say, You went to so much trouble to please me. Taken aback, since she certainly didn't consider herself as needy as such a declaration implied, she deliberately lightened her voice. "That is, however did you manage this? Skating rinks don't grow on trees, and there's certainly never been one in Altaria."

"I have an acquaintance in the amusement business in Trieste. I made a phone call. He took care of the rest."

He was obviously downplaying his role. Even if his friend had all the equipment to put together an ice arena in less than twenty-four hours, Kaj still would've had to secure the site, get a permit, arrange for power and water hookups and take care of a dozen other things she was no doubt overlooking.

"The most challenging part was having it ready by this afternoon," he confided. "It seems this much water takes a certain amount of time to freeze."

"Surely you realize I could have waited a day."

He shook his head. "I promised you a surprise. As I believe I've mentioned before, I always mean what I say."

To her dismay, his declaration made her suddenly remember something he'd said last night. *Make no mistake, Catherine. I want you. And I intend to have you.*

And just like that her mouth went dry and her nipples tightened. Hastily she crossed her arms, reminding herself sharply that that had been *before.* Before she'd made it clear that marriage wasn't for her. Before he'd conceded the most they might ever be was friends. Before he'd demonstrated his good faith by bestowing a kiss on her that had been a model of respect and restraint.

As for the tiny but willful part of her that persisted in hungering for more—it was her cross to bear. While Kaj's explanation for putting a halt to their encounter out on the bluff had eased the worst of her hurt and embarrassment, it wasn't an experience she had any intention of repeating. And surely, given time and familiarity, the shivery feeling she got when she was around him, as well as the zing of pleasure she experienced at even his most innocent touch, would dim. It had to, since the alternative was simply unthinkable.

"What about the children?" she asked. "What made you think to invite them?"

"Self-preservation." At her startled look, the skin around his eyes crinkled. "Given recent events, and your effect on me, princess, I thought it would be best for us to be chaperoned."

Some of her anxiety eased. "I'm glad you did. Otherwise, I suppose I'd have to skate alone, since I don't imagine they do much ice-skating in Walburaq."

"You forget I went to school in England."

"You skate?" She tried to picture it and couldn't.

He was simply too big, too intent, too seriously masculine for something so lighthearted.

A rueful smile curved his mouth. "In a manner of speaking. My mother's family has an extensive holding in Northumberland, and my cousin Joffrey and I spent our winter holidays there. He made certain I learned the local pastime. Initially, I've no doubt, because he enjoyed seeing me fall."

She considered his wry expression. "You're not serious."

"Ah, but I am."

"But I've met your cousin. Blond, rather serious, lovely manners?" He nodded his confirmation, and she couldn't contain a protest. "He seemed so civilized."

"A facade, I assure you," he responded dryly. "A devil in tweed would more accurately describe him."

As if a veil had been torn away, she suddenly heard the affection underlying his tone. "The two of you are close?" As fond as she was of her own cousins, she'd never spent much time with them. The idea that Kaj had a warm relationship with a member of his family, particularly one who seemed so different from him, was oddly endearing.

"Very. Despite his limitations as a skating teacher. Not to worry, however. Today I thought I'd limit myself to just being an observer."

She forgot all about their respective families. "No. You can't!"

One elegant black eyebrow rose. "I can't?"

"No." The mere idea of being watched by him made her skin tingle; she didn't want to think how her body would react to the real thing. "You can't go to all this trouble and then just sit on the sidelines like some kind of all-powerful pasha expecting to be entertained.''

"But I *am* a pasha, dearest Catherine, albeit an Arabian one.''

"Not today,'' she said firmly. "Today you're a participant.''

Their gazes met. He studied her a moment, and then his face softened and he inclined his head. "Very well. If that's what you wish.''

Her stomach did an unexpected flip-flop, and once more she tried to tell herself the cause was nothing more than sexual chemistry. Only, this time she didn't totally believe it.

She liked him. Or at least she could, she quickly amended, if this was the real him and not some carefully constructed act. Which she didn't think it was.

Not that *that* was necessarily good. She could handle being physically attracted to him, though it wouldn't be easy. But to actually become friends, to have someone in her life who was genuinely interested in her, who wanted to know her in more than just the Biblical sense...

She drew in a shaky breath. Giving him a second chance had seemed like the right thing to do last night. But now she wasn't so sure. Could she trust her instincts? Could she trust *him?* Or *was* she really so needy, so starved for attention, she'd lost all perspective? Even worse, what if she was just looking for an excuse to go after what she'd already decided she shouldn't have?

"Catherine.''

She jumped as he touched his palm to the small of her back. "What?"

"Quit thinking so hard." He urged her toward a bench near the curving, puffy plastic wall. "Today is about having fun. Relax." He motioned to a young man standing next to a large chest.

"I am relaxed." It wasn't a total lie, not really. As soon as she put some space between them—and got away from the delicious weight of his hand resting against her—she hadn't a doubt she'd feel much, much calmer.

She took a jerky step and abruptly sat down on the end of the bench, feigning interest in the youth approaching with a pair of large, square boxes. He set them down, retrieved two pairs of skates, and in no time at all she and Kaj were booted and laced.

"You're certain I have to do this?" Underlying Kaj's inquiry as they headed for the ice was a distinct note of reluctance.

"Yes."

He uttered a faint sigh, and to her surprise, she found she wanted to smile. Although it was hardly to her credit, there was a part of her that was looking forward to seeing him be less than his usually competent self.

But first she had a more immediate concern. The instant she stepped onto the ice, children approached from every direction, drawn to her like filings to a magnet. "We've been waiting and waiting for you," Marko exclaimed.

"Watch me, Princess Cat!" Christian demanded, doing an awkward pirouette.

"Look at my skates!" Isabelle pointed at her feet. "Aren't they pretty?"

"Will you skate with me?" Elizabeth asked.

"Me, too?" Nicco chimed in.

Just for a moment Catherine wondered what it would feel like to be free of obligation. The thought quickly faded, however, as she looked around at the faces turned hopefully up at her. If there was one thing she understood, it was a child's need for adult recognition. She summoned a smile. "Of course I will—"

"But later," Kaj said firmly. "First Her Highness needs to practice." He ignored the chorus of dejected oh's that greeted this pronouncement and leaned close to Catherine, his warm breath tickling her ear. "Quit looking so surprised. You deserve some time just for you." Straightening, he addressed the children. "I, however, would be delighted to skate with you. Or perhaps some of you might prefer to have a ride on my shoulders?"

There was an instant uproar. "I want a turn!"

"Me first, me first!"

"No, me!"

He raised a hand to silence the jangle of young voices, looking around until his gaze settled on Amalie, who was hanging back as usual. "What about you, little one? Would you like to go skating with me?"

She considered, then shyly nodded.

"Very well." As easily as that, he leaned down, turned her around and gently lifted her up, settling her squarely on his broad shoulders. "Don't worry," he murmured as the child took a death grip on his hair. "I won't drop you."

"Promise?" came her tremulous voice.

"On my honor."

Amalie thought about it, then relaxed enough to give him a tentative pat on the head. "'Kay."

He took in the other children's disappointed expressions. "Everyone who wants one will get a turn," he said, and the youngsters' faces immediately brightened. He turned to Catherine. "If you'll excuse us?"

Hopelessly if reluctantly charmed, she nodded. "Of course."

He nodded back, then turned and skated away, skimming over the ice so effortlessly he might have been born with blades on his feet.

So much for incompetence! She'd been conned, and though she told herself she ought to be mad, it was impossible. Still, she couldn't allow him to escape completely unscathed. "Has anyone ever told you you're a scoundrel, Sheikh al bin Russard?" she called after him.

He executed a graceful half turn so he was gliding backward. His teeth flashed whitely. "As a matter of fact, yes. I believe they have."

Oh! The man had more nerve than anyone she'd ever known. Which was precisely what made him so entertaining.

Deliberately she turned her back on him, doing her best to ignore the amusement dancing through her like sunlight on water. Still, she couldn't seem to stop smiling even as she took a few tentative steps of her own. To her delight, so quickly did she find her footing, it might have been days instead of years since her last outing. In no time at all she was lost in the sheer exhilaration of flying over the ice, and the next hour flew by. By the time she finally conceded to a break to catch her breath, she felt as giddy as a teenager.

And every bit as mischievous. Gliding out of the far corner, she eyed Kaj, who stood down the rail, standing to one side of a half circle of attentive children. Carefully judging velocity and distance, she sped up, then slid to a showy stop—a move that just happened to spray a certain Walburaqui chieftain with a shower of ice.

The children gasped. Then the gasps turned to smothered giggles at the sight of the frosty coating clinging to the sheikh's face. "Uh-oh," Marko murmured as said sheikh turned to consider Catherine.

Kaj deliberately wiped the clinging crystalline droplets from his face before raising one black eyebrow. "Having fun?"

She smiled sweetly at him. "Yes. I am. Thank you for asking. And you?"

His gaze flicked to her upturned mouth. Just for an instant something hot and dangerous seemed to flare in his eyes. Then he smiled and his whole face changed, leaving her to wonder if she'd just imagined that torrid look. "Yes, I believe I am. Despite a certain person's warped sense of humor."

"We're all having fun," Christian chimed in brightly. "But it would be even better if you'd skate with us, Princess Cat."

Wrenching her gaze away from the sheikh, she glanced around to find the children all staring expectantly at her. Grateful for the distraction, she nodded. "I'd be delighted."

"Good!"

"I want to be first," Isabelle declared.

"No, me!" Marko chimed in.

Christian pursed his lips. "How about if we all hold hands? Then everyone can skate together!"

There was a moment's silence as his suggestion was considered, then a sea of small heads bobbed up and down.

"Is that all right with you, Mr. Kaj?" Elizabeth asked, staring up at him with a worshipful expression.

"Certainly." He glanced at Catherine. "What do you say? Want to give it a try?" He held out his hand.

Once again she looked into his handsome face, her heart giving a familiar little stutter as their fingers brushed. "Yes," she said impulsively, "that would be—"

"Perfect!" Christian thrust between them, bristling with importance. "You can be on the inside, sheikh, because you're the biggest. And Princess Cat can be at the other end—" he took Catherine's hand and tugged her toward the rail "—because she's the fastest. And everybody else can be in between." He gestured at the other children to fall in.

Catherine glanced over her shoulder at Kaj, expecting him to protest. When instead he gave a philosophical shrug, she felt a prickle of disappointment.

She looked away, telling herself not to be foolish. The last thing she needed was to hold hands with the sheikh like some sort of vapid schoolgirl. Yet she couldn't deny the pang she felt when she glanced back and was just in time to see him reach down to clasp little Isabelle's skinny fingers with his much bigger ones.

In that instant she knew she'd been deluding herself.

Despite all her protestations to the contrary, what she wanted from Kaj al bin Russard was not a platonic friendship. So what, exactly, did she want?

Kaj strode along the headland path, moonlight lighting his way. Like a lover's playful fingers, the ocean breeze skimmed over his face, plucked at his white silk shirt, tugged at his pulled-back hair. He barely noticed. He was far too intent on identifying the cause of the uncharacteristic restlessness powering his steps.

He tried to tell himself it was merely the result of his longing for home. As had often happened during his school years in England, he was fed up with well-ordered gardens, constricting clothes, too many people and too many rules.

He wanted—no, he needed—to strike out with a few trusted kinsmen, to lose himself in the vast silence of the desert where he could travel for days seeing nothing more than a sun-drenched horizon or the endless black dome of a star-spangled sky. He needed to shake off civilization, speak his native tongue, drink in the hot, dry desert air and not this softly misted imitation fluttering in off the Tyrrhenian.

And it certainly wouldn't hurt if somewhere in there he could take Catherine to bed.

The last thought brought a sudden, reluctant smile to the tense line of his lips.

Very well. So perhaps there was more to his present mood than mere homesickness. Something resembling an ocean-size pool of lust that rose with each passing day, threatening to breach the dam of his restraint.

Ah. And I suppose that explains why finding a way to coax a smile from Catherine has become such a priority. Or why she's constantly on your mind. Yes, and let's not forget the growing need you have to protect her from any and every hurt.

He stubbornly gave a mental shrug. The truth of the matter was he'd always had a penchant for defending those weaker or less fortunate than himself. How could he not? Both his parents had been so self-absorbed while he'd been growing up that someone had had to look out for the hundreds of people who looked to the Russards for guidance, protection, support. He'd had no choice but to step in and do what had to be done.

As for Catherine, she understood duty and obligation, was exceedingly nice to look at, had breeding as well as style—just as he'd foreseen when he'd chosen her to be his wife. Of course he wanted to protect her. She now belonged to him, whether she wanted to or not.

That he found her interesting was simply an added bonus. As was her underlying kindness and the vulnerability she did her best to hide with her tart tongue and that raised, elegant chin. He was beginning to understand her well enough to know she'd deny she needed, much less wanted, a champion. But he hadn't missed her extreme surprise and genuine delight today at the skating rink—and he was glad for the chance to make her happy. If nothing else, having her depend on him could only benefit the long-term success of their marriage.

Yes, of course. But how does that square with your growing possessiveness?

Kaj hunched his shoulders and lengthened his stride. There was no way he could outpace his own misgivings, however, and after a moment he had to concede that that development was a trifle unsettling. Although he'd always viewed women as fascinating and complex, he'd also seen them as fairly interchangeable. If an association with one didn't work out, there was always another charming creature waiting to step into the breach.

Yet for some reason he didn't feel nearly so cavalier about Catherine. She was *his,* and while it made perfect sense that the idea of her being with anyone else was absolutely unacceptable, at some point during their little skating party today he'd realized she was the only woman he wanted. At least for the present—and even that was unprecedented.

Not to mention crazy. If he didn't get a firm hold on such fanciful thinking and soon, the next thing he knew he'd be wondering if perhaps he was on the verge of falling in love.

He abruptly stopped walking, which was just as well, since he'd reached the farthest point of the promontory. Thrusting his hands in his pockets, he blanked his mind, disgusted that he would entertain such a ridiculous idea even in passing.

With an iron will he forced himself to concentrate on the waves down below, watching as they dashed themselves against the projecting jumble of rocks, retreated, then came rushing in again.

He wasn't sure how much time passed before he realized he found the age-old action decidedly suggestive.

The discovery startled a laugh out of him, and like a puzzle piece snapping into place, he suddenly realized he'd been correct at the start of his walk. His uncharacteristic mood really *was* just frustrated desire. Catherine was the first woman to hold herself aloof from him, and as Joffrey would put it, he was in a "bad way." The fact that such a thing had never happened to him before explained why he'd allowed himself to get caught up in all these other unacceptable thoughts and uncertainties.

But now he knew. He wanted Catherine, pure and simple—and not just to fulfill the dictates of his father's will. Oh, no. He was way past the point of making her his solely out of duty. When he finally claimed her, he wanted her hot, slick, wet, whimpering with need, straining against him, her legs locked around his back, begging him to sheath every thick, aching inch of himself in the tight glove of her womanhood.

Even as his body throbbed at the images tumbling through his mind, he breathed a sigh of relief. Looking back on the day from this new perspective, he thought it safe to say he'd made definite strides toward achieving his goal. The skating idea had been nothing short of inspired, and Catherine had clearly been pleased. Add in his gentlemanly behavior, and he'd made definite progress in winning her over.

The next step would be more of the same. After

that, he'd find a way to get her off by herself, away from the palace, away from her friendly group of orphans, away from all other distractions.

Once he got her truly alone, she'd have no choice but to focus solely on him. And once she did, it shouldn't take much to get her into his bed. Then finally all these disturbing and uncharacteristic doubts would be vanquished for good.

As for the fantastical notion that he could be falling in love—it was absurd. Truly, absolutely, unequivocally absurd. Hadn't he seen what "love" had done to his parents and everyone around them? Hadn't he vowed never to get caught in a similar trap?

Absolutely. And he had no intention of changing his mind, now or ever.

No matter the temptation.

Six

"You, my dear *chaton*," Kaj said, "are a menace."

Accepting his steadying hand as she climbed out of the gleaming-hulled cigar boat, Catherine turned to look up at him the instant her feet touched the palace dock. "I beg your pardon?"

"You heard me." He jumped lightly down beside her. Wrapping his long fingers around her upper arm, he gently urged her toward shore as the dock attendants moved in to secure the mooring ropes. "Was there some purpose in cutting in front of that ocean liner? Other than giving me a heart attack? Or attempting to make my hair turn white?"

She glanced at the hair in question. Black as a winter night, as shiny as a raven's wing, several of the thick, straight strands had come loose from the leather thong anchoring them at his nape and now framed the strong angles of his sun-kissed face. Her fingers suddenly itched to touch him.

She looked away, filled with the by-now-familiar confusion she'd been immersed in since they'd gone skating.

The past handful of days had been amazing. She and Kaj had spent most of their waking hours together, engaged in activities from horseback riding to dancing the tango at Altaria's hottest nightclub. They'd gone on a picnic, spent an afternoon hang gliding, flown to Rome for a day of shopping, stayed up an entire night playing a cutthroat game of baccarat, which Kaj had waited until after he'd won to cheerfully inform her was Walburaq's most popular pastime.

Such were his persuasive abilities, he'd even convinced her to show him Altaria from the water—no mean feat since she hadn't gone near a boat since losing her grandfather and father.

Most amazing to Catherine, through all the things that they'd done, was how they'd talked. Perhaps not about their most private feelings—she still couldn't bear to discuss her father or the circumstances surrounding his death—but about more than fashion or the weather. To her surprise she'd shared happy memories of her grandmother, admitted how as a child she'd longed to go to a real school rather than be tutored, had even talked about her Connelly cousins and how she'd always envied them their bonds with each other.

For his part, Kaj had regaled her with tales of his schooldays in England, disclosed some of the difficulties he'd had growing up caught between two cultures, revealed an unexpectedly sentimental side when he'd described the ancient fortress built around an oasis that was his home.

And though none of their conversations had seemed particularly serious at the time, at some point Catherine had realized she knew that Kaj's parents' marriage had been an unhappy one, that he had no intention of repeating that particular bit of family history, and that for all his easygoing charm, he took his responsibilities seriously.

She'd also learned firsthand that he really was a man of his word. Just as promised, except for legitimate reasons like holding her when they danced, shielding her from the occasional paparazzi or helping her in and out of various vehicles, he'd kept his hands to himself. He'd been gallant and gracious, thoughtful and polite, concerned at all times with her comfort and pleasure—the perfect gentleman.

And it was starting to make her a little crazy. When they were apart, she wondered where he was, what he was doing and with whom. When she was with him, she wondered what he was thinking. And all the while her senses seemed to be operating on overdrive. A part of her was constantly tracking everything about him—the tone of his voice, the warmth that emanated from his skin, his scent, his relative proximity, his facial expression.

She was starting not to recognize herself. She'd tried to convince herself that her unusual behavior was the result of prolonged sleep deprivation, since she hadn't slept through an entire night since their first meeting at the ball—but she didn't really believe it. Something else was happening, and she was very much afraid she knew what it was.

He was getting under her skin, sweeping her off her feet, making a place for himself in her heart.

She had no intention of letting him know that, though. What she felt was too new, too unexpected, too fragile and ultimately uncertain to share. She was having a hard enough time explaining it to herself.

Suddenly aware that he was still waiting for a response to his accusation that she'd tried to scare him, she did her best to match his light manner. "Don't be such a baby. Everyone knows that big ships are notoriously slow. Plus we had scads of clearance time, and I was only at three-quarters throttle. Although I have to admit, I did love hearing the warning horn blare out. It sounded wonderfully dramatic, don't you think?"

His response would have been deemed a snort had it been made by anyone half so sophisticated.

She felt the corners of her mouth start to curve up, but quickly controlled herself. "In any event," she said, trying to sound austere, "I'd watch whom I criticize, sheikh. Let's not forget just who it was who attempted to take that wave sideways and very nearly flipped the boat. In the future you might want to consider sticking to those things you know."

"Very well. If you insist." He ceased his unhurried walk and pulled her around to face him. Then, his movements deliberate, he moved his hand slowly up her arm, slid it under her hair and cupped the back of her neck. "I'm just not sure where around here—" he lowered his head so she felt his warm breath against her lips, and her eyelids suddenly felt heavy "—I'd be likely to find a camel. Do you?"

It took a second for his words to sink in. When they did, her lashes snapped up and she found he was mere inches away.

He raised an eyebrow at the same time that a slow, devilish smile transformed the perfection of his lips. "What? You were expecting me to ravish you?"

She laughed. The sound burbled softly up, the result of an odd combination of exhilaration and embarrassment. "The thought did cross my mind," she admitted recklessly.

He shook his head and a loose strand of his hair tickled her cheek. "Not until I receive an invitation."

"Yes. So I understand." And finally she did. With a sense of wonder, she realized she trusted him. Enough to take a chance.

Her gaze locked with his, she brought her hand up and brushed his hair behind his ear. The errant lock was silkier than she'd expected, as was the arch of his ear. Intrigued, she traced the curve of his jaw with her fingertips. His bones felt larger, denser than her own, but his skin was surprisingly smooth despite the faint prickle of beard that lurked just beneath the surface.

"Catherine—"

"Shh." Then she breathed in, filling her head with the essence of him, a heady combination of spicy aftershave, soap, saltwater and sun, and suddenly such limited contact wasn't nearly enough. Sliding her hands around his neck, she pushed his collar out of her way, took a half step forward and buried her face in the warm hollow where his neck met his shoulder.

As it had that day on the cliffs, pleasure enveloped her. Only this time there was none of the frantic urgency, the uncertainty of being completely out of control, to distract from the experience of being close.

She closed her eyes, soaking up sensations like a sponge. She felt the steady thud of his heart against his chest, the hardness of his thighs through the finely spun material of his slacks. His chest was broad, solid, warm, a welcome refuge protecting her from the breeze blowing in off the water.

It was the smooth, taut, velvety texture of his skin beneath her cheek that made her head spin, however. With a sigh of pleasure, she snuggled closer, more than a little intoxicated by the pleasure of being in his arms.

She wasn't sure how long they stood there, bodies pressed together. Finally Kaj made a sound that was midway between a chuckle and a groan. "I was right," he murmured, his lips brushing her temple. "You *are* a menace." The words might have stung if hadn't added, "A beautiful, much too desirable one." His movements firm but gentle, he reached up, disengaged her arms from around his neck and set her away from him. "Now come." Linking his fingers with hers, he resumed his unhurried walk. "Let's see if we can't find some refreshment. I find I'm feeling a little overheated."

Any embarrassment she might have felt was banished by his admission. "I believe I could use something cold to drink myself," she conceded, breathless but happy as she strolled beside him. "And something to eat. All of a sudden I'm famished."

In companionable silence they reached the end of

the dock, crossed a swath of emerald lawn edged with bright splashes of blooming flowers, and proceeded up the wide stone staircase that led to the palace's main back terrace.

They hadn't taken more than a step or two across the tile floor of the gallery when a movement in the shadows of an archway to her right caught Catherine's eye. Her attention arrested, she came to a halt, tensing as Gregor Paulus emerged from the darkness.

He inclined his head. "Your Highness. Sheikh al bin Russard."

Something in the way his gaze flicked from her to Kaj and back again made her suspect he'd been watching them for some time, an idea she found extremely distasteful. "What is it, Gregor?" she demanded.

"Might I have a moment of your time?"

"Is it really necessary?"

"Yes, Your Highness. As much as it pains me to interrupt your…tête-à-tête, I believe it is."

She bit back a sharp reply. Sinking to his level would accomplish nothing. "Very well." She glanced at Kaj. "Would you excuse me? This shouldn't take more than a second."

Flicking a speculative look at the servant, he nodded. "Of course. I'll wait here for you."

She smiled, then turned away. As she approached Gregor, he stepped back into the gloom of the shadowed archway, beckoning her to follow with a crook of his long skinny fingers.

She barely had time for her eyes to adjust to the change in light when he came straight to the point. "I found this among His Highness's private papers this morning. I thought you'd like to have it.'' He held out a palm-size envelope, that she instantly recognized as bearing the crest and distinctive gold-edged design of the stationery used exclusively by her father.

A knot coiled in her stomach, part hope, part dread. Yet years of practice helped her retain an outward calm. ''Thank you,'' she said, taking the missive from him. She waited, willing him to leave. When he didn't budge, she managed a cool smile. ''Don't let me keep you. I'm sure you have other, more pressing duties to see to.''

''How gracious of you to be concerned.'' Despite his words, he made no move to depart. ''But before I take my leave, may I say how glad I am to see that the prince's death hasn't had an adverse effect on your enjoyment of the water?'' His unblinking gaze didn't leave her face.

Catherine recoiled. Although the words were perfectly benign, the sentiment behind them was anything but, as was obvious from the chilly dislike in his eyes.

Then and there, she made a vow to speak to Daniel about the man's insufferable attitude. In the meantime, she lifted her chin and said with all the hauteur she could muster, ''Leave me. Now.''

For the briefest instant he looked surprised, and then he inclined his head. ''As you wish.'' He made a cursory bow, turned and walked away.

She waited until he was out of sight, then slipped her finger under the envelope flap. She slid out the heavyweight piece of card stock. Her hands trembled slightly as she looked down and her father's distinctive handwriting jumped out at her.

Daughter,
I see no need for further discussion between us. Sadly, your decision to indulge your own desires rather than do your family duty doesn't surprise me. I will see to it your grandfather receives your regrets.

It was signed with Prince Marc's trademark looping *M*.

For a moment she couldn't seem to breathe. She'd been distraught when she believed her father had never received her e-mail message; now it appeared he had, but not only hadn't he cared, he'd continued to believe the worst of her, and oh, how it hurt.

It also served to revive her guilt: *she* should have been on the boat that day with King Thomas. If she had, perhaps she would have noticed something or somehow prevented the tragedy.

She suddenly could no longer contain her pain. She sagged back against a marble pillar and squeezed her eyes shut, fighting for control.

I will not cry. I will not. After all, this really isn't any great surprise. Father was angry; he hated having to dance attendance on Grandfather and clearly he wrote this before he had a chance to cool off and get over his pique. He didn't mean it, not really...

"Catherine? Has something happened?"

It took a moment for Kaj's concerned voice to penetrate her misery. Realizing how ridiculous she must appear, she straightened her spine and opened her eyes, doing her best to pull herself together. She dredged up a determined smile. "No, of course not."

"Then what's the matter?"

"It's nothing. I'm sorry I kept you waiting—"

"Don't," he said sharply. "Don't lie to me. Tell me. Now."

There was no mistaking his absolute determination to hear the truth. Still, she continued to resist, not entirely comfortable with sharing either her feelings or her problems. "Truly, Kaj, there's no need for you to be concerned."

His jaw hardened just for a second, and then his face abruptly softened. "Please." He reached out and lightly laid his palm against her cheek. "I'm not going away, nor do I intend to take no for an answer, so you may as well tell me what's upset you and be done with it."

His kindness nearly undid her. She swallowed, forcing down the tears suddenly clogging her throat as she conceded defeat. For all his gentle manner, it was clear he meant what he said. And she was in even less of a mood to argue with him than she had been with Gregor. Reluctantly she handed him the card.

He read through it in a handful of seconds, then looked at her questioningly.

She drew in a shaky breath and tried to put her thoughts in some sort of coherent order. "The day my father and grandfather died, I was supposed to be on the boat," she began. "Grandfather's eyesight was failing and I knew he didn't feel safe piloting the boat by himself anymore, but he was such a proud man. He absolutely refused to acknowledge that he needed help, so for several months I'd been going with him on one pretext or another.''

She couldn't contain a shaky sigh. ''But that day—that day I wasn't feeling well—I was suffering from some sort of nasty food poisoning—so I called Father and asked him to go in my place. He said he would, but it was obvious he wasn't happy about it, and before I could explain that I was ill, he accused me of being selfish, always thinking of myself, just like my mother. God forgive me, but I lost my temper. I told him he was absolutely right, that I was begging off because I had an absolutely essential appointment for a facial and manicure, and he—he hung up on me. The instant I heard the phone go dead, I realized how childishly I was behaving. I called him back but he wouldn't come to the phone, and as I was too indisposed to leave my room, I sent him an e-mail, asking if we might talk when he got back.

''This—'' she tapped the note card still in his hand ''—was his answer. His man Gregor, who's in charge of putting his affairs in order, apparently just found it.''

The line of Kaj's mouth had turned grim. Not at all certain what he was thinking, she turned to look blindly out at the last of the sunshine sparkling on the water. She cleared her throat. ''I should have been the one on the boat that day,'' she said, finally saying aloud what she'd been thinking for months. ''No matter how ill I felt, I was a better driver than Father. If only I'd been there—''

''That's nonsense,'' he interrupted harshly. ''For all you know, you would have been killed, too. You have to accept that accidents happen.''

"I'd like nothing better," she said fervently. "But it wasn't an accident."

"What? What do you mean?"

She felt his gaze sharpen but continued to stare out at the horizon. "At first we just assumed it was some terrible, unforeseen mishap. Then there was an attempt on Daniel's life in Chicago, and he and his family began to wonder. They hired an investigator, who's since found evidence the boat was sabotaged." Gathering her courage, she turned to face him. "Don't you see? If I'd been there, I might have seen something, or sensed that something was wrong—"

Looking into her anguished face, Kaj felt something fierce stir to life deep inside him. "And what if you hadn't?" he demanded, catching her by the arms and pulling her into the shelter of his body. "It would be you who was gone—and *that* is totally unacceptable to *me*."

In point of truth, while logically he could see that any ongoing threat most likely centered around Daniel and the succession, he felt a stab of anger that nobody had seen fit to even consider that Catherine might also be in danger, much less provide her with added protection.

Until now. Resolve hardened his voice. "What happened was not your fault," he said flatly. "It was a terrible thing, one we will talk about in greater detail in the future, but for now there's something else we need to discuss."

Clearly confused by his manner, not to mention the sudden change of subject, Catherine tipped her head back to directly meet his gaze, still looking pale and fragile from too much emotion. "And what is that?"

Her hair slid like silk against his hands; he ignored the instant stirring in his groin. "I have to leave for a few days. There are some things that demand my attention at home."

For the merest second her lips trembled, and then she got herself under control. "Oh."

He hesitated, but only for a moment. Cupping her chin in his hand, he stroked his thumb over her lips. "I don't want to go without you, Catherine. Come with me."

Seven

"**Y**ou're very quiet, *chaton.*"

Taken aback by Kaj's observation, Catherine considered a moment, then realized it was true. She gestured at the view beyond the tinted glass limousine window as their driver negotiated the busy downtown streets of Akjeni, Walburaq's main city. "There's so much to take in."

That was a decided understatement. Everywhere she looked there was an eclectic mix of East and West, old and new. Shiny new high-rises pierced the azure sky several blocks away, while directly around her sprawled the low stone buildings of what Kaj called the Old City. Booths from a variety of small markets or *soukhs* crowded the side streets. As the limo slowed to negotiate around a donkey-powered cart, she glimpsed swatches of jewel-colored silks, the glitter of gold jewelry, vast stacks of baskets and piles of colorful rugs all in a single narrow alley.

And the crowds! Clustered on the narrow sidewalks, men in traditional white headdresses and the long white robes that Kaj called *dishdashas,* rubbed shoulders with men in European-style suits. Similarly, women wearing the newest New York and Paris fashions looked like bright butterflies as they flitted among their more conservatively attired, black *abaya*-wearing sisters with their modestly covered heads.

It was all very exotic, and for an instant she almost convinced herself what she'd told Kaj was the truth—that her silence stemmed from a preoccupation with her surroundings. Augmented, perhaps, by continuing distress about yesterday's encounter with Gregor Paulus.

Except, Catherine the princess had traveled the world and had seen far more startling sights than this prosperous and beautiful city. And Catherine the daughter had long known better than to allow her father's manservant to upset her.

More to the point, much as she might like to pretend otherwise, Catherine the woman knew that the true cause of her reticence was sitting right beside her.

She still found it hard to believe she'd actually confided in him the way she had yesterday afternoon. For as long as she could remember, even when her grandmother had been alive, she'd kept her own counsel. No matter what the provocation, the public Catherine always raised her chin and put on a show of regal indifference. Tears and fears, hurts and disappointments, even hopes and dreams, were handled alone, in private.

Until Kaj. From the moment he'd thrust himself into her path at Daniel and Erin's ball, he'd managed to get beneath her practiced reserve. And though she'd long recognized the power of his personality—it had been her primary reason initially for wanting to avoid him—in the past twenty-four hours she'd come to see that she'd underestimated his sheer charisma and commanding presence.

That had never been more evident than earlier today when they'd stepped aboard his private jet and set course for Walburaq. A subtle transformation had come over him. Although he'd been as polite and attentive to her as ever, there'd been a tone in his voice when he'd dealt with subordinates, a decisiveness about his every move, an ease of manner that had made her more aware than ever that he was accustomed to being in charge and enjoying instant obedience.

And though that was hardly a surprise, her reaction to the palpable power he exuded was. Not only was she even more hyperaware of him than usual, but for the first time in her life she also felt a desire to cede control, to lean into his big, hard body and simply let go.

It scared her to death. And excited her no end.

"Shall I turn down the air-conditioning?"

Kaj's concerned inquiry penetrated her musing. She turned to look at him. "What?"

"You're shivering. Are you cold?"

"Oh. No, I'm fine."

Despite her assurance, his concerned gaze swept over her like a lick of fire and her nipples promptly puckered. She felt them pressing against the lace of her bra and a splash of heat burned her cheeks since she knew very well her reaction had nothing to do with the temperature and everything to do with him.

In the next moment he seemed to realize it, too. Realized it, but still—thankfully—misunderstood.

He reached across the plush leather seat, captured her hand and brought it to rest against his muscled thigh. "It's all right, you know. Even here in Walburaq our agreement still stands. Nothing will happen between us without your express permission. However much—" his voice dropped ever so slightly, at odds with the twist of amusement that lurked at the corners of his mouth "—I might like to lock you in the seraglio and keep you solely for my pleasure."

"Seraglio?" Her lips parted in surprise. "You have a harem?"

He gave a theatrical sigh. "Yes—and no. I have the structure to house one, but not the requisite concubines. Fortunately—or unfortunately, depending on one's viewpoint—my great-grandmother put a stop to that."

"Really?" Grateful for any diversion to keep her mind off his proximity, she cocked her head. "How on earth did she manage that?"

His silvery eyes, so startling, framed by his inky lashes and bronze skin, warmed. "Her name was Anjouli, and the story goes that she was very young and very, very beautiful. She was also exceedingly clever and wise, and it is said that it took Khahil, my great-grandfather, a very long time to coax her into his bed. Once he finally did, he was entranced. So much so that when she eventually gave birth to his first son— until then he'd been blessed only with daughters—he impulsively told her he would give her anything her heart desired. I can't help but believe he thought she'd request her own palace or a trunkload of jewels, but instead she asked that he be hers exclusively. He agreed, and that—'' his teeth flashed in a rueful smile ''—set a precedent for future Russard sheikhs.''

His smile was irresistible and she answered it with one of her own. ''Oh, dear. Is that regret I hear?''

He shrugged, careless, elegant, infinitely masculine. ''I think not. Even without a harem, I've managed to acquire a more than adequate amount of carnal knowledge. Enough to know what—and whom— I want.'' Once more, his gaze played over her, then settled on her face, riveting her in place.

Another shiver went down her spine, and this time she didn't even attempt to deny that he was the cause. Yet some proud and obstinate part of her still wasn't quite ready to reveal the depth of her growing desire for him.

Not here, not now, not yet. Not when she still wasn't sure if she intended to act on what she felt or keep him to his word and make this trip a purely platonic one.

Doing her best to look thoughtful and nothing more, she nodded. ''I see.''

Outside, the city fell away and the road opened up. Fine white sand stretched in every direction, framed in the west by the aquamarine glimmer of sky meeting sea and to the east by the jagged upthrust of the Kaljar Hills.

After a score of miles, their driver turned onto a side road that climbed through a series of rising sand dunes. Eventually the road leveled out and in the near distance Catherine could see the brilliant green foliage of a large oasis, ringed by a cluster of buildings whose rooftops could be seen over a mammoth, crenellated wall. Behind them, soaring upward, was a storybook palace built of glistening white stone, with gilded domes and exquisitely shaped towers that looked as if it had been plucked from the pages of *1001 Arabian Nights*. "Oh, my," she murmured.

"Home," Kaj informed her, pride and affection unmistakable in his voice. "It's called Alf Ahkbar—which roughly means a thousand shades of green."

"I can see why."

Minutes later the limo swept through the compound's main gates, then slowed as it advanced down a narrow stone road set between a double row of chenar trees. Off to one side was a plaza where a spring bubbled up to fill a large, rectangular reflecting pool. Several dozen people, mostly women and children, looked up from various tasks, smiling and waving as the car went past.

The vehicle approached another set of gates, these fashioned of elaborate ironwork. Their driver spoke into the car phone, and the gate opened, then slid shut behind them. Five hundred feet later the limo pulled into a circular courtyard and came to a stop before the massive front doors of the palace itself.

Catherine drew in a deep breath as the full magnitude of her agreeing to come here sank in.

For the first time in her life she was alone with a man on his home ground. And she still didn't know what she wanted to do. Marriage, of course, remained out of the question. But did she really want to spend the rest of her life as a virgin?

* * *

A faint knock jarred Catherine awake. Blinking the sleep from her eyes, she shifted on the azure velvet divan, taking a moment to get her bearings.

The tiled ceiling overhead was ornate, decorated with an intricate pattern of vines and flowers in shades of turquoise, indigo and celadon green. Thick blue-and-cream rugs covered the stone floor, and diaphanous silk panels lavishly embroidered with silver thread draped the arched doorway that opened onto the balcony. Matching silk panels encased the bed, which boasted a delicately carved headboard inlaid with lapis lazuli and a peacock-blue bedcovering scattered with tasseled pillows in shades of green and blue, amber, orchid and rose.

Unlike the more sedate furnishings of her rooms in Altaria, the chamber was lush, playful and exotic, a feast for the senses, and Catherine felt a return of the delight she'd experienced when she'd first laid eyes on it.

Which had been two hours ago, she realized with a jolt as she glanced at her wristwatch. Appalled, she sat up and swung her feet to the floor, doing her best to quell her fascination with her surroundings and force herself to think.

She remembered climbing out of the limousine, and her surprise at the sweet scents of roses and jasmine that had laced the crisp desert air. She recalled crossing the courtyard and passing through a tall, arched doorway. Once inside, she'd given a sigh of pleasure at the lovely detail of the tile and latticework walls, the tall ceilings and the cool serenity of the interior that had greeted her. There had been a wide staircase with shallow steps that climbed unhurriedly up to a long gallery, a formal-looking reception area furnished with exquisite Georgian furniture to the left and a mirrored hallway dappled with shadows and sunlight to the right.

But it had been the view directly ahead of her that had most enchanted her. A series of carved arches had opened onto a shaded inner courtyard. Stands of bamboo had whispered beneath a nearly imperceptible breeze, while plants in enormous pots provided brilliant flowers in shades of magenta, scarlet, and lavender. Small, colorful birds darted among the foliage, and a peacock strutted along a paved path past a three-tiered fountain that was the courtyard's centerpiece.

It had been hushed, soothing and beautiful and Catherine had loved it on sight. She'd been nearly as entranced by the rest of the palace when Kaj had given her a quick tour. If she'd also felt relieved when he'd escorted her to her own quarters, tacitly revealing that he didn't expect her to share his room, well, that wasn't surprising given the current turbulence of her feelings. But it certainly did not excuse her lying down to rest for a few minutes and promptly sleeping away the afternoon—

Another knock at the door interrupted her musing. Positive it must be Kaj wondering what had become of her, Catherine shook off her languor, scrambled to her feet and raked her fingers through her hair. "Come in," she called, stepping forward as the door opened. "I'm so sorry—"

She broke off in confusion. In place of the tall, powerful figure she expected, there was a slim, pretty girl of perhaps fourteen. *"Masa'a alkhayr,"* the teen said, making a quick curtsy. "I am Sarab."

Catherine shifted gears, trying to remember some of the Arabic words she'd been studying. *"Marhaba,* Sarab." Hello.

The girl's dark, liquid eyes sparkled with interest. "You speak Arabic?" she asked.

Catherine shook her head. "No. Only a very little. I'm sorry."

"That is very much all right, Highness," the girl assured her. "Most fortunately, as you can surely tell, I speak the English very, very well. That is why my *jaddah* sent me to assist you."

"Jaddah?"

"My grandmother. She is the sheikh's…how do you say?…keeper."

Although she knew the choice of word certainly had to be a mistake, Catherine couldn't contain a smile. "Keeper?"

The girl nodded earnestly. "Yes. For many years now she has had the charge of the entire palace."

The pieces fell into place. "Ah. You mean house-keeper."

"Housekeeper, yes." Sarab nodded enthusiastically, then flashed Catherine another melting smile. "Please, I may come in?"

"Yes, of course." Stepping back out of the way, Catherine gestured for the girl to enter.

Sarab crossed the threshold, looked around and headed straight toward Catherine's suitcase, which lay open on a stand next to an enormous satinwood wardrobe inlaid with mother-of-pearl. She glanced politely at Catherine. "It is approved by you that I unpack your things?'' Catherine nodded, and the girl began the task, her slender fingers deft as she started to transfer clothes to the wardrobe's padded hangers.

Catherine watched, feeling strangely ill at ease. Although she'd lived her entire life surrounded by servants, she'd never known one so young, and it bothered her. ''Have you worked for the sheikh long?'' she asked after a moment.

''Oh, no, Highness!'' The quick shake of the girl's head was accompanied by a small, amused giggle. ''I'm just visiting while my parents attend a conference. They are doctors.'' Her pride was unmistakable. ''My mother grew up here at Alf Ahkbar and has always been exceedingly clever, so Sheikh Kaj sent her to medical school as was her dream. He never forgets his people. He's a very great man, you know.''

This last was said with such reverence that Catherine was tempted to roll her eyes. Except that at the same time she felt a swell of something akin to pride.

Where on earth had that come from? she wondered, a little unnerved.

Sarab removed a stack of lacy lingerie from the suitcase. Holding the items as if they were made of cobwebs, she opened one of the wardrobe's drawers and laid them carefully inside. Worrying her lower lip, she appeared to ponder something, then turned to Catherine. ''A thousand pardons, Highness, but... might I ask you a question?''

Even temporary help in Altaria knew better than to be so forward. Catherine parted her lips to say no, then hesitated. ''Yes, I suppose,'' she said, her curiosity getting the better of her. Besides, it was better than trying to sort out the confusing mix of her feelings for Kaj.

"Are you going to marry the sheikh?"

So much for a diversion. "Why would you ask that?" she demanded.

Hot color tinged the girl's smooth cheeks. "Just…everyone is wondering. Sheikh Kaj has never brought a woman here, you see. He has a house in Akjeni where he…entertains. Not that I'm supposed to know that," she added hastily. "But you're so very beautiful and you seem so very nice, and Jaddah and my mother—all the village really—think it's time for him to settle down, even if one didn't have to consider Sheikh Tarik's most unfortunate will—" She broke off, her face growing even more flushed as she seemed to decide she'd now completely overstepped her bounds. "You do know about that, yes?"

There was nothing like having everyone know your business. Catherine felt a sudden sense of kinship with her host, as well as a perplexing protectiveness. "I believe the sheikh has mentioned it," she allowed.

Sarab continued to stare at her expectantly.

She lifted her chin. "As for the other, I haven't decided."

"But—" The girl swallowed whatever she'd been about to say, Catherine's cool tone apparently registering. She looked thoughtfully down at the open suitcase, then reached in and extracted two of the four negligees Catherine had impulsively brought with her, and placed them in the wardrobe. She delicately cleared her throat. "Sheikh Kaj is very handsome, is he not?"

"He is."

"And he would give you many pretty babies, yes?"

"Yes, I suppose."

"And he is generous and kind, brave and smart, tall and vigorous and very strong. He has much wealth and many beautiful homes and— Oh!'' The girl's eyes rounded and her hand flew to her mouth. "Oh, no!"

Catherine jerked her thoughts away from the idea of having Kaj's baby, which she found absurdly appealing. "What on earth is the matter?"

"I forgot!" the girl wailed. "Jaddah said I was to tell you the sheikh would be most pleased if you'd honor him with your presence in the Peacock Garden. And I forgot!"

"Oh." Her initial alarm faded. "Is that all?"

"All? You cannot keep him waiting. He is the sheikh!" The teenager made a vague, shooing motion. "You must hurry!"

Catherine started to protest, then reconsidered as she took in the girl's very real distress. Her expression softened. She agreed, "I suppose I shouldn't keep him waiting."

Yet even as she allowed Sarab to lay out fresh clothes and help her with her hair, Catherine couldn't quell a prickle of amusement as the girl's words about making Kaj wait kept playing through her mind.

Poor Sarab, she thought wryly, if only she knew. Compared to what else I've been keeping Kaj waiting for, this is nothing.

But perhaps—just perhaps, since she still hadn't made up her mind—that was about to change.

* * *

Kaj stretched his legs, pleased to feel the familiar comfort of the fine white cotton of traditional Arab dress against his skin.

It was good to be home. Settling a little deeper into one of the oversize garden chairs in the inner court-yard, he soaked up the familiar sound of the soft splash of water from the fountain. He could hear the usual evening breeze blowing beyond the sheltered walls of the courtyard, but within the compound the flower-scented air was still. The only movement came from the scores of candle-filled lanterns illuminating the garden, their flickering light painting gilded shadows on walls and foliage.

The only thing more beautiful, he reflected, as he lifted his iced coffee and took an appreciative sip, was his company.

He regarded Catherine across the intimate width of their wrought-iron table-for-two. With her elegant bones, creamy skin and gleaming, shot-with-fire hair, he'd always considered her lovely. But tonight there was something different, something special about her. And after painstaking consideration, he'd finally figured out what.

"So." He took another sip of coffee. "Are you going to tell me what has you so amused?"

Her eyes widened slightly—but not before a telltale gleam of comprehension sparked in their emerald depths. "Pardon me?"

He unhurriedly set down his tall, narrow glass. "Ever since you joined me there's been the ghost of a smile lurking at the edges of your mouth. It was there all during dinner and dessert, it's continued to tantalize me as the sun has set and the moon has risen, it's teased at my senses during our every conversation I'd simply like to know if you're ever going to share its source with me.''

Her eyes gleamed mischievously. "I don't know. I'm not sure that I should.''

Like a silken vise his desire for her tightened its hold on him.

He ignored it. Instinct told him that here, in what was indisputably his territory, it was more important than ever that *she* come to *him*. If keeping his hunger for her in check had also become a point of honor, an exercise in willpower that had his intellect pitted against his libido, so what? Eventually he *would* emerge the winner. "And why is that?''

Her lips curved a fraction more. "Perhaps because I think your ego is already more than healthy.''

He raised an eyebrow. "You don't say.''

"I do. Although you've proven to be such a gracious host I suppose I might make an exception.''

"How generous of you.''

"Yes, isn't it?''

Their gazes locked. Again his body stirred, and again he disregarded it. He took another sip of coffee. "Well?''

"Oh, all right.'' She gave an amused little sigh and made a production of crossing one leg over another. "It appears you have a fan club.''

He told himself sternly not to notice the way the thin fabric of her dress clung to her rounded breasts and slim thighs. "I do?''

"Mmm-hmm. Your housekeeper's granddaughter couldn't refrain from singing your praises.''

"Ah, Sarab. A lovely child. And exceedingly intelligent, too."

"You don't say?" She made no effort to hide the irony in her voice as she repeated his earlier words to him.

"But I do. What's more, I think it's extremely unkind of you to keep me in such suspense. What did she say?"

"I'm afraid I don't remember exactly." Her voice was airy. "Something about you being tall. And healthy, for someone your age. And I believe the word *handsome* may also have been used. But then, she *is* just a child."

The tartness of her humor pleased him. Too much. Suddenly restless, he came to his feet. "One with excellent taste," he said, stepping around the table and holding out his hand. "Come."

She was clearly puzzled by the abrupt change in his manner. "Where?"

"The moon is up. Let's take a walk."

To his gratification, she asked no further questions but pushed back her chair, took his hand and came to her feet, following his lead as he made his way to the far side of the garden and up a narrow set of stairs. He unlocked the gate at the top, and they stepped out onto the wall walk.

"Oh, Kaj," she murmured in an awestruck voice.

Bathed in pearlescent light, the desert seemed to stretch endlessly before them, still and silent except for the invisible play of the wind, while to the east a full moon lay low in an immense cobalt-blue sky. Not to be outdone, stars shimmered overhead, some spilled in swaths like vast rivers of sequins, some solitary and immense like the finest of diamonds.

It was breathtaking. But not half so much as Catherine's upturned face as she turned toward him, her eyes shining with reflected starlight. "It's beautiful. Absolutely beautiful."

There was something in her expression.... He tensed with anticipation, expecting her to come closer, to reach out and touch a hand to his arm or face or shoulder, to finally tell him she wanted him.

Instead, as their eyes met, her expression changed, transforming from warm delight to something he couldn't identify. Puzzled, he tried to put a name to what he was seeing—doubt, longing, chagrin? Before he could reach a conclusion, a trace of brilliant light streaked across the sky and Catherine hastily turned away to watch it. "A shooting star!" she exclaimed. "How perfect."

He considered her averted face and stiff spine. Whatever she felt, her body language spoke for itself. She may as well have donned a sign that said Don't Touch Me.

Frustration and what felt alarmingly like need roared through him. "I suppose it is," he managed.

She fixed her gaze on a distant spot, gingerly ran the tip of her tongue over her lower lip, then quietly ventured his name. "Kaj?"

"What?"

"Thank you for asking me here. For being—" she paused, as if searching for just the right words "—such a good friend."

Friend? She couldn't mean it. What about *lover?* He clenched his jaw, excruciatingly aware the cotton pants that had been loose earlier in the evening now felt damnably confining—a ridiculous state of affairs for a man of his age and experience.

"A ridiculous state of affairs, period," he could just imagine his cousin Joffrey drawling in his usual amused way.

The thought of what else his relative would have to say about the current situation made him grimace. Yet it also served to remind him of what was at stake. He wanted Catherine to be his wife, not just a one-night stand.

And not because he had designs on Joff's painting, he thought impatiently. But because he was now more convinced than ever that she was the perfect choice for him. She was smart, interesting and beautiful, generous of heart but nobody's pushover. He had every confidence she'd be a caring mother to his children, a thoughtful and responsible guardian of his people, a gracious hostess, an asset to his varied business dealings. She was clearly not inclined toward promiscuity, but still spirited enough that he doubted he'd ever suffer from boredom.

And hadn't he learned by watching his parents the incalculable value of making a well-thought-out match, of never letting his body or emotions overrule his common sense?

Of course he had.

He slowly let out his breath. "I'm honored to be your friend, *chaton*. Thank you." Bracing himself against the increased desire that touching her, no matter how innocently, always brought him, he reached out and clasped her small, elegant hand. "Come. I'll take you to your room. It's been a long day and you must be tired.''

She parted her lips as if to protest, then appeared to think better of it. "I suppose you're right," she said in a subdued voice.

By way of an answer he walked over and opened the gate, indicating with a flourish of his hand that she should precede him down the stairs. Avoiding his gaze, she did as asked. Congratulating himself on his self-control, he closed the gate and started after her.

And that was when he discovered his mistake. All it took was one look at the firm, rounded cheeks of her derriere flexing beneath her thin dress to send his testosterone level soaring again.

Scowling, he flicked a baleful glance at the heavens, knowing he was doomed to spend yet another restless night alone.

Eight

———

Coward.

Catherine paced her bedroom, her self-condemnation gaining ground as she replayed her exchange with Kaj over and over.

Despite what some of the men in her past had assumed, her virginity didn't make her either naive or unworldly. And while she was currently of the opinion that that didn't always qualify as an advantage, she still couldn't escape the truth: the moment she'd stepped into the courtyard tonight and seen Kaj sitting there, something inside her had shifted and she'd known he was the one she wanted to be her "first."

The reasons then—as now—seemed obvious. She admired how comfortable he was in his own skin, the way he could be commanding without being a bully, the fact that he could make her laugh. She liked his strength and tenacity, his willingness to stand up to her, his wry sense of humor. She cherished his unexpected kindnesses and respected his honesty.

Young Sarab had gotten it right when she'd said he was a good man.

That he was also heartbreakingly handsome and wonderfully exotic Catherine had always known. But seeing him this evening, dressed as befitted the Arab half of his heritage, so clearly at ease with himself and so assured of his masculinity, she'd also realized how tired she was of fighting her attraction to him.

So she'd let down her guard just as she had after her encounter with Gregor. Only this time instead of telling Kaj her troubles, she'd given herself permission to reveal her softer, more playful side. She'd done her best to make sure he knew she was enjoying herself. And that she enjoyed being with him.

And everything had gone well—until the time to speak up had come and she'd faced the prospect of admitting she'd changed her mind, that she wanted him in every way the word *want* could be defined. Looking up at him, her fingers tingling with the urge to touch him, to brush back a stray strand of his glossy black hair, to trace the line of his eyebrow, to explore the muscular contours of his chest, she'd panicked. Not only hadn't she confessed she wanted to make love with him, she'd actually thanked him for being her friend.

Just thinking about it made her wince.

In stark contrast to her sorry performance, Kaj had been an absolute gentleman, not pressing her to deliver what they'd both known she'd been promising.

Which might not have been so bad if she hadn't clearly seen both the desire, the surprise and the disappointment in his eyes in the moment she'd lost her nerve and turned away.

But she had. And she couldn't get his expression out of her mind. Making matters worse, no matter how many times she went over it, she didn't understand why she'd behaved as she had. After all, her decision to have sex with Kaj hadn't been a sudden whim. Over the years she'd known plenty of attractive men but had never felt the slightest urge to share her body with any of them. Yet, where Kaj was concerned, one way or another she'd been thinking of nothing else ever since they met.

So why, why, *why,* having finally made a decision, had she acted the way she had?

Restless, uneasy, agitated, she reached the far end of the room. She started to turn to retrace her path, only to freeze as she caught sight of her shadowy reflection in the mirrored wall of the bathroom a dozen feet away.

Her long, nearly transparent silk robe of peach, pale-green and cream clung to her bare shoulders. The flimsy garment did nothing to hide the way her ice-green satin nightgown molded to her high breasts or rounded hips or the long line of her thighs. Her hair was tumbled around her shoulders, her cheeks were flushed, her lower lip plump and swollen from being gnawed on.

She looked like a woman who'd just rolled out of her lover's bed. Or a woman in a fever to climb in....

She whirled away, unable to bear her own image, much less the ideas it provoked. Pacing back the way she'd come, she felt as if she couldn't breathe. Her heart began to pound; her skin felt tight; the walls seemed to close in, making the same space that earlier had been such a source of pleasure now feel like a gilded cage.

Unable to stand it a moment longer, she fled toward the balcony, threw open the French doors, took a half dozen steps outside—and just as suddenly jerked to a halt, sucking in what little breath she had left.

Twenty-five feet to her right stood Kaj, his head bowed, his back to her, his hands braced against the parapet. He was barefoot and naked from the waist up, and, despite the distance between them, thanks to the moonlight she could see the muscles in his wide shoulders and lean waist bunch with every slight shift of his weight.

Her stomach hollowed. Her throat went dry and she felt a sudden throbbing at the apex of her thighs. Most alarming of all, however, was the way her heart squeezed at the tension of his posture.

In a burst of clarity, she understood what she'd refused to face only minutes earlier.

She cared about him. More than she'd ever cared about another person. Enough that earlier tonight some self-protective part of her had made one last desperate attempt to keep him at arm's length and keep her heart safe. Enough that the only word powerful and exclusive enough to describe what she felt was...*love*.

She remained stock-still as the idea washed through her, half expecting her sanity to return and tell her to stop being ridiculous. She didn't love Kaj. She couldn't. Hadn't she long ago decided that love wasn't for her?

Yet as the seconds ticked by, as the sensual play of the wind cooled her cheeks, tugged at her hair and ruffled her gown, her inner voice remained silent. With a growing sense of wonder, she realized that loving Kaj al bin Russard simply felt…right. That this time there were no doubts.

She wasn't sure how long she stood watching him, her heart hammering in her chest, her throat tight, her eyes stinging with her newly realized feelings.

But eventually, watching him wasn't nearly enough, while the need to touch him became overwhelming.

She began to walk, drawn to him like a compass to true north. Desire beckoned, tempting her to keep going until she was pressed against his gleaming bronzed back. Only her sense of fair play held her back, insisting he deserved something more.

Something better.

She stopped when a mere arm's length separated them. "Kaj."

His head jerked up. Although only an instant passed before he swiveled around on the balls of his feet, she was so attuned to him she saw the slight shudder that went through him before he turned. Nevertheless, he didn't look happy to see her. "What are you doing out here?"

Raising her chin, she stood her ground. "I need to tell you something."

He was shaking his head even before she finished. "Whatever it is, I'm sure it can wait until morning."

She might have been discouraged if not for the

sheen of perspiration suddenly sleeking his skin, the tautness rippling his abdomen, the effort he had to make to control his breathing as his gaze flicked over her. Despite his attempt to convince her otherwise, he was anything but indifferent to her. "No," she said softly. "I don't think so."

Impatience flashed across his face. "Catherine—"

She stepped close enough to reach up and press her fingers to his mouth. "I want you, Kaj. Make love to me."

He went still as a statue. His eyes locked on hers, not wavering even as she allowed herself the luxury of stroking the strong line of his jaw.

He cleared his throat. "What did you say?"

"Make love to me. Teach me how to make love to you."

For another second he remained anchored in place. Then he slowly let out his breath, looped his hands around her waist and tugged her close. "Damn. I was beginning to think you'd never ask." Bending his head, he covered her mouth with his own.

Magic. Madness. Bliss. Her body seemed to melt like a candle overrun by a forest fire. She molded herself against him, exulting in the satin-over-bronze texture of his skin, the flat planes and rounded curves of muscle in his chest and arms, the sleek power of his legs as he pulled her into the cradle of his thighs.

He became her universe. His breath fed her lungs, his strength held her up, the beat of his heart dictated the rhythm of her own. A rhythm that began to race as he slid his hands lower and gently squeezed the sensitive curve of her bottom.

She whimpered and pressed even closer.

His mouth still fused to hers, he swept her off her feet and into his arms. She vaguely registered that he was carrying her somewhere, but it didn't matter. What did was the delicious heat of his tongue tangled with hers, the sweet sensation of having one of his hands press the side of her breast while the other cupped her hip. Then there was the way the swelling ridge of his erection pushed against her with his every step.

Angling sideways, they passed through a doorway. Surprised by the faint smell of sandlewood and cloves, she broke the seal of their mouths, lifted her head and looked around.

She knew immediately she was in Kaj's bedroom. It was larger than her room and more lavishly decorated, the walls embedded with bands of gold and silver tiles in a diamond pattern. An opulent rug covered most of a pale marble floor. She had an impression of dark gleaming furniture, dimly realized the soft, exotic music she heard was spilling from hidden speakers and that the scents that had first caught her attention were coming from a dozen glowing candles grouped together in a wall niche.

But it was the oversize bed that quickly became her focus. Backed by a massive headboard of gold and silver latticework, it was framed by gold cloth drapes that swept to the floor. The matching satin comforter lay folded across the bed's foot, exposing rich black sheets. The effect was uncompromisingly masculine and breathtakingly handsome.

Which perfectly described the master of Alf Ahkbar, she thought, her gaze swinging back to Kaj as he set her on feet. Cupping her face in his palm, he brushed his lips over her cheeks, jaw and brow. "You're sure?"

Tenderness flooded her. For all that his voice sounded calm, she felt the slight tremor in his hand. "Yes."

"Very well." He took a half step back, unwound the band of fabric at his waist and stepped out of his pants. Her breath lodged in her throat as his erection sprang free and she had her first unobstructed view of what a real man looked like.

Massive. Impressive. Impossible. The thoughts tumbled through her mind a little hysterically before her reason reasserted itself. After all, men and women had been procreating for untold centuries, she reminded herself, and everyone seemed to survive. At least everyone she'd ever known.

Then Kaj slid her robe off her shoulders and her gown over her head, and her thoughts fragmented yet again as she glanced up to find *him* looking at *her*. Too aroused to be self-conscious, she watched, flattered and fascinated as the skin across his nose and cheekbones drew tight at the same time a muscle ticked to life in his jaw.

"Ah, princess… Do you know how beautiful you are? How perfect?" He brushed the pad of his thumb across the straining tip of her left nipple. "How much I hunger to make you mine?"

His thumb strafed her tender flesh again and her knees nearly buckled. Instinctively she stepped forward to clutch his broad shoulders for support, only to shiver as she felt his thick masculine length press firmly against her stomach. "As a matter of fact—" she did her best to ignore the heat she felt rising into her cheeks "—I believe I do." She pressed a kiss to the shallow valley between his pectoral muscles.

His response was midway between a groan and a chuckle. Gently weaving his hands into her hair, he tipped her face up to his. "Why do I suddenly have the feeling you're going to make me as crazy in bed as you do out of it?"

"I can't imagine. Perhaps because you're beginning to know me?"

Although her words were lightly spoken, as he looked down at her his amusement drained away. "Yes," he said, slowly running his thumbs over the curve of her cheekbones to frame her mouth. "I think perhaps I am." With that he leaned down and once more began to kiss her.

The play of his lips was even more drugging than before. A fever of need seemed to spread through her, and instinctively she locked her arms around his neck and hoisted herself up, wrapping her legs around his hips.

Her action obviously surprised him; for a moment his whole body stilled. Then he made a fierce sound low in his throat and wrapped an arm beneath her to brace her, lifting her higher and deepening the kiss.

She felt the broad tip of his staff nudge against her at the same time his tongue stabbed possessively into her mouth. Excitement, anticipation and need went from bud to blossom, deepening the ache pulsing at her center. "Kaj. Yes. Oh, yes." Loosening her hold on his neck, she sank down and felt him slip shallowly inside her.

"Catherine, darling, slow down. I don't want to hurt you."

"You won't," she assured him breathlessly. "You couldn't. I want you, Kaj. Inside me. Now." Trembling, she wrestled the tie out of his hair, thrust her hands into the thick, inky locks and dragged his head to hers. "Please." Copying his action of a moment earlier, she breached his mouth with her tongue and mimicked the slow thrusting motion that had set her own blood on fire.

He made a strangled sound of protest. Or was it surrender? The answer came as he abruptly tightened his hold on her and flexed his powerful hips.

Catherine felt a brief, unexpected flash of pain as he slid deeper, then a stinging discomfort as her body stretched to accommodate him. The latter was more than bearable, however, offset as it was with other sensations: the drugging warmth of his lips plying hers, the delicious friction of her nipples rubbing against his hard chest, the unexpected sense of security she felt being in his arms. "More," she urged impatiently.

A shudder passed through him, shaking them both. Then he bent his knees and pushed.

The slow slide of him inside her seemed to last forever and left them both out of breath and trembling. Fully buried, he dragged his mouth away from hers to brush kisses over her cheeks and eyes. "Are you all right?" he murmured.

"Mmm," she answered, her focus inward. "Don't stop."

"No. I won't." Shifting his hold on her, he pulled back slightly, then rocked his hips.

It was like dragging a match over a strike strip. Heat flickered, expanded, flared. It was only a tiny flame at first. Until he repeated the motion. And then she caught fire. "Oh!"

Again he moved, settling into a steady pumping rhythm that soon had her rocking back.

"Kaj."

"What?"

"It's not—" She sucked in air, her voice shaking. "It's not enough. I want...I need...you. Deeper. Harder."

"Aw, Catherine. Sweetheart, you're killing me." Tightening his grip on her to keep them joined, he walked toward the bed, where, the muscles bulging in his upper arms, he slowly lowered her until her upper body rested on the high mattress.

Bracing his legs, he pulled back until he was almost out of her. Automatically she tightened the lock of her legs on his waist. "Kaj, please—"

"Shh." To her disbelief, instead of immediately acquiescing to her plea as she expected, he shifted his hands so that one supported her bottom while the other slid over the top of her thigh. Then one big finger skated sideways, zeroed in on the swollen seat of her need and rubbed. She cried out in shocked pleasure, and that was when he drove forward.

For one mind-altering moment the world ceased to exist as she knew it. Her stomach hollowed, her skin flushed, her back bowed, her every muscle clenched as she was swept by a monumental explosion of pleasure.

Powerless against such hot, mindless delight, she felt herself tighten around Kaj as he pumped full into her. He gave a guttural shout, then she too was again crying out as a second, even stronger explosion rocked her.

Catherine gladly bore his considerable weight when he collapsed on top of her moments later. And she knew, even as he wrapped his arms around her, keeping her close as he rolled onto his side, that nothing in her life would ever be the same.

Kaj lay sprawled in the center of the bed, one hand tucked beneath his head, watching with lazy interest as fingers of sunshine reached through the window tops to paint shimmering golden stripes on the ceiling overhead.

He felt boneless. Satiated. Beyond content. But then hours and hours of incredible sex with an incredible woman could do that to a man.

He shifted to look at Catherine. She lay nestled against him, her head cradled on his shoulder, her arm draped across his chest, her fingers lightly tracing the path from his ear to his collarbone. Although she'd stirred awake some twenty minutes ago, they had yet to speak. There was no need since their shared silence was so comfortable they might have been lovers for years.

Kaj had never experienced anything like it. Or like the night they'd just shared. His hunger for her had seemed to grow as the hours passed. Their every kiss, every touch, every joining had only made him want to hold her closer, thrust himself deeper, feel her shudder and cry out yet another time. And though he'd managed to cling to some semblance of control, to leash his strength so he wouldn't hurt her, he hadn't been able to stop. He doubted they'd slept an entire hour altogether.

Which might have concerned him far more were it not for the fact that, as often as not, it had been Catherine who'd initiated another round of lovemaking. She was definitely unique, a jewel to be treasured, he thought, idly rubbing his thumb over the silken skin of her hip. "Good morning, princess."

Her fingers stilled and she angled her head up toward him. "Good morning yourself," she said softly.

"How do you feel?"

"Tired. Marvelous." She gave a small, delicate yawn. "What about you?"

"Me?" He considered. "As if I just ran the world's longest marathon." He smiled. "And won."

She smiled back, and he realized she looked different. For the first time since they'd met she'd lost her usually guarded expression.

The discovery made him feel even more protective and territorial than usual, and he gathered her even closer. "I've pictured you here, in my bed, you know. I imagined the way you'd look against these very sheets, with your white skin and Titian hair. But my imagination didn't begin to do you justice."

"Oh." Pleasure colored her cheeks, but she glanced away from him and ran her hand over the exquisitely soft fabric that draped their hips. "*I* never imagined black velvet sheets. I always thought satin sheets would be the preferred choice for…worldly pursuits."

He shook his head. "No. Satin feels either too hot or too cold. Plus it's slippery."

"Ah." She considered a moment, then nodded thoughtfully. "No traction. A definite drawback."

His lips twitched at her serious tone. "My, aren't you a quick study."

"I suppose I am." She shifted to look at him. "Is that a problem?"

"Absolutely not. Your intelligence is one of the reasons I chose you to be my wife."

For a long moment she was silent. Then she said with a touch of amusement as well as something else he couldn't quite identify coloring her voice, "Do you know, sheikh, I remember agreeing to a lot of things last night. But a marriage proposal wasn't one of them."

He twisted a lock of her hair around his finger. "I rather imagine that's because I was too busy with other things to ask. But I will. And when I do, you'll say yes."

You'd better. Because you're mine, sweet Catherine, in every way that matters. And I intend to keep it that way.

The sudden violence of his emotions caught him by surprise, and he felt an abrupt stab of uneasiness.

He promptly shrugged it off. After all, he'd already acknowledged she inspired a host of unique feelings in him: possessiveness, protectiveness, an unprecedented tenderness. Just as he'd admitted that, though he didn't love her, he cared about her in ways he'd never cared about another woman. The fact that he wanted to please her, to make her happy, was a miracle all by itself.

A miracle that should help ensure that theirs would

be a successful marriage. "Trust me, *chaton*. We're meant to be together."

Her face softened, but to his surprise all she said was, "I'll think about it."

As responses went, it was totally unacceptable, and for one very long moment he was tempted to press the issue, to do whatever it took to bend her to his will. He hadn't a doubt that if he put his mind to it he could make her give him the answer he desired.

Yet, after a bit more thought, he realized such a power play was unnecessary. Given what had occurred between them in the past twelve hours, it was obvious she had deep feelings for him. All he had to do was be patient and she was bound to come around to his way of thinking and see the advantages of a union between them.

The realization sent a surge of energy through him. "Very well. In the meantime—" gently shifting her off him he climbed out of bed "—it occurs to me there's someone you should meet."

"You can't be serious."

"Oh, but I am."

Yawning again, she made a shooing motion. "You go ahead. Visit whomever you like." She snuggled deeper into the bed. "I'll stay here. I'm afraid I'm not in the mood to make conversation."

"That's quite all right. My friend isn't big on talk."

"Kaj—"

He held out his hand. "Please?"

Her gaze touched his proffered hand, took a leisurely dip lower, then slowly rose to his face. She chewed her full bottom lip. "Would we shower first?"

Given that he was once again as hard as a rock, it seemed like an excellent idea. "Yes."

"In that case..." She tossed off the covers and reached for him.

Nine

"So?" Kaj stood next to his friend, one hand resting on the big fellow's muscular shoulder. "What do you think?"

"Are you serious?" Catherine stared in awe at the huge orange tiger, who from whiskers to tail had to measure over nine feet long. "He's incredible. And utterly beautiful."

Kaj cocked his head. "You sound surprised. Did you think I was making things up that day at the orphanage when I told the children about him?"

"I wasn't sure," she admitted.

He made a faint tsking sound. "You need to have more faith in me, *chaton*. Although I've been known to withhold information during business negotiations on occasion, I don't lie. And certainly not to children."

"Yes. I know that. Now."

"Good. Now come say hello to Sahbak. Like me, he has a penchant for beautiful, red-haired women."

She didn't hesitate to do as he bade. Partly because she'd been raised to always show courage when confronted with a challenge. But also because she trusted Kaj not to put her in danger. Moving forward to stand at his side, she offered her hand to the big cat to be sniffed.

"Have you known that many?" The words popped out of her mouth before she could stop them.

"What? Redheads?" He gave her a lazy smile that made her feel warm all over. "Personally, just one. Sahbak, however, is acquainted with a number of such ladies. Although the captive Amur tiger population is considered to be stable, his genes are still very much in demand."

"I've never heard of Amur tigers."

"You've probably heard them referred to as Siberian tigers."

"I thought Siberian tigers were white."

"No, those are actually Indian tigers."

She rolled her eyes, and without warning, Sahbak took a friendly swipe at her hand with his long pink tongue. It was not unlike being stropped by a damp emery board and she gave a slight start. "Oh!"

"He likes you." There was no mistaking the satisfaction in Kaj's voice. "Good."

"You make it sound as if I've passed some sort of test." She tried not to sound as pleased as she felt as the cat licked her again.

"I'd say you have." Kaj scratched behind the animal's rounded ears, and the beast promptly began to make a low rumbling noise that was clearly the tiger version of purring. "After all, we've known each other a long time, he and I. I was just seventeen and he was a mere cub when he was given as a gift to my father. He's usually quite a good judge of character."

Unable to help herself, she rubbed her hand over the ruff of white fur that encircled the tiger's neck. "Then perhaps you won't be offended if I tell you I'm not sure I approve of an individual person, rather than a zoo, having this kind of animal. In Altaria, trading or owning any sort of endangered species is illegal."

"As it should be everywhere, since there are less than a thousand Amurs left, wild and captive. But the man who acquired Sahbak as a cub has never concerned himself with legalities, no matter the country, much less cared about wildlife conservation. And my father always believed *he* was a law unto himself. It took me several years just to convince him to have Sahbak's name entered in the International Tiger Studbook, and he only agreed then because he knew no one could force him to give the tiger up."

"Your father sounds rather difficult."

"My father was impossible," Kaj said simply. "He could be charming when he chose, and he did have some qualities I admired, but the majority of the time he wasn't an easy man to be around, particularly in the latter years of his life. He had to be in control, and he was willing to do whatever it took to get his own way."

Catherine reached out and touched her hand to his arm. "I'm sorry."

The strain on his face abruptly vanished. "Yes, I know you are. And while it's not very noble of me, it's a relief that you understand. Which is another example of why we're so well suited."

"Now, sheikh," she admonished, amused by how quickly his mood had turned around, "let's not ruin a perfectly lovely afternoon by bringing that up again. I told you I'd think about us. And I will."

With a wry smile he squeezed her hand. "Very well. But in an attempt to redeem the family image, allow me to at least explain that, except for a female with cubs, tigers are by nature solitary creatures. They don't do well in groups, which can put a real strain on zoos and other captive habitats. Because of that, and because I have the resources to provide a very large and customized enclosure, Sahbak is better off here than he would be any number of other places."

"He certainly appears to think so." She watched as the tiger, apparently tired of all their talk, leaned against Kaj and nudged the sheikh with his large head, clearly impatient to be petted again.

Ever dutiful, Kaj again began to scratch between the animal's ears, although he had to strain to stay on his feet as the contented beast slouched more and more against him.

"How much does he weigh?" Catherine asked curiously.

"Six hundred sixty pounds. And at the moment—" with a grunt, he gave the tiger's shoulder a shove that seemed to affect the placid Sahbak not at all "—I'm feeling every one of them. Lazy bounder."

"Pardon, Mr. Kaj." They both looked over as the younger of the two men Kaj had introduced as the tiger's caretakers spoke up from just outside the enclosure gate. "You have a phone call. Mrs. Siyadi transferred it from the main house to the office here. She says to tell you it's the call you've been expecting."

"Thank you, Jamal," Kaj answered. "I'll be right there." He motioned to Saeed, the other handler, who'd been quietly standing vigil several yards away, poised to intervene if the big cat made any unexpected moves. "If you'd be so kind as to take over. Sahbak seems to have a number of itches that need to be scratched."

"Certainly, sir." Walking slowly, Saeed went to stand opposite Kaj and began to knead the animal's neck. Snuffling happily, Sahbak shifted his weight toward the source of this new pleasure, barely taking note as Catherine and Kaj made their way out of the enclosure.

Clasping Catherine's hand, Kaj interlaced their fingers as they walked up the slight hill toward the airy stone structure that housed Alf Ahkbar's stables. "Praise be for phones," he said dryly. "Another few minutes and Sahbak would have been on top of me. An experience I've had previously and would prefer not to repeat."

"Did he hurt you?"

"Only my dignity. But being a tiger's doormat is not the image I want you to have of me."

There was slight chance of that, Catherine thought wryly, her pulse racing merely from the innocent contact of their fingers.

But then, where Kaj was concerned, she seemed to be ultrasensitive in all sorts of odd places—the backs of her knees, ears and neck, the inside of her wrists, the bottom of her feet—that until last night she'd never considered erogenous zones.

Even more confounding, her lips and breasts, as well as the inside of her thighs, actually ached. And not from being tender or tired as might be expected. No, they ached for *more*.

For the first time in her life she understood what it was to hunger for a man. To hunger for Kaj.

Coming on the heels of last night, it surprised her. She'd just assumed that once they made love the sharpest edge of her desire for him would be dulled. That she'd feel relaxed and fulfilled. That the compulsion to be close to him would ease and that the little things like a warm look from him or a husky tone in his voice would lose their power to affect her.

Clearly that hadn't happened. And didn't seem likely to in the immediate future.

Kaj let go of her hand and motioned for her to precede him into the large, air-conditioned office just inside the stable block. "This should only take a second," he promised, giving her arm one last, proprietary squeeze. Moving across the well-appointed space, he propped a hip on top of a large, curved desk, turned the phone around, put the receiver to his ear and punched a button. "Russard."

She looked around, taking note of the state-of-the-art computer workstation, the floor-to-ceiling stainless steel file cabinets, the inviting seating area that occupied the room's near corner. But it was the display of framed photos on the far wall that drew her. To her delight, a closer inspection proved that although most of the pictures were of horses, Kaj also appeared in some of them.

In one he couldn't have been more than two or three. Nevertheless he sat proudly atop a lovely dapple gray mare, a smile of unabashed delight warming his small face. Even then he appeared to have a light grip on the reins.

In another he was perhaps five years older. His face was thinner, his body long and rangy, his expression oddly guarded for someone his age. All of the joy that was so evident in the first photo was gone.

In the next several shots there was again a jump of several years. But to her relief, in these he appeared happy again, something she attributed to his company—a smaller boy with gilt hair and an impish smile who could only be his cousin Joffrey.

Smiling, she admired a teenage Kaj and his horse done up in full native regalia, caught her breath at a shot of him in formal English hunting attire atop a big bay taking an enormous cross-country fence, nodded her approval as he was caught leaning down to accept a blue ribbon and silver plate atop the same horse.

Next on the wall were several snapshots of him as a tall, elegant youth on the cusp of manhood, a tiger cub that had to be a young Sahbak in his arms. There was also a larger, more formal picture, this one with a man who had to be Kaj's father, and the cub. Boldly inscribed across the bottom in black ink was an inscription.

"My dear sheikh. May my humble gift to you grow to be as noble and fierce as his new master. Your servant, The Duke."

She frowned, disturbed but not certain why. Something about that last seemed almost familiar....

"Catherine? Is something the matter?"

With a start, she realized Kaj was standing beside her. "No. I don't think so."

"Then why are you frowning so?"

"It's just that this picture..." She trailed off, feeling silly. Surely the use of that title was just a coincidence. Lord knew there were lots of dukes in the world.

"What about it?"

"Do you know the man who wrote this?" She indicated the inscription.

"I know him, yes. His name is Georges Duclos. The other is an appellation I'm sure he gave himself."

"He's not a real duke?"

He grimaced. "No."

"What does he do?"

He gave her a puzzled look. "Why do you want to know?"

"I just do."

He considered her a moment longer, then sighed, no doubt at the determination that most likely was stamped on her face. "Very well. If it's important to you. The duke is a middleman of sorts. He made a vast fortune as an illegal arms broker in the 1980s, then retired and did his best to become part of the so-called jet set, befriending a number of influential European and Arabic royalty.

"Because he still had criminal contacts and a total lack of scruples, he gained a reputation as a fixer, if you will. He was—and is—someone who can provide a prominent, married friend with the name of a person willing to put a scare into an ex-girlfriend who threatens to go to the tabloids, for instance. Conversely, he's also been known to connect a wealthy crime lord who wishes to see a certain law watered down or eliminated altogether with a down-on-his-luck but still-well-connected aristocrat.''

Catherine turned to stare blankly at the photo as she digested what he was telling her. ''I see.''

Kaj laid his hand on her shoulder. ''Now tell me why he's of interest to you.''

''It's probably nothing, just a coincidence. But a few weeks ago I used my father's computer to check his e-mail. I was trying to see if he'd read my message, the one I told you about. More to the point, there was another e-mail. I don't remember the exact wording, but in essence it assured my father that things were in order and that as long as something continued to go on unhindered, a loan he'd taken out would be retired.

''I honestly didn't think much of it at the time, since my father often did favors for people and I'd only recently learned he owed a great deal of money, and I had…other things on my mind. But I do remember it was signed exactly the way your photo is: 'Your servant, The Duke.''' Ignoring the sick feeling twisting through her stomach, she forced herself to meet Kaj's gaze without flinching. ''The more I consider it, the more likely it seems that your duke and mine could be the same man.''

''Yes.'' Kaj's voice was unexpectedly gentle. ''I think you're right.''

They both fell silent, considering.

Catherine was the first to speak. "Given this Duclos's reputation and the kind of people he knows…" She swallowed. "Do you think he could have anything to do with what happened to Grandfather's boat? Or the attempt on Daniel's life?"

Kaj shook his head. "Doubtful. Or at least, not personally. Remember, he always acts merely as a middleman. As for the third party he was representing, if you're accurately remembering what was in that e-mail, it sounds as if everything was under control. Why would anyone commit murder if they didn't have to?"

"Yes, I suppose that's true."

"In any event, when we get back to Altaria we can make a hard copy of the e-mail and let the king and his people take it from there. That is, if that's all right with you?"

"It's fine." It was more than that, really. Having someone she could confide in, whose judgment she trusted and who treated her like an intelligent partner, was a rare and precious gift.

"Now, quit worrying." Wrapping an arm around her shoulders, Kaj drew her toward the door. "This will all work out, I promise you, although it may take some time to get all the answers."

They stepped into the stable aisle, and as if there to provide a distraction, a good two dozen priceless Arabian horses, their necks extended over the bottom halves of their stall doors, nickered as they caught sight of Kaj.

Catherine raised her eyebrows. "My, you're popular. Let me guess—these are all mares."

"Of course not." He gave her a smug, supercilious look that was so unlike him she had to choke back a laugh. "Such is the strength of my appeal that I'm appreciated by all of my horses."

She did laugh then. "Oh, really? I don't suppose it could have something to do with the carrots you were handing out earlier?"

"Certainly not." Pulling her close to his side so they were pressed hip to thigh, he urged her toward the end of the corridor. "Now enough of this nonsense. We're falling behind schedule."

"We have a schedule?"

"Yes."

"I don't suppose you'd be willing to share it with me?"

"But, of course. First we're going to eat the lovely late lunch Mrs. Siyadi has prepared for us. Then I think we could both use a nap so we'll be well rested for tonight."

"What are we doing tonight?"

"Now that, *chaton,* I can't tell you. After all—" he swung her around, planted a kiss on her lips, then pulled quickly away, a devilish glint in his smoky-gray eyes "—if I did, it wouldn't be a surprise."

Kaj pulled the blindfold loose from Catherine's face and took a step back.

He watched with a now familiar combination of tenderness, expectation and lust as she made a slow circle, her long legs flexing in her high, spike heels, her body slim and supple beneath her thin blue sheath. She took her time, examining every detail of her surroundings.

The tiny oasis, with its handful of palm trees and its deep crystalline pool. The pair of glossy-coated horses and the stacks of supplies he'd had brought in so he and Catherine might stay as long as it suited them.

The airy pavilion, draped with silken hangings, lit against the night by dozens of hanging brass lanterns. The priceless jewel-toned carpets piled to create a floor over the soft sand. The large *dawashak,* or mattress, covered in dozens of pillows.

And surrounding everything, for as far as the eye could see, the desert. Empty. Mysterious. Eternal.

By the time Catherine's gaze finally came to rest on him, her beautiful green eyes were wide and awestruck. "I feel as if I've stepped into a dream," she said softly.

"You're not disappointed we didn't go into Akjeni to sample the nightlife, then?" He'd been afraid after he'd assisted her into the Land Rover instead of the limo that, blindfolded or not, she'd guess they were headed somewhere more remote than the capital.

"Don't be silly. Although—" she did her best to shape her lips into a pout "—when you told me to pack an overnight bag I did think it was possible I'd get a chance to see your apartment there. Or do you call it a love nest?"

Damned if she wasn't always surprising him. Every time he started to think of her as sweet and malleable, she drew a line, threw in a little spice and reminded him that she hadn't been referred to as the Ice Princess for nothing.

And he was glad. The occasional tartness of her tongue coupled with her refusal to worship at his feet pleased him. Immensely. "I can see I'm going to have to speak to Mrs. Siyadi. Sarab talks too much."

"Don't you dare."

"Very well. If you feel that strongly." He closed the space between them and cupped the back of her neck. "But I'm afraid my cooperation will come at a price."

She tipped her head up. "Blackmail, sheikh?"

He leaned down and lightly kissed one corner of her mouth. "I prefer to think of it as taking advantage of an irresistible opportunity."

"Lucky me." She turned her head and captured his lips with her own.

Their kiss was tender, teasing, full of mutual understanding and silent promises about the night to come. Kaj had never experienced a kiss quite like it, and while his body reacted predictably, his mind marveled. *This is what you've been waiting forever for. This closeness, this silent communion, this sense of rightness.*

Out of nowhere, unease slithered down his spine. Irritated, he brushed it away, telling himself it meant nothing, that it was simply the result of his lifelong habit of limiting whom he trusted. Given that he intended he and Catherine would be together for the rest of their lives, it was clearly time he started letting down a few barriers. As for the rest, they'd just have to see. Maybe with time…

He ran his hand down the silken valley of her spine. Urging her closer, he savored the slowly accelerating drumbeat of desire pounding through him. She was so very lovely. And he was so intent on exploring the sweetness of her mouth, it took him a moment to register that her hands were pressed against his shoulders, pushing him away.

He released her instantly. "Catherine? Sweetheart? What's the matter?" Even to his own ears, his voice sounded ragged.

She drew in a shaky breath of her own. "Nothing."

"Then why—"

"I have a surprise for you, too."

"Trust me." He reached for her. "Whatever it is, it can wait."

"It could, but that would also ruin it." She stepped back out of range.

"Catherine—"

"Indulge me, Kaj. Give me a minute and allow me to change into something more comfortable. Before I punch a hole through your carpets or break an ankle in these shoes."

"Take them off. Better yet, take everything off."

She smiled. "Try to be patient. Now, where did you put my bag?"

He took a firm grip on his temper and reminded himself that every woman he'd ever known had certain idiosyncrasies. If Catherine didn't want him to see her in her pantyhose, or something equally ridiculous, he supposed he could live with it. It wasn't as if he were some randy youth, after all; he was a grown man who for good reason prided himself on his self-control.

Still, he couldn't resist a small, long-suffering sigh. "Your bag is in the back of the tent, behind the partial wall."

"Thank you. You may not believe it now, but I think you'll appreciate the delay." Going up on tiptoe, she bussed his lips, then turned on the balls of her feet and headed inside.

Determined not to add to his own torture by watching the sway of her hips, Kaj resolutely turned away. Yet he couldn't seem to get Catherine's "surprise" completely out of his mind. What could she possibly have planned that was worth delaying their mutual satisfaction?

Clasping his hands behind his back, he walked over to where the supplies were stacked and made sure everything was in order. Next he checked the horses, who, unlike some people, seemed to welcome his company. Finally he walked back to the entrance to the pavilion and, desperate for a diversion, raised his face to the clear night sky and began to count stars, alternating between Arabic, French and English in a last-ditch attempt to keep from turning and walking inside.

Wahid, deux, three, *arba, cinq,* six…

He'd gone all the way to *sitten*—sixty—when Catherine's soft voice saved him. "Kaj?"

He turned. And looked. And looked some more.

Gone was his modern, sophisticated princess. In her place was a barefoot siren in diaphanous emerald-green trousers that clung to her hips and a matching jeweled bra that appeared to be at least one size too small for her full, high breasts. Her sleek, pale midriff was bare, exposing the shallow indentation of her navel. In sharp contrast, her hair and face were modestly veiled, leaving visible only her kohl-rimmed eyes, the lashes demurely downcast.

"Allah save me." He fell silent, forced to swallow

as he discovered there was no moisture left in his mouth. "Where did you get that outfit?"

"Mrs. Siyadi. According to her, Sarab's mother once flirted with the idea of being a dancer."

"You're not serious."

"I am."

"What about you? Do you also have aspirations to dance?"

"Oh, no. I thought we might explore more of the pleasures we shared last night. That is, if the idea pleases you…master." She finally lifted her eyes to him and he saw the hint of challenge in them, so at odds with the rest of her meek, harem girl mien.

It fired his blood the way nothing else could have. To his shock, he realized his hands were shaking. "Oh, it pleases me, woman. It pleases me mightily."

"Good." She closed her hand around his. "Then come."

He didn't require much urging. His breath was already labored, his body hot, tight and ready.

He let her lead him under the tent awning to the mattress. He reached for the buttons of his shirt, but when she brushed his hands away he allowed her to undress him. He even managed to keep his hands to himself when she stepped back to look at him in all his naked glory.

"I didn't know," she said softly, her gaze once more demurely downcast.

"What?"

As light as a feather, she traced a line from his throat to his navel with her finger. "That a man could be so beautiful."

He closed his hand around his erection, already so hard he almost hurt. "Even here?"

She reached out and nudged his hand away, replacing it with her own. "Especially here."

She gripped him, too gently. He parted his lips to tell her so, only to shudder with an overload of sensation as she tightened her hand and stroked her thumb over the broad, swollen tip of him.

It was clearly time to take control. Before she did him in.

He carefully unclasped her hand, eased down onto the mattress and stretched out on his back. Looking up, he held out his hand. "Come here."

"Do you want me to undress?"

"No." Executing an effortless stomach curl, he came up, caught her around the waist and pulled her down so she was straddling his lap. "Not yet. Or rather—" he reached around and deftly unfastened her glittering top "—not completely."

Her breasts spilled free as he tossed the jeweled fabric away. With a groan of pleasure, he cupped the soft, firm globes in his hands, then rubbed his smoothly shaven cheek over one taut, supple nipple. "Ah, but you're perfect. So soft. So very soft."

Sinking back, he propped his head on a pillow. He tugged her forward and down, pushed her face veil out of his way and began to suckle, first lightly licking just the tip of her nipple, then sucking gently, then working the erect bud with his teeth, carefully increasing the pressure until she began to rock against him in a tight little circle, chasing release. "Kaj—"

"Shh. There's no reason to hurry." He turned his head to her other breast, filled with an almost primitive satisfaction as he found that nipple already swollen and tender, just waiting for his mouth.

Catherine whimpered. What he was doing felt so very, very good, yet at the same time with every tug of his mouth she felt a growing tension. Pressing against him, she felt her warm center become slick with need.

With a faint smacking sound, he released her breast, gently gripped her shoulders and eased her up. "Such beautiful eyes you have, princess," he murmured, his thumb coming up to touch the corner of one above her veil. "Do you have any idea how exotic you look with your bare breasts and your veiled face?"

She shook her head.

"Well, you do." His hand dropped away from her face and he slid his warm palms beneath her arms. His thumbs brushed her nipples, then his hands drifted down even further, coming to rest just above the feminine swell of her hips. She held her breath as he spread his right hand and his thumb slowly stroked her silk-covered dampness. "No panties?"

She swallowed, feeling her pelvis begin to sway as the throbbing inside her grew. "No." Her voice was a mere whisper.

There was no mistaking his satisfaction. Or that the heat pouring off his golden skin seemed to originate in his silver eyes. "Good." With carefully calculated strength, he gripped the flimsy fabric between his fingers and yanked, splitting open the trousers cleanly at the crotch.

"Kaj!"

Ignoring her startled protest, he took a long look at

the dark auburn curls now framed by the emerald silk. "Ah, Catherine, you're like a picture of paradise. Come to me, *chaton*. Come to me now."

Her throat too tight to speak, she nodded. Then she came up on her knees, moved him into position and sank slowly down, exulting in the way he filled her like a broadsword sliding into a sheath. Biting her lip in order to stay focused, she waited until he was buried in her as far as he could go. And then, guided by an instinct she didn't question, she rotated her hips.

Kaj's control snapped.

Clamping his hands around her waist, he dug his heels into the mattress, lifted her up, then guided her back down as he thrust.

The pleasure was intense. Arching her back, Catherine braced her hands on his thighs and closed her eyes. So intent was she, she barely noticed when he rasped, "I want to see you. I want to see you when your pleasure comes," and reached up and tugged the veils from her hair and face. Instead, her entire being was focused on the quickening inside her as he drove in and out, slowly picking up speed like the piston of some great steam engine.

Again and again, they rocked together. Then Catherine felt him stiffen, felt his hands spasm against her hips, heard the low choked sound of exultation coming from his lips. She felt the hot, wet surge of him inside her, and her own body answered, contracting around him and rocking in wave after wave of pleasure.

When the storm finally passed, she fell bonelessly against his heaving chest, fairly certain she'd never be able to move again.

It was a long time before either of them spoke.

"Have I told you you're incredible?" Kaj murmured.

His breath tickled her cheek. "Umm. I can't really remember." She stroked his hair with her fingers, feeling drowsy, peaceful, replete. "Have I told you that I love you?"

He went very still. A second later he rolled to his side, propped himself up on an elbow and gazed down at her. "Do you mean that?"

She gazed steadily back at him. "Yes."

Just for an instant there was something in his expression—a twinge of sadness, a flicker of regret?—and then it vanished, replaced by a look of absolute resolve. "Then make me the happiest man on earth. Say you'll marry me. Please, *habibi.*"

Habibi. She knew the word meant beloved, and her heart lifted. It might not be the declaration of undying love she longed for, but it was early yet. And it was obvious he cared. Plus she couldn't imagine her life without him. "If I did say yes, when would you want the ceremony?"

He didn't hesitate. "Next week."

"What?"

"Why wait?" He clasped her hand in his and pressed it to his heart. "I'm not some callow schoolboy. I know my own mind and I want you to be my wife. Not next month or the month after that. And just so we're clear, there's still half a year before my father's deadline, so it's not that."

She looked into his eyes and he looked steadily back. "Marry me, Catherine."

The last of her resistance crumbled. "Yes. Yes, Kaj. I'd be honored to be your wife."

Ten

"Darling, you look exquisite,'' Emma Rosemere Connelly said to Catherine, her gaze sweeping approvingly over her niece's ice-pink ball gown with its strapless beaded top and full tulle skirt. She paused the barest instant. "Exactly as a Royal should.''

Catherine smiled fondly at the older woman. "Compared to you, Aunt Emma, I feel like a child playing dress up. You look perfect, as always.''

It was true. The former Altarian princess, who'd shocked her parents and the world more than three decades earlier when she'd renounced her title to marry an upstart American businessman, had the sort of classic beauty that was timeless. She also had impeccable taste. Tonight she was wearing an elegant, plum-colored Chanel gown that was the perfect complement to her dark-blond hair and willowy figure.

Framed in the entrance to the suite of rooms that were now always kept ready for her at the royal palace, she looked at least a decade younger than her sixty years.

"I realize I'm here early," Catherine said. "But I wanted to see you and Uncle Grant for at least a few minutes without half the kingdom in attendance."

"And I'm glad you did." Putting an arm around Catherine's slender shoulders, Emma drew her inside. "Grant should join us in a moment. He's on the phone with Elena, your cousin Brett's new bride." Motioning her niece toward one of a pair of chairs grouped cozily together in the lavish sitting room, Emma sat down on the other. "They've been trying to connect with each other for the past two days."

Catherine made a face. "It has been hectic, hasn't it? I keep telling myself I'll get some sleep after the wedding."

Emma laughed softly. "From the way your sheikh looks at you, I wouldn't count on *that,* darling. As for all this feverish activity, you have only yourself to blame. First you call out of the blue from Walburaq to announce you're getting married. Then you ask Grant to give you away. And *then* you reveal you intend to hold the ceremony in barely more than a week!"

Catherine did her best to look contrite. "I know, and I am sorry. But as I believe I've mentioned, Kaj was quite insistent."

"Yes, and from the little I've seen of him, he's a very persuasive man. I must say, he reminds me more than a little of my Grant."

Catherine's gaze met her aunt's and for a moment the years between them fell away and they were simply two women discussing the men they loved. "I can see how he might. And not because they both have black hair and gray eyes."

Emma shook her head. "I should say not. What they share is an air of command, coupled with an indefinable something that proclaims they're all man." Her voice softened. "Not to mention that way they have of looking at you as if you're the only woman in the world."

"Are you two ladies talking about how wonderful I am again?" Still dynamic and vigorous at sixty-five, Grant Connelly strode into the room, instantly making it seem half its previous size.

Emma gave her husband a chiding look. "Did I also mention a healthy ego?" she inquired.

Grant winked at Catherine. "Of course I have a healthy ego." Pouring himself a brandy from the sideboard, he walked over and sat down on the sofa across from them and stretched out his tuxedo-clad legs. He took a shallow sip of his drink. "It takes an exceptional man to catch and tame an Altarian princess."

"Really, Grant," Emma protested. "You make Catherine and me sound like bucking broncos."

"Never, sweetheart." Grant's eyes twinkled. "I was thinking more along the lines of Thoroughbred mares. Spirited, headstrong and totally without equal. As I believe I mentioned to Catherine's young man at lunch today, he's marrying into exceptional stock. Just look at us. Thirty-five years and eight children later and I still think you're the most beautiful woman on earth."

His wife's smooth cheeks flushed with pleasure. Yet as Catherine knew, Altarian princesses of the old school had been raised to observe a very strict protocol, one that didn't allow for making intimate conversation with a man in public—even if that man was one's husband.

True to form, her aunt demurely changed the subject. ''How was Elena?'' she asked Grant. ''Is she still feeling well?''

''Yes. Except for a slight case of exasperation. She claims that by the time the baby comes, Brett will have cornered the market on childbirth books and infant supplies.''

Emma smiled. ''Good for him. I hope you told her to take it easy.''

''I did.''

''And?'' There was a brief silence as the two locked gazes. Finally, sounding faintly vexed, Emma elaborated. ''Did she learn anything more about Ms. Donahue?''

Grant's expression abruptly sobered. ''I'm sure Catherine has better things to concern herself with than our family problems, Em.''

''Nonsense,'' his wife replied. ''I know she'll want to hear about this since it concerns Seth. The two of them have always been particular friends. Haven't you, dear?'' She glanced at her niece for confirmation.

''Yes, we have.'' And for good reason, Catherine thought. Seth was the third Connelly son, but he wasn't Emma's child; he was the product of a brief affair Grant had had early in his and Emma's marriage, when the conflicting styles of his driving ambition and her royal upbringing had resulted in a short separation.

Like Catherine, Seth had also been given up by his mother. And though he hadn't come to live with the Connellys until he was twelve and Catherine just four, an unlikely but very real bond had formed between the two cousins.

"So what did Elena say?" Emma asked.

Grant gave his snifter another swirl. "She finally managed to locate Angie and talk to her. Angie," he added for Catherine's benefit, "is Seth's biological mother. And though Elena didn't say so straight out, it's obvious she has some misgivings about her. Apparently, not only did the background check Elena did on Angie turn out too good to be true—Elena's words, not mine—but when they talked, Angie reportedly told Elena more than once how much she now regrets giving up Seth to us."

Emma's spine straightened. "You're not serious," she said, not even trying to hide her disbelief.

"I am."

"Well." For a moment Emma simply sat there. Then she lifted her chin just a fraction and said with obvious conviction, "Let us hope, for Seth's sake, that she's sincere."

"Yes. Let's." Grant looked at his wife with obvious admiration. "Have I mentioned lately how lucky I am to have you, Emma?" he said softly.

Emma Rosemere Connelly smiled at him, and for a moment they might have been alone, so thoroughly absorbed did they appear to be with each other.

And then Altaria's former princess seemed to remember who and where she was. She turned toward

Catherine. "Now, enough Connelly family drama," she said briskly. "Let's talk about you, darling. After all, that's why we're here."

"Your aunt's one hundred percent right," Grant chimed in. "I like your sheikh, but I can't say I'm wild about this hurried-up affair. You're not going to give me a grandniece or nephew in eight months, are you?"

"Uncle Grant!" Catherine protested.

He looked at her indignant face and chuckled. "Well, somebody had to ask."

There was a solid knock on the door. "I'll get it," Catherine announced, springing up and hurrying toward the entry. Briefly pressing her hands to her warm cheeks in an attempt to cool them, she took a breath, then opened the door.

She gave a start of surprised relief. "Kaj! What on earth are you doing here?"

Her fiancé, looking tall and dashing in exquisitely tailored evening wear, gave her an appreciative, all-encompassing look. "I came up to escort you downstairs, and your maid said I'd find you here. And from the look on your face, I'd say my timing is perfect as usual."

"Happy?" Kaj asked her as he expertly navigated a path for them through the crush of other dancers.

Catherine gave her head a slight shake. "No. Not really."

As she'd imagined he might, he instantly raised an eyebrow. "Pardon me?"

The waltz they were doing was one of her favorites, a fast step-step-whirl done while revolving around the floor. She smiled at the way the skirt of her dress billowed around her as they danced. It gave her almost as much pleasure as the sight of the large square-cut emerald and diamond ring glittering on her finger.

But neither meant as much as the solid weight of Kaj's hand against her hip, or how safe and protected she felt being in his arms. "Happy is far too tame a word to describe how I feel. Ebullient? Ecstatic? Deliriously thrilled? None of those are exactly right, either, but they come closer."

His gaze skated over her. "How about exquisite?" he said, tightening his hold as they twirled toward the far end of the ballroom.

"If I'm exquisite, it's merely reflected glory from being close to you." The cool air from the open French doors washed over them and she gave a soft sigh of appreciation.

"Hardly. There isn't a man in this room tonight who doesn't envy me. And for excellent reason."

"Are there other men here?" she asked. "I hadn't noticed. While you...I've missed you the past few days," she said softly. "I wake up during the night and wish you were beside me."

He gave her an indecipherable look. Then to her surprise, he abruptly altered course and danced them right out through the doors and onto the terrace.

She gave a gasp of laughter. "Kaj!"

"Hush. I wanted to do this that first time we danced, but controlled myself. I'm not about to give up a second opportunity." Without missing a beat, he led the way around a corner and backed her up against a short section of balustrade hidden by an enormous planter. "You're a menace to my peace of mind. You know that, don't you?" Pulling her flush against him, he found her mouth with his own.

Their kiss was mutually hungry, fueled by the past several days of deprivation. Although they'd managed a few other stolen kisses, it seemed they'd only served to heighten their desire for each other. Now, tongues tangled, hands feverishly searching for any available patch of bare skin, they clung together, desperate to touch and taste.

When finally they eased apart, Kaj tipped his head back and blew out a frustrated breath. "Three more days until the wedding," he said with disgust. "We should have eloped."

"I know." Smoothing her hands over the back of his jacket, Catherine rested her cheek against his black satin lapel. "Sometimes I don't think I can wait, either."

His concern immediately shifted to her. "Just how are you holding up to all this craziness? Every time I call you on the phone, that tyrant of a palace operator says, 'I'm sorry, sir, the princess is unavailable.'"

He sounded so insulted she had to smile. "I'm fine. Between Erin doing all the planning for tonight and Aunt Emma arranging the wedding, all I've had to do is say yes or no when they've asked my opinion. Although it's time consuming—"

"That's an understatement," Kaj muttered into her hair.

"—everything has gone far more smoothly than I expected. Except for missing you. And being unable to show you and Daniel that e-mail…" Although she did her best to keep the regret out of her voice when she got to that last part, Kaj wasn't fooled.

"I've told you, it doesn't matter that the e-mail was erased. It's the connection you drew between it and the photograph at Alf Ahkbar that's important. And now that you've told Daniel about it, he'll pass it along to his investigators who'll be sure to look into it. You needn't worry about that."

"I know. It's just…sometimes it doesn't feel right that I should be so happy, while Father and Grandfather—" She broke off, chiding herself for being negative on such a special night. "I'm sorry."

As he so often did, Kaj seemed to understand perfectly. "There's a reason the old cliché Life Is for the Living is an old cliché," he said gently. "I know you and your father had your differences and that King Thomas wasn't terribly demonstrative, but I don't think either one of them would begrudge you a chance at personal happiness. Do you? Truly?"

"No. I suppose not."

"Good. Now come here and let me help you forget your troubles."

He didn't have to ask again. Linking her arms around his strong neck, she leaned against him, heat instantly rising through her as his firm, warm lips moved over hers. Kissing him was better than drinking the headiest champagne, she thought. It made her feel bold and brave, hopeful, incredibly alive. It made her believe that anything was possible….

When they finally came up for air, Kaj gave a raspy chuckle. "Sweet, sweet Catherine. I'm afraid we'd best go in…while I still can."

She sighed, reluctantly released her hold on him and stepped back. "I suppose you're right."

They took a moment to straighten their clothes. "Ready?" he murmured, reaching for her hand.

"Yes."

Hand in hand they strolled from their trysting place across the terrace and on inside. They'd barely cleared the door when a familiar male voice said, "Ah, there you are."

Materializing out of the throng, Grant Connelly smiled at them. "I've been looking for you, Catherine. Do you think I might steal my niece for this next dance, sheikh?"

"As much as I hate to give her up, I suppose I must," Kaj said with a gracious smile, "seeing as we're soon to be family. Speaking of which, I need to see if my cousin's finally arrived, anyway. He was catching a late flight in. So if you'll excuse me?" Giving Catherine's hand a brief kiss, he nodded at the other man and strode away.

Grant watched him go for a second, then turned to Catherine, held out his hand and gestured to the dance floor. "After you, Your Highness."

Her smile, which had been feeling slightly strained, became genuine. "Thank you, Mr. Connelly."

With the ease of years of training she went easily into his arms, gracefully following his lead as the music started up again. "I believe I owe you an apology, Catherine," Grant said seriously. "I didn't mean to insult you earlier. Or imply that I don't have the highest regard for your character—"

"No, Uncle, please. Not another word. I know you

were kidding and trying to look out for me. It's all right, truly. It's rather nice to know that you care.''

"Of course I do. You're a special young woman, my dear. I hope you know how proud your aunt and I are of you.''

Touched, Catherine squeezed his hand. "Thank you.''

Comfortable with each other, they danced without speaking for several turns of the floor. "Did your aunt tell you about the twins?'' Grant finally inquired.

"Drew and Brett? What about them?'' Her twenty-seven-year-old cousins were the only twins she knew.

"No. Douglas and Chance Barnett. Soon to be Barnett Connelly.''

She felt her eyes widen. "You and Aunt Emma are adopting?''

He smiled ruefully and shook his head. "No. Of course not. The boys—men, actually, I guess—are mine. They were conceived by a woman I knew in college, before I ever met your aunt. Their mother chose not to tell me she was expecting. Or to tell them my identity. At least not until she fell mortally ill, and by then they felt they were old enough to take care of themselves.''

"Good heavens.''

"Yes. Oddly enough, it was all the publicity about Daniel coming here, to Altaria, that made them decide they might like to get to know me and the rest of the family.''

"I'm not sure what to say. It all seems sort of fantastic, like something out of a movie.''

"I couldn't agree more. It's been hard on your

aunt—hard on us both, really. But the good news is from what I can see, in addition to having the Connelly good looks—'' that faint rueful smile flashed again ''—they're both hardworking and resourceful young men. Chance is a Navy SEAL and Douglas is a doctor. We're having a big party to welcome them to the family once Emma and I get home. Jennifer is taking care of everything.''

Jennifer was Emma's social secretary, a blond, pretty, single mother about Catherine's own age whom she'd liked very much the one time they'd met. ''Are Tobias and Miss Lilly going to be there?'' Grant's parents were two of her favorites.

''Yes, they are. For once they're actually interrupting their annual Palm Springs hiatus—can you believe it?''

She shook her head. ''I'm sorry I'll have to miss it.''

''Now, none of that. You'll have plenty of time to see everyone some other time,'' Grant said easily. ''While with any luck, you'll only get married once.''

Catherine smiled.

And then, out of all the myriad conversations floating around them, a laugh from overhead arrested her attention. Looking over her uncle's shoulder, she caught sight of Kaj and Joffrey standing upstairs on the balcony.

Pleasure exploded like champagne bubbles through her veins at the sight of her fiancé, and she had a sudden urge to be with him, to touch him and share her overwhelming happiness with him. It was all she could do to uphold her end of the conversation for the remainder of the dance, and she could only hope the manners that had been drilled into her since birth stood her in good stead as the music came to an end.

She hoped she thanked Grant for the dance, but she couldn't be certain.

Then she dismissed the concern. And picking up her skirts, she turned and headed for the stairs.

"They may be a tad on the formal side, but these Altarians do know how to throw a party," Joffrey said, gazing admiringly down at the crush below. "This is quite the impressive affair."

"Don't forget the new king and queen are Americans," Kaj said. "And in case it's somehow escaped your notice, I happen to be quite fond of Altarians. At least, one in particular."

"Yes, I know. I've been meaning to talk to you about that."

Kaj groaned. "Spare me, Joff. I assure you I already know more than you ever will about the birds and the bees, nor do I need you to lecture me on the responsibilities of marriage. Particularly when you yourself are in possession of neither a wife nor even a significant other, as I believe they're called. As for love, you don't have any more experience with it, dearest Joffrey, than I do."

"One does not need to be a poet in order to understand great verse," the Englishman said with dignity.

Kaj made a deliberately rude noise. "Please. If I remember correctly, your last prediction—something to the effect that I'd have a difficult time making a certain princess aware I was alive—didn't pan out."

The other man made a vague, dismissive gesture.

"One slight miscalculation hardly disqualifies me to speak my mind."

"One? In case it's slipped your mind, it is currently March 26, my ring is on the aforementioned princess's finger, and you'll simply have to take my word as a gentleman that I fulfilled the third requirement of our wager. Speaking of which, when should I expect to receive my new Renoir?"

Joff grimaced. "I've been wondering when you'd be ill-mannered enough to bring that up. And I can't help but point out that you're being incredibly short-sighted. That painting clearly belongs in my drawing room. You yourself are always saying how perfect it is for the space. Think about how much you'll miss seeing it there when you come to England to visit."

"I'll survive. We had a wager, I won, and now—" He narrowed his eyes as Joff's gaze drifted to something beyond him. Accustomed to Joff's tendency to try to distract him whenever his cousin felt he was on the verge of losing an argument, Kaj pretended not to notice when the other man stiffened in seeming alarm. "Now I expect you to pay up. Just as I haven't a doubt you'd be pressing me to ship you Tezhari if the tables were turned."

"Kaj, shut up."

Damned if Joffrey didn't sound genuinely distressed. He stared at his cousin curiously. Then, with a faint shrug, he turned to see for himself what, if anything, was causing Joff's odd behavior.

Catherine stood no more than ten feet away, her gaze riveted on him, her face whiter than his shirt.

He swore under his breath. "Would you excuse us, Joff?" he said, never taking his eyes off his betrothed.

"Certainly."

He felt Joff withdraw. And then it was just Catherine and him.

This, Catherine thought, as she stood frozen in place, must be what it felt like to be struck by lightning.

She could hear the blood rushing through her ears, feel her pulse pounding, taste the metallic flavor of crushing hurt on her tongue. Her skin burned, but at her core she felt colder than death.

As for her heart... She couldn't feel it at all.

"Catherine, don't look like that," Kaj said sharply. Striding close, he reached out and clasped her cold hands in his own. "I'm sorry you had to hear that, but I assure you it meant nothing."

"You—" She stopped and wet her lips, which felt bruised and stiff. "You and your cousin had a bet? About me? About us?"

"Yes. But I promise it was made well before I got to know you, and was nothing more than the sort of stupid posturing that men are prone to."

"I see." And she did. She believed he was telling the truth. Unfortunately, that wasn't what had her rooted in place, feeling as if she'd had her soul torn out. It was what he'd said so casually to Joffrey before the bet had even come up:

"As for love, you don't have any more experience with it, dearest Joffrey, than I do."

She took a deep breath, then swallowed, trying to dredge up the courage to ask what she was very much afraid she already knew the answer to. "Do you love me, Kaj?"

Just for an instant he seemed taken aback. Then his expression cleared. "I want to spend the rest of my life with you, Catherine," he said persuasively. "I want you to be my wife, the mother of my children—"

"That's not what I asked you. Do you love me?"

"I care for you more than I've ever cared—"

"So the answer is no."

"Catherine, sweetheart, you're not listening—"

She jerked her head up at that. "Oh, no, you're wrong, Sheikh al bin Russard. For the first time I really *am* listening. And I'm hearing what you're saying. Or perhaps to be accurate, what you're *not* saying.

"And it's not your fault. You told me right from the beginning that you intended to marry me. I was just foolish enough to delude myself that, like me, somewhere along the way you'd fallen in love." Somehow she managed a slight shrug. "I love you, Kaj. And because of that, and what we've shared, for the first time in my life I feel worthy to be loved."

She pulled her hands free of his, slipped the beautiful emerald and diamond engagement ring he'd given her off her finger and pressed it into his hand. "So while you might be willing to live in a loveless marriage, I'm not." She looked him straight in the eye. "As of now, this engagement is off."

Then, not giving him a chance to respond, she turned and walked away.

Eleven

———

"So, are you going to go after her? Or are you just going to stand up here all night like some sort of lovelorn statue?"

Joff's ultrapolite voice punched through Kaj's paralysis. Slowly, feeling not unlike he had when he was fifteen and a spooked stallion had tossed him to the ground and stomped on him, he turned and addressed his cousin. "Go to hell."

Whatever he saw in Kaj's face chased every trace of amusement from Joff's expression. "I very likely will. Someday. In the meantime, why don't you tell me what happened?"

"What do you think happened? Catherine overheard our conversation and decided she'd prefer not to marry me."

"Because of the bet?" Joffrey said in amazement.

"You can't be serious. I mean, it was obvious she was upset, but I was sure once you explained and assured her how much you love her—" He broke off, his eyes abruptly narrowing on Kaj's face. "You *did* tell her you love her, didn't you?"

Confronted with his cousin's probing gaze, Kaj set his jaw and looked away.

There was a thunderous silence. And then Joff said carefully, "Would you care to tell me why you didn't?"

For a moment Kaj considered just walking away. Only the knowledge that his cousin would hound him clear to Walburaq and beyond until he had an answer prompted him to reply. "Because I care for her too much to lie."

There was another silence. This one, however, was much shorter, shattered as it was by Joff's snort of disgust. "Bloody hell! If that's not the most ludicrous thing you've ever said, I don't know what is!"

Kaj stiffened. "Spare me, please. I find I'm not presently in the mood for your opinion."

"Fine. But at least let me ask you this—if you don't love her, why the big rush to get married?"

"I beg your pardon. Apparently you've had so much to drink you've already forgotten our wager."

"To hell with the wager. It had nothing to do with this wedding, and you know it. All you had to do was be engaged by month's end. So I'll ask again—why the hurry?"

"Does it really matter?"

"Yes."

"Then my answer is, I don't know," Kaj said impatiently. "I suppose I wanted to get it over with."

"Ah. This from a man who's been dodging every beautiful, intelligent, eminently suitable woman intent on tossing herself at his feet or any other body part for longer than I can count? A man who could have married any female he ever dated with just a snap of his fingers? Who in the past decade became so well-known for his avoidance of the altar that his own father felt he had to blackmail him into wedding to ensure the family bloodline?" He sniffed in the particularly contemptuous way that only the English could really pull off. "Sorry, old boy, but I don't buy it."

"Then that's your problem."

"Hardly."

"And just what's that supposed to mean?"

"Just that if you're any kind of man, you'll also consider your princess. Because it's obvious she loves you. Just as it's also obvious—at least to me—that for the first time in your entire always-in-control-of-yourself life, you're in love as well."

"Really? And on what do you base your conclusion, if I might be so bold as to ask?"

"That's easy. Every sense you possess has been engaged by her from the very start. I've never seen you so single-minded about a woman, much less feel free to be your real self the way you are with Catherine. Most telling, just being with her clearly makes you happy. And I think all of that is because you fell in love with her that very first night, in this very palace, on that dance floor down below, when you first held her in your arms."

"Are you finished?"

"No. I also think you're scared. Scared because for

some reason you think if you acknowledge your feelings, things will go sour. That Catherine will turn into a tease like your mother and you'll become like your father—jaded, selfish, embittered.''

"I believe I've heard more than enough. If you value our friendship at all, Joffrey, you'll drop this now."

"Very well. But my leaving isn't going to change anything. Whether you admit it or not, your feelings aren't going to vanish merely because you want them to. And by refusing to face them, by insisting on basing your life on your parents' past, you'll get none of the joy you so rightly deserve—only misery. And that *will* make you like your father.''

Back rigid, face set, Kaj refused to respond, simply stared at the other man until Joffrey gave a slight, regretful shake of his head and retreated. Then Kaj swiveled back around and resumed his unseeing contemplation of the ballroom below.

Joffrey was wrong, he thought mutinously. Dead wrong. He was not in love with Catherine. Nor was he afraid—of anything. And he was most certainly not worried that he would ever turn into someone as empty and cut-off from real life as his father.

Really? So why, for the first time in your life, does the thought of going home to Alf Ahkbar bring you absolutely no pleasure? And why does the mere thought of living out the rest of your years without seeing a certain smile, hearing a particular laugh, having the right to touch and watch out for one special individual leave the taste of ashes in your mouth? As if you just burned down the only bridge that ever mattered—or ever will?

The future suddenly seemed to stretch out before him like a barren wasteland.

Unable to stop himself, he slid his hand into his pocket and drew out the ring Catherine had returned to him. On her slim, graceful hand it had shone, full of life and brilliance. Now, without her warmth, her fire, her vibrancy to define it, it seemed dull and lifeless.

Just like his heart.

In that moment he knew that somehow, some way, no matter what it took, he had to get her back.

Catherine sat huddled on the edge of the mattress in the dark sanctuary of her bedroom. Although she couldn't seem to stop shivering, she felt too listless to bother with a cover for her bare arms and shoulders. In much the same way, she couldn't summon the energy to reach over and switch on the bedside lamp.

Soon, she promised herself. Soon, she would pull herself together. She'd stop this ridiculous shaking and turn on a light. She'd climb to her feet and make her way to the powder room, where she'd smooth her hair and retouch her makeup. Then she'd lift her chin, plaster a smile on her face, go back downstairs and find Daniel or Erin or Emma or Grant and inform them the wedding was off. Surely they would then make some sort of announcement. One that would preclude any but the vaguest of explanations.

Because while there would no doubt be endless speculation, despite her brave words to Kaj she didn't think she could survive the whole world knowing that he simply didn't love her.

If she didn't hurt so much, it would almost be funny. Consider: after years of believing there was something about her that prevented the people she loved from loving her back, Kaj hadn't even had to dupe her into believing he cared. She'd done a more than adequate job of deceiving herself.

She made a small hiccuping sound. To her horror, it sounded almost like a sob. Clenching her teeth, she choked back the emotion threatening to spill out. She was not going to cry. She was *not*.

A sharp rapping sound momentarily startled her from her misery. For a second she couldn't imagine what she was hearing. Then, as she realized someone was knocking on her sitting room door, she nearly gave way to panic. She wasn't ready to face anyone yet. Not her maid, not her family. She needed more time, time to lick her wounds, to gather the cloak of her composure around her.

As abruptly as the knocking had started, it stopped. She held her breath as she heard the doorknob briefly rattle, and then the distinct memory of herself turning the lock surfaced in her mind. She sagged in relief, only to jerk to her feet at the violent sound of splintering wood.

There was a sudden flash of light as a lamp in the other room was snapped on, and then the carpet-cushioned thud of a long-legged stride she would have recognized anywhere.

"Catherine?" Kaj stood in the doorway, outlined by the light behind him. She couldn't see his face.

She didn't want to. Nor did she care for him to see hers.

Not now. Not like this.

"That locked door was a signal, Sheikh al bin Russard. It indicated my profound desire to be alone." Miracle of miracles, her voice sounded deceptively strong, even if her stride was unsteady as she made her way toward the balcony doors. Hugging her arms to her chest, she stopped before the tall panes of glass and pretended to gaze out. "In plain words, I don't want to see you. So please go away." She shut her eyes, praying he'd do as she asked.

"You're shaking." It was a statement, not a question.

She managed a shrug. "It doesn't concern you."

"Catherine—"

"Go away."

"What a stubborn woman you are."

Something marvelously soft and warm slid around her icy shoulders. With a start, she realized it was Kaj's evening jacket. And that he must be right behind her. She frantically reached down and fumbled for the door handle. If she could just get out onto the balcony she could escape—

Too late. Reaching around her, Kaj caught her gently by the arm and turned her around to face him. "No doubt that's one of the reasons I love you."

She stared blankly up at him, telling herself she couldn't possibly have heard him right. "I'm sorry. I must have misunderstood. What did you say?"

"I'm a fool, *chaton*. And a stubborn one, at that. I've spent so many years determined never to repeat my parents' mistakes that somewhere along the way I lost sight of the truth. I blamed love for the failure of their marriage. But the reality is that what they had wasn't love at all.

"I know that now. Because of you. Right from the start you made me feel more alive than I ever had. You challenged me, you beguiled me, you infuriated and moved me. Most of all, you made me want more. Of your temper and your laughter, your passion, your insight, your heart. For the first time ever, I want to share my life. With you. I love you.

"Marry me. Be my wife. I can't promise it will be perfect—nothing ever is. But I swear you'll never again doubt how much I love you. Please, Catherine. Give me another chance."

She searched his face, the strong lines and planes starkly illuminated by the moonlight pouring in. He looked unwaveringly back at her, his chin firm, the curve of his mouth resolute. But it was the sight of his eyes, usually so steady, so direct, so forceful, that stole her breath and mended her aching heart.

They were sheened with tears, filled with uncertainty, alight with hope. For the first time they were totally open to her, nothing hidden, nothing held back.

"Yes." She reached up and cupped his lean cheek in her hand. "Oh, yes."

His thick, inky lashes swept down for an instant as a shudder of relief went through him. Then he leaned down and captured her mouth with his, kissing her with a sweet tenderness that was totally new.

Catherine didn't know how long they stood there, holding each other, exchanging kisses. All she knew was that when the first flash of brilliant light filled the room, for a second she thought it was just a reflection of her happiness.

Then another blazing burst lit up the grounds outside, and they turned just in time to see a pinwheel of colored light explode above the very cliffs where they'd shared their first passionate embrace. Another barrage followed and then another and another until the entire sky was painted with shimmering fireworks.

"Oh, I had no idea! How beautiful," Catherine breathed.

"Not half so beautiful as you, *habibi*."

And with that Kaj took her left hand, pressed a kiss to her palm and slipped her ring back on her finger where it belonged.

Epilogue

The first bell began to peal as Catherine and Kaj stepped out of the ancient chapel where Rosemeres had been getting married for more than two centuries.

A cry went up from the waiting crowd. Old ladies wept, the working men removed their caps, children waved, matrons called out their blessings. Then more bells began to ring, until the chiming seemed to stretch the entire length of the Kingdom of Altaria.

It was, Catherine thought, a joyous sound as much as one of thanksgiving. But it didn't compare to the sweetness that filled her every time she looked up at the tall man beside her.

Her husband.

She supposed that to anyone else, this moment right now—with Kaj in his formal gray cutaway and her in her pearl-encrusted satin gown, her long sheer veil held in place with a tiara of diamonds and flowers, their hands clasping each other's—would seem like the perfect fairy-tale ending.

But not to her. She knew this was just the beginning. That they had a whole life ahead of happily-ever-afters. And she couldn't wait to get started.

Kaj's fingers brushed her cheek. "Are you ready?"

"Yes. Absolutely."

He smiled. "Then let's go."

Her right hand held safely in his, she picked up her skirt with the other. Together they began the dash down the steps toward the waiting limousine, laughing as a shower of rose petals fell all around them.

* * * * *

MILLS & BOON®

Bestselling novels by favourite authors for you to enjoy!

LOVING THE LAWMAN

Featuring
Montana Lawman
by Allison Leigh
&
Lily and the Lawman
by Marie Ferrarella

0407/064a

0407/39

There's the life you planned and there's what comes next...

DRAGONFLIES AND DINOSAURS
by Kate Austin

Randy Roman is taking a leave of absence from her life, and hitting the road. With each passing mile of farmland and prairie, she feels the thrill of freedom. But fate has a surprise for her, which will give Randy the courage to take a risk that will change her life...

OUT WITH THE OLD, IN WITH THE NEW
by Nancy Robards Thompson

Kate Hennessey is turning forty and has to confront the fact she no longer trusts her husband. Her world is ripped apart, but Kate might just find that putting the pieces together in a whole new way can bring unexpected rewards...

Because every life has more than one chapter...

On sale 20th April 2007

Available at WHSmith, Tesco, ASDA, and all good bookshops
www.millsandboon.co.uk

MILLS & BOON

THE BABY TRAIL
by Karen Rose Smith

Baby Bonds

When someone abandoned a baby girl on Gwen Langworthy's doorstep, she couldn't just hand little Amy over to social services and forget her; so she hired tough, ex-FBI agent Garrett Maxwell to discover what had happened to the baby's parents.

A FATHER'S SACRIFICE
by Karen Sandler

Jameson O'Connell returned home to discover that a night of frenzied passion with Nina Russo had resulted in a baby boy. He insisted on claiming Nina as his bride. With their insatiable hunger for each other, would this ready-made family have a happy ever after?

THE WAY TO A WOMAN'S HEART
by Carol Voss

When widow Nan Kramer was forced to confront her son Justin's troubles, she didn't know where to turn. But then an old friend arrived on her doorstep, offering a shoulder to cry on and much, much more…

0407/38

MILLS & BOON®

*Super*ROMANCE™

THE PRODIGAL TEXAN by Lynnette Kent
Home To Stay

Back in town for a short while, local boy Jud Ritter had a surprise encounter with Miranda Wright, the girl he'd teased mercilessly in high school. She'd become an attractive, successful woman – and the town's mayor. Now Jud's back to make amends with his family, the town…and Miranda.

UNEXPECTED COMPLICATION
by Amy Knupp
9 Months Later

Libby Wilson gave up a prestigious medical position to search for her father. And she desperately needs Carson Dodge's help to find him. But Carson is recovering from a serious accident. Can he be the man Libby needs him to be? They both have everything to prove…

THE GIRL WHO CAME BACK
by Barbara McMahon

When Eliza Shaw was sixteen, her life was torn apart by a lie. Twelve years later, Eliza has returned to the house she grew up in to reconnect with the only mother she's ever known. But she must also face Cade Bennett – the only *love* she's ever known…

A MAN SHE CAN TRUST
by Roxanne Rustand

Jill Edwards is pregnant and stunned. Grant had walked out on her because she wanted to delay having kids, but now *she's* pregnant and *he's* back – and someone's threatening them. As much as she hates it, Jill's life, and their baby's, may depend on Grant's help…

On sale from 20th April 2007

Available at WHSmith, Tesco, ASDA, and all good bookshops
www.millsandboon.co.uk

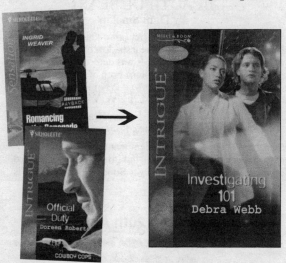

MILLS & BOON

INTRIGUE™

RILEY'S RETRIBUTION
by Rebecca York
Big Sky Bounty Hunters

A master of disguise, Riley Watson infiltrated Courtney Rogers' Golden Saddle ranch to capture a sinister fugitive. Riley was caught off guard by the pregnant ranch owner and he vowed to protect Courtney from a deadly showdown…

MORE THAN A MISSION
by Caridad Piñeiro
Capturing the Crown

She'd murdered the heir to the throne, and now the assassin was firmly in undercover agent Aidan Spaulding's sights. But Elizabeth Moore looked more like a princess than a prince-killer…and she faced the greatest threat of all: one to her heart.

BEAUTIFUL BEAST
by Dani Sinclair

When an explosion ended Gabriel Lowe's military career and left him scarred, his life became a shadow of what it once was. But the beautiful Cassy Richards was determined to warm his heart before an old enemy cut short both of their futures.

CAVANAUGH WATCH
by Marie Ferrarella
Cavanaugh Justice

When Janelle Cavanaugh's assignment took a deadly turn, she was given a ruggedly handsome, but infuriating, bodyguard. Risking his life was part of Sawyer Boone's job. Risking his heart was quite another matter.

On sale from 20th April 2007

Available at WHSmith, Tesco, ASDA, and all good bookshops
www.millsandboon.co.uk

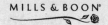
MY SISTER, MYSELF
by Alice Sharpe

When Tess Mays discovers she has an identical twin, she thinks her life is finally coming together. But with her sister in a coma, Tess stumbles into an arson investigation, assuming her sister's identity to exonerate the father she never knew.

THE MEDUSA GAME
by Cindy Dees
Bombshell – The Medusa Project

Isabella Torres is part of the Medusa Special Forces team. She must protect an Olympic figure skater receiving death threats – then the Medusas discover something far more sinister. With Gunnar Holt as her partner, can Isabella keep her cool?

STRANDED WITH A STRANGER
by Frances Housden

Wealthy, pampered Chelsea Tedman never expected to be climbing Mount Everest with a mysterious, alluring stranger. But only Kurt Jellic could get her up the perilous mountain to solve the mystery of her sister's fatal fall.

STRONG MEDICINE
by Olivia Gates
Bombshell

The Global Crisis Alliance had been Calista St James' life – until she'd been blamed for a botched mission and dismissed. Now, the GCA want her back for a dangerous rescue operation and Calista must work with the gorgeous man who'd fired her.

On sale from 20th April 2007

Available at WHSmith, Tesco, ASDA, and all good bookshops
www.millsandboon.co.uk

From No. 1 *New York Times* bestselling author Nora Roberts

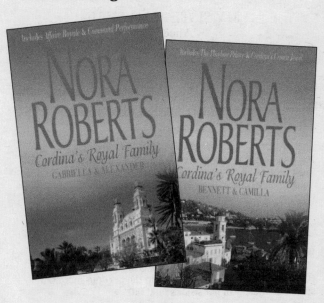

Romance and intrigue are woven together in these classic stories about Cordina's royal family

Gabriella & Alexander
Available 2nd February 2007

Bennett & Camilla
Available 4th May 2007

www.silhouette.co.uk